Praise for *The Last Shootist*

"Action-packed, funny, impressively researched, and often tenderly romantic, *The Last Shootist* is a rambunctious Western and a youthful, zesty homage to Glendon Swarthout's forty-year-old classic."

—Ron Hansen,
author of *The Assassination of Jesse James by the Coward Robert Ford*

"Miles Swarthout's crisp prose and earthy details bring the rough reality of the Texas border at the turn of the twentieth century into vivid focus. *The Last Shootist* is a worthy and entertaining finale to Glendon Swarthout's classic tale of shootist J. B. Books."

—Lucia St. Clair Robson,
New York Times bestselling author of
Last Train from Cuernavaca

"Swarthout is an accomplished Western writer. . . . If you enjoyed *The Shootist,* saw the film, or just want to read a very good Western story, I recommend this book." —*Historical Novel Society*

"An excellent Western novel that seamlessly picks up the complex characters and transitioning West of El Paso, Texas, that made the elder Swarthout's original so popular. Miles's prose is lean with richly developed characters, tight dialogue, and well-researched historic border towns and mining camps of Texas, New Mexico, and Arizona."

—*True West* magazine

The Last
SHOOTIST

Miles Swarthout

A Tom Doherty Associates Book / New York

This is a work of fiction. All of the characters, organizations, and events portrayed in this novel are either products of the author's imagination or are used fictitiously.

THE LAST SHOOTIST

Copyright © 2014 by Miles Swarthout

Photograph on page 389 courtesy of the El Paso Public Library, Aultman Collection

A Forge Book
Published by Tom Doherty Associates, LLC
175 Fifth Avenue
New York, NY 10010

www.tor-forge.com

Forge® is a registered trademark of Tom Doherty Associates, LLC.

ISBN 978-0-7653-7679-4

Forge books may be purchased for educational, business, or promotional use. For information on bulk purchases, please contact the Macmillan Corporate and Premium Sales Department at 1-800-221-7945, extension 5442, or write to specialmarkets@macmillan.com.

First Edition: October 2014
First Mass Market Edition: September 2015

Printed in the United States of America

0 9 8 7 6 5 4 3 2 1

For

Glendon

and

John "Duke" Wayne

the *real* shootists

Acknowledgments

The 1954 black-and-white photograph of the famous alligator pond in El Paso's downtown San Jacinto Plaza is reprinted by permission of the El Paso Public Library from their Aultman Collection, with the assistance of librarian Danny Gonzalez.

I'd like to thank publisher Tom Doherty of Tor/Forge Books for allowing me another book in print and editor Bob Gleason for once again helping with good story notes. Assistant editor Kelly Quinn and copy editor Susannah Noel were also helpful in readying this text.

Former Northland Press editor Tom Carpenter from Flagstaff and frontier-weapons expert Phil Spangenberger from Leona Valley, California, both provided their expertise, as did Los Angeles producer/filmmaker Marcos Cline-Marquez with my weak Spanish. Mr. Spangenberger can also be enjoyed on two of Mark Allen's DVDs, *Gunplay Made Easy* and *Gunplay: The Art of Trick & Fancy Gun Handling*. Wes Patience is a Western historian retired to Bisbee, Arizona, who pointed me in right directions research-wise.

And lastly, my dear mother, Kathryn Swarthout, for her help removing modern words from these Old West characters' mouths. Without these experts' wise suggestions, this Western tale could not have been polished.

As for the master storyteller himself, the great Glendon, well, he *knows*.

The young lions roar after their prey, and seek their meat from God.

—Psalm 104:21

Prologue

The Final Scene from Glendon Swarthout's Western Novel *The Shootist*

Gillom Rogers inched through the doors of the Constantinople. Eyes watering from the smoke, he gaped at Jay Cobb and Serrano and Koopmann, and at Jack Pulford, seated against the wall.

Skirting the three bodies near the bar, avoiding the blood and brains as best he could, he looked over the bar, then scuffled in wonder through the carnage of glass behind it. A dollar bill stopped him. He put it in his pants pocket that held the other money. A black-handled Remington lay in the walkway. He picked it up and holding his breath approached the prone man, who seemed small to him now, even puny.

"Mister Books?"

He saw the torn coat and the blood on it and the right arm extended stiffly, gun aimed. He moved slowly to Books's side, bending.

"It's me, Gillom," he said.

He got down on his knees. Books was incapable of

speech. His chin was clamped upon his left wrist. Gillom did not care to look into the face, but the eyes arrested him. They considered. They considered not only the archway, as though something implacable waited on the other side, but something transcendent beyond that as well, far beyond.

"Mister Books, it's me, Gillom."

The mouth opened. Nothing inaudible issued from it, but the lips formed two words: "kill" and "me."

"Kill you?"

Gillom chewed his lips.

"Sure thing," he said, then stood, moved behind the man, straddled him, and put the muzzle of the revolver he had picked up to the back of the head. He turned his own head away, shut his eyes tight, gritted his teeth—pulled the trigger.

The hammer *clicked*.

"Shit," he groaned.

He despaired, aware on the rim of his consciousness of the smoke and the reek of the air and the solemnity of the fans. He got down on his knees again beside the prone man and worked at the fingers clenching the pearl handle of the second Remington, prying them free until he possessed that weapon, too.

He stood again, straddled the prone man, and put the muzzle of the revolver to the back of John Bernard Books's head a second time, into the hair. He turned his own head away, shut his eyes tight, gritted his teeth, and pulled the trigger.

· · ·

He walked out of the Constantinople into chaste air. A crowd of men and boys had gathered across the street. Waiting for a buggy to pass, then a buckboard, he crossed the street to the crowd.

"What happened in there?" at least six asked.

"They're all dead," said Gillom.

"Who?"

"J. B. Books. Jay Cobb. Jack Pulford. A Mex name of Serrano, a rustler. And some guy I don't know who. A big guy. He killed 'em all."

"Who?"

"Books."

Someone had counted. "Five! *Whooeee!*"

"Jesus Christ, boys, he killed every hard case around!" someone exulted. "Jesus, boys, we fin'ly got us a clean town!"

"Oughta put up a statue of the murderin' bastard!" someone else enthused.

"These are his guns." Gillom held them up for all to covet. "He gave 'em to me before he died."

"Look at that!"

"Short barrel, no sight, specials by God—hey, kid, wanna sell 'em?"

"Hell, no," said Gillom. He grinned and waved at the Constantinople. "Okay, folks, step right over and see the show! Drinks on the house!"

As the crowd tided across the street, Gillom Rogers strode away down it, swinging a gun in each hand. An alchemy of false spring sunlight turned the nickel of the Remingtons to silver. He strode head up, shoulders back, taller to himself, having sensations he had never known before. One gun was still warm in his hand, the bite of the smoke was in his nose and the taste of death on his tongue. His heart was high in his gullet, the danger past—and now the sweat, suddenly, and the nothingness, and the sweet clean feel of being born.

One

One thing he knew for a fact: he had to get these pistols hidden quick or his mother might kill him, too. They were much too valuable to flash around town. *Sweet bearded Jesus!* He now possessed J. B. Books's matched Remingtons!

Gillom Rogers slowed his walk, wondering where he would get a double-holster rig to house these legendary nickel-plated Remington .44s. Or should he have a silk vest made like Books's, with leather holster pockets sewn on either side of the chest, angled forty-five degrees inward for a cross-handed draw? Too late to get J. B.'s own now. That special weapons vest was all shot up and bloody on his corpse. Books was too heavy to clothe Gillom's skinny frame anyway.

If I can just learn to handle these pistols as well as Mr. Books did, quick draw, spinning tricks, a sharpshooter, I can become as famous a shootist as that old man was! With a little gambler's luck, if nobody fills me fulla lead, makes me look like a colander. Famous and *feared.*

"Hey, kid! *Kid!* Wait up!"

Gillom halted in El Paso Street and stepped back from the steel trolley tracks to turn to see who was hulloing. Shading his eyes against an afternoon sun, he squinted at the hullabaloo stirring around the Constantinople saloon, spectators shouting, hurrying in and out of the opened front doors. A spindle-shanked fellow in a striped suit and derby hat galloped out of the crowd and waved at Gillom.

"Dan Dobkins! Daily Herald!"

Gillom Rogers nodded as the young journalist caught his breath. "You interviewed Mister Books at our house."

"Well, almost. Before that cranky old bastard booted me out." Dobkins pointed at one of the shiny revolvers Gillom held. "His pistol?"

Gillom straightened, displaying a nickel-plated Remington in either hand.

"J. B. Books himself gave 'em to me the moment before he died."

Dobkins couldn't resist running an index finger along the five-and-a-half-inch sightless barrel of the made-to-order Remington.

"You *stole* 'em off a dead man."

"I did *not*! It was our deal. If I told Cobb, Pulford, and Serrano over in Juarez to meet Mister Books in the Connie today at four, when the shooting was over, Mister Books said I could have these specials."

Dan Dobkins only had about ten years on this callow youth, but he surveyed the teenager with a cynical eye. "So you *took* 'em off a dead man?"

Gillom reddened. "*No!* He asked me to finish him off. Hell, he was all shot up anyway, almost dead. So I pried this loaded pistol from his fingers and did what he asked."

Dobkins's mouth fell open. "*You* issued the coup de grâce?"

"The what?"

"Executed him?"

"Yup." Gillom Rogers raised his narrow chin defiantly, risked twirling the revolver in his right hand by its finger guard, just once.

The star reporter of the El Paso *Daily Herald* noticed bystanders halting to overhear. He grabbed the teenager by the shoulder, turned him round, and marched them both toward the swinging doors of the Pass of the North's best-known saloon, the Gem.

"Let's get a drink. I'll make you famous, kid, but I need your whole story."

Opened in the fall of 1885, the Gem Theatre was a full-service establishment with a restaurant and saloon in front and its gaming rooms moved upstairs by order of a reformist town council. A stage at one end of the barroom hosted variety musical shows with singers and dancing girls, sometimes even dog fights and boxing matches, which were heavily bet.

"My name's not kid. It's Gillom Rogers."

"Fine. But hide those guns, Gillom, or somebody will shoot *you* to steal 'em."

Gillom stuck the Remingtons carefully under the

waistband of his woolen trousers, covered by his light wool coat. Dobkins steered him into one of the red leather wine booths in a back corner.

"*Two* beers, Jimmy! McGintys!" Pulling a small notebook and pencil from his coat pocket, the ace reporter got right down to business. "So at J. B. Books's behest, you summoned Jay Cobb, Jack Pulford, and that Mex, what was his name?"

"Serrano. El Tuerto. Cross-Eye, they called him. He was one bad *bandido* from Juarez."

"So why were all three of these gunslingers summoned to the Connie today?"

"'Cause they were all good with guns. Mister Books was dying of cancer and expected one of those gunmen would save him the trouble of doing himself in."

"*Cancer?* Books?"

"Yup. Doc Hostetler told him he didn't have much time to live. That's why my ma let him stay on in our bottom guest room even after all our other boarders fled, after those two jaspers tried to shoot him in bed earlier this week. He had nowhere else to go."

Dobkins chewed his pencil. "Fits. I did hear a rumor Books was dying, but after what he did to me . . ." The journalist made a face at the sour memory of the great gunman booting him ignominiously in the ass off Mrs. Rogers's front porch.

The rotund barkeep put one huge mug of warm beer in front of Mr. Dobkins, but he gave the young customer the fisheye. "Kid's too young to drink in here, Dan."

The reporter shook his head. "Not today he isn't,

Jimmy. This is the young man who just killed John Bernard Books."

The barkeep gave Gillom a long stare. "On the house then. For helpin' rid El Paso of our last *pistolero*." Jimmy left to go draw another beer. Dobkins slid his stein of ale across the table to young Rogers, who grinned as he sucked it down. The teenager found killing worked up a thirst.

Dan gave him a smile oily enough to grease a locomotive.

"Okay, Gillom, who shot who first?"

"Well, most of the blood had been spilled by the time I snuck in there. Books had shot 'em all—Cobb, Pulford, that Mex, and some other joker I don't even know. All the hard cases he invited to his funeral."

Gillom gulped more beer as Jimmy approached with another huge mug, named after the McGinty Band, El Paso's famous musical drinking society. The journalist's eyes drifted to the ceiling.

"Invitation to a funeral . . . or, or, a gunfight. What a headline. . . . Or the title of a book . . ."

Gillom nodded, remembering. "Yeah, the gunsmoke and pistol fire echoing off those tile floors burned my nostrils and deadened my hearing. Heavy . . ."

Dobkins nodded, transported. "A vibrating mantle . . . of death. Like something out of Poe."

Gillom slugged his beer. "Who?"

"Edgar Allan Poe. Dissipated Baltimore poet you might like."

"Listen, Dan," said Gillom. "It's after five. I gotta get home for supper."

The reporter snapped out of his wonderment. "Me, too. Gotta see if that photographer's gettin' those death photos. Crucial with a headline. So Books actually asked you to shoot him?"

"He was bleedin', wounded bad, dyin' anyway. Whispered 'kill . . . me.' So I blessed him with a bullet."

Dan Dobkins listened transfixed. "A bullet's *blessing* . . ."

Gillom's chair scraped as he got up, remembered his manners. "Thanks for the beer."

Dobkins hastily rose, too. "Sure, kid, uh, Gillom. Gonna make you famous. Tomorrow's paper."

They shook hands a little awkwardly under the circumstances.

"Thanks, Dan. Maybe this'll lead to a good job. Something exciting involving firearms is what I fancy."

"Finish your schooling first. You're a game young man, Gillom Rogers. More education, you'll go far."

"Already on my way, thanks just the same." With a spring in his step, Gillom was off, checking the weighty guns in his waistband as he bounced through the Gem's swinging front doors. Dan Dobkins smiled as he dropped four bits on the table, leaving an uncharacteristically decent tip. Headline story this hot might make *him* famous, too.

Two

The McGinty Coronet Band, its brass blasting and drums rattling, marched up El Paso's main street to its free Saturday night concert in the Gem. Dobkins elbowed his way through the marching throng to reach the bottleneck outside the Constantinople's front doors.

"Make way for the press! Please! *Daily Herald* coming through!" A strong hand pushed back his chest. The imposing, red-necked man was one of the smaller marshal's muscles. Turning to catch Walter Thibido's eye, the deputy got the nod to let the press in.

Dobkins stepped carefully into the saloon's mess. He noted the bullet holes in the carved mahogany bar, the jagged glass teeth left in the wide, shattered mirror behind it. Amazingly only one light fixture, designed like a cluster of glass grapes, was broken. The burnt gunpowder filled his nostrils with an acrid scent of sulphur, like the devil's vapor trail.

Moving around the big stranger's body near the front door, Dobkins gave a kick to a short-haired mongrel licking brain slime off the green and white floor tiles next to the gaping hole in Jay Cobb's head. The dog let out a yelp, but circled out of boot range to go lap more blood from the viscous pool around the other stranger's torso.

Marshal Thibido mopped his brow with a blue silk handkerchief. "Books hasn't any relatives I know of, so I'll handle his personals until this shooting investigation's finished. Where are his guns?"

The lawman was addressing Skelly, the photographer, who was propping Books's upper body against the bar's mahogany front, closing eyelids over vacant orbs, arranging the corpse in a position more suitable for infamy. The gunman's skeletal features, emaciated by his prostate cancer, were ghastly gray to look at, but aside from wiping away blood splatters, there was nothing much Skelly could do to improve J. B. Books's gaunt death mask. No time to get any face powder, makeup from his studio. Skelly had to tilt the gunfighter's Stetson to cover up the hole on one side of his head. Luckily the bullet hadn't exited through the face or he couldn't shoot a saleable photograph.

"No weapons on him. No watch, no wallet, no money. He was robbed, Marshal."

"Goddammit, he used those guns. *Deputies!* I want these shooters' guns confiscated, especially Books's. *Find 'em!* They're valuable . . . evidence."

Dan Dobkins curried favor. "Kid's got those pistols, Marshal. Gillom Rogers took 'em before finishing Books off, that shot to the head there."

"You saw those Remingtons?"

Dan nodded. "Ten minutes ago, talked to Gillom. He's gone home."

Thibido blew relieved air. "Well, least we know where they are."

Mr. Skelly positioned his equipment, angling the maple Conley eight-by-ten camera on its tripod down on Books before ducking under green baize cloth to adjust the focus on its twelve-inch rectilinear lens.

Pushing his opening, the lanky reporter began to drill. "So, Marshal, what have you concluded from this gory mess?"

Thibido surveyed the big saloon. "Well, all of El Paso's hard cases seem to have convened to gun each other down. I'll propose to the city council we pay for these burials, since they've done us a civic favor. No innocents lost in here today."

"Any idea who shot first, or why?"

"Nope. Except to burnish their bad reputations? Pulford and Serrano were mankillers. Jay Cobb was just a pimple-faced punk, a sharpshooter only with his mouth. Jerk didn't stand a Chinaman's chance against these gunslingers. And J. B. Books, well, his reputation rode into town before he did." The marshal sighed, exhausted at just the thought of how much legal trouble cleaning up this big mess was going to be.

"I'll tell you straight, Dobkins. We've had bloody hell here these past ten years, since John Selman blew Wes Hardin's brains out in the Acme in '95. Then Scarborough killed Selman. Then some tough killed Selman. Before that marshal Stoudenmire shot Hale Manning and his brother Frank retaliated, killing the marshal." The short, well-dressed lawman gestured around the barroom with vigor.

"Now I'm standing at six-shooter junction. If these shootists don't stop invading our fair city to assassinate each other, there's going to be nothing left of El Paso but burnt dirt!"

Both men were distracted by the sight of two young boys playing with Jack Pulford. The cardsharp was slumped against the back wall of the Constantinople. J. B. Books had killed him from sixteen feet, both men standing and firing at each other. One shot, right in the heart. But the bullet, stopped by fibrous heart muscle, hadn't exited, and now the two boys, who must have snuck in the back door, were bent over Pulford's corpse, playfully lifting his slack left arm up and down. With each lever action of his pump handle arm, blood swelled from the wound in the deceased's chest. The mischievous boys were pumping a dead man dry.

Appalled, the city marshal yelled to another deputy. "*Jackson!* Get those damned kids outta here! Playin' with the corpses. *Christ!*"

"So Marshal, you have *no idea* how five noted gunslingers managed to show up in the same saloon at the same time in broad daylight for the shoot-out of the century, right under your nose?"

Walter Thibido had had enough.

"No, by ginger, I *don't*! And I've had quite enough of *you* today, too." His face flushed red, one neck vein began to pulse as he shouted. "I want *everyone* not involved in this police investigation out of this saloon *right now*!" The marshal pulled his own pistol to wave above his head. "That includes children, dogs, *and* journalists!"

At that moment, Skelly puffed hard into the brass pipe in his mouth, squeezed the bulb, and his exhalation blew the alcohol flame through the rear of the tin trough he was holding and ignited the magnesium powder in the trough. For a second the barroom lit up like the Fourth of July.

Everyone—children, dog, deputies, the marshal, frightened bystanders—jumped. They might have all been standing in Hades' waiting room. The photographer quickly extinguished the flame, put down his flashpan, and began fanning away the cloud of smoke. Five corpses never moved a muscle.

Three

Gillom avoided details over his mother's supper that night, saying only that people had been shot in the Constantinople that afternoon, probably Books, too. Bond Rogers had decided to move her son out of his smaller upstairs bedroom and open that one up to another boarder, if any roomers *ever* showed up on her doorstep again after all this bloody mayhem. She wanted Gillom staying in J. B. Books's larger downstairs room. The shootist had left nothing behind but his notorious reputation and the fact he'd shot two country cousins who'd tried to kill him in that very corner room only a week ago. No respectable person would rent a room housing those murderous ghosts till long forgot. She also thought it would be easier to keep track of her delinquent son in a main-floor room, right below hers.

Gillom was happy to help his mother move his clothes downstairs to Books's suddenly vacant quarters. His nostrils still caught scent of the faint mix of flaming gunpowder and urine from when Books had doused the burning bedsheets with the contents of his piss pot after those two jaspers had tried to murder him right there. His mother had bought new bedding and a mattress, to which he quickly gave a bounce test. Gillom rose from the refurbished bed and went to the west and then the south windows, sliding their wooden sashes higher to let in more cool night air. *These glassed downstairs windows will make my comings and goings easier,* he realized.

Gillom returned to bed, pulled his bedspread up higher against the spring chill. But he was restless, squirming under stiff, new sheets, nerves still taut from the events of his momentous day. The seventeen-year-old jerked again from bed, padded in nightshirt and bare feet to the curtained closet. He groped the top shelf inside where he had dumped his cowboy hat and leather baseball glove and pulled Books's whiskey bottle from a cubbyhole his mother had missed. A corner of redeye remained.

Hurling himself back into bed, Gillom made the wooden frame sway and creak. Nestling with his prize, he pulled the cork with his teeth, grimaced as the whiskey seared his palate. He mused: *Men drank whiskey, tough men like J. B. Books. I'll have to get used to this harsh taste. My sarsaparilla days are over.*

Burning alcohol slid down his teenaged gullet and mixed with the warm beer he'd gulped six hours earlier. Gillom Rogers relaxed, remembering the first time he'd encountered the famous gunman, just a week ago. Books had spotted him spying, grabbed him by the throat and yanked him right up to this very room's window. Nearly choked him out before the sick old man had collapsed on the windowsill, exhausted. Gillom dozed.

He awoke to whispers on the wind. Curtains in the west window to the side of his headboard moved in the morning breeze. Bright sunlight. A giggle and a loud *sssshh*. *I'm not dreaming, somebody is spying on me!* Eyes wide, Gillom leapt out of bed, jumped to the open window, thrust his head outside.

"*Hey!*" The gigglers jerked back in fear, surprised by the teenager's suddenness. "Don't you spy on *me*! I'll whup your setters so hard, you'll stand for a week!"

Then he launched right through the open window to do it. Frightened by this angry young man right in their small faces, the two peepers turned tail and skedaddled across the grassy yard. A skinny tyke with black hair and big ears and a taller towhead.

Both boys flew over his mother's picket fence on the bounce.

Must have talked to someone, heard what I did, Gillom thought. *Gol-lee! I'm notorious before breakfast!*

His mother sat at the head of the long dining table, *Daily Herald* in hand. Her right hand quivered as she turned the front page to continue reading about El Paso's killings yesterday. Her intake of breath startled the silence. She'd read her son's name again in the newspaper.

Gillom slunk into the dining room. He'd heard her crank telephone in the front parlor ring several times, but had dozed until little boys whispering outside his window had pulled him from conflicted sleep. He could see from the *Herald*'s headline how deep he was in. . . .

INVITATION TO A GUNFIGHT! J. B. BOOKS KILLED IN EL PASO BLOODBATH!

His mother lowered the paper to search him with haunted eyes. She shoved her untouched plate of eggs and biscuit and unsipped cup of coffee along the tabletop.

"*You* eat my breakfast. I have no appetite."

"Ma, *please*."

"Please. That's a funny word, isn't it? How one can twist its meaning into something completely different. You *displease* me greatly. My son, the only child I have born, is now a killer."

"Did him a favor, mother. Mister Books asked me to. It was . . . merciful."

Her face was drawn, but her voice remarkably level.

"It was a bloody slaughter. Which you evidently helped arrange. For some kind of payoff. Oh yes, I read you took his guns."

"It was our deal. His pistols for my service. Mister Books didn't wish to die in bed, so he committed suicide."

"In *public*. And by assisting him in this public slaughter, you've brought shame upon us. Disgraced our family's proud name . . . around all of Texas. Forever."

Her son waved his hands to stop. "*Mother!* People are saying Mister Books did El Paso a public service. Rid this town of all its hard cases. And I helped him do it."

Her eyes flared. "I didn't read that in here." She tapped the inky newsprint with a sharp fingernail. "You are named the assassin's *assistant*. . . . Where are they?"

"What?"

"His guns."

"Oh. They're well hid."

"We'll have to turn them in. To the marshal. I'm sure they'll be wanted."

"Be damned if I will."

"Gillom!"

"Look, I'm not breaking any law. Thibido will just sell 'em, after the court work is done. He's a shyster, a peacock. His deputies do all his dirty work."

"Well *you're* already infamous, taking his guns and using them on poor Mister Books. If you're seen on the street with those pistols, somebody will try to shoot you, too, to steal them. Until we're rid of those bad luck weapons, wash our hands thoroughly of this shameful business, more trouble will follow us. I feel pain in my bones already."

Gillom rose from the table, his loaned breakfast untouched. "Be goddamned if I give up those guns. To anybody. I earned 'em."

His threat hanging heavy, the young man stomped back down the hall to his room. His disobedience, again, finally cracked his mother. Bond burst into tears, slamming both palms onto the hard wooden table.

"Damn you, John Bernard Books!"

If anybody but the Lord had been listening, they'd have been shocked. It was the first time Bond Rogers had ever sworn.

Four

Gillom left by a side window in his back bedroom, a new convenience keeping his mother from interrogating him coming and going from their house. He stopped to pull his new guns from their hiding hole in the woodpile next to the storage shed. He fondled his prizes. These were 1890 Remingtons, basically the 1875 model with the webbed underbarrel assembly cut away. They were chambered for centerfire .44-.40 brass cartridges blasted through 5½" barrels. A hot lead load of 40 grains of black powder, the bullets of which could be used interchangeably in the famous Winchester '73 rifle. He stuck them inside his leather belt, butts forward, out of sight under his blue wool sack coat. Gillom stepped over the yard's white picket fence and hurried downtown.

He headed up Overland, turned one block north onto noisy San Antonio Street, one of the main merchant byways of booming El Paso at its hard turn into a new century. He strode past the Liberty Bakery,

Gamozzi's Ice Cream Parlor, C. S. Pickerell's Confectionary, any of which might have tempted his sweet tooth. He headed toward the meat markets farther down the chuck-holed, sand-and-gravel street. Two gigantic Percheron draft horses pulled a long wagon loaded with barrels of beer fresh from the brewery bound for one of the ninety-six saloons crowded all over this border town.

On the northeast corner of Mesa and San Antonio streets stood his favorite, the old Acme Saloon, where he normally would have snuck in the back to check the day drinkers and drunks dozing off a long night before. It was in the Acme's front barroom where the West's most notorious shootist, John Wesley Hardin, was rolling dice for drinks on a hot August night in 1895. John Selman stepped inside the batwing front door and dropped his prey like a stone with one lucky shot right in the back of Wes Hardin's head. Selman got off on that murder charge even though Hardin never had a gunfighting chance. For even as an older man, Hardin was still quite dangerous and generally disliked around El Paso.

The Acme Saloon was thus consecrated ground to Gillom. But this crisp spring day he bypassed his shrine. Jim Dandy's Leather Goods was near some of the meat markets on San Antonio Street, close to the source of the cowhides they worked into their leather products. And the stench from Jim's tanning vats blended in with the smell of butchered beeves aging on big iron hooks in the meat markets, so those butchers didn't complain. To them that stench smelled like money.

Gillom found the proprietor behind a wooden counter in back and told him what he wanted: a double-holster rig in good condition. Mr. Dandy, or whatever his real name was, peered over bifocals.

"New or used?"

"Uh, new."

The proprietor pulled off a peg a brown leather holster and cartridge belt with a bronze buckle in front and cartridge loops around the back. Two more leather strips were spaced apart and stitched across the gun pockets to strengthen them and support each pistol. Gillom took the double-loop rig and strapped it on.

"Stiff."

Jim nodded. "It's new. Leather loosens as it's broken in, gets comfortable around your waist."

"How much?"

"Forty dollars. We'll embross that leather for you, your name, any design you want, for an extra ten."

Gillom frowned. "Got anything cheaper?"

Mr. Dandy sucked his teeth, moved to a darkened corner and pulled open a bottom drawer of an old desk. He returned blowing dust off another double rig, this one naturally brown.

"This is a moneybelt. Cowhide's doubled over and stitched together on top. See this slit inside here you can slip coins in to hide safely? You slide the belt's billet into this slit, so your coins won't fall out. Your silver dollars will add weight to this double rig, but no one's the wiser when you're travelin'."

The single-loop holster had several dull-colored silver conchos attached around the belt and on each gun sheath. Its worn leather was very flexible when the young man strapped it on.

"Conchos are a little scratched, but they'll shine up again, that buckle, too," Mr. Dandy added.

This time Gillom drew the six-guns from beneath his belt and slid them into the holsters, then raised and lowered the revolvers several times with his palms on each grip, testing for a smooth pull.

He smiled, liking the feel. "How much?"

Mr. Dandy eyed the teenager, calculating. "Twenty-five dollars, for those fancy conchos."

"Throw in some silver polish?"

"Dollar extra."

Gillom tried a quick draw with his stronger hand, his right, but caught the revolver's barrel on the sheath's lip. There was no front sight on either pistol's barrel to cause this, so he adjusted the height of the rig on his slim hips. He tried again, cleared leather easily.

"Be faster, you soap that leather good, then oil it," said Jim.

He tried another draw with his off hand, his left, and was successful. Gillom grinned. He drew both guns. The three-pound revolvers seemed made to fill his strong hands and slid out of their protective pockets slicker than greased piglets. Cocky, pleased with his first attempts, Gillom spun the .44 by its trigger guard, like any teenager trying to show off a flashy spin before jamming his gun back into the leather. His index finger tapped the Remington's trigger, however, and that was all it took. A bullet banged into the store's upper wall, ricocheted off the arched wooden ceiling, and zinged harmlessly into the wooden wall directly behind him. A three-bank shot! Jim Dandy disappeared.

Two Mexican leatherworkers piled out of the rear workroom, one of them pointing a revolver! Mr. Dandy rose from behind the counter red-faced.

"*Jesus,* kid! Put that pistol away until you learn how to use it!"

"Sorry." Gillom unbuckled quickly and folded holster and guns to lay on the counter. "Trigger's a little touchy."

"Are they even *yours*?" The shop owner was angry at how scared he'd shown.

"Yes! J. B. Books himself willed 'em to me . . . after he died. They're special Remingtons, custom-made."

"Books, huh? You're the kid mentioned in the paper today."

Gillom nodded. Jim Dandy eyed him with new appreciation.

"Books prob'ly had 'em sweetened. Gunfighters like to file down the notch on the hammer, loosen the spring on the trigger so it'll pull sweet. Damn trick guns'll go off if you breathe on 'em. Oughta get those fixed, before you blow your toes off."

"I'm sorry. . . ." Gillom paid with clean bills folded in his pocket—Books's money left for his mother, which he'd stolen. He didn't dare complain when Mr. Dandy charged him another dollar each for the saddle soap, bottle of gun oil, and tin of silver polish.

Gillom left the leather shop in a hurry, his ill-gotten goods wrapped in burlap. His mother was right. He couldn't be seen wearing these famous guns around El Paso, at least until some of the trouble stirred up by Books's fatal gunfight had died down. Gillom had only John Bernard's word he could have these weapons, regardless of the outcome of the bloodletting. Books's letter to his mother that Gillom had found in his room, leaving her a sum of money, $532, he'd destroyed, so that the secondhand man who quickly showed up that night to take possession of Books's few personals hadn't been able to snatch his famous guns in the bargain. Gillom professed ignorance of their whereabouts, though Mr. Steinmetz hadn't believed him. But his bill of sale from Books said nothing about the Remingtons.

"Too bad for that old peddler!" he laughed later.

Gillom would turn eighteen this summer, a grown man. He couldn't hide something as exciting as these big pistols forever, especially from his pals. As spring weather began to warm the Pass of the North, his restless thoughts turned from readin', writin', and 'rithmetic, to gamblin', guns, and gunmen in pretty quick order. Girls, too, figured somewhere in his brain-scrambled equation, but an amateur gunslinger needed time and money for courting, two commodities that had only just fallen his way.

Gillom knew where his pals might be. They often liked to wander down to the muddy Rio Grande after school, to skip stones across the slow-moving water, or watch an occasional train chug across the Mexican Central Railroad trestle heading south into Juarez. Maybe they'd sip a little cheap whiskey or smoke hand-rolled cigarettes if they could steal any liquor or tobacco, or bribe some cowhand to buy these prohibited goods for them.

Five

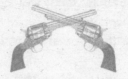

Gillom found Bee Dunn, Ivory Bean, and Johnny Kneebone, Jr. in the thicket of cottonwoods and tall brush at the river's edge, smoking and joshing as Bee splashed about in the turgid water, hoping to stir up a frog. All three youths attended the old Central School where four upper classes met weekdays in rooms on the second floor. All three were pleased to see their compadre when he hailed them.

"Gillom, lad! Bring an offering to the party?" yelled the blacksmith's big son.

"I *did,* Mister Kneebone! A nip of the cacti to go with a relaxing smoke after a hard day in the class-room." Gillom broke through the brush to his pals, pulling a bottle out of his bag, which he'd purchased out the back door of one of the cantinas clustered along the road to the border crossing. He'd bought that Mexican's tobacco pouch, too.

He held up a small pint bottle of golden liquor with

a blue agave on the label. Gillom pulled the cork with his teeth as he strode up to them. *"Mezcal!"*

Young Ivory smiled. Named for his thin blond hair and pale skin only a shade darker than an albino's, this teenager's delicate skin forced him to wear a felt cowboy hat always, even in cloudy weather like today, just in case of sunshine.

"Missed an arithmetic test today, Gillom. It was a wooly booger!"

Swallowing a first snort, Mr. Rogers breathed through his mouth, exhaling alcohol fumes. "Had more important things to do. Like buy a holster for these beauties." Proudly he pulled his holstered specials from the burlap.

His three mates were dumbstuck, mouths opened.

"J. B. Books's guns?" gaped Ivory.

"Matched Remington .44's. Told you he left 'em to me. Books had 'em sweetened. Filed down the notch on the hammer, loosened the spring on the trigger so they'll fire quicker." He passed both pistols gingerly to the young men. "Careful. You breathe on 'em hard, they'll go off."

The blacksmith's son filled his hand. "No front sight."

"Faster pull. Mister Books did his killing close in. He had sharp eyes, good reflexes, but he told me careful aim wasn't as important as a close distance to your man."

"Gol-lee fishhooks. . . ." Bee Dunn petted one pistol like you'd stroke a cat.

Johnny Kneebone, Jr. closed an eye, extended his gun hand. "Let's try 'em."

"Shots echo off this water. Somebody's sure to come

down here, see what's going on," said their most pragmatic pal, young Mr. Dunn.

"Bee's right, Johnny. Don't." Ivory was the mortician's son, well acquainted with the tragic results of gun trouble.

Gillom stuck out his hands. He took both pistols and slid them carefully back into leather sheaths. "Bought saddle soap and oil, to shine up this old leather. I'll get a new holster someday."

"Was that Books's, too?" Bee asked.

"No. Just bought it at Jim Dandy's. Books left me some of his savings."

Ivory yelped. "Christmas in *April*!"

Gillom turned to young Kneebone. "Get your own pistol, Johnny, you wanna become a dead shot."

"I wanna practice with the shootist's smoke wagon. See what made him so good."

Bee snorted. "So *good*? He got killed, remember?"

Gillom shook his head. "Not a chance of usin' these guns here."

"Buy one from yah." Kneebone appraised his thinner pal. "Thirty dollars."

Gillom shook his head again. "This matched pair's worth hundreds. To collectors."

Johnny cat-eyed his compadre. Gillom returned his stare. He and Johnny were friendly rivals among a group of senior boys, but since Gillom had recently dropped out of high school and then had the luck to get involved in Books's big shoot-out, his esteem had grown in the other boys' eyes, his reputation for toughness burnished. Now the green-eyed monster reared its ugly head.

"Bet you. Remington for my Barlow knife. Mumblety-peg."

Gillom scowled. "That's no fair bet, knife for a fine pistol."

"Plus thirty dollars."

Gillom chuckled nervously, looked round at his classmates. "You don't have that kind of money."

"I win, I'll scrape it up. You keep Books's revolver till I do."

Gillom was reluctant, but he saw the eager faces about him. A *dare*!

Bee, his closest friend among the bunch, was the first to compromise him. "C'mon, Gillie. You need a good knife to go with those *pistolas*."

"You'll still have one, if you lose," chimed Ivory.

The gauntlet had been tossed. Reluctantly, Gillom Rogers nodded.

Kneebone pulled out his three-bladed clasp knife and wiped its four-inch steel blade clean on his corduroy trousers. "Yank yer boots off."

"*Yeah!*" yipped young Mr. Dunn. "Bare feet makes it interestin'!"

Both boys bent to unlace their brogans, which were made of leather heavy enough to support mine workers. Cocky with his own weapon, Johnny flung it by the handle, sticking the knife into the riverbank's moist soil, next to the work boot Gillom was unlacing.

"*Hey!* Not ready!"

A crooked smile crossed the bigger kid's face. "You won't be, either, when I stick that steel between your toes."

Gillom pulled the pocketknife from the soft dirt and wiped the blade off. He chewed his lower lip. He leaned and tossed the sharp knife into the dirt a foot and a half from Johnny's foot. Kneebone slid his bare foot out to reach the blade, then yanked it out to lean across his body and stick it a foot-length the other side of Gillom.

Boys in west Texas grew up playing mumblety-peg, graduating from small penknives to single-bladed hog stickers. More dangerous barefooted, this match bid to be a good contest. Over pretty quickly, too, at the rate these limber youths were reaching, sticking, then spreading their legs wider, almost doing splits now. First one to miss sticking the knife blade in the dirt, handle up, would lose more than his pride.

Showing off to the grinning lads, Johnny held his steel blade by its sharp point and flipped it end over end to stick another eight inches beyond Gillom's left little toe.

"Nice throw!" yelled young Bean.

Johnny smirked. "I need that Remington to practice my aim, so's when asked whether it's gonna be guns or knives, won't make no difference which one my victim chooses."

Gillom leaned far to pull the knife. He was spread wide, with not much length left in his legs to maneuver. But he managed to reach and stick the blade again four inches beyond Johnny's far foot. Kneebone reached and pulled. The longer legs he inherited from his tall blacksmith daddy gave him an advantage. Showing off again, Johnny took the blade point between thumb and forefinger, leaned and flipped his knife. The sharp steel rotated end over end, but the teenager miscalculated the arc and stuck Gillom right on top of his foot, back of his little toe.

Gillom fell backward. "Owww! *Damn!* You cut me deliberately!"

"Gillie, I'm sorry."

Gillom rolled on his back, holding up his bleeding foot. "Yes you did!"

"*No*, Gillom. I just missed."

Gillom's juices were running now, bringing him to his feet, limping around on one bleeding foot. "If you've made me a gimp, swear to God I'll kill you!" He was as angry as the other boys had ever seen him. Bending to his bundle, Gillom ripped the two prized pistols from the burlap.

"Trying to hurt me, put me down so's you can grab my new guns! I'll show *you* who lays the chunk!" Barely aiming, he pulled a hair trigger, blasting a bullet near Kneebone's bare foot. Johnny jumped as if from a hot foot!

"Dance, Kneebone, *dance!*"

Bullets from Gillom's six-shooters kicked up clods of dirt at Kneebone's feet, with Johnny frantically hopping about. "I'm sorry, Gillom, *sorry!* Didn't mean—"

A ricochet cut him off, bruising Kneebone's instep. The gunshots, flying dirt, *mezcal* coursing through their veins, scared the other boys. Bee Dunn and Ivory Bean backed away, turned to make tracks. Young Mr. Kneebone wasn't far behind, leaving his work boots lying as he galloped off in big bare feet.

"Yeah, pull your freight for home, Kneebone! Taste a what you'll get, you ever try to stick me again!" Gillom fired one last shot at the retreating trio, over their heads.

"*You're pure-dee crazy, Gillom!*" Bee yelled back.

Gillom sat down suddenly, breathing hard from the pain, his fury, and his frustration with his confused life and his abandonment by his old pals. He pulled a fairly clean handkerchief from his jacket pocket and wrapped his bloody foot, trying to squeeze off the pain. He rested his foot and picked up his new Barlow knife. He balanced the knife in his palm, musing upon his predicament, and then softly, for only the third time since he was a little boy, Gillom Rogers began to cry.

His mother was waiting as he limped in the front door. She herded him into her kitchen and got out the antiseptic. His explanation of mumblety-peg with the boys at the river didn't wash well, either.

"At least your friends are *in* school. Why don't you go back with them, finish your senior year together?"

"Aw, I can't now. Word's around I was involved in that gunfight. Teachers would mark me down for bein' dangerous. Girls wouldn't talk to me and the fellas would be botherin' me to show 'em those guns, just like the boys this afternoon."

She hesitated before dousing a clean rag with carbolic acid. "You had Mister Books's pistols out in public?"

"No. But the boys sure wanted to see 'em."

She rubbed disinfectant right onto his wound, causing her son to jerk straight up!

"Sufferin' Jesus!"

"Wound doesn't look too deep. I think you'll walk again." A little more scrubbing by her and a lot more grimacing by him and his cut foot was freshly bound.

"Gillom. If you won't attend school now, you need a job. Keep you busy, out of more trouble, while you learn a trade."

"Given it some thought."

She waited while he wriggled his foot about to see if it still worked. *"And?"*

"Well, I'm now known for my weapons skills. So something to do with security. Bank or train guard, maybe."

"And get shot." She frowned. "To go along with your toe-cutting today? I think not. Something *not* involving weapons. Cashier in a bank perhaps? You're good with figures."

Gillom tested his weight on his wounded foot. "Could be a bouncer in a saloon, but I'm not full-grown yet. Might not win the fistfights."

"Or sales clerk in a mercantile. You'd meet lots of people in a store, nice girls."

"Boring. Like a little excitement with my pay."

His mother shook her head. "I'll ask around, Gillom, at church, my ladies' club. See if anyone respectable is looking for unschooled help."

Gillom moved well enough to limp back toward his

new bedroom. "Sure, Ma." He hesitated. "Thanks. Foot feels better already."

Taken by this little tenderness, the only empathy she'd had with her son in too long a while, Bond Rogers nodded.

Six

Marshal Thibido nailed him as he walked out of the Fair, a dry goods store on the corner of West Overland. Gillom had his arms full of new clothing and saw the lawman standing outside on the sidewalk, masticating a cigarillo.

"Word with you, Rogers." Thibido steered him to the end of the long glass display window fronting the mercantile, next to Phil Young's Café.

"Where'd you get the money for these fancy duds?"

Gillom lugged a pair of black wool, pin-striped California pants and a black morning coat to match, plus the black and silver threaded shirt he was wearing under a brown-collared calfskin vest, adorned with two rows of silver conchos. He had on a pair of blue denim Levis tucked into his new brown leather boots with yellow lightning bolts stitched into their scallop-cut tops. The silverbelly-colored beaver fur Stetson atop his shaggy head had a Carlsbad crease down the front of the crown and sported a six-inch brim.

"Against the law to go shopping?"

Thibido scowled as he tapped the black rubber Tower brand rain slicker Gillom was also carrying, along with a set of brown leather saddlebags into which he'd stuffed cloth bandannas and several pairs of underdrawers, wool socks, and gray cotton undershirts.

"Heard you were buying out the store. All this new gear must run a hundred dollars, easy. Where'd a ruffian get that kind of *dinero*?"

"If it's any business of yours, Marshal, J. B. Books paid me to run messages for him, do errands."

The marshal leaned in, pinning the youth and his full armload tight against the window glass. "Heard you grabbed his pistols, too. Where are they?"

"Who told you that?"

"Answer my *question*! Where are Books's guns?"

"I don't have 'em!"

"*Liar!*" Thibido pinched Gillom hard by the elbow and began steering him down the boardwalk. "Think you're a real rooster, don'tcha? Regular cock of the high school walk. Let's see if a night in jail doesn't settle your sass."

Gillom could only yelp as the short, muscular lawman gave him a side kick in the seat of his stiff new jeans to hurry him across the busy street.

Walter Thibido gave Gillom Rogers another hard boot in the pants seat to launch him inside the jail cell. A deadbeat was sleeping off a drunk on the lower bunk.

"What's my crime again?"

"Withholding *evidence*! From a murder investigation! I want Books's guns!"

"I don't have 'em!"

"*Horseshit!* I heard you did!"

"Truth's a hard cat to skin, Marshal."

The lawman clanged the iron door shut, made a production of locking it, then spun the big key ring on his index finger, gunfighter-like.

"Letcha stew in here awhile, till memory serves."

Gillom tried to shake the bars in his anger. "My mother'll miss me, Marshal!"

The marshal smiled, insincerely. "I'll tell dear mother first thing in the morning, I've found her runaway. She brings me Books's pistols, you go home. Then she can skin you there, too. Otherwise . . ." Thibido jangled the keys at his new prisoner.

"Can't hold me on a *rumor*!"

"Sleep tight, Sonny Boy."

The only people who slept tight that night in those small cells in that raucous jail were the snoring drunks. Gillom dozed fitfully, pondering his mostly uneventful past, at least until last week when J. B. Books arrived, and his disturbing future, now that Mr. Books was gone. His young life had been turned upside down and he couldn't have been more surprised than if he'd just spotted the baby Jesus wearing short pants. *What in holy hell do I do now?*

But good to his word, by ten the next morning, one of Walter's deputies had informed Bond Rogers. She hurried to El Paso's jail, recently rebuilt for expansion. The short marshal, in a tan leather vest, white shirt, and butternut pants, escorted the widow and her companion, the Reverend Henry New, down the walkway past the crowded cells, so they could see the bad company her only child would be keeping if he didn't cooperate.

Thibido couldn't resist a little snide showmanship, gesturing. "Your prodigal son."

A hand to her mouth. "Oh, Gillom . . ."

Gillom sat on the top bunk dangling new boots, his pile of new clothing beside him.

"I'm sorry, Ma. Reverend. He arrested me for no good reason."

The Reverend New, full of thirty-three years of rectitude, nodded to his young parishioner. "Whatever the reason, let's get you out of this filthy place and home to put you on the stool of repentance."

Thibido frowned. "Gave him my best cell. God help he should meet some of our other incorrigibles." For punctuation, the drunk still sleeping on the bunk beneath Gillom groaned and shook a little in his delirium tremens.

Henry New steepled his fingers. "The way of the transgressor is *hard*. Why *is* he in here, Marshal?"

"Withholding evidence. He's got J. B. Books's revolvers and won't give 'em up. For my murder investigation."

Gillom jumped down off the top bunk to grab the cell bars. "That investigation's *done*! Mister Books shot everybody inside the Constantinople and then that sneakin' barkeep shotgunned him in the back. There's no mystery about that, no more to learn."

The marshal folded his arms. "Property of the court."

"My *ass*! He wants Books's pistols to sell as high-priced souvenirs!"

"And you'll stay in my jail till you cough 'em up, thief!"

Mrs. Rogers blanched. "Marshal, *please*. Release my son and we'll locate those guns for you within a couple days."

El Paso's finest considered her. "Missus Rogers, I checked at Central School. Evidently he took some shots at Johnny Kneebone, the blacksmith's kid. Made him dance down near the river day before yesterday, after class. Blacksmith isn't demanding an arrest, he just wants Gillom relieved of those weapons. Gillom can't go back to school for a while, either. The other kids are afraid of him."

Henry New looked solemn. "*I'll* work with Gillom, Marshal. No more pistol shooting. His temperishness is finished. We'll find a job to fill his idleness. The way the twig is bent, that way it shall grow."

Marshal Thibido considered the offer as he shifted from one foot to another in squeaky brown shoes. Finally, a reprieve.

"I defer to your wisdom, Preacher. And to your promise, ma'am." With a last flourish, the marshal produced the brass ring, unlocked the iron door, and Gillom Rogers was free. The reverend and his mother followed Gillom up the jail corridor, past curious inmates. Marshal Thibido followed the chastened family right out his rebuilt jail's front door, hollering after them as they crossed the street.

"*Hooligan's Troubles* is playing down at the Myar Opera House, Gillom! Maybe you can get a starring role!"

Seven

His mother ordered him to stay home that afternoon, out of further trouble, while she visited several lady friends to spread word her son was seeking employment. Gillom watched her walk off in high-button shoes, stepping high, like her feet hurt with the task. The house was silent as he stood in the bedroom where J. B. Books had killed two midnight assassins only a week ago. Until echoes from that bloody set-to died down, Bond Rogers wouldn't have to slave afternoons cooking more big meals for boarders. They were all gone.

Sure his mother was gone, Gillom left the house and headed for Mose Tarrant's livery stable. All he needed now was a horse and tack. *With that damned marshal chasing me and my pistols,* he decided, *I gotta get the hell out of El Paso for a while.*

He hurried along Overland Street, keeping his head down under his new Stetson. Tarrant's stable was on Oregon Street, a cross street. He walked south, toward the river and Mexico. Glancing back, Gillom saw two Mexicans riding slowly along the street after him. Gillom had noticed these two young men sitting beside the dirt road under a shade tree, holding their horses' reins and conversing as he passed.

Gillom checked behind before entering the stable, and sure enough, the two Mexicans on horseback were still dogging him. Inside, Mose Tarrant was attempting to curry an anxious stallion tethered outside its stall.

"*Mose!* I need to buy a horse!"

"*Whoa*, settle down there." Twisting the stamping stallion's bridle, the liveryman turned the gray horse's rear hooves away from his new customer.

"Got any money?"

"Yes, I do," nodded Gillom. "Mister Books left me a little."

"Really? After that shitty trick you pulled, sellin' me Books's horse without his permission?"

"Well, said I was sorry. Thought we settled our personal differences . . . before his shoot-out. You still got his horse?"

"Yessir. Dollar. His fistula's healin'. Expensive animal, though."

"How expensive?"

"Three hundred dollars."

"*What!* That horse ain't no racer."

The older stable owner gave the teenager a mercenary look. "Son, that horse *belonged* to John Bernard Books."

"Well, I just need a fit animal to ride. Doesn't have to be blooded stock."

"I'll look around. When do you need this mighty steed?"

"Oh, next couple days. You still got Books's saddle?"

"I do." The tall, stooped white man gave the stallion's mane a couple last swipes with his brush, then led the restless bangtail back into its stall.

"Hundred and fifty dollars for all his tack."

Gillom shook his head. "Pretty dear."

"Hey, that's a Myres saddle, a good double rig. Where you ridin' to?"

"Oh, north, probably. Into the mountains."

Mose Tarrant ran long, dirty fingers through his own thinning hair, brushing loose straw from the tangle.

"Then you'll need a breast collar, too, so that big saddle won't slip back when you're climbing. Might throw that in for the price."

"See what I can afford."

"Tomorra's Sunday. Come back Monday, see if I've found anything can still trot."

Gillom grinned. "Gallop would be preferred. Thank you, Mose."

Mose Tarrant cleared his throat, expectorated into the pungent dirt on his stable's floor. "Don't forget to bring your money, Junior. *All* of it."

Gillom stuck his head round the barn's corner to peer both ways, up and down busy Oregon Street. He saw several Mexicans going about their business, but not those two young vaqueros.

. . .

Next morning, his arm hooked into his mother's, Gillom attended church. Methodists occupied the greatest number of churches at this turn of El Paso's century, five, and Gillom was seated in a pew of the oldest, Trinity Methodist South, on the corner of Texas and Stanton. His mother wanted his attendance noted but not to put Gillom on display, so they were seated near the middle of the congregation. Bond Rogers sat on the aisle, so her son couldn't escape.

From his pulpit, the Reverend Henry New was excoriating his flock about sinners swimming in "hot *agua*," and how he'd rather be a doorkeeper in the House of God than dwell outside forever in the tents of wickedness. Biblical hot air drifted over Gillom like sleep until a rap in the ribs from his mother startled him awake. The preacher was climaxing about the Lord leading him to a sacred rock that was higher than *he* was, when the youth's bored glance out one of the side windows caught sight of two Mexicans riding slowly up to one of the tall oaks in their church's backyard. The young vaqueros halted and bent to speak to one of the girls skipping rope outside now that Sunday school had released. Gillom sat straight up in his pew seat. The little girls gabbed with those same Mexicans and pointed toward this church!

Gillom was restless through the final hymn and benediction, while the riders sitting their horses under the big oak were patient, quiet. After the service, Gillom tried to bound down the front steps past Henry New, but the reverend was too quick.

"*Gillom!* Any luck with the job hunting?"

"No, sir. But I plan on goin' lookin' tomorrow."

His mother wedged in her two cents. "I heard Jay Cobb's parents need somebody to deliver milk from their creamery, after what happened to their poor son in the Books tragedy."

Reverend New's smile folded into a funereal frown. "Their *only* son. Those who live by the sword, or the six-gun in young Jay's case, shall *perish* by it. I must step round with my condolences." He turned back to Bond's wayward son. "Milk deliveries would be a starter job, Gillom, until you found something better. Did you find those pistols?"

Gillom wasn't partial to a Sunday grilling, especially with other parishioners hovering.

"Nope." Gillom pushed from the knot of people awaiting the preacher's blessing and down the front steps. The reverend, however, always liked the last word.

"Hope you're not back in jail before you find a job!" he yelled at the retreating young man.

Bond Rogers stood embarrassed. Realizing even he might have overstepped the bounds of propriety, the parson patted Mrs. Rogers's wrist.

"A wise son maketh a good father, but a foolish son is the heaviness of his mother."

Mrs. Rogers gave her preacher a hard eye before marching away from the gossiping churchgoers.

There was no stopping Gillom as he strode toward the big oak up the grassy rise. Seeing him coming fast, the two Mexicans were already turning their horses.

"*Hey,* you fellers! Wait up!" The vaqueros gave their mounts the spurs. Only their dust lingered.

. . .

That afternoon Gillom told his mother he was going to see his pals.

"I can't look for work, it's Sunday. Maybe Bee or Ivory will know of a job, or they can spread the word at school tomorrow. See if anyone's dad's looking for someone full-time."

"I'm surprised those boys would have anything to do with you after you shot at them."

"That was just at Kneebone, *after* he stuck his knife in my bare foot. Don't believe everything the marshal said, Ma. I'm still friends with most of the kids at school. They ain't scared a me."

Mrs. Rogers rubbed worry from her hands. "I certainly hope not. You'll never find any job if people are afraid of you, or hear even a whisper you're dangerous."

"I'll be back for supper."

"Think you'll find those pistols?"

Gillom's grin turned downward. "Don't bet on it."

"Don't make J. B. Books your dime novel hero, Gillom. He was nothing more than a shootist."

"Maybe, but he also made history." Then he was out the front door, bounding down their whitewashed steps. He gave his mother a backhanded goodbye as he strode out their front gate. He halted on their wooden sidewalk to check up and down Overland Street, looking for Mexicans.

No spies in sight, so he turned left, away from downtown. When he saw his mother had closed the front door of their two-story brick house, he sidestraddled their back fence, ran to the woodpile behind their backyard tool shed. Moving some firewood, Gillom dug out Books's revolvers again from their burlap swaddling. He'd soaped and cleaned the leather late last night in his bedroom closet, then oiled the old holster to preserve it and speed his draw.

I've gotta practice, he realized. *Fire these pistols before somebody tests me. These two Remingtons are gonna be my only protection from thieves and pistoleros trying to prove their speed, so I better get comfortable with 'em. These guns and I need to become friends.*

Eight

The bundle tucked under his wool coat, Gillom
hopped the fence again and walked west, headed past
the growing city's fringe. He knew of denser thickets,
north of the Rio Grande, that were crossing points
south for smugglers of guns, ammunition, cattle, and
horses, with outlaws and tequila returning north
through the same overgrown area. That dark country
should be safe enough in the daytime, though, if he
stayed on his guard.

Three miles outside El Paso, Gillom turned off the
rutted road to hike into a bosque, a thicket of cottonwoods and heavy scrub brush just north of the river.
Gillom recalled a big flood four years earlier in 1897
that had caused the Rio Grande to change course, iso-
lating pieces of land between the old and new river-
banks. Gillom walked over the dry watercourse onto
one such island, no longer legally in either America or
Mexico until diplomats crossed sharp pens over the
dispute. Brush-breaking was tiring, so he stopped to

belt on his holster to free his hands. Ahead was a small clearing with a well-used firepit in the middle. He was entering bandit country!

Gillom sat down on a rock next to the fire ring to catch his breath and remove his coat. He picked up a small canteen he'd carried along, took water. He rolled up his shirtsleeves and took off his stiff new Stetson to enjoy some afternoon sun. Rising, he adjusted the single loop holster on his hips, making sure the double rig was belted low enough so his arms and big hands rested just below the revolvers' trigger guards visible in their leather pockets for a fast pull. He loosened the leather tie-downs over the hammers to keep the guns snug in their leather sheaths. Then, first with his strong hand, he drew the pearl-handled .44 Remington smoothly but slowly, extended his right arm, closed his nondominant left eye, thumbed the hammer back, and fired. Gillom Rogers hit the tall tree he was aiming at, but not the target joint of its low-hanging branch.

He took a deep breath. *Speed and accuracy need to be better,* he realized. Adjusting his gunman's stance a little wider, he reholstered his right revolver, stuck his empty right hand out for balance. He quick-pulled the gun on his left side with his off hand, extended his forearm, closed his dominant right eye, thumbed the single-action again, and pulled the trigger. This time his aim was wide, clipping a branch. His second shot was muffled by the dense underbrush. *Wonder if my gunfire will attract any attention?*

Now that the hammers of both pistols rested upon empty chambers, the safe way to practice in case he dropped a gun, he could practice firing without worrying about shooting himself in the foot. So practice Gillom did—fast draws, right hand, left hand, both hands, twirling the nickel-plated revolvers on his index fingers within their steel trigger guards, one revolution, two spins round, backward, forward, to make his reholstering look fancy. Again and again—quick pull, trying to make his hammer cock and the aim off his hips merely a reflex of hand and eye, without squinting, flinching, without even breathing.

Dropped the pistol! *Damn! Be careful!* Wiping sweaty palms on his Levis, he sucked breath and tried again. Right, left, both, again, until he had his fast draw fairly smooth with either hand.

Gillom stopped for a gulp of water. Since his first shots hadn't drawn any unwelcome attention, he tried a trick he'd only heard about, never seen attempted. Pulling both revolvers suddenly, he cocked and fired his right Remington, then spun its pearl handle backward and flipped it into the air. While the first revolver somersaulted in the air, he quick transferred the black-handled grip from his weak left hand to his strong right, while attempting to catch the first pistol in his left palm as the gun spun round in the air. And *missed*!

He brushed dirt off its silver nickel plating, reholstered, and tried once more. This time he flipped the pearl-handled revolver higher, giving himself more time for the catch after the transfer, and achieved it. To celebrate he cocked and fired the black-handled pistol without carefully sighting and was rewarded by splinters flying from the cottonwood's girth, seventy-five feet away. The border shift was tricky but essential to learn, for it allowed a gunfighter with an empty pistol to exchange it for a loaded weapon rapidly while under fire.

He dropped a pistol again, then made another successful transfer. Gillom began to complicate his draws, rotating each revolver once right out of the holster pocket as he spun them on each index finger and extended his right and left forearms, earring hammers back and firing at the end of each reach. Another drop. A blister formed on his right finger.

"Damn this is hard!" Gillom said aloud. Over and over, Gillom's quick reflexes and sharp vision helped him whang chunks out of the distant tree almost every time. *Maybe I've got the goddamned gift of gunfighting,* he thought. *What did that journalist call it—a bullet's blessing?*

He was reloading from a box of cartridges in his coat pocket when a bush snapped. While jamming cartridges in the revolver's chambers, Gillom saw the crown of a wide hat above the breaking brush, a man on horseback. Now brush was crackling behind him, too! Spinning, he kept his left hand on his gun butt, his right revolver cocked and pointed at a black sombrero moving toward him.

Damn! That looks like one of those . . . Mexicans . . . been followin' me! How in the bejesus did they find me out here?

The vaqueros had him sandwiched as they halted their scrawny horses in the brush either side of the clearing's edge. Each wore a pistol on his hip, but both young men kept their hands on their reins as they sat cheap-looking saddles.

"You boys been *followin'* me!"

The Mexicans held their tongues. His next question was a little more plaintive.

"Whatdya want?"

"Señor Gillom?"

"Yeah?"

The taller guy, who looked tougher, more aggressive than his younger partner, smiled. Maybe it was his black sombrero that intimidated.

"Ahhh, Señor Gillom. Did you invite Señor Serrano to his shooting?"

Gillom Rogers hesitated. "I guess."

"An' Señor Books kill him?"

Gillom slowly nodded.

Black sombrero waggled a finger. "*Sí.* It was you. Senor Serrano is his *tio*." He pointed at the younger Mexican across the clearing. A flash of a gold tooth in a mouthful of pearlies. "Married to his sees-ter."

"His uncle?"

"*Sí. Tio.* Un-cle. Now he must kill you. *Caballerismo.* Hon-or his *familia*."

"*What?*"

The older young man nodded. "*Sí.* You help thees assassin, Señor Books."

Gillom was astounded by this primitive logic. "*No!* I was just Mister Books's messenger."

"But you invite his un-cle to his murder. Mess-age of *muerte*, death. An' then you shoot Señor Books, no? *Journalista* say. So Cesar must kill you. *Justica. Por* his *familia*."

Their logic might have been crazy, but they didn't appear to be fooling. Gillom pulled his second pistol and cocked it, training his left hand on the younger *hombre* to the south. The older vaquero grinned. "You prac-tice, *pendejo*. But no more bul-lets!"

They're testing me, Gillom figured. *Gotta show 'em.*

Crouching to provide a smaller target even though he was standing all by his lonesome in the middle of a bare clearing, Gillom extended his right arm and squeezed the trigger of Books's big revolver. The .44-.40 slug clipped a branch of brush next to the mean Mexican, causing his horse to snort and shy side-ways.

"Hokay, *pendejo*! *Mi* mis-take!" The twenty or so year old got his frightened horse under control, while his cousin across the clearing ducked, put his hands on his pistol's butt, readying to draw. "No shoot you today, *gavacho,* but *watch out*! Serranos *owe* you!"

Touching a finger to his forehead goodbye, the black-hatted tracker began backing his skittish animal out of the thicket. His younger relative on the other side of the clearing began retreating, too. Gillom noted how underfed and unkempt their horses appeared.

My God! I can't have these backshooters following me around El Paso, trying to kill me any goddamned time they please! That dark thought propelled him into an equally scary plan.

"You boys want a fair fight, meet me tonight!"

The older vaquero turned in his saddle. "Where?"

Gillom had to think a moment. "The bandstand in San Jacinto Plaza. Midnight!"

The Mexican pondered. *"Hokay!"* His gold front tooth flashed like a character flaw. *"Mucha suerte, gringo!"* He clucked to his horse and after fearsome moments of brush cracking, the vengeful young men were gone.

Gillom Rogers uncocked his Remingtons and reholstered. Bending, he put both hands on his knees, took another long, deep breath, and exhaled slowly. *God-almighty. What have I done now?*

Nine

"**How about working as** a bellhop at the Grand Central? Finest hotel in all the southwest, three whole stories, and you'd meet important guests. Maybe lead to something better if you were polite and gave good service. Plus the gratuities, my goodness." Gillom's mother had a long index finger to her temple, helping her think.

"I'm not toting anybody's bags, Ma, just cause they're rich."

"Well. . . . I read about the four C's of growth in our region—copper, cattle, citrus, and climate. They never mention the fifth C, consumption. El Paso is paradise for the pulmonary invalid. We've got more consumptives and asthmatics in our sanatoriums than anyone can count, with more coming out every day to where sunshine spends the winter. They need strong, young aides to move those patients around. That could be a good starting job for you, health care."

"Ma, I ain't wheelin' any lungers around. You want

me to catch somethin' bad, get sick, too?" Gillom threw his linen napkin down on their long dinner table, vacant now except for the two of them, his beefsteak half-eaten. "I'll find a job, eventually. Maybe work in a gun shop, for a gunsmith. Learn that trade."

"Guns." Bond Rogers blew frustrated air through her lips, like a tired horse.

"Just give me some time to get my life straightened out after all this trouble."

"You seek trouble like a moth does the flame."

With a backhanded dismissal, Gillom headed back to his room. There, by the light of a coal oil lamp in the sanctuary of his clothes closet, behind the curtains, he cleaned Books's revolvers. With a wooden pencil he poked an oiled rag down the Remingtons' barrels to clean out old powder from an afternoon of tree blasting. He oiled the cylinders and replaced the .44-.40 cartridges and spun them shut. He didn't leave one empty as a safety under the hammer, for he knew, barring a miracle, he'd be using these guns tonight. Hope to God I don't need all twelve cartridges. What was it Books said about shoot-outs?

"It isn't being fast, it's whether or not you're willing. The difference is, when it comes down to it, most men are not willing. I found that out early. They will blink an eye, or take a breath before they pull the trigger. I won't."

That's how he'd done it all those years, Gillom thought. Survived. Gunmen of all stripes, fast and slow, young and old, white or whatever race, trying to shoot him, blast him dead. But his steel nerves, quick reflexes, and steady aim always saved his ass. J. B. Books—the shootist. *Well, a cool countenance and a calm hand will save mine, too.*

Gillom got to his knees. Just in case, he put more cartridges into both pockets of his wool coat, for quick reloading. He buried the double holster under some dirty clothing on the wooden floor and was backing from the closet when his mother walked into the bedroom.

"What are you doing in there?"

Startled, Gillom turned, then deliberately calmed his emotions, practicing control.

"Cleaning my boots." He graced his mother with his most conciliatory expression. "Ma, I'm sorry for our arguments. We've both been greatly aggravated by all this . . . bloodshed. Mister Books shook this house up but good. But he's gone now, I doubt to a better place, so we can try a fresh start. I'll look for a good job tomorrow. And find one. I promise."

Her smile finally bloomed. "Oh, Gillom. You can do it, I know you can, dear. Learn some decent, respectable profession. And finish your high schooling. Go back to Central School next year, after this awful business dies down."

Now Gillom smiled. "Maybe." He was careful in the hug he gave her, so she didn't feel any cartridges rolling around in his coat pockets.

Gillom heard his mother lightly snoring upstairs through his thin ceiling, so he had no trouble slipping out his bedroom window later that night. He chanced wearing his double rig under his wool coat. It was Sunday and long after dark, when even the six hundred gamblers in the forty licensed gambling halls and the hundreds of whores in the bagnios and cribs and dance halls lining Utah Street all the way down to the Rio Grande had to catch their breaths after another weekend's lucrative work. The local saying was, "When anybody has a dollar in his pocket, he heads hell-bent to El Paso to get rid of it."

Gillom had been to San Jacinto Plaza many times with his mother. Peering through the darkness as he walked up to it, he noted the two highest structures· in the block-long plaza—the bandstand and the fountain in the middle, constructed of rocks and mortar from which a large plume of water shot up in the air during the daytime, when it was turned on. A stone catch basin around it was filled with water five feet deep. Grass grew around this fountain in a ring between the water pool and a chain-link metal fence anchored by iron poles that encircled the whole layout, at least thirty yards wide.

The metal fence had been constructed to keep little boys out and the alligators in. Local kids had a penchant for poking the alligators with sticks and throwing stones at them while they dozed in the grass beside their waterhole, seeing if they could be provoked. According to local legend, six baby alligators had been shipped by train from the swamps of Louisiana by a friend of one A. Muhsenberger, a mining man, as a joke. Having no way to care for them, Mr. Muhsenberger had prevailed upon the city council to add the gators to the plaza menagerie. A few had survived attacks by eagles, owls, coyotes, and little boys to thrive on a diet of horse and cow carcasses, stray dogs, and the occasional child. Several of these pet gators had grown to be a good ten to twelve feet long.

The most famous incident happened after a convention of dentists, drinking too late in an El Paso saloon, got into a loud argument over how many teeth an alligator actually had? A number of these dentists, armed with more booze and torches and ropes, set off into the dark midnight to actually find out, but were stopped by deputies before they could conduct any alligator dental examinations.

Gillom had no interest in arousing the ancient beasts as he walked delicately across the long plank bridging the stone basin to several rock steps leading up to the top of the rock fountain in the middle of the gators' pond. Looking down into the murky water, he could see several pairs of orbs as red as fireholes glowing in the cairn beneath the fountain he was about to climb. Stone masons had thoughtfully hollowed out an underwater grotto underneath the fountain where the gators could rest in peace out of the hot sunshine and away from rock-throwing kids.

The raised fountain gave the crouching gunman good vantage of the whole plaza in every direction, and by moving around its uneven, eight-foot-high stone sides, he could have cover. Still, it was unnerving, perched atop rough rocks in the dark, watching an occasional ripple cross the pond to lap upon the gravel rim at the edge, or to hear an exhalation from the grotto beneath, a shivery breath from a prehistory entirely foreign to this high school dropout. Gillom Rogers was very aware of what lurked below.

He didn't have long to wait. Serrano's vengeful relatives showed up half an hour early, similarly thinking to gain an advantage. The cousins rode slowly north up El Paso Street from the Juarez bridge, dismounted to loose-tie their horses to another chain-link fence that had been erected around the whole park to keep horses and rabbits from grazing its flowers and grass under its pepper trees down to nubs. The young Mexicans didn't pause, hopping the waist-high fence, then pulling their old pistols to move out along either side of the plaza, heading toward the raised bandstand.

Gillom slid down the far side of the fountain from them. He'd left his new Stetson at home, to present less of a profile against the lamplight from the windows of the luxurious new five-story Sheldon Hotel fronting the north side of the plaza. Several saloons along the south side of San Jacinto Plaza were still open, but other stores and commercial buildings around the park were closed this late Sunday night and the plaza deserted. He hugged the rocks of the fountain's construction and slid over the top to the opposite side again as the two Mexicans passed him on either side, looking cautiously about everywhere but up at the fountain itself, for no one would dare venturing into that alligator pond after dark.

The vaqueros wore dark clothing, one had a sombrero, and when they reached the covered bandstand only ten yards north of the pond, the taller man dashed up its five wooden stairs to get better vantage. Serrano's closer relative waited below, bouncing nervously on the toes of his boots, steeling himself for a bloodletting. Gillom could hear their Spanish whispers. *Might as well start the ball,* he figured. *Didn't come here to hide from a fight.* He chewed his lip as he rose to stand atop the flattened top of the rock tower, where the brass nozzles of this big fountain's three pipes blew towering spray from these rocks in the daytime.

"*Buscaderos!* This is your *chance!* Take your best Sunday shot!"

"*Cuidado,* Cesar!" yelled the man leaning on the bandstand's low railing. His jumpy relative below was already jerking his *pistola* up and firing a wild shot at the shadowy figure standing atop the rock tower.

Gillom knew it was gospel among gunfighters that the man who survived a shoot-out took his time. So he took his precious time, too. As a second, errant bullet flew past, he sighted down his stretched arm and with one shot, plugged the kid right in his breadbasket. The young vaquero staggered at the slug's impact and fell on his seater, the shock of a stomach wound paralyzing him. The older Mexican clattered down the bandstand's stairs to his cousin's aid, who sat slumped forward like a rag doll with the stuffing knocked out of him.

"Cesar! Cesar!"

His cousin couldn't answer, gurgling blood instead. This enraged the aggressive youth who had instigated this vendetta, and he jumped to his feet.

"*Pendejo!* You kill him!" Firing his own pistol, Gold Tooth winged a bullet off the rock under Gillom's boot. Jumping at the ricochet, Gillom pulled his second revolver and cocked and fired both .44's from his hips at once! One of his lead slugs caught the second Mexican, spinning him around and down on the dirt walkway next to the bandstand. Gillom couldn't take any further chances. Straightening from his crouch, he extended his right arm, thumbed the hammer, and aiming down the unsighted barrel of his Remington, went cat-eyed in the dark.

"Buenas noches, hombre!" His careful shot from twenty-five yards, aiming downward, found its target again, hitting the second troublemaker in the chest and knocking him flat. Gillom didn't stop to admire his shooting, but quickly reholstered and clambered down the rock tower's side. He heard a band in a distant saloon essaying a standard, "Where the Lilies Bloom," as he tiptoed rapidly across the plank board bridging the pond.

With one gun drawn again, Gillom kicked the older, more dangerous man to ascertain if he was dead. Not worried about his relative still slumped, breathing raggedly nearby, Gillom quickly unbuckled Gold Tooth's holster and took his pistol, then rifled the young man's pockets finding some dobie dollars and a pocketknife. *Don't leave anything identifying him behind,* he remembered.

He was pulling the dead man up when he heard a loud *hiissss* behind him. *The alligators! Christ, they hunt at night!* His mind raced. *And eat dead meat!* Gillom turned to see two bright pairs of eyes staring unblinkingly at him from dark water. One of the beasts had its elongated flat snout resting on the pond's concrete lip, several of its eighty long teeth glistening in the moonlight.

Gillom heaved, waltzed the dead Mexican around, closer to the chain-link fence, then with a big hoist and a shove, pushed his stalker over the low, iron-poled fence backward into the pond with a splash. Gold Tooth had barely hit the water when several big splashes signaled the alligators were into him, grabbing the body from either side and shaking it with their sharp teeth.

"Damn! They smell the blood!" Gillom was breathing heavily, but didn't have time to watch the frenzy, the big beasts dragging the body underwater to swim it down to their lair underneath the stone pile. He was already unbuckling the other teenager's holster, picking up his revolver, too. The *bandido* groaned at the movement and his chest wound bled badly.

"Sorry, amigo, you asked for this. Can't leave you . . . to recruit Serrano's other kin. You ain't gonna recover anyway."

After rifling his pockets, he pulled the younger Mexican to his feet, hoisted him over his shoulder.

The vaquero groaned "Noooo" as he tried to grasp the pistols in Gillom's holsters. Gillom staggered under the young man's weight, but got himself turned round and lunged forward several steps to push the youth over the metal barrier to drop him on his butt inside the pond with another splash. The cold water woke the teenager from his lead-shocked daze. But his blood was already in the water.

Gillom hurriedly gathered his plunder outside the fence, the worn holsters and old, scratched pistols, the Mexican money and small buck knife. He saw several people moving outside the entrance to the hotel across the way, trying to ascertain the source of the gunshots in the night. A couple drunks weaved outside one of the saloons across from the park's south end, but they were shouting and singing.

As Gillom picked up Gold Tooth's gun belt and holster, with a *schlooosh* the biggest alligator, twelve feet long in the darkness at least, leapt out of the water and grabbed the sitting Mexican kid by the left shoulder in its mighty jaw. The crunch of collarbone through his coat was unmistakable.

"Aiiiyeeee!" The youth was yanked backward by the gator's savage grip. The beast's thrashing and heavy weight dragged its second victim into the pond and underwater into its death roll with only a muffled moan and a furious roiling of water.

"The gators got something!" one of the hotel guests yelled and started to run over. Gillom ran south along a plaza pathway, arms full of his antagonists' weapons. He was horrified by the alligators' blood thirst, had never seen anything like their attacks before, and felt no satisfaction in the killings. He was simply grateful to be alive, his guts still intact.

Gillom slung himself and his booty over the iron fence around the plaza, then yanked the Mexicans' horses' reins loose, drooped their holsters over the second one's saddle horn. As he trotted his prizes away, a policeman's whistle shrilled through the midnight air.

Ten

Bond Rogers was surprised to find her son already up and heating a coffeepot on her woodstove when she appeared in the kitchen early next morning.

"My, you're serious about finding a job today."

Gillom wore new Levis and dark brown cowboy boots; his long gray undershirt was rolled down to his waist as he pumped water into the kitchen sink to wash. *Probably should shave,* he thought, *but no time for that now.* He toweled off as she poured their coffees.

"Ma, I am going to find a good job, but not in El Paso. Have to leave today. For a while."

"What? Why?"

"Well, I got into a . . . shoot-out . . . last night. Late. In San Jacinto Plaza. Shot a couple of young Mexicans, Serrano's kin, who've been followin' me."

His mother paled. "My God. You've turned into a mankiller . . . just like Books." Suddenly out of breath, she sat down hard.

"Ma, they trailed me on the street outside here, to church yesterday, then down near the river when I was practicin'."

"Practicing? With those guns?"

"My *gosh*! I have to be able to defend myself!" He paced as he wormed back into his undershirt. "Those two vaqueros stalked me! Mister Books killed their uncle in the Constantinople. A rustler named Serrano, a real *bandido*. I delivered Books's saloon invite to him, across the border. So his young relatives decided they had to kill *me*! It's their blood honor or some crazy Mexican vendetta. It would have gone on and on, so I had to end it last night. Pronto."

"My son. A *shootist*." She was dazed, not quite comprehending his wild story or his reasoning.

"It was them or me. Younger one shot first."

"You just left them wounded, lying there in the dark?"

"No. They were next to the alligator pond. I think their bodies have been disposed of. Nothing left to connect to me." He wrung the towel in his hands, fretting. "But their relatives will come looking for them. And if they talk to Thibido, and he puts two and two together, he'll come right to our front door. You know the marshal wants those fine revolvers, or me in jail."

His mother stared at him, unhappy and dismayed.

"Why can't you just give Marshal Thibido those guns? Buy him off this . . . this endless trouble."

"No, I've got to vamoose. I have those Mexicans' horses and pistols. I'll sell 'em, out of town. Then take the train to Santa Fe. Always wanted to see that old trading post. I'll find a job, bank or train guard, something honorable, where my gun skills are useful." Gillom reached for her hand. "I'll be fine. I'll come back in a year or so, after these shootings are forgotten. Thibido may even be out of a job by then, and leave you and me and my guns alone."

His mother started to cry, gulping air in and out as the finality of all this bloodshed washed over her. "How can . . . our stars . . . have gotten so crossed? What did we do . . . so awful . . . to deserve John Bernard Books . . . showing up at our front door? *Cursing us!*"

Gillom had the Mexicans' horses saddled in an hour. He ground-reined them in his mom's grassy backyard, away from the nearby street's prying eyes. These horses were stolen and he was taking a risk, but he didn't intend to keep them long.

His mother cooked him a hurried breakfast of oatmeal and bacon, then loaded her only child up with half the foodstuffs in her pantry in a canvas bag. She was filling his bulging warbag with a small frying pan, while he tightened one hemp cinch underneath the big saddle and hopped onto the black horse, the friskier of these *caballos*.

"Got your wool mittens?"

"I've got new leather gloves in my bags, Ma. Weather's mild, won't even need 'em."

"Nights get cold in the desert. You'll catch a chill." She couldn't look at him.

"I'll be fine. Sell these horses and tack when I get into New Mexico, catch a train for Santa Fe."

"Write me often. So I know where to reach you when it's safe to come home."

"I will, Ma. I promise." He leaned down to buss her cheek. That set her tears flowing again. "I won't rest in jail again, either."

"Couldn't bear to lose you, Gillom. Not after Ray. I'd grow old. Alone."

"Year or two at the most, Ma. When this all blows over, I'll come back."

She clutched his arm. "Promise you'll stop this pistol-fighting. *Please!* Don't shoot anybody else!"

He jerked the black horse's head sideways, turning the gelding out from behind the house toward their front yard, led the smaller bay filly along behind by its mecate reins. He'd buried his choice revolvers in his saddlebags until he got out of town or she'd be trying to grab those, too.

She was crying, semihysterical. "Gillom! *Please!* No more killings! It's not *right*! It's not our way!"

He didn't favor his distraught mother with a wave, or even a look back.

Gillom surprised Mose Tarrant in his stable so early, feeding his paying guests. Mose asked where he'd found these two nags, if the kid had gotten a good deal? Gillom lied and resisted the horse wrangler's entreaties to buy Books's overpriced horse, Dollar, instead. But he did swap the worst of the Mexicans' saddles for Books's custom saddle and open reins, a snaffle bit with a high port and several ornate cheek pieces on a split-ear, leather headstall, plus one hundred and fifty dollars. Books's saddle was a Myres double rig with a low wooden horn, bow fork, and a square leather skirt. Mose had found a brown leather breast collar that sort of matched, which he'd tied onto the front of the saddle to prevent slippage. Double cinches made the big saddle more secure, with less movement on the horse's back during jarring movements like sudden stops. Gillom wanted something more comfortable to ride on, for he was going a long ways, and it was why he'd decided to trail two horses instead of one. Old Mose wet-thumbed his money, hiding it in his leather snap-top purse, pleased to get monetarily even with this snaky kid, as Gillom rode away. Neither bid the other farewell.

He avoided the downtown's center around San Jacinto Plaza, the scene of last night's hellish confrontation. *God knows what body parts might have floated up today,* he mused. But Gillom did stop at his favorite haunt, the Acme Saloon, Wes Hardin's infamous headquarters. A bleary bartender didn't blink at selling a pint of whiskey to a minor, since there were no Laws about that early to catch him doin' it.

"Long as you don't drink it in here, kid."

Gillom was stuffing the bottle into a saddlebag when Dan Dobkins spotted him as he strolled out of a nearby breakfast parlor. Dobkins had on another loud, checked suit that didn't match the yellow-and-black shoes he danced across the street in.

"Young Rogers!"

Gillom winced as the newspaper reporter sped over.

"A packhorse? Going somewheres distant?"

"Visiting some relatives. You made it too hot for me here, Dan, writing that stuff in the *Herald*."

Dobkins cleaned what was left of breakfast from his teeth with a matchstick.

"Power of the press. Promised I'd make you famous."

"Notorious is more like it. Now I can't find a job here, can't go back to Central School. And Thibido's tryin' to steal J. B.'s guns, even after Mister Books promised 'em to me."

The newsman shook his head, feigning empathy. "Price of infamy, kid. You get collared as a killer, it'll haunt you."

"You done?" Gillom mounted up. "What did John Wesley Hardin say? 'My enemies are many, but my sword of retribution is my six-shooter.' "

The newshound eyed him speculatively. "You're a real cocked pistol, kid. You get over into New Mexico, stop in Tularosa, ask directions to Gene Rhodes's ranch, west across the white sands up in the San Andes Mountains. Eugene's a tough bird. He's that aspiring fictionist I mentioned. He's got a weakness for desperados ridin' the Owl Hoot Trail, so it's reported."

Gillom had the black gelding moving, but he just nodded, leading the dark brown packhorse away.

Dan watched him go. "*Owe* you one! You come back to the Pass, Gillom, I'll buy the drinks and you tell me your adventures!"

Gillom turned in his saddle to give Dobkins a hard smile, but he didn't wave goodbye.

Eleven

Gillom rode north from El Paso aiming for
Tularosa, the only destination that stuck in his head
from Dobkins's advice. He knew only that after last
night's nightmare with the alligators he had to get
the hell on his horse, or these two stolen ones, and
get gone for a long while.

He still had two hundred and fifty dollars of Books's
inheritance burning in his saddlebag, plus the young
Mexicans' old revolvers and holsters he'd trade for
supplies along the way. *I hope those crazy boys are still
missing,* he thought. It was street wisdom among El
Paso's youth that their park's famous alligators hid
their victims underwater in their rocky grotto to gnaw
on later for snacks. *Hope to God parts of those vaqueros, Serrano's kin, don't float up to give me away!*

The black horse was feisty under its new rider, chewing its snaffle bit, shying sideways, but Mose had told
him this bar bit with a hinge in the middle was easier
on a horse's mouth. Gillom gave the gelding a little

iron of the new spurs he'd also picked up at the Fair store. He nearly lost the reins of the packhorse following as he clung onto the saddlehorn during the bucking that followed. *Lucky Mose sold me that breast collar,* he thought, *so my damned saddle won't fall off!* Gillom aimed the big horse upslope on Mt. Franklin until its consternation subsided.

El Paso had grown up on both sides of this milehigh wedge of limestone and granite shaped like a horseshoe, and he rode along the rocky foothills of the western side of Mt. Franklin, which gradually sloped down to the big river to the south.

But Gillom was headed away from the Rio Grande, weaving through patches of lechugilla and yucca, enjoying a morning sun filtering through mountainside stands of live oak and juniper trees. He was confident enough to ask an old Mexican goatherder chopping down a piñon pine, "How far to Tularosa?"

"Tularosa? *Tres dias,*" the old man answered, scratching his chin hair.

"One hundred miles?"

The old Mexican understood English. "*Mas o menos.*"

I'll tire these ornery animals ridin' forty miles on each of 'em these first couple days and then just ease in that third day for a layover till I get my bearings, Gillom decided. *Tularosa's supposed to be a tough town. Excitin'!*

He rode down the mountainside and out of the coffin corner of Texas.

. . .

It was dark when he reached a stream leading into Old Coe Lake, out in the lower middle of the long Tularosa Valley. The lake was too big to be anybody's fenced-off waterhole, but too small to be good for fishing. Even if he knew how to fish, Gillom was too tired to try. His thighs and butt and lower back ached from a full day in the saddle, which this town boy wasn't used to. He staggered as he pulled the sweaty Navajo double blanket and saddle off the bay horse he'd switched to riding midday, to give each mount a breather from the packed saddlebags and man they had to carry. Taking hardtack from the food sack in his warbag, Gillom led both tired horses down to the stream. While they guzzled noisily, he unbuckled his new twenty-five-dollar Bianchi spurs, yanked his boots and socks off, and splashed into the chilly flow alongside his stolen horseflesh. The spring freshet felt so good, he flung off his new felt hat and cotton shirt to sluice his sweaty chest in a whore's bath.

Gillom managed to find in the dark the leather hobbles Mose Tarrant had thrown into his tack sale. One was unusual, a fore and hind leg "cross-hobble," which he finally attached to the reluctant gelding's hooves by the rising moonlight. Their reins removed, the two horses were left to browse as he untied his canvas-wrapped bedroll with wool blankets inside, rolled up in them and, still chewing a chunk of hardtack, fell into exhausted sleep with his head against J. B. Books's own saddle.

He awoke to one of the horses nibbling grass near his ear. While stretching the stiffness out of his legs,

Gillom gathered sticks for a small fire, filled his coffee-pot and canteens in the stream. He stuck head and shoulders underwater and blew bubbles to wake fully up, then walked back to his fire shaking water from his wet hair like a dog. He'd decided to eat mostly on the move, holding off regular meals until Tularosa, where he could rest and figure out what to do next.

If this Rhodes fella ain't there, I'll ride west, over the mountains to Arizona, he decided. *Prescott's the territorial capital, so it should be a hoppin' town. Or maybe ride down to Old Tucson in the Sonoran desert, before their summer heat hits. Tucson's a famous old tradin' post I'd like to see.*

After horse and rider loosened their leg muscles, Gillom booted the bay mare into a hard trot, wanting to put long miles on while the day was still cool. He aimed northeast, trying to hit the El Paso and North Eastern rail line, which had been completed across the Tularosa Basin only three years before in 1898.

A wide sky sprayed light blue with thin swatches of clouds, across which birds winged. The vast emptiness of the Tularosa Valley was so peaceful Gillom's worries from the two weeks since John Bernard Books had ridden up to his mother's front door took wing, too. He crunched one of Bond Rogers's biscuits.

He kind of missed school, sorry that his run-in with the marshal and Books's shocking suicide and his own temper had all conflagrated so quickly to make him a pariah even among his buddies, an undesirable at high school. *Ahh, to hell with my senior year! Wish they could see me now. Free as a bird and rich to boot! Bee, Ivory, and Johnny would be jealous of my free-ridin' life. Green with envy, especially Mr. Kneebone, Jr.* The thought pleased him no end.

Lunch was hardtack washed down with water, while he lazed in the grass giving the horses a half hour blow and a hatful of corn. Then he switched tack again, putting Books's saddle on the black gelding. The bigger horse didn't fight the bit so much today, the unfamiliar saddle, so Gillom didn't have to grip tight with his sore thighs, alert to the sudden buck or occasional sidestep by an anxious horse.

To relieve the boredom of his slow ride, Gillom practiced. That morning, concerned about highwaymen, he unpacked Books's guns and strapped them on. He reversed the handles of the black and pearl revolvers so he'd be less likely to knock them out of their holsters if he suddenly had to do any hard riding. Gillom practiced his cross-handed draw with each hand a few times, then both at once. Spinning the nickel-plated beauties on his index fingers like Catherine wheels, forward, backward, halting quickly with a twist of his wrist to slip them reversed back into the leather holsters. *Gosh! Did I leave the chamber under the hammer empty like Books warned me to do?* He checked each cylinder. *If I shoot myself or one of these horses in the leg accidentally, I'm in a damned pickle. Be careful, buddy.*

But of course he couldn't be for long. Careful. Boys with guns for toys just had to play with 'em, spinning them upward, downside on one crooked finger. Gillom wrapped the long reins of his follow horse around his saddlehorn, so he could take aim with each hand, squinting at fence posts, rabbits bursting from the brush as he passed. When that game paled, and since he didn't want to call attention to himself by actually firing for marksmanship, he got fancy, pinwheeling a Remington up in the air, catching it by the handle again after a full rotation as the butt dropped naturally into his palm. Reversing the revolution, too, by tipping the five-and-a-half-inch barrel with his forefinger so that it tossed up butt first, and brought his left hand into play, so it was ready for work, false-fanning the hammer when he caught the big pistol again by its handle on its drop. He was quick, very quick. His reflexes, hand-to-eye coordination, distant vision, Gillom Rogers had it all, the lightning-fast instincts of a gifted athlete, or a gunfighter.

It was only when he pushed his tricks too far, flipping the .44 up from behind his back with a twist of his wrist and lowering his right shoulder, that he missed a catch. The heavy revolver bounced off the horse's flank and then to the dirt, spooking the animal. Gillom had to grab the saddlehorn and unwrap the reins of the follow horse to get both startled animals calmed down after a few bucks and snorts. The gunslick dismounted and walked the skittish horses in a circle before retrieving his Remington from the dust. *Better leave the gunplay for standing up,* he realized.

His fingers were as sore as his legs when he made camp at a grove of cottonwoods early evening. The horses he watered at another small stream and since it was twilight he risked a fire. In the dimness smoke wouldn't show much and it was still light enough for his tiny blaze to be invisible at a distance. Any Indians around, though, could smell the smoke with their keen noses. Apaches had raided regularly throughout southern New Mexico, but this was a new century, although he'd heard there were still some wild ones left down in the Sierra Madres. Gillom pondered noises in the night now drawing about him while he enjoyed his first full meal of beans and bacon in nearly two days. He licked the skillet clean before nodding off with a slice of moon for dessert.

He awoke to a chilly wind blowing across his blanket. Dust began to swirl. Gillom blinked. *Damn! Another spring dust storm!* When the spring temperature was in the seventies, conditions grew ripe for winds around El Paso to blow in from the west. These big dust storms, hundreds of miles across, could reach fifty miles an hour, gusting higher.

"Clean sand is healthy for your character," his dad used to tell his tyke. "It polishes up the town."

Gillom wasn't as sure of the medicinal qualities of flying dirt as he choked down a dry biscuit while saddling. A last drink of water for the horses, a faceful for himself, and then wet handkerchiefs tied round his neck and pulled up over his nose, trying to filter out the grit. These sandstorms every spring stung like a slap across the face, reminding one the Southwest still wasn't fully tamed.

They moved northeast to Gillom's reckoning, riding slowly into blowing sand for what seemed like hours. Finally he raised his head, squinting against the scratchy dust, for they'd reached a rise in the hard-packed ground.

A railroad track! Coughing, he dismounted to take a piss. Relieved, he gulped water from a canteen and washed his dirty neckerchief to retie over his nose. It was too difficult in this strong wind to switch saddles, so Gillom moved his bedroll and warbag from the back of the Mexican's saddle he hadn't traded to Mose Tarrant and tied this gear onto the back of Books's big saddle atop the gelding he'd been riding all day, turning it into his packhorse. Adjusting the narrow, leather-covered Oxbow stirrups, tightening the single cinch, he climbed atop the smaller mare and set out again into the storm, pulling his worn black horse along behind.

An old El Paso adage that the wind went down with the sun once again proved true. He saw lights beginning to twinkle in a town in the distance. But Gillom still looked like the sandman, so he reined his horse and dismounted. The teenager partially stripped, shaking like a dog, then stretched, trying to shed grains of sand which seemed to have embedded themselves in every crease and crevice of his pale skin. He rebuttoned with one hand while chugging the last of his canteen water with his other. Gillom switched horses again, too, back to riding the black gelding.

Gotta look good, he thought, *hittin' Tularosa.*

Twelve

Tularosa had the black reputation of an outlaw town, where unsmiling men arrived by horse or stage, between two suns and one jump ahead of the sheriff. Laws there were minimal and their few enforcers indulgent. It was a community of small farms growing alfalfa mostly, worked by Mexicans with a liberal splash of gringo blood running the town's businesses. Swift Tularosa Creek watered the long and narrow town with fingers and thumb of orchard and farmlet via *acequias* off the smoother ridges as they fell away from the narrow shelf of land below the Sacramento Mountains, which loomed barrier-long to the east. Transplanted Texans ran their cattle near springs in the stony hills and slopes extending up into the mountain range and fed their herds and horses on that alfalfa during the harder winters.

Gillom rode past mud-daubed adobes and a couple more substantial structures, the Santa Fe railroad office and the post office. It was a town of little shade.

He smelled the stable at the south end of the town before he rode up to it. The old stableman was more interested in his supper, but they bargained a wash and a couple days' feed for his two tired horses.

"Gene Rhodes? Yeah, I think he's in town. Either at his wife's house, or at the Wolf, playin' cards. Right down this street, right-hand side."

"Where can I get a good meal, maybe a bath, this time of night?"

"Tularosa House, center of town. Expensive, though, if they ain't already full." The proprietor scratched his stubble. "The Wolf, too. Bed down in their storeroom, them that's over-indulged." The old man smiled, displaying partially vacant gums. From the odor off him, this wasn't the man to ask the whereabouts of a bath.

The Wolf was better than he expected, with its head of the predator painted larger than life over the bat-wing front doors. A real grey wolf's head was mounted over the bar inside, jaw stretched, yellow teeth frozen in a snarl. Intimidating, especially on a dark night with a few whiskeys in your gut.

Gillom limped to the long counter, feeling every muscle ache after three days in the saddle, by far the longest ride he'd ever taken. The tall bartender eyed his young, grimy guest skeptically.

"Mister, I need a bath and a bed for the night."

The barkeep smoothed his waxed mustache. "Can throw your bedroll in our back storeroom for a dollar. Wash trough out in the alley is free. Towel's your own."

"I could also use a beefsteak, burnt, fried potatoes, and a beer."

"That's *two* dollars. In advance."

Gillom dug into his grimy new jeans for two singles, which he thumbed from a wad.

The bartender took his money. "Drop your gear in back. Time you clean up, your supper'll be ready."

Gillom Rogers smiled for the first time in three days. Sauntering down the long bar, his limp forgotten, he noted the free lunch set out—pretzels, sausages, mustard, olives, crackers, and cheese. He helped himself to a pickle, crunching it, letting its sour juice run down his chin as he went out back to clean up.

Refreshed, Gillom sat at a table near the bar, demolishing his steak while he looked around the long barroom, lightly patronized this spring weeknight with a scattering of players at the monte, faro, senate, and poker tables, ending at an empty billiard table in the rear. In this outlaw town they had no trouble with a teenager drinking, so Gillom motioned for another brew. As he was served, he queried the nattily dressed bartender.

"Lookin' for Eugene Rhodes."

"Sure. If Gene's not up at his horse ranch, he'll be over at the little house west of town he's renting for his wife, May, who's expecting. But he'll be in here sooner or later. Mister Rhodes is fond of poker."

Gillom stopped in midchew. "I'll be here a day or two, restin' my horses."

The barkeep smoothed his silk vest. "Who's lookin' for him?"

"Friend of a friend. From El Paso."

"Uh-huh." The bartender gave him a cool stare.

· · ·

After an exhausted sleep on a hard floor, Gillom was up next morning for that bath and a haircut at the barber shop, turning in his dirty clothes at the Mexican laundry and having a big breakfast at the Oasis Café. He took his time checking on his horses at the stable, then bought a calfskin wallet at a leather goods. Nothing doing at the blacksmith's, so Gillom had a gunsmith clean his Remingtons while watching the process, then bought gun oil, a brush, and some rags to do it later himself.

Gillom relaxed outside the gun shop, letting a boy with a shoebox spit-shine his boots, the brown ones with a yellow lightning bolt on each leather top. He watched a couple schoolgirls idle down the boardwalk window shopping. The Wolf's bartender walked into his view from a side street on his way to work.

"Mister Rhodes was tending his yard not a half hour ago. Said he'd be in the Wolf tonight."

A long nap that afternoon left him rested, so Gillom was in good fettle as he finished another beefsteak that evening. Friday night's arrival had aroused the saloon business and the gambling tables along one side of the Wolf were busy. The bartender, whom he'd been tipping well, caught Gillom's eye and nodded toward the stocky man who'd just walked in the front door. Short-framed, maybe a hundred and fifty pounds after a big meal, Eugene Manlove Rhodes had a handsome head of unruly blond hair. He caught the bartender's eye, too, and followed his nod to the teenager's table.

"You the sprout making inquiries after me?"

Gillom dropped his knife and fork and rose up. "Yes, sir, Mister Rhodes. Please, take a seat. Can I buy you a drink?"

Gene slid out a chair. "Only imbibe coffee or wate'. Whiskey's the cause a most of the killings in the West and I don't carry a gun."

Gillom pantomimed drinking from a cup to a bartender. "Only take an occasional beer myself. Noticed your crooked nose. Thought you might be a scrapper?"

Rhodes grinned. "Neve' walk away from fisticuffs or a wrestling match. But when weapons come out and the combatants get blood-crazed, I head the othe' direction." He thanked the bartender who served him his coffee. "You a two-gun man, I see."

It was Gillom's turn to smile. "Carry one for either side of the border."

Eugene Rhodes eyed the teenager thoughtfully. "What *are* you doin' here, kid?"

"Well, I needed to get outta El Paso awhile, catch some fresh air in some new country. Dan Dobkins, of the *Daily Herald,* mentioned your horse ranch up in the mountains."

"Dan and I share an interest in writing and American history. Dobkins is a newspape' man, always reporting on the wilde' characters in this lawless land, whereas I make my Western stories up. I've had a couple articles published in *Out West* magazine from Los Angeles, so

Dan encourages me during my visits to his sinful city." The rancher scratched his bent nose. "I can understand why you'd want to leave a twenty-four-hour town like El Paso. Helluva fast city for a kid to grow up in."

Gillom played with his new Stetson, curling the sides of the brim upward with his long fingers. He had to listen hard, for Eugene Rhodes spoke with a slight lisp, dropping his "r's" due to a cleft palate he tried to conceal under his broad mustache. The tough rancher didn't seem self-conscious, though, even of his high-pitched voice.

"Oh, I'll get back to the Pass. My mother lives there. My dad was a railroad engineer, died when I was just a tad, so I've gotta look after my mother."

Rhodes nodded. "I'll take you to the San Andes when I pack a load of supplies up for my wrangle' day afte' tomorrow. Gotta hang round the house here awhile for May. Married a widow with a young son and she's expecting our first baby in a couple months. Horse ranch is too lonely for youngsters."

Gillom started to thank him, but they were interrupted by a commotion outside the saloon. A horse squealed and someone yelled in pain as Gene took off from the table at a fast trot in his high-heeled boots. Gillom hurried behind his new host through the bat-wing door.

Outside a roan horse was hot-eyed and kicking, having loosed its tie-rein from the hitching post. A long-haired cowboy was down on both knees attempting to crawl away from the stamping bronco.

"What happened to you, fella?"

"Stom-ach cramps. Godamighty," groaned the cow-hand. "Somethin' I et."

"Ohh," smiled Gene. "And a big bruise to go with 'em. Miste', you'd betta see a docta', get some purgative."

"Yah . . ." The cowhand crawled slowly away from his trouble.

Gillom joined the older rancher gentling his snorty horse in front of the crowd of gawkers who had run outside for the excitement.

"What was that about?"

"We've been plagued by saddle thieves. Few weeks ago I lost my best saddle right here in front of the Wolf. They ride off into the night, let you' horse loose to return, but you' saddle's headed somewheres else. So I trained this raw bronc Indian-style, to be mounted from the right instead of from the left. That jaspe' tried to mount him regula', on the left side, and got a hoof in the belly for his dirty work." The explanation drew chuckles from the Wolf's patrons. "Any a you boys see that jaspe' spookin' you' horses again, give him a good kick for me, wouldcha?"

To shouts of "Sure will, Gene," and "He ain't welcome round here," the drinkers and gamblers filed back in the saloon.

Gene Rhodes tightened his half-broke horse's cinch and hoisted himself back onto his second best saddle from the wrong side.

"You a gamble', son?"

"Nope. Can't afford the expense of learnin' poker."

"Good. Hold onto you' money. Poker's *my* affliction, so I'll cut the wolf loose in he' tomorrow night."

"Okay, Mister Rhodes."

Gene wheeled the anxious animal and booted him down the hard-packed street.

"Call me Gene!"

Thirteen

Walter Thibido was not in a positive frame of mind as he clomped up the few stairs to Bond Rogers's front porch. The marshal usually left domestic difficulties to his deputies and he hadn't enjoyed dickering with this imperious widow and her sassy kid in his jail. But those special guns were too valuable to ignore.

The mother answered his hard knock. "Marshal?"

"Missus Rogers. Those pistols turn up?"

"No, I'm sorry to say, they have not. I've no idea what happened to them."

"I want to speak to your son."

"Well, he's not here. Gillom left."

"For where?"

"I don't know. He rode out of town and said he was going to catch a train, probably headed west."

El Paso's top lawman glared at her, frustrated. He had not removed his Stetson in deference, and out of courtesy, she had not invited him inside.

"Probably took those Remingtons with him."

"Gillom was not armed when he left here, that I saw."

"When was that?"

"Three mornings ago. Early."

"Uh-huh. We had a well-chawed body turn up in our alligator pond, San Jacinto Plaza, that same day. Young Mexican, nephew of this Serrano, from Juarez."

Mrs. Rogers acted perplexed. "So?"

"Serrano was a cattle rustler, an all-purpose *bandido*. One of the bad boys J. B. Books killed in that shoot-out in the Constantinople. Now Serrano's cousin turns up as alligator bait on our side of the line, and his relatives are looking for another missing young kin to this same *bandido*." The tightly wound lawman paced about in a little circle on her porch, thinking aloud. "Now your son's flown the coop, too. All three young men are connected to the Books shoot-out and I wanna know how closely?"

"I didn't read about any alligators eating Mexicans in the paper?"

"No, we're keeping that quiet. Frightens the tourists. But there were .44-.40-caliber slugs in that Mexican kid, so the alligators didn't grab him first. I'm gonna put out a wanted bulletin for your Gillom."

"On what grounds?"

"He's a witness in a murder investigation. And suspected of gun theft. That's enough for the law to pick him up, anytime, anywhere he turns up."

No arguing with this bully. Mrs. Rogers shut her front door. Walter Thibido shouted through it.

"You see or hear from your son, tell him to save

himself more trouble, turn himself in. He's got more explaining to do!"

Bond Rogers rested her head against a framed tintype on the wall, of her mother and father and her brother, with her standing in front, all smiling on a sunny day somewhere else. She caught her breath and fought back tears.

Gillom Rogers spent another day lazing around Tularosa, browsing the limited goods in their general store. He got in more practice with his pistols in the alley out behind the Wolf, dry-firing only, not disturbing their peace. He spent another hour under an arch of cottonwoods on a bench in their little plaza writing a letter to his mother, Bond, reassuring her he was okay and had already met a fella who was going to teach him to wrangle horses. Gillom licked a pencil lead and listened to the mockingbirds in the cottonwoods' branches. The Wolf's bartender walked by late afternoon again on his way to work.

"Gotta move your gear outta our storeroom, son. Holding a fight in there tonight."

"Then where do I sleep? I paid for that bare corner!"

"You can move back in after the fight's over. That spot's for drunks anyway."

Gillom nodded to the older man, who waved as he walked off. *At least the locals are warmin' up to me a mite,* he realized.

• • •

Gillom was finishing another dinner steak when Gene Rhodes strolled into the Wolf.

"*Gillom!* You bet on fights? We got a dog and a badge' goin' at it tonight!"

"Oh, no. Don't gamble, but I'll watch."

"Okay. Maybe we'll let you referee."

Gene asked his buddy the bartender for a glass of water, drank half of it, and then clambered from a stool on top of the bar counter.

"Okay, you topers! You betting fools! We've got a badge' going against a kille' dog in the storeroom tonight! Phil's got the most ferocious canine I've ever seen and I've got a hundred dollars says so!"

A Texas cowboy jumped up. "Take half a thet bet!"

Card games were hastily concluded, cattlemen rising from the tables, pushing away from their suppers and grabbing their drinks to shuffle off to the back room. *Can't miss this,* Gillom figured.

Rhodes pointed to one of the bigger wranglers. "Phil, get you' vicious beast."

The tall cowboy nodded and headed outside. Another drinker shouted, "I'll put fifty on a badger's nose any day!"

Gene jumped down from the bar counter, took Gillom by the arm, who asked him, "Where is this badger?"

"Got him in a barrel, in back. Too mean to let around loose."

They followed the pushing crowd into the back storeroom, where stood a large wooden rain barrel in the middle of the bare dirt floor with a clothesline leading under it. Oil lamps held by several customers threw murky shadows among the wooden cases of bottles and supplies in the saloon's dusty storeroom. There came a loud barking as Phil Early led his large mongrel in, half wolf itself, at the end of a stout rope. Bettors moved away as the fighting dog was led up to the barrel and got a whiff of what was inside. The dog snarled saliva as it cut loose with another volley of barking.

Another cowboy jumped into the lamplight's circle. "Another hundred dollars on that vicious mutt!"

Gene Rhodes held up both hands, stepping forward. "*Wait!* We've gotta have a referee! . . . Gillom, you do it."

"Awww, he's a friend of yours," a local complained.

"No, surrah! Just rode into town. Barely know him and he's not bettin', eithe'. Gillom will pull fai'."

Time held still as everyone looked at the teenager.

"Well, okay, I guess."

"I'll cover the badger!" yelled a sport.

Shouts of enthusiasm as one of the badger bettors grabbed Gillom by the shoulder to talk low in his ear. "Don't pull too hard, kid. Choke the badger and he won't fight as good."

Gillom scratched an ear. "But I *like* dogs."

Bets were made and wads of cash flashed as Phil Early dragged his thoroughly enraged mastiff away from its enclosed prey, passing close enough to mutter to the kid, "Twenty dollars for yah, you half choke that badger."

Chewing his lip, Gillom was confused, uncertain who to favor, since either betting contingent was certain to be unhappy with the outcome, and hence with him. All eyes were on the young referee now, as he rubbed sweaty palms on his clean Levis and moved forward to pick up the end of the clothesline.

In the stillness, a lone voice. "Be fair now. Give 'em room to scrap!"

The sportsmen edged back against the walls and boxes in the stuffy, darkened room, as the bartender readied himself behind the barrel. Phil knelt beside his excited dog, growling encouragement in its pointed ear.

"Kill 'im, Cajun. Rip 'im apart!"

The bartender looked the young ref in the eye. "Ready?"

An overexcited spectator couldn't stifle. " 'S gonna be bloody!"

The barkeep tipped the barrel backward and Gillom Rogers gave a tremendous yank on the line and out of the bottom of the barrel popped a porcelain chamber pot, which bounced and rolled across the floor with a hollow ring.

The surprise stretched across Gillom's face suddenly gave way to anger as he realized he'd been played the fool. Hoots and laughter exploded on all sides with the betting men convulsed, backslapping one another.

"Didcha see him choke that badger?"

Quick as a fox, Gillom's Remington was in his right hand and cocked as he blasted the chamber pot to porcelain bits. A startled silence among the laughers, then Gillom Rogers smiled.

"*Killed* 'im, too."

It was safe again to laugh, so the pranksters did.

Back in the saloon, the bartender raised a beer mug and tapped Gillom's glass. "Here's to that badger."

Gillom smiled good-naturedly and met his new friends' toast.

"And a two-gun Texan," offered the mastiff's owner.

"We're just green-hazin' yah, kid," added another.

His mentor drew him by the arm away from the laughing crowd.

"You' a good sport, Gillom. That chamber pot's had a long lineage here in the Wolf, and now you' part of that tradition, too. You ready to ride tomorrow up to horse camp?"

"Yessir!"

"Afte' breakfast. Gotta pack a couple horses. Meet-cha, say, at nine, down at Tom's stables."

"I'll be ready, Mister Rhodes."

"Meanwhile, the pasteboards are callin'. Git a good night's sleep."

Gillom watched the decade-older man stroll off to the gaming tables, poker fever already upon him. "You, too, boss."

Gene Rhodes evidently had a big night at the poker table, for he showed up half awake and a half hour late next morning at the stable. And they still had to stop at the general store to pick up supplies. Gillom was surprised to see this teetotaler pack three bottles of whiskey carefully in among his canned goods and sacks of flour and beans in the packs he cross-tied behind the saddles of the two horses he was using for baggage, besides his saddle horse.

"Thought you weren't a drinker, Gene?"

"I'm not. But my wrangle' up at the ranch asked me to bring him some whiskey. For the snakebite, you know?" He winked at Gillom as they mounted and reined their five horses down a residential street, headed at a slow walk west across the Santa Fe railroad tracks till the animals adjusted to their loads.

"How far?"

"Oh, twenty-five miles. That notch you see up in those mountains is my pass. I run a stock ranch for the *remuda* from the Ba' Cross Ranch, big spread the other side of the San Andres down toward Engle. I've got two hundred wild cattle I let graze loose up there, and invite some of the Ba' Cross men up in the fall to help brand 'em and drive my steers down to Engle to sell. Ain't gettin' rich on a herd that small, but it's a livin'. Engle's another cattle shipping town like Tularosa, out in the middle of the Jornada del Muerto. Eve' been there?"

Gillom shook his head. "Never been out of El Paso. 'S why I need to see some of this big country."

Gene continued his interrogation. "So you finished you' schoolin', set off to scratch you' restless itch?"

"Umm, got into a little trouble, had to quit this senior year, before graduation. School wasn't that excitin', just had to commence my travels a little sooner."

"Well, nobody will bother you up in the pass. I've given refuge to a number of hard-faced hombres who passed over that lonesome divide while paying attention to thei' back trail. I've cooked fo' several of the Dalton gang, as well as Bill Doolin. The King of the Oklahoma outlaws himself stayed with me for about three months between his criminal escapades. Helluva crack shot. Bill shot a horse that had me tangled up in the rigging, draggin' me. I could have been seriously hurt if Bill Doolin hadn't put him down."

The buckaroo looked back over Gillom's mounts and tack. "You worked horses much?"

"No sir. We're town folk, never owned any. I picked these two up . . . cheap, for this trip."

"Well, maybe you'll get you' chance. I also do that for the Ba' Cross, break thei' green colts and drive thei' refreshed horses down to help out at thei' spring and fall roundups."

"You're a horse man then, mostly?"

"Yup. Cows are dumb, smelly animals fit only for eatin'. But I sell a few range cattle."

Gillom agreed. "I'm no cowpuncher, either. Who's this other wrangler up at your ranch?"

Gene smiled. "Call him Jones. He's a rooste', so I wouldn't ask him too many questions, kid. But he takes a shine to yah, Miste' Jones might teach you a trick or two."

Gillom Rogers' eyes shone.

Fourteen

About ten miles west of Tularosa the legendary white sands began. Gene halted the horses for a breather and dismounted to stretch his legs. Removing his beat-up cowboy hat, he ruffled his unruly thatch of blond hair that rose up in a crest like a cockatoo's. The broncbuster waved a hand toward the rolling dunes of sparkling white sand as Gillom hopped down, too.

"The gypsum sea. Ain't she beautiful?"

The teenager nodded, drank deep from his canteen. "Makes me thirsty."

"Those white sands look pure, but they hide treachery and tragedy. The only creature who sleeps out here with his eyes closed is dead."

"The sands are a dangerous place?"

"Bet you' boots. Not as bad as the Jornada Del Muerto on the othe' side of those mountains, though. That's where the Apaches used to attack, constantly. Known as Scalp Alley."

Gillom watched his companion take a sack of Bull Durham out of his shirt pocket and begin to roll a cigarette. The wrangler's hands were rough and one finger appeared to be permanently cramped.

"What happened to your finger, Gene?"

"Oh, knife fight, cut the tendon. Same bout bent my nose. Don't carry a gun, but I fight when challenged."

Gillom shifted his heavy saddlebags off the black gelding and onto the Mexican saddle of the bay mare he'd been riding. "Gonna ride my stronger horse through the pull of this loose sand."

"Good idea," agreed the shorter wrangler, striking a sulphur match off a copper rivet on his jeans. "Smoke?" He offered his lit cigarette to his companion.

"No thanks."

"Bad habit." Rhodes pulled a green coupon from the tobacco sack, and held it up for inspection. "But I'm hooked on these coupons. Four of 'em are good for a dime novel from Munro's Library in New York City. They've got all the best stories—Dickens, Conan Doyle, Robert Louis Stevenson. I'm gonna read all three hundred and three a those books if I don't cough up a lung first."

Gillom grinned. He liked this literate horseman with a penchant for harboring killers like himself. He now understood why lonely bank robbers and cow thieves sought this genial host out. The kid swung back up onto J. B. Books's big saddle.

"Daylight's burnin', boss."

. . .

Their plod through the sparkling white sands was slow going and the glare off the dunes shimmering in the afternoon sunlight really tired one's eyes. But finally they were through the dunes and began pulling the last five miles of double track wagon road up, up into the deep notch in the San Andres Mountains. On either side westward ran a ridge of black cedars drawing the two men and five horses higher until they reached a dark mountain at the head of the pass, seventy-four hundred feet high. Around this summit was a hidden country of grassy parks and cedar motes, gentle slopes and low rolling ridges of juniper, with wide, smooth valleys falling away to the north and south.

"My ranch up here is homestead land, and since I control the spring on it, my cattle can range free out into miles of unfenced graze all about in these mountains. I just have to flush 'em out come spring and fall to burn my '61' brand in and sell 'em. Hell, I'm better at breaking horses and driving cows than I am at owning them," Gene explained as they rode ever upward.

They reached Five Springs at dusk, greeted by bats from a nearby cave dipping down for evening drinks in one of the springs. Rhodes's ranch was a single-room, flat-roofed fortress of red stone, maybe fourteen feet by eighteen, with a fenced yard on a low red flat expanse, looped about by the canyon. Out behind were several horse pens, but the maybe twenty mounts were all resting tonight in the biggest, farthest water pen in which another spring bubbled up. To its rear the ranch was protected by a mountain of red sandstone, while across the trail on the other side it faced a mightier mountain of white limestone. Five springs gushed forth at the contacts of red stone and white. It was a fine spot for a horse ranch.

"My daddy Hinman's house was only six miles away, that's how I came to know this hidden spot. Man could get lost up here for months. *Hallo the house!*"

They reined up outside the fence and waited, so as not to startle anyone inside. Gillom saw smoke rising from the stone chimney. There were no windows in the cut stone, so the front door opened tentatively until they were recognized.

"Gene, you rascal! Welcome to what's left of supper!"

"We can cook some more, if you'll help wrangle these packs."

A fair-skinned six-footer with reddish blond hair ambled out to help Rhodes untie his packs. The man was built from the ground up and armed with some kind of pistol in his right holster. He was somewhere over forty, 170 pounds, and he never took his pale blue eyes off Gillom.

"Who's this smiling gallant?"

Gene Rhodes watched both armed men take the measure of each other.

"This is my new friend, Gillom. From El Paso."

The heavily freckled man with the sandy mustache hefted loaded saddlebags, but never turned his back on the young stranger as he sidestepped back to the house.

"Gillom *who*?"

Rogers hoisted his own heavy saddlebags to follow the men inside.

"Gillom's good enough. What's yours?"

Gene Rhodes stopped at the doorway. "This is Mister Jones. And don't you bulls start pawing around fo' turmoil ah I'll kick you both off my ranch."

They watered their horses and fed them in the dry pen, away from Gene's unfamiliar string that first night. The two riders washed themselves in the near spring and toweled off in the darkness as they walked back to the little house.

Mr. Jones had a couple more steaks sizzling on a long-handled spider skillet set up in the soapstone fireplace in the middle of the back wall. A pot of beans hung from a crane hook swung over the blazing logs and a pot of coffee bubbled in the hot ashes. No beds could Gillom see inside, only bedrolls against a wall, and a rough wood table with a couple benches and stools around it. The only luxury in the place was a beautifully turned rocking chair Gene mentioned he liked to read in by coal oil light.

The horse wrangler knifed their dinners out of the flames and pulled utensils from a box as his dining companions chucked off spurs and unpacked their personals.

"You can put those big pistols away, kid. I promise not to shoot you in your sleep," laughed Jones as he accepted a bottle from his host. "Gene don't drink, but join me in takin' a jolt of the critter, junior?"

Gillom looked at his host, then nodded, trying to be sociable. Two cups were filled and Mr. Jones tapped his to Gillom's with a tinny clunk.

"To *love,* wherever her pretty ass may be."

Gillom tried to match Jones's big gulp, but the harsh

liquid and the fumes burning his throat and nasal cavities caused him to gasp like a landed fish.

"Not used . . . to," he rasped.

"Me, neithe', Gillom." Gene smiled. He sat down on a bench at the wooden table with the teenager across from him. The hungry horsemen dug into their meals, while the stranger, who had already eaten, nursed his toddy from the rocking chair.

Gillom took a more tentative sip. "How come you abstain from hard drink, Mr. Rhodes?"

"When I was a wild-assed youth like you, I couldn't afford liquor. At seventeen I was riding as a nonenlisted guide fo' the Army during the Geronimo outbreak of 1885. We didn't catch the wily Apache then ah catch up with much liquo' in the field, eithe'. What little money I saved from my service went toward my education at the University of the Pacific over in Stockton, California. Methodist school. Had to work as a harvest hand between school terms and even then I could only afford a couple years of college before I dropped out, broke, and came home to New Mexico to get back to horse wranglin'."

"Don't need college to learn ranchin'," groused Jones.

"No, unless you want to study accounting ah animal care, become a vet. But I took courses in history, philosophy, and literature, learned to love the great books and good stories. That little education is what's compelled me to try some writin' myself."

The drinking hombre put another oar in. "Ahh, book learnin' jus confuses a man's mind. Start questionin' everything, before you know it, you can no longer think straight."

"Well, schoolin's quite like whiskey then. Just makes men dumbe' and quarrelsome, right?"

"Exactly," said Mr. Jones, draining his cup of hooch and helping himself to another. "Shall we shuffle some pasteboards tonight, Gene?"

"Played all last night, pard." Rhodes finished a last bite of steak. "Long ride today, need some shut-eye. Gillom can play if he wants?"

"I'm tired, too."

"*Damn!* You jaspers been havin' too much fun in Tularosa, shootin' its lights out and kissin' the dawn, while I've been holdin' down the fort by my lonesome up this damned mountain. Then, when I want to play—"

"Let's have a smoke outside. Got news of you' brothe'."

This got Jones's attention and he clumped out the low front door swigging cheap whiskey straight from the bottle. Gene Rhodes looked at Gillom and pointed to a water pail near the fire.

"Dishes."

Rogers scrubbed dirty dishes with a bar of soap in the wooden wash bucket and was laying them out to dry on the wooden plank shelf jammed into the stone wall. The front door was open and he could barely hear the two men speaking low as they strode the front yard in the stiff-legged gait common to men riding constantly in high-heeled boots.

Suddenly Jones let out a squall, a long, shrieking

howl that rose from his bowels and stretched his mouth wide in mortal pain.

Somebody got stabbed! Gillom was startled alert. He almost dropped a dish, but quickly put it down and ran out the front door. There he saw Jones, head up and eyes wide, wandering into the darkness, moaning at the moon.

"Is he hurt?"

"Only in his heart." Eugene Rhodes shook his head, looking forlornly after his mysterious friend. "Told him something unfortunate about his younge' brothe'."

Gillom forgot his host's admonition about asking personal questions. "What?"

"He just got hung." The older horse wrangler put his arm over the teenager's shoulder, as they watched their companion wander off, taking a huge swig of red-eye from his half-empty bottle.

"Let him drink it off. We need sleep."

But they didn't get much rest, for a few hours later they were awakened by more human screeching and bullets flying into the house's wooden door. Rhodes was up in an instant, running to his damaged door in his long johns, flinging it open and jumping outside. Gillom took a little longer to roll from his bedroll and fumbled about for a coal oil lamp and lit it, then rose to peer cautiously outside to see what in hell was going on? In the darkness, Gene Rhodes appeared to have his outlaw caretaker in a headlock, one arm around his neck, squeezing, his left arm stretched trying to wrestle the revolver away from the thoroughly drunk, bigger man. Another report in the moonlight!

Gillom ducked, but still held his lantern above him in the doorway. A fourth shot missed it but cracked the door frame, so the teenager pulled his hand and the light back out of range. He heard a big *oomph!* then a thud and he had to peek out again. By the lantern's glimmer he could see that Gene had flipped Jones over onto his back, yanked the pistol loose, and was now astraddle the larger cowboy with his knees digging into his heaving chest, almost riding him like a jockey in his bare feet.

"*Stop* it, Sam! Don't want to hurt you!"

His midnight plea didn't faze the inebriated outlaw, who sputtered and yelled and heaved like a wild man in his grief. Gene grabbed the Colt from where they'd dropped it in their fray and with a mighty swing, cracked his guest upside the head, squelching his howling and putting him out of his misery, for a while at least. Mr. Jones let out a final moan and was still.

Eugene Rhodes got shakily up off his knees and stood over his victim a moment in his underwear, panting, then wobbled back into his ranch house carrying the other man's gun, while Gillom lit his way.

"*Damn it!* Hate to poleax a man with his own weapon, specially when he's drunk."

"Throw some water on him?"

"No, just leave him lie. He'll have a headache in the morning to remembe' this foolishness by. Sam'll be all right. He won't bother us again."

Maybe not, but as Gillom lay down in his underwear again and damped the lantern near his bedroll, he noticed his host had barred the front door and took his guest's gun to bed.

Fifteen

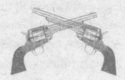

They found Mr. Jones next morning sprawled on his back in the grassy front yard that had been nibbled short by hungry horses and bold rabbits, sleeping his drunkenness off. A purplish welt rose from his hairline, so they left him alone and went out back to break a bale of alfalfa for the Bar Cross's horses in the larger pen. Gillom had even more respect this morning for his host, who had wrestled down a drunken gunslinger quite a bit larger than himself.

Walking to the smaller holding pen, Gene tied nosebags onto the two best horses they'd ridden up on the day before, making sure these new arrivals got good helpings from the sack of oats they'd carried up with them. Gillom's bay mare, the slowest walker in the string, had ankles swollen from the tree stumps she'd bumped into on the two-track trail up their mountain. The kid watched as Gene doctored the lame animal by pouring coal oil from the oil can he used for their lamps down the mare's front legs. The wrangler rubbed the soothing alcohol gently into the swollen skin with his work-scarred hands.

"Like rubbing alcohol on a lame child. Cheap medicine," he explained.

"Mister Rhodes, last night, what you said about Jones's brother, being hung."

"Let that slip, huh? Emotional fo' him. You'll read it in the papers. Laws just hung his younge' brothe' ove' in Clayton."

"Who?"

The wrangler eyed his young companion speculatively.

"I guess we'll test you' discretion. . . . Tom Graham."

The kid was surprised. *"Blackjack?"*

Gene Rhodes nodded. "Murdere'. Train robbe'. Horse thief. And just about everything else il-legal."

"And this is his older *brother*?"

"Sam Graham. One of five kids born in San Saba County, between Abilene and Austin, over four decades ago. Sam's the othe' bad apple in the bunch."

"San Saba, Texas, is where J. B. Books grew up." Gillom turned to watch the bad man lurch about the corner of the rock house and walk unsteadily past them to one of the five springs outside the horse corrals. Red-eyed and reeling, Sam Graham paid them no never mind, but waded right into the small pond and bent to splash water over his face and hair, soaking his smelly shirt. Then, shaking off water like a dog, Graham stalked back toward the house.

"Ready for dinne', Miste' Jones?"

"The *hell* with you and your horses." The grieving brother didn't even look back at them, but disappeared dripping around the house corner. Gene turned back to his protégé.

"*You* ready to fork a bronc? Little ridin' will work up an appetite."

The horse Gene roped out of the big corral was a *grullo*, the color of a Maltese cat, a sleek, velvet slate-blue with a dark mane, tail, and socks, clean-legged as a deer. Handing the lead rope to Gillom, Rhodes threw another lasso around the *grullo*'s neck and between the two of them on either side, they walked and pulled the half-wild, dainty-nosed mare into the smaller corral, from which they'd moved the five new horses they'd ridden in on into the bigger corral with the others from the Bar Cross string. Tying both ropes to two fence posts, Gene had Gillom hanging from the small horse's neck. He explained that this mare was further along in her training and had been saddled, but never ridden.

"They forget a few things between my trips to town, so I usually have to bust 'em twice. I've rarely seen a bronc who believed it was saddled the first time ah eve' doubted it the second."

Gene was able after a couple tries to saddle the anxious, stomping animal and cinch it tight. Fitting the snaffle bit in and the headstall on took more effort and earned him at least one good nip of his fingers.

"*Ouch! Damn!*" Rhodes poked the horse in its sensitive nose and tried again to bridle, successfully. "At least this one accepts the bit. Some of 'em you gotta use a hackamore on and then work you' way up to a snaffle. Don't have time for all that nonsense today."

Finally the feisty mare was ready, but Gillom turned down the boss's second offer to be first on her.

"Rather learn bronc riding from a master."

Gene smiled at the compliment, a good rookie ploy, as he approached the nervous horse from the left to get one tentative foot in the stirrup. But the *grullo* kept backing away.

"Damn you, fiddlefoot, stop dancing!" He looked up at Gillom riding the railing. "Snub the lassos tighter! Let's get hobbles on these front hooves, too."

Gillom snubbed the neck ropes and retied them to the fence posts a few yards apart and soon they had the cold shouldered mare's head tied right against the top wooden rail. Gene fastened leather hobbles onto the horse's two front hooves, tying them together like prison irons. Then he could lift himself up in the left stirrup several times, rising up and then back down before finally swinging his right leg up over the mare's hindquarters and easing himself into the saddle so the skittish horse could get used to his weight. Gene mounted okay but kept his right leg hooked around the saddle horn so as not to get his leg banged into the hard railing when the horse shied. At his command, Gillom unbuckled the front hobbles and removed one lasso from its neck, causing the horse to shy sideways on its remaining tether. Gene gathered the reins in his left hand and slid his right leg down into the wooden stirrup. The bronc master was ready.

"All I want to do is walk a circle, but I can feel he' gettin' ready to ignite."

At a nod from him, the teenager unsnubbed the

second lasso and suddenly the rodeo was on, with Gene grabbing the saddle horn as the unbroken horse reared up and pawed for the sky, cloud-hunting. Rhodes maintained his seat, leaning back in the saddle, so the *grullo* tried another tactic, cat jumping and spinning to its right in a fast, tight spin as Gene hung on for dear life.

Then it was a bucking contest for a long minute around the smaller corral, with Gene uttering several yelps of pain as the snorting, angry animal banged hard into the wood railings trying to knock off its unwanted jockey.

The commotion drew Jones back out of the house. The infamous train robber walked shakily up to hang onto the top railing beside Gillom just as the bucking session was concluding. Panting heavily, the pretty blue horse now paced about the pen, one rope still trailing from her lowered neck. Atop her, Gene Rhodes breathed hard, too.

"Ready for you' morning ride, Miste' Jones?"

"Fuck you, Eugene." The big cowboy spat, causing him to groan. "Still tryin' to get the snakes outta my boots."

The horsebreaker reined the tired, skittish animal closer to the two men and slid off to the ground.

"You' turn then, young man. Horse is tuckered, so you shouldn't have much difficulty stayin' on."

Now he was trapped. No excuses in front of these hard men, for Sam Graham was giving him a bloodshot eye. So, against his good sense and health, Gillom Rogers climbed over the railing and jumped into the horse pen. Gene Rhodes waited, holding the reins tight under the *grullo*'s slobbering mouth. He removed the last lariat from around the horse's neck, to reduce the chance of the mare stepping on the rope and injuring herself.

The youngster got one foot in the stirrup and both hands on the saddle horn, but the shadow jumper kept edging away, bouncing the expectant rider on one foot until Gene shouldered the rank horse into the railing so she could be mounted.

"Got a temper like Satan's," Gillom offered. Swinging himself slowly up into the small saddle, his spurs jingling, he leaned forward to grab the reins from his host's grasp.

And then they were off to the rodeo again! Gritting his teeth, rocking back, his bones jarring, Gillom clung onto the saddle horn and almost dropped the reins after one two-legged kick.

"Lean back! *Ride* that wringtail, cowboy!" shouted Gene from a top railing.

The wild bronc reared one more time, pawing the air with its front hooves. Gillom blew his stirrups and his death grip on the horn, slid rapidly off the back of the saddle and off the horse's hind quarters. He let go the reins or the frantic horse might have fallen backward atop him. With a last buck and a snort the sweaty mare capered away, free of half its problem.

Gillom staggered to his feet and jumped aside as the riderless horse brushed past him.

"Get back on he'. Show he' who's trail boss!"

Gillom brushed his jeans and clambered back up on the rail where he sat bent over, sucking air.

"Not today."

"First thing tomorrow then. You fall off a horse,

you gotta get back on. Don't let this bronc beat you, boy, or you'll be scared a horses the rest of you' natural life."

The teenager nodded.

"You bent, kid?" asked Graham.

"Jus' my pride."

"You did okay. Everybody gets unhorsed sometimes," added the ranch owner. "By the time we get all these bangtails finished off, you'll be a broncbuste'."

Gillom's smile was tight. "*If* I'm still walkin'."

Gene Rhodes slapped him on the back as they stepped gingerly down to walk back to the ranch house. "Let's get some grub. Unsaddle that switchtail for me, Sam!"

This brought Sam Graham up short. "You *told* 'im?"

"He asked about you' loud grievin'." Mr. Rhodes pointed at his mysterious guest. "Gillom's not going anywhere for a while. An' by then, Graham, you'll be headed another direction."

Sam Graham glared at his host. "I frown on loose discussion."

After a noon dinner of burnt beef and beans, respecting Sam Graham's delicate stomach from its prior night's sousing, the three enjoyed long afternoon naps under the shady cedars out back of the corrals, lulled by sweet breezes eddying down off the nearby mountaintop. Gene read one of his dime novels he'd gotten with his Bull Durham coupons, *The Woman in White* by a British writer, Wilkie Collins, which he said was a mystery tinged with sadness. He offered to lend it to Gillom when finished.

Sore from two hard riding days in a row, the three men took turns bathing with one bar of soap in the biggest cold spring which burbled up away from the horse pens, where the red soapstone of the mountain behind them met the white limestone of the mountain to the front of their stone house. They rested in the altogether in the early summer sunshine, contemplating life on their mountain.

"I ain't gonna tell anyone I metcha, Mister Graham, I promise."

The big cowboy slanted his pale blue eyes toward the naked teenager sunning on the sandstone nearby. "Easy to say, kid. Up here." The outlaw pointed into the distance eastward. "Different story down there, when you're looking at reward money headlined on a poster featuring a rough sketch of yours truly."

"Naw, I don't need that kind of money." The young tough looked at his patron. "Gene doesn't, either. I'm sorry to hear about your brother. Lots of stories kickin' round El Paso about Blackjack. All bad."

Sam's blue eyes flashed as he sat up suddenly. "That *was* his problem. Tom did pure-dee crazy things without thinking them through. That was my little brother's real name, Tom. Blackjack is just an alias lots of brush *bandidos* use to confuse people. My oldest brother, Greenbriar, and I kept cautioning him to slow down, but . . ." The middle brother warmed to his memories, soaking up heat from the smooth rock.

Gene Rhodes smiled ruefully. "Told me when they

hung Blackjack over in Clayton a few days ago, he dashed up that gallows' thirteen steps, his one good arm lashed to his back and yelled, 'I'll be in hell before you start breakfast, boys!' "

"God damn." Sam Graham fingered the knot on his forehead. "Sounds like Tom. Crazy bastard. He knew fate was coming for him after he got his arm shot-gunned in his one-man train robbery near Folsom. A doc took the arm off in the penitentiary, but nobody could get in there to help him get out, too heavily guarded. They wouldn't even release him back to Arizona for the big reward for his crimes over there. They were hot to hang him here in New Mexico as a warning to other train robbers." Tom Graham's older brother shook his head sadly. "Tom was a tiger, though, insane temper. Absolutely fearless. Everybody said so. Hope he had a long rope and a short drop."

"My witness said that when they put the black sack ove' his head, he yelled, 'Let e' rip!' They pulled the trap and ripped his head clean off."

"Oh *no*!" Sam Graham jerked straight to his feet. "His head came off? *Jesus Christmas!*" Upset and buck-naked, the older brother stalked off.

Gillom stared at Gene Rhodes. "Why would you tell him something like that?"

The rancher watched the agitated bandit disappear around the house's corner.

"Ohh, Sam's a big boy. Maybe his brother's awful demise will keep him on the straight and narrow. Or at least, a little less crooked for a while." He turned upon Gillom a thoughtful eye.

Sixteen

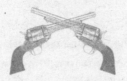

That afternoon Gene showed his student more horse-breaking tricks, like using his hands to touch sensitive areas such as its ears and belly and upper legs above the elbows, to get a horse used to people.

Another big buckskin gelding was a step further along, so Gene had Gillom rub his Navajo saddle blanket all over to get the animal adjusted to a different-smelling and -feeling cloth. The horse wrangler then very gently laid a saddle atop this pad and took it off again and back on several times so the horse could get used to the extra weight on its back. Cinching caused a blowup with the buckskin, and with saddle and blanket dumped several times in the dirt, Rhodes decided he'd had enough vexation for that day, too.

"Bucketheaded son of a bitch," he muttered as he let himself out of the corral.

They left Sam to his misery and whiskey again that night. He was already down to his third and last bottle, which was another one of his problems, whiskey fever. Gene showed Gillom how to rub sharp-smelling horse liniment on his lower-back aches and bruised thighs for relief. Then they retired to different corners of the small house so they wouldn't have to smell each other all night.

Next morning they busied with getting another green-broke paint horse ready to ride around the corral until it either stopped bucking or its rider got launched. Gene Rhodes went first, showing Gillom a few riding tricks. This wild horse was a high roller, leaping with all four hooves off the ground at the same time, with a sharp kick of its rear hooves straight out as a finish. Rhodes even got in a little spurring as he fought to keep his high bootheels in the stirrups and his butt in the small saddle. The older wrangler wasn't graceful, often showing daylight between his tight ass and the saddle, and his spurring wasn't smooth, but even flailing about, Gene managed to stay on these wild horses one awkward way or another.

Gillom borrowed Gene's kidney belt to protect his tender guts from further misadventures. This was a leather belt eight inches wide buckled by three straps around his middle to hold himself in, sort of like a woman's girdle. The youth's second tries were often near wrecks, ending up with the reins between his teeth and both hands pulling leather, but he could now sometimes ride a bucker to a standstill. Gene coached him through his loose management of these tiring mounts.

"Few more days buckin' and bangin' and you'll be an A-number-one bronc rider, kid."

Gillom brushed off his no longer new jeans one more time, grabbed his dusty hat, and limped to the railing. "Like I said, *if* I can still walk."

But Gillom swallowed his pain and determinedly carried on with Mr. Rhodes's horse wrangling invitation for another hard day. Sam Graham didn't partake in this rodeo, either. They let him stay up past their bedtime that night, nursing his last bottle and wallowing in sad memories, then sleeping it off again. But the whiskey had run out and Blackjack was no longer mentioned when on their fourth afternoon together, Sam returned from a bath and a shave in the springs just as the student and his teacher were rising from their afternoon siesta.

"Saw you carryin' those fancy pistols up here, youngster. Can you shoot worth a shit with either of 'em?"

Gillom scowled. At least Blackjack's older brother appeared sober.

"I can hit a mark. I've been working on my speed and gunplay regular since I inherited those weapons."

"From who?" Gene Rhodes inquired.

"John Bernard Books."

"J. B. Books? The famous *shootist*?" Sam Graham, the notorious train robber, looked skeptical. "I heard Books went down in a big shoot-out in El Paso, the Constantinople I believe it was, in broad daylight not too long ago."

Gillom nodded.

"*You* were involved in that bloodbath?" asked Gene.

Another nod. "Mister Books was shotgunned in the back, both barrels, by a treacherous bartender in the Connie. J. B. had already killed everybody else in that fancy saloon, five of 'em, but he knew he was dyin' there behind that bar. He had a cancer, too, up his ass, which is why I helped him arrange that shoot-out in the first place. So John Bernard begged me to finish him off. Promised me these matched pistols for doing him the favor."

Gene Rhodes figured it out. "Then that makes *you* the kid who shot the legendary shootist, John Bernard Books."

Gillom Rogers did not smile. "Yes I am."

"My God." Sam Graham blew some air. "Well, fetch along some rounds, kid, and let's see what kind of gun-slick you are."

They retrieved their revolvers and strapped them on, and Gillom dug a box of .44-.40 cartridges from his saddlebag. The horse-breaking scholar was thinking over what he'd just learned.

"Books lived in Tularosa fo' a couple years with a woman named Serepta Thomas. Must have been ten years ago. Something went wrong between them and she took up with a freighte' named Pardee. They had a couple girls togetha, but Pardee's gone now, too. He used to beat he' regula', so he wasn't missed." Eugene shook his tousled head. "Serepta used to be a looke'. Blonde."

"Didn't know that," said young Gillom. "But some older gal came to visit him in his back room at our boarding house. Maybe it was her?"

Gene made them hike a fair ways up the mountainside behind the house so as not to scare the horses too badly. He tramped along to watch.

"I don't want to referee any fuss, so let's just practice friendly, fellas. No shooting each othe' ah you' own feet, okay?"

Sam grunted and Gillom nodded as they took stances apart in a clearing amidst black cedars and junipers, looking out over the pass through the San Andres and Gene's small ranch below. The teenager safety-checked the empty cylinders beneath the hammers of his two Remingtons. Sam Graham stroked his bushy mustache, watching.

"Okay, rooster."

"I've only had these pistols from Mister Books a coupla weeks. Not much time to practice."

"Gunfighters don't get excuses."

So Gillom performed his fast draws, first with his right hand, then with his off-hand, his left. Pulling both guns at once with respectable speed, he began spins with his dominant right hand, rolling the gun over several times out of the front leather lip of his holster as his arm extended from his crouch. He reverse-spun the big revolver by its trigger guard several times around and slipped it smoothly back into the holster from the rear.

Sam Graham nodded at the kid's display. "You're pretty sudden, kid."

"What I'd like to do for work. Bank guard, law enforcement, some job lets me handle weapons and use 'em if necessary."

"You've got quick hands and fast reactions fo' gunplay," agreed Gene.

Sam Graham snorted. "You join the Laws, only thing you'll succeed in arresting is your own life!"

Mr. Rhodes frowned. "Listen, you whiskey-sucke'. Don't lead this young man down that outlaw trail. Might end up like your brothe'."

The big train robber scowled, spat, and concentrated on his gun handling. Sam slid his leather holster across to the left side of his gunbelt. He reversed the holster's opening so that his was a right-handed cross-draw across his waist above his center brass buckle. He tried a few pulls with his walnut-handled Colt .45 with impressive speed.

"Show you a trick my brother Blackjack invented." Graham took a deep breath, settled into a slight crouch, and drew rapidly, cocking the Colt as he extended his right arm to one side and fired. In a blink, Sam dropped the gun forward on its trigger guard and turned it underneath his wrist as he pulled it back across his body, passed the grip into his left hand, thumb-cocking the revolver again to fire as his left arm reached out. Two shots in only a couple seconds at opponents coming from either direction!

Gillom was open-mouthed at this fancy move.

"Very pretty," agreed Gene Rhodes.

"Quick pass is better than a toss, which you might drop when they're comin' at you from all directions." His last shot echoed down the valley leading north and south off this high pass. The men could see they'd gotten the horses' attention in the two corrals down below.

"That's a move John Wesley Hardin could have made," Gillom added.

"Hardin hurrahed drunks and bullied hotheads who neve' stood a chance against his gunplay. That's how he ran up such a body count at such a young age, before they locked him up in Huntsville. Wes Hardin killed men just to see them kick."

"John Wesley never shot anybody who didn't have it coming," replied Gillom with a little heat. "He was a good man compelled to do bad deeds."

"Neve' showed an ounce of remorse. Wes Hardin was a Baptist preacher's son who thought he was full of God's own grace, when it was really just piss and vinega'," replied Mr. Rhodes.

Graham ended their argument by pulling out a deck of playing cards.

"Hardin used to shoot playing cards and sell them as souvenirs or give them to gals. Neat trick if you can do it." Sam strode five long paces, maybe fifteen feet, to lodge a couple lower denominations in branch notches of the nearest cedar. "See if your aim's as good as your draw?"

Gillom drew and took his time, cocking and placing four of five shots around a five of spades. The outlaw nodded. Sam Graham proceeded to place all three of his remaining bullets in a tighter grouping. Gillom retrieved the targets while Sam reloaded from his own box of cartridges.

"You're a marksman, Mister Graham."

"Aim is what counts. Ain't the guy who shoots first, unless you're real close in, but the steadiest hand who walks away. To shoot again, another day." His pale blue eyes twinkled at his little rhyme and the other two men smiled.

Sam admired the rough triangle of three bullet holes Gillom handed him, then gave the youth two more cards from his deck to place again in the tree.

"Noticed you holdin' your breath, Gillom. Try suckin' it in, then lettin' out a little air before you fire, so you're not puffed up tight. Let your soft pull surprise your finger."

Gillom walked back reloading and followed the outlaw's advice to let out some breath before thumb-cocking and firing one, two, three, four, five steady shots! This time he didn't miss.

The kid was grinning as Sam went into another crouch, cross-drew suddenly and held the trigger of his .45 against the guard as he fanned three shots with his left palm against the hammer of the gun in his right hand, the echo of one explosion fusing with the bang of the next round. Graham not only missed the target, but the entire tree.

"*Damn!* Never could hit the near side of a barn, fanning. Makes this single-action as fast as a double-action revolver, but it's not very accurate. Don't try that in a gunfight unless you're in real close." Now Graham took his time, extending his right arm and sighting along the short rear sight and through the removable front sight of his shortened 4¾" barrels. Three shots! He didn't miss, either.

"*Wooo!*" exulted Gillom.

"One bullet in the right spot, kid, is all the truth you'll ever need."

Gene Rhodes roused himself from the stump where he'd been observing.

"Nice shootin', boys. That's probably enough scarin' the horses for today."

Gillom reloaded and offered his revolver to the older wrangler.

"You wanna try, Mister Rhodes?"

"No thanks, son." Gene hitched up his short frame. "When I was a little boy on our family farm I watched one of the field hands remove his glass eye at lunch one day to wash it. Being four years old I thought that was some trick and I tried to remove my own eye, too. Hurt like a sumbitch and I've had a weak left eye eve' since. Can't see worth a damn at distance. I'd be a dange' to all mankind shooting pistols."

They lingered over coffee and the dessert Gene had cooked in his dutch oven in the fireplace—"spotted pup," rice cooked with raisins and brown sugar.

"You gotta gift with guns, Gillom. Which is probably you' misfortune."

"I don't know about that, Gene," replied Sam Graham. "Pistol fighters can always find a job out West. Earn plenty of respect to go along with a payday, too."

"And an early grave." Rhodes shook his head.

"Maybe not. If I stay on the right side of the law," argued Gillom.

"Yes, *if*," added Gene. "And you respect what the old cowboys used to call the code of the West."

"What's that?"

Gene Rhodes rubbed his small belly to aid digestion.

"Well, it's sort of a rattlesnake's code, to give fai' warning before you strike. It's to the death after that, the barbarous code of the fighting man. Neve' take unfai' advantage of someone. Neve' use sneaky tricks in a business deal ah a fight, like shooting someone in the back when he's unarmed. You cannot eat a man's food and then stand up and shoot him. You can't kill someone without warning them first you're out to get them, but then ambush is okay, since they've been fai' warned. And keep you' word. Do what you say you' gonna do. Always."

His reddish-haired friend snorted. "That's how most of these gunfighters' reputations were made, Gene, back-shooting and killing drunks and ignorants. John Wesley Hardin's, for instance."

"Yeah and it caught up with him, didn't it? Hardin got shot in the back of the head in the Acme by an angry old lawman, who got off scot-free fo' his murder."

Sam scratched his chin stubble. "John Selman got shot himself not long after for that crime."

"That's what I'm sayin'. You cross the law's line, it'll catch up with you, soone' ah late', one way ah anotha. You' brothe's fate is gonna be yours, too, pardne', you don't straighten up," Gene lisped.

Graham scowled at the family reference, got up from the table to pour more coffee from the kettle resting in the fireplace embers.

"You're good with guns, too, Sam. We just saw. You'd make a helluva bank guard ah even a small-town sheriff yourself, somewheres fa' away, unde' another' name."

"My fate lies somewheres else."

Gillom had gotten up to take out his revolvers, unload them, and pull out his cleaning rod, gun oil, and a tiny screwdriver. He held up one of the .44-.40

Remingtons, admiring its silver shine in the lamplight as he spun an empty cylinder.

"What should I call 'em, fellas? Fire and Brimstone? Shouldn't I name these guns, like that fair warning you mentioned, Gene? Blood and Death maybe?"

Gene Rhodes's lecture on fair gunplay hadn't quite taken.

Gillom took a respite the next day, letting Sam follow Gene in breaking one of the last wild horses. The kid's tailbone was aching from several days' banging in the saddle, so he watched from the rail and grinned as Graham launched off the back of a big sorrel whose white socks flashed as it crow-hopped around the corral, celebrating unhorsing a rider.

"You *did* let him buck, Miste' Graham!"

"Jesus to Genoa." The outlaw got gingerly to his big feet, brushing off his pants and his pride.

Rhodes caught the bronc and led him back docilely by the reins to the jockey. "If at first you don't stay on—"

"All right, damn it. My ass says no, but my pride says go. But if I take another circus tumble, Gene, you'll have to iron this nag out for me."

"My pleasure," grinned Mr. Rhodes, helping his house guest back aboard. The horse just stood there, breathing hard as Sam lifted the reins, adjusted his fanny in the saddle. Then he gave it a little spur with an iron rowel.

The tall horse was off instantly, sun-fishing with all

four legs in the air while it twisted to show its belly, with Sam yelling and grabbing its blond mane. But his saddle weight wore the scared horse down and its buck jumping gradually lessened with Graham yipping and Rhodes yelling at his pupil. "Lean back! Keep its head up!"

The reddish horse pranced by them at a hard trot. "You can bust broncs for me anytime, cowboy!"

"No, one's enough today. Don't wanna push my luck!" yelled the Texas cowboy as he slid off the saddle and let Gillom take the reins of the skittish horse. Gene got the cinch loosened and the saddle off and the teenager yanked the headstall off the feisty animal, which leapt away with a last cow kick at its captors, narrowly missing Sam's head.

"*Whew!* I'll leave the horse wrangling to you, Gene. Ain't my favorite line of work."

The ranch owner put the sweaty tack atop a railing to dry, and the men tromped off with towels to the bathing spring to dunk their sore butts.

Snow melt burbling up into the two rock pools laved their undersides and made the chilly water bearable. Gillom lay back against the smooth sandstone. Gene joined him in the larger pool, leaving the smaller one to the big bandit.

"Those fou' horses are green-broke now, so I need to drive 'em down to the Ba' Cross for the boys to use as replacements and get 'em cattle-trained before fall roundup. I'll ride down to Engle tomorrow for supplies. It's thirty miles to that cattle depot on the railroad, which will take you anywhere you want to go. You wanna go down with me, Gillom, ah stay up here fo' a while?"

"Oh, I probably should put more miles between me and my trouble. I don't know where to go, though, besides west?"

Graham stopped soaping his head. "Oughta try Bisbee. There's a real fast town. All that copper money has dolled it up pretty good and those free-spending miners keep their saloons open all night. Douglas is building another big smelter a little south right near the border, and it's starting to hop, too. Tombstone nearby has slowed way down since its silver mines mostly played out, but Clifton to the north has got rich copper diggings, I hear. Bisbee's cornered most of the excitement, though, kid. Hottest town in the whole southwest, besides El Paso."

"You can pick up a Santa Fe express in Engle, Gillom, and be in Bisbee in two days," said Gene.

"Aways wanted to see that Arizona Territory. Can I sell my horses and tack in Engle and buy a ticket?"

"Sure. I know Slim, the stableman."

"Bisbee's got the mine and bank jobs you're seeking, kid, guarding all that mineral wealth," added Sam from his nearby bath.

"Sounds good. What are *you* gonna do now, Mister Graham? Why don't you come along with me?"

"No, too well known in Bisbee. I'll stay up here till Gene gets back from Engle. Then I'll push off for Texas. Need to tell my kin what happened to brother Tom."

Their host was trying to remove soap from an earhole with a knuckle.

"You'd be wise to stay shy of New Mexico, too, Sam, for quite a while."

Sam Graham stretched his muscular body. "Central Texas is home. Lotsa good outlaws come from that underbelly of America between Abilene and Austin. Ed Bullion was a train robber, so were the Kilpatrick brothers, George and Ben, the notorious Tall Texan. Will Carver left our gang to join up with the Wild Bunch for some of their better-planned escapades. John Wesley Hardin, too, came from San Saba County. I remember the trouble Blackjack and I got into in San Saba. We were just little kids, but Tom got thrown out of church one Sunday for chasing a barking dog down the aisle."

Gene Rhodes marveled. "Thrown out of *church*?"

"Yep. Even as a little boy he was a shit disturber. Guess a rope burn was inevitable, but Tom didn't deserve to have his head yanked off. Can't tell that to my kin in Texas or a few of 'em's liable to ride back here to even the score with these uncivilized New Mexicans."

"No, we can't have that," agreed Gene.

Seventeen

After a big meal and a long nap, the three made the hike up to the clearing on the mountainside again. Gillom had more energy this breezy spring day since he hadn't done any horse breaking that morning. As he placed playing cards in their shooting tree, he noticed Sam rubbing his aching ass.

"Look a little butt-sprung, Mister Graham."

"That horse broke *me*."

"Aw, Sam. Horses are noble steeds. The cowboy's best friend," replied Gene Rhodes.

"Not mine. Horses are strictly transportation. Can't see making pets out of 'em."

Gene took a tender seat on his stump to watch the fireworks.

"Why, Mister Graham. You'll neve' make a good cattleman with that attitude."

"Exactly," agreed Sam as he checked his Colt Bisley.

Gillom started practicing his gun juggling, tossing one revolver by the handle to catch again after a full rotation in the air. With his right hand he essayed a tougher toss, catching his other Remington by the barrel after one full flip. Then he was pulling both pistols at once, tossing them across his body in the air, catching them in opposite hands and reverse-twirling the guns back into his dual holsters at the same time.

"You oughta join Buffalo Bill's Wild West show, Gillom," applauded their ranch host.

"You pull that fancy stuff in a gunfight, they'll be nailing your coffin shut before you can take a bow," warned Graham.

"Just tryin' to warm up my hands."

"Just remembe'," offered Gene, "you' playin' with three pounds of steel a foot in front of you' face. Dangerous doesn't begin to describe those tricks."

"Gettin' shot hurts like a sumbitch, too. Like someone stuck you with a hot poker," added Sam. Reloaded, their bank robber friend got to his feet. He laid his big Colt flat in the palm of his hand, barrel forward. "Ever see the border roll?"

Sam suddenly dropped the pistol down, caught his forefinger in the trigger guard, and flipped the weapon into normal position in his hand, cocking with his thumb and thrusting the gun forward to fire. All in the blink of an eye.

"Or, you can hand it over butt first." He offered Gillom the gun butt first, who reached to take it, but Sam instantly rolled and reversed the revolver in his hand.

"Wes Hardin pulled that trick on Wild Bill Hickok in Abilene back in the 1870s. Move's become all the rage in Texas."

Gillom tried the road agent's spin both ways and after several awkward fumbles, once even dropping his revolver to the grass, seemed to get the hang of the quick maneuver.

"Road agent's spin is mostly useful when you're getting arrested, 'cept most Laws now know that trick."

Tired of gun tossing, Gillom took his stance, drew, and cocked and fired at the playing card in the tree maybe twenty feet away, then pinwheeled the revolver in his right hand, thumb-cocked and fired again, then pinwheeled a second time to fire. He hit a black king with his second shot.

"*Damn!* Gotta work on my aim."

Gene nodded. "All those tricks are sure flashy, but if you can't hit much, what's the point of going around heeled?"

Sam answered, "This is a Colt Bisley Flattop Model built for target shooting. Perfect balance. Bigger grip for a better feel in my hand and improved accuracy with these special sights. Best revolving pistol ever made. And my 4¾" barrel is shorter than your 5½", easier to draw. Know the first shootist to use these shorter barrels?"

Gillom shook his head.

"Bat Masterson. Marshal of Dodge City. Ordered 'em special from the Colt factory. Many imitators followed."

"Books's sweetened Remingtons have only á two-pound pull, J. B. said. Hair trigger."

Sam Graham nodded, impressed. He crouched, drew cross-handed, cocked, fired, fanned his second shot, did a Texas rollover of one spin forward and cocked and fired a third round. He hit the jack of diamonds twice, all in a few seconds.

"Beats me." Gillom shook his head as he strode off to change targets. They were using smokeless cartridges, so no powder lingered in the air to obscure their vision.

"Nice shootin', Sam." Mr. Rhodes nodded.

Gillom plodded back but Graham stopped him as he started to reload. Reaching, he turned the youth's pistol around butt forward in his right-hand holster.

"You show up to a gunfight with your gun butts forward, you'll intimidate 'em before they even start shootin'."

Gillom tried the different draw several times, starting his wrist backward, then snapping it outward, while they watched.

"It's just a flashier draw, not faster?" he questioned.

"Exactly. Just somethin' different to practice, that they may not have seen before. You distract 'em with a flashy trick, then kill 'em with your sharp aim."

Gillom suddenly drew both guns, cocked, and blasted away at the card targets, hitting them both.

"Shoot to kill with both hands!" he exulted.

"Head shot's the deadly one," offered Graham. "But tougher to make. Wes Hardin was a head-shooter. But you hit a man in his bigger target, his stomach, that lead bullet's such a shock to his body, he's paralyzed and will have a more difficult time returning fire. That's where the Apaches always tried to shoot their poisoned arrows, right in a man's wide gut."

At all this talk of killing, the horse wrangler roused himself.

"You boys blast away all you want. Scare off the game for miles around while I start supper."

"One more thing," said Sam to his protégé. "If you have only one shot, take it between your two heart-beats as you surprise the trigger." The master gunman raised his target pistol at arm's length, squinted, listened to his own blood pulsing and then triggered his short-barreled Bisley. A smokeless slug ripped into the queen of hearts twenty-five feet distant.

Young Gillom was open-mouthed again at his instructor's accuracy. The fast gunmen smiled at each other as Gene Rhodes lumbered back down the mountainside, holding his sore ass. They didn't hear him whimpering.

They had a peaceful night's sleep since Sam had finally run out of liquor. They assembled in front of the stone house after breakfast. Gene had saddled the easiest of the four horses they'd taken turns breaking and was going to drive the other three broncs in the cavvy ahead of them down to the Bar Cross Ranch on their way to Engle. Gillom had saddled the black gelding, with the smaller bay mare he'd taken from the Mexican cousins packing his personals. He left the last of his food supplies at Gene's since the horse wrangler had refused any payment for Gillom's stay.

Sam Graham idled near the front door while the other two tightened cinches and pack ties.

"You ever come up against a man who covers his pistol with his hat, watch out. 'Cause he's probably drawing his gun beneath it or from behind his back while he's talking to you." The train robber demonstrated with a sly smile.

Gillom matched his grin and shook the outlaw's hand after he'd reholstered.

"I'll watch out for that, Mister Graham. Sorry our trails never crossed, but it's been my pleasure."

Sam stretched to his full six feet as his pale blues watched the teenager mount.

"You're a real whizbang with those *pistolas,* kid. Your calling cards. Hope they're not your funeral."

Gene Rhodes whistled and shook his lasso at the three loose horses.

"*Hi-ya!* Git along, horses! I'll be back up from Engle late tomorrow, Sam, with more grub. Can I get you anything else?"

"You know my taste for barbed-wire extract, boss." The tough outlaw waved. "So long, you saddle-bumpers! You run across any old ladies or dogs need kickin', send 'em along to *me!*"

Eighteen

The long ride on the wagon road Rhodes had laid down from his high valley to the Bar Cross Ranch was uneventful, with only short stops to change saddles among the six horses, especially the four green broncs Gene was still training to work the roundups. Not many bucksnorts did either man endure as they schooled these rank horses to a riding saddle. Gene did have to put the Fish to one bangtail when it started acting up, chousing it around the neck with his Fish brand rain slicker, hazing the nervous horse until it settled down, worn out, most of the fear of its new rider exhausted.

They rode across the southern fringe of the notorious Jornada del Muerto, the Day's Journey of the Dead Man. Here sand dunes rose occasionally from broad swales where yuccas grew in groves and alkali flats dipped across the desert prairie, where even scrub greasewood barely held its own. The yuccas, man-high and sinister at a distance in the morning light, deceived

Gillom's sharp eyesight at first. *If I got stuck out here, fighting Apaches, I'd be a goner,* he thought.

Working together they were able to chase the three half-wild horses into a smaller corral next to a large one full of horses behind the big ranch house above Engle they arrived at in the late afternoon. The cowboys were still off working, but a short, stocky man came out of the barn to greet the two wranglers.

"Gene Rhodes! Whaddya know?"

"Less and less, Cole." Gene dismounted and nodded to Gillom to do the same. The two wranglers shook hands. "This here's Johnny Jones, Mister Railston. From El Paso. Johnny stayed with me, helped break these broncs. He's a natural."

Gillom smiled. "I was happy to lend him a hand and a hard seat for a few days for a roof over my head."

"You're learning horse breaking from a master. You want to continue your education, we can probably use another hand around the Bar Cross, at least through fall roundup."

Gillom pulled his refreshed mounts out of the trough, as they shook and blew water from their nostrils.

"Thanks, Mister Railston, but I'll be movin' along."

"Johnny's takin' the train tonight to Bisbee. Gonna get a job as a bank guard, so he can get paid to play with his pistols."

Mr. Railston eyed Gillom's matched revolvers.

"Uh-huh. Not much call for gunwork on a cattle ranch. Nothin' much to do here but stretchin' wire and movin' cattle around to fresh grass. Not enough

excitement for Gene either, huh pardner?" The foreman slapped his compadre on the back.

"No si'. I'd rathe' be a horse wrangle' than a cattle
prodde'."

"Okay. Here's sixty dollars for breaking these three.
You goin' to town?"

Gene nodded. "Need supplies. I'll stay ove' in
Engle tonight."

"Stop in on your way back up the mountain. Got a
couple more outlaw horses here. If they're too wild to
finish for saddle broncs, maybe you can get 'em to pull
harness."

"Okay, Cole, I'll give 'em a try. Thanks." Gene pock-
eted his sawbucks.

"See you at poker tonight? So I can win that hard-
earned money back?" inquired the older cowboy with
the twinkling eyes.

"You neve' know. Gotta help Johnny sell his horses
and tack first."

The ranch foreman grinned as the cowboys remounted and jigged the reins to urge their tired animals on.

"You bet. Goodbye, boys!"

As they rode away from the Bar Cross, Gillom had
a question.

"You gonna break two more broncs all by yourself?
Sam doesn't like to ride 'em."

"Oh, he'll help. Especially if I was to get bunged up.
Sam's only workin' fo' whiskey an' food and a place
to hide while this stink about his brothe' dies away.
Sam swears he's reformed, no longe' robbin', but he's

still wanted for a long list of crimes. So keep you' word, Gillom, and don't tell anyone you met him, ah trouble will surely follow."

"I owe you for your hospitality, Mister Rhodes. So I never met Mister Graham, or you, either."

"I'm okay to talk about, just forget you've been to my high camp. I already got a sullied reputation for sheltering outlaws in the San Andres. But I gotta have somebody up there to feed those horses while I'm down with May and her boy in Tularosa. That horse ranch is my livelihood."

Gene told him Engle was half the size of Tularosa, all oriented toward shipping cattle on the railroad from the ranches spread about the edges of the desolate Jornada del Muerto, many of them nearer the water of the Rio Grande running along the western side of the Fra Cristobal Range to the north and the higher Caballo Mountains to the south. A mercantile, several restaurants and saloons, a small bank, post office, blacksmith and stable, besides the stock pens near the depot of the El Paso and North Eastern railroad, made up all of Engle's business district that Gillom could see. Few families cared to take up residence in this barren burg unless commerce called.

They stopped first at Slim's, which must have been a joke on the pudgy hostler who waddled out to greet them. Slim was another friend of Gene's, and all these tough men were used to his lisp and high-pitched voice and didn't kid him about it. Slim led their three horses inside a corral next to his barn.

"Gene, Gene. You gonna leave a little long green on our poker tables?"

"Might do that, Slim. Feelin' lucky tonight. And my friend Johnny here, from El Paso, would like to offe' you a chance at purchasing these two fine horses, the black and the bay, and the tack that goes with them. Am I correct, Johnny?"

"Yes, sir."

They unsaddled the horses so the hostler could get a good look at the gear as the men hoisted Books's forty-pound saddle and six-pound Navajo blanket onto a top railing to dry.

"Well sir, I have enough horses here now to meet occasional demand, but come fall, roundup cowboys'll need extra. Good saddle like this double rig, though, is always appreciated." The fat stableman patted Books's padded saddle seat with its dual leather cinches hanging below. Gillom didn't point out J. B. Books's name branded onto the leather skirt but covered by the back jockey, even though being owned by such a famous gunfighter would have made it worth much more. The teenager didn't wish to be traced back to that El Paso bloodletting.

"I've got this one good saddle and the black gelding that goes with it, and I could ship both out if I don't get a fair price. The mare's a gentler horse for a woman or child, with that other saddle. I'll take three hundred dollars for both horses and gear."

"*Whoa,*" said Chubby. "Not much call for saddle mares for the few ladies in this town. Mexican saddle's pretty much used up. Give you two hundred dollars for the lot."

"No chance!" The kid looked exasperated, but was bargaining like a man. "That good saddle alone is worth a hundred dollars. And this black beauty is fit and fast."

"He is, Slim. I've seen him run," lied Gene.

"Two-twenty."

"Two seventy-five."

"Two-forty is my final offer."

"Two-sixty and they're yours."

Rhodes was hungry. "Ahh, split the difference at two-fifty and let's go have some dinne'." The two horse traders reluctantly shook hands.

Gillom lifted two sets of saddlebags to each shoulder, as Slim went to dig his money out from somewhere he'd hidden it.

"Tired of steak," said Gene. "Let's eat at Lupita's."

Gillom received his money and Rhodes's horse was led off to be attended to, so they decided on a farewell dinner of spicy tamales and stringy beef enchiladas at the only Mexican joint in Engle. Liquor wasn't sold in this small, fly-specked family place and Gene didn't drink anyway, so the teenager contented himself with a warm sarsaparilla, even though he'd thought back in El Paso his sarsaparilla days were over.

"Thanks for puttin' me up for a few days, Mister Rhodes. The grub was good and the company, too, but my tailbone may never be the same."

The short wrangler laughed. "You're young, you'll recover. Anything you learned about hangin' onto a horse will be useful if you keep travelin' around this rough country. Trains and stagecoaches are fine between the bigger towns, but only horses will get you out to where the real beauty of the Southwest lies."

"I'll own more horses someday. Are you going to keep writing for that journal in Los Angeles?"

"Sure." The broncbuster nodded between bites of his cheesy enchilada. "But I'm thinking about a bigge' canvas than short stories and essays. May try writing a novel. Like to see my name in a library. Somebody needs to record the adventures of these notorious outlaws I keep running into up at my horse ranch. I get to know 'em and earn thei' trust, they sometimes tell me about thei' families and the scrapes they've been in. Thei' true stories are priceless, Gillom, and as this country gets tamed, you're gonna see fewe' and fewe' of these wild bandits still on the prowl. Civilization and better law enforcement will tie 'em up. Bill Doolin, for instance, was known as the King of the Oklahoma Outlaws. A rough, tough hombre, unforgettable. Same with those bad Graham bothers. Maybe I'll immortalize 'em in prose, as well as on thei' wanted posters."

"I'd sure buy *that* book, Gene." Gillom nodded. "I was never too partial to fiction, but I remember one poem we read in English class. Let's see. . . .

When all the world is young, lad,
And all the trees are green;
And every goose a swan, lad
And every lass a queen;
Then hey for boot and horse, lad,
And round the world away;
Young blood must have its course, lad,
And every dog his day.

"Charles Kingsley, I know it!" Gene Rhodes crowed. "Too bad you didn't finish you' education, Gillom. Mighta made a good teache'."

"No, I'm ready for some real life learnin'."

Gillom treated his host to dinner and together they strolled over to the train depot smoking small Mexican cigarillos, the teenager coughing. His passenger train south was a three-hour ride to the end of the Santa Fe's line, supposed to get to Deming by midnight. The ticket clerk showed them on a wall map how the kid would have a layover till morning to catch the next Southern Pacific express out of El Paso on to Lordsburg and over Stein's Pass with a long chug into Arizona Territory and Benson. They shook hands a last time in the small depot.

"Can't thank you enough, sir."

"I wish you luck, son, buckets of luck. You' problem will come when anyone learns you were involved in Books's big shoot-out and those are his special guns. Someone will want to test you, see if you are as good as that famous shootist was. And if you pass that first test and kill again, you' a marked man the rest of you' limited days."

Gillom Rogers clapped the shorter man on the back. "Now, Eugene. Long as I stay within the law, my future can't be that grim."

"Someone will hea', someone will see you practicing, and hence will come the challenge. You're a feisty kid, Gillom, loads of sand, but you'll want to demonstrate you' prowess. And then . . . young blood will have its course, lad. . . ."

As unpredictable as the wind, Eugene Manlove

Rhodes spun round and walked out of the train station. Gillom just stood there, watching the bowlegged cowboy amble away.

"And every *dog* his day, Gene!"

But the horse wrangler never turned back to wave goodbye.

Nineteen

Since he'd never ridden a railroad before, Gillom knew he wouldn't be sleeping much, so he purchased a second-class ticket for five dollars, which didn't include a sleeping berth. He watched as a few folks got on the passenger train after this every-other-night express pulled into Engle about 9:00 P.M. More families got off in that little station after their shopping excursions to Albuquerque, mothers carrying sacks of new clothes and dads boxes of foodstuffs, their kids clutching new toys. One gent carried a new saddle over his shoulder as Gillom brushed past him looking for an empty seat in the day coach, after he'd passed his saddlebags and warbag to a baggage man on the platform.

Gillom pushed past an overweight man dozing on the aisle and took a seat next to the window. Electric lights in the cars were on during its half hour stop in Engle. He could see cattle waiting to be shipped out of pens across the tracks. Gillom was settling into the comfortable upholstery when the whistle suddenly shrilled, the train cars jerked, and couplings clanked, and the steam engine began its hard pull forward.

The fat man next to him was already snoring, so Gillom restlessly got up. The parlor car was half-filled with cattlemen and traveling salesmen, drinking at the stand-up bar or sitting in plush chairs smoking or reading a selection of newspapers or books from racks above the cushioned wall seats. Women weren't allowed to drink liquor with the men to discourage the many traveling prostitutes, and he'd already been warned by a conductor who looked at his ticket that he wouldn't be served, either. Gillom paused to have his boots blackened again by a white kid who also served as the train's butcher boy, selling lollipops, fruit, and cigars to the passengers. The boy wanted fifty cents for his snappy shine, which Gillom thought high and thus declined to tip, earning a scowl. He watched one woman shuffling cards with a few boisterous men at a poker table, but she didn't appear to be drinking anything stronger than iced tea. He spotted a writing table nearby and commandeered it, using the free pens, ink, and paper to dash off a brief note to his mother.

Gillom then walked the Persian carpeting through a concertina-pleated vestibule between cars, to spare travelers discomfort from wind or rain. He peeked into the dining room, where white-jacketed Negro waiters were tidying up while several tables of diners lingered over their coffee and pie. Gillom wasn't hungry, so after getting an evil eye from the uniformed black porter in the next sleeper car to the rear, he trudged back to his second-class car. There he crammed beside the snoring fat man and rested his cheek against the cool glass of the window. Squinting, Gillom could just make out the ghostly shapes of occasional cows as they ran away from the scary fire-breathing snake as it roared down dark rails under a silvery moon.

Deming, New Mexico, sat at the conjunction of two major railroads, so all the passengers had to disembark from the Santa Fe after midnight and fend for themselves until picking up the Southern Pacific headed west out of El Paso the next morning, or early next evening when another SP train arrived from the West Coast headed on to the main city of West Texas. Gillom reaffirmed this from a conductor after they arrived in Deming and he learned his options for the night. Passengers served themselves according to their needs—families hiring a carriage to drive them and their luggage into the railroad crossroad for some fitful sleep at a small hotel. Single men, after seeing their bags into safe storage at the depot, might walk into town for a nightcap at one of Deming's tough saloons. This wasn't the most prudent course, for in the early 1900s this was a brawling railroad town so lawless that outlaws rounded up in Arizona were often booted into the next territory with a one-way ticket to Deming.

So he'd been warned. Gillom picked up his saddlebags and wandered off to an outside corner of the depot building, as far away as he could get from the few people milling about inside the station, uncertain what to do with themselves till dawn. The teenager had had enough excitement this very long day, and he nodded off under a starry sky, a bag of unshelled peanuts in one hand and a bottle of fizzwater in the other.

Come morning and after depositing his gear in the baggage room and purchasing another six-dollar ticket to Benson, Gillom strolled into the dusty burg to wolf down breakfast at the Beehive Café. He mailed his letter to his mother in the little post office inside Deming's only mercantile, which opened at 8:00 A.M. His westbound wasn't due in until after ten, so he dawdled down the town's small main street of shops and saloons and took a gander at its real business—an extensive rail yard composed of an engine roundhouse and train repair shops and freight car sidings shared by two of America's mightiest railroads, the Atchison, Topeka and Santa Fe, and the Southern Pacific.

Gillom had heard fuel oil was starting to replace coal burners on some Western railroads, but those sleeker, cleaner engines hadn't arrived on the Sunset Route yet. He marveled at the size of the Mogul locomotives being worked on by mechanics. Then a distant whistle keened and the youth hustled back to the depot to reclaim his bags as the big ten-wheeler chuffed into town spraying cinders and smoke.

Gillom watched better-dressed passengers debark for a morning constitutional around the platform before resuming their journey. He was transfixed by one pretty blonde brushing her linen duster off with gloved hands after she removed it to shake soot off her wardrobe. The teenager snapped out of his daze to get his saddlebags to a porter and clamber aboard the

Southern Express himself. They were rolling westward not long afterward.

Gillom awoke from exhausted sleep after noon, oblivious to the comings and goings of others in their second-class car. What should have been a fast, uneventful trip on the bumpy roadbed wasn't, for this Southern train was no express, but a milk run, requiring a stop at every way station between El Paso and Tucson. As they screeched into yet another small depot, he complained to a man reading a newspaper next to him.

"We're stopping again?"

"Southern Pacific has the only twice-weekly train running across the bottom of this country, kid, so they milk their business for all it's worth. Even making less than thirty miles an hour, it's still faster than a bumpy stagecoach. No Indian attacks, either."

Gillom nodded. His mouth was dry from sleeping wide open, catching flies, as his mother used to say, so he roused to stretch numbed legs. This train was much more crowded on its main run than the mixed passenger and freight train he'd ridden in from Engle, and the bar car was its hub. Gillom bought more soda water to wash from his mouth leftover salt from the peanuts. One nattily dressed gent seated alone at a small table against the wall caught Gillom's eye and beckoned him over, gesturing to the one empty chair left in the parlor car.

"Sit down, young man. Take a load off."

Gillom did as bid.

"Nice brace of pistols. Where's a young gun hand like you headed?"

"Bisbee. Hear that's a fast town."

"It *is* indeed. To do *what* there, may I ask?"

Gillom admired the middle-aged man's fancy clothing, his ruffled white shirt under his black silk vest which displayed hand-painted red and pink roses on its wide lapels.

"Oh, somethin' to do with protection—bank guard, stage shotgun, mine security, eventually maybe law enforcement."

The stranger nodded. "All that copper mining in Bisbee, precious metal shipments, ought to be lots of protection jobs for an aggressive young fella like you. Dangerous work, though."

Gillom just smiled.

"So you're a risk taker. Betting your life on your nerve and quickness, your steady hand under fire." The man reached inside a pocket of the black broadcloth coat he'd draped over the back of his chair and withdrew a deck of cards, which he fanned in one hand, then bent back and riffed rapidly into the palm of his other. Gillom saw the heavy gold rings he sported on either hand.

"Care for a little pasteboards? To pass the long hours till you reach your mining mecca."

"I'm no gambler."

"Ahh. Ever tried three-card monte? It's simple and fast. The *right* game for a lad with sharp eyes like yours." The flashy stranger flipped over the top card to show him the ace of hearts, which he laid onto the table faceup. The next two were the king of spades and the queen of clubs, which also went onto the bare table. The dealer slid the rest of his railroad bible back into his coat pocket, then turned the three cards over again, facedown.

"Remember where that ace of hearts was? Keep your eye on her now." The man began moving the three face cards around beneath his big hands. He stopped and spread his hands wide. "Where is that red ace, sir?"

Gillom aimed an index finger at the card on his left. With a broad smile the gent flipped over the ace of hearts. It was easy.

"Excellent. Okay, let's make it interesting. Five dollars?"

After a pause, Gillom nodded. The ace was turned back over again and the three cards began their little dance. This time Rogers watched the ace end up on the right.

The gambler nodded. "Your eyes are quicker than my hand, young sir. Ten dollars?"

"After you pay me my five."

"But of course. You're a careful manager of your money, sir. I respect that in one so young." Pulling out a leather change purse from a back pocket, he removed a five-dollar bill and handed it over. Again, the cards were circled, then reversed. Now the ace was in the middle, which the youth pointed to. The gambler shook his head at the correct call, made a production of pulling several Mexican five-dollar coins from his change purse to roll across the hardwood. "Give me a chance at twenty?"

But Gillom shook his head no.

"Oh, c'mon. Surely you're enough of a sport to allow me a chance at winning my money back?"

Another young man stepped up to the table now, who'd been watching this pasteboard manipulation keenly from a distance.

"I'll go you for that twenty, mister."

"Weeell, all right. At least *someone's* got sporting blood."

Gillom looked this young man, in his early twenties maybe, over. A derby hat, a tan-and-black-checked suit, soft brown leather dress boots completed this young buck's ensemble. No weapons visible. A traveling salesman of some type of flashy, unnecessary merchandise probably. The sport watched the cards move again and with a grin, fingered the red ace.

"Pay up, pardner."

"*Damn!* You boys are bleedin' me to death." The gambler rubbed perspiring hands across his brow, then off on his shirtsleeves, shooting his French cuffs. "But I'm a sporting man. I'll take another chance." He paid off with a small twenty-dollar gold piece.

"Let's go fifty." The new bettor agreed. The cards seemed to move faster now under the gambler's paws, but when he at last paused his shuffle, Gillom's eagle eye was fixed upon what he figured to be the high heart. He also noticed that one corner of that card seemed to be tipped, bent slightly upon one edge. The new player must have noticed this, too, for with a chuckle of satisfaction, he pointed to that same card. With a grumble, the gambler turned over the red ace once more.

"*Damnation!* I cannot win for losing today. You

eagle-eyed, young bucks are plucking me bare." This time he peeled off two twenty-dollar bills and a ten-spot to push reluctantly across the table to the flashy bettor.

"Double or nothin'. My last hundred." For emphasis, the monte man withdrew a one-hundred-dollar bill from his pouch and laid it on the edge of the small table, smoothing it out with his big hand. He stared at the new bettor, but the sport in the derby shook his head.

"I don't want to take *all* your money, mister." The sport looked directly at Gillom. "Kid wants some of this, it's his turn."

The gambler now stared at Gillom. "Fair enough. You clipped me, too."

A small crowd had slowly gathered to watch this table action and from it pushed an older gentleman in a blue hat and coat, a silver watch chain dangling from his vest. He took Gillom by the elbow.

"May I see your ticket, son?"

"Huh? Oh, sure." Gillom fumbled in his pants pocket, but found the ticket and gave it up.

The conductor looked at the ticket, then steered the youth from his seat and out of the small crowd. "Come with me a moment."

The big gambler was immediately on his feet. "*Hey!* This young man was about to bet!"

"Gamble with your own kind, Doc." The railroad employee pointed at the young sport in the checked suit. "Like your partner there."

"Mister, I wanted to bet that card," Gillom protested as the train conductor pushed him to a free corner of the parlor car.

"You saw the bent corner on that ace? Well, I guarantee you that ace was about to be replaced by a bent face card instead," hissed the older man. "That's Doc Davis, son, notorious cardsharp. Seen his sleight of hand too many times. That young bettor was his 'capper,' helping him set you up. We can't stop 'em from buying tickets, but I *can* stop them from running that old monte ruse on our unwary passengers."

Gillom squinted, peering back at the two cardsharps who were fuming loudly to bystanders near their table.

"I didn't realize. . . . Thanks."

The graying conductor finally smiled. "The Southern Pacific is trying hard to stop card cheating on its rails." They shook hands. "Save your money, kid. And stay away from the gaming tables."

Gillom nodded thoughtfully and started for the front exit of the parlor car. He was hungry after his brush with poverty, so he splurged on a full dinner in the dining car, seated at a table for two with white linen and silver service, where he was served by an Ethiopian waiter in a spotless white tunic. The teenager enjoyed foods he'd never tasted before, including salmi of duck, baked veal pie, French slaw, and sweet potatoes, with mince pie, vanilla ice cream, French coffee, and a sampling of cheeses for dessert. For $1.50.

Feeling like an overfed potentate, for the rest of the train ride Gillom dozed in his coach seat and stared out the window at the two-horse towns they had to stop at to take on or put off a mailbag, boxes of goods, or a couple passengers. It was dark when the Southern Express pulled into Benson, a somewhat larger depot on the slow train ride toward the territory's biggest town, Tucson.

Gillom grabbed his saddlebags from a porter unloading the baggage car and spotted the friendly conductor, who offered a final word of advice.

"Careful with those guns you're toting, young man. I'd hate for them to put you on the night train to the big *adios*."

The teenager waved him away, as with another shriek of its whistle, the Southern Express chugged off into the West.

He ambled into Benson loosening stiff legs. Because it was midweek, Gillom was able to find a spare bed at the first boarding house he came to. Their communal supper had already been served, so the landlady pointed him toward a nearby saloon. There he ordered the chicken stew, which seemed tasty until the beer slurper stooped over beside him at the long bar remarked it was actually prairie dog. Gillom immediately wished he was back on the train, fine dining.

Next morning, Gillom Rogers rode the 11:00·A.M. train out of Benson with maybe thirty passengers in its two rail cars, other boxcars filled with store goods. The ticket clerk had explained that this faster express run had just been inaugurated to get the Western mail into Bisbee in time for same-day delivery.

"Business is booming in Bisbee," the clerk told him,

"so the Phelps Dodge Company built their own fifty-five miles of track when they couldn't get Southern Pacific to run a spur down there from Benson."

So Gillom rode the small Arizona and Southeastern Railroad on its two-hour run, enjoying the scenery and conversing with a well-dressed gentleman on the seat across from him.

"Going to Bisbee on business, young man?"

"Yessir. I hope to find employment guarding the mines, banks, something in the protection line," replied Gillom.

The gentleman had been idly blowing smoke rings from his cigar, but he now focused on his fellow traveler.

"That's necessary work, with all the money generated by the mining industry. You look a little young to be a deputy."

"Probably. They like you to have a few years' practical experience before law enforcement will hire you."

"As well they should. Dangerous job." The older man blew another smoke ring and was pleased with the result. "Copper is a wondrous metal, son, and as long as its price holds up, a lot of us in mining are going to ride its glittering back to our fortunes. Copper is nearly indestructible and I know you've seen it conducting electricity through telephone wires. But it's also used in ship hulls, cookware, and roofing. Why, those pistol cartridges in that belt around your waist, every one of them contains half an ounce of pure copper in its brass."

Gillom looked down at his belt to inspect a round. "I didn't realize."

"The ore out here is very low grade compared to Michigan's high-grade deposits. It takes a hundred and fifty pounds of smelted copper to equal the value of one ounce of gold or fifteen ounces of silver. That's why Phelps Dodge built this little railroad, to lower their connector freight rate on smelted ore down to a dollar a ton. Beats those old mule-drawn ore wagons they used to run up to Benson by six times on price."

"You must be a mining man?"

The businessman smiled. "Work for Anaconda Copper, the big boy up in Butte, Montana. Copper Queen Consolidated is going to shut down their old smelter in Bisbee. Copper Queen's building a better smelter down in Douglas, right on the border, twenty-three miles away. They've got more well water there and cheaper land to expand on."

"Huh." Gillom was impressed. "Maybe I'll look for work there."

"You should," agreed the equipment broker. "But they haven't found any copper around Douglas. It's all up there, hiding in those Mule Mountains."

Gillom pressed his face to the train's window glass as he followed the mining man's pointed finger.

"See those two peaks? Think they look like two big ears on a mule?"

"Not really," said Gillom. The buyer laughed. "How many folks live there?"

"Oh, about eight thousand, I heard." The equipment broker leaned closer to the window, looking out across the sun-baked plains leading up to mountain crags sparsely forested with Apache pines. "They used to call this isolated place 'the country that God forgot.' But that's certainly no longer the case with Bisbee."

No *indeed*, Gillom Rogers thought, *and I can't wait to get there*.

For they sow the wind, and
they reap the whirlwind.

—Hosea 8:7

Twenty

Gillom steamed into the Bisbee depot the afternoon of a Thursday. Miners of three nationalities, mostly white, the American-born, the Irishmen, and the elite diggers, the Cornishmen, trudged up Tombstone Canyon, headed toward the second, late shift in the Copper Queen shafts, after the day drillers got off. These tough men looked over the passengers getting off the short Arizona and Southeastern train, especially the few women, but paid a teenager little mind. So he shouldered his saddlebags and canvas warbag and headed across the tracks up infamous Brewery Gulch.

Buying an *Arizona Daily Orb* for a nickel, Gillom stopped in the first saloon he came to at the junction of the town's two main thoroughfares, the canyon and the gulch, which split the heart of the empurpled peaks of the Mule Mountains. He was out of breath from his walk, for this isolated town built around an ore load nestled at fifty-three hundred feet. Panting a little, he was conscious of a vile odor assaulting his nostrils, but figured it was the sulphurous red-brown smoke blowing from the smelters' smokestacks.

The Bonanza was one of the bigger drinking establishments among the over-forty in town, but except for a lazy mutt soaking up some late-afternoon sun outside its batwing door, it didn't seem very crowded. After dumping his gear in a corner and joining a few men wearing calluses on their elbows at the long bar, he addressed a bartender with muttonchop whiskers framing a full browse of red hair. The young barkeep was dressed in black wool pants and a white shirt. A black string tie and black sleeve garters completed this mixologist's outfit. He looked Gillom over when he ordered a beer. He saw the kid had made a distant journey with all that gear, plus the matched pistols on his hips, so the bartender decided his new customer was man enough and poured him a mug from a keg.

"Seems sorta quiet today."

"Give it an hour. Then the day shift gets cleaned up from the mines and the girls stroll in to entertain 'em. Oh, it'll be rippin' in here later tonight, right on through the weekend. Bisbee's a twenty-four-hour town."

Gillom nodded as he flipped through the six pages of their daily paper, scanning the ads.

"Lookin' for a room to rent. Don't see any mentioned in your paper."

"Town's always full. The Richelieu is right up Main Street. It's first class, expensive. Bessemer House is our biggest hotel, but they are hot-bunking that joint. One miner leaves for his shift, another just getting off work takes his same bed."

"No, don't want to share beds. Mining's not my choice job anyway."

"Well, a miner who lived near me just got killed in an accident, so widow Blair may have a spare room. I get off my afternoon shift at 8:00 P.M. We can go see her then. You lookin' for work, kid? They're building the Copper Queen Hotel, just up the canyon. Forty-four bedrooms. Supposed to cost 175,000 dollars. Building it in the Italianate style, whatever that means. It'll be the fanciest hotel in the whole territory. Should bring us in some classy customers."

Gillom shook his head as the barkeep polished a drinking glass.

"Nope, I'm not a builder, either. Interested in security, guardin' valuables."

"Well, try our Bank of Bisbee, opened last year, just a block away, up Main Street. We've got armed messengers on our trains, security up at the mines, too. Somebody around here always needs somethin' protected. You good with them guns?"

"Try me." Gillom smiled. "Thanks for your suggestions. I'm gettin' somethin' to eat, but I'll be back at eight. Whatcher name?" He reached across the bar to shake hands.

"Ease Bixler."

"Gillom Rogers." He left his new acquaintance four bits as tip.

Gillom needed a haircut to look presentable at job interviews, so he stopped at the City Barber Shop and got his peach fuzz shaved, too. He dropped his roady clothes off at the Warren Laundry, which was run by a couple large white women, not the usual Chinese. When he commented on that, the heavyset lady manning the cash register explained that Bisbee was a "white man's camp."

"Celestials are allowed in during daylight hours to sell their vegetables and fruit they grow on their little farms around Fairbank, but we don't want 'em livin' in town running their laundries and chop suey houses and opium dens."

"Or undercuttin' our miners' wages!" chimed in a laundrywoman working over a steaming tub in back.

Gillom walked out with his laundry ticket. *Bisbee is gonna be different,* he thought. *Never been around mining people, but I heard they're as tough as they come.*

He ladled up greasy soup floating a few wads of maybe mule meat in a hole-in-the-wall up the gulch, but the sourdough bread was filling. Gillom didn't complain about the bad food, for he needed to make new friends in a hurry, not start by aggravating the local cooks.

He walked back to the Bonanza under his burden of bags. Ease Bixler clapped his hands when he saw Gillom clomp tiredly back in.

"*There's* that curly wolf! Told you this joint would be jumpin' later."

Ease was right. The poker tables were filling up, the faro and craps, all run by well-dressed dealers in their suits and string ties, clad in fancy footwear and big jewelry. The cowboys and teamsters were recognizable in dirty jeans and big hats, often unshaven from their travels. The miners were tough-looking, in wool pants, vests, and derby hats often, but they were more likely to be shaven to help keep mining dirt off their faces.

And the women had arrived to entertain them on these ladies' night shifts, all races, colors, and ages. Gazing around the cavernous saloon, Gillom saw that half the women were Mexican. The Bonanza wasn't the toniest saloon in Bisbee and they were close to the border, but Gillom had been aware of a distinct segregation among the prostitutes in El Paso, with the Mexican women confined to the cribs and cantinas and cheaper bagnios. In Bisbee it looked like the races mingled more freely and the rough and tumble miners appeared more tolerant in their tastes for painted flesh.

"Let's go find ya a roof to sleep under!" The barkeep polished off his own beer, hung up his apron, and led the youth outside, offering to shoulder one of Gillom's saddlebags since the kid seemed to be drooping. Then they were off, strolling up a street filling with thirsty customers heading into the darker reaches of Brewery Gulch.

"Bisbee comes alive at night," explained Mr. Bixler. "Then you don't notice all the garbage thrown in the creek, dead animals about, open cesspools, nightsoil on the streets."

"Is that what I'm smellin'?"

"Yup. The housewives just throw their garbage and bathwater down these hillsides, trash gets pitched out the back of restaurants, and outhouses drain into the creek. By spring that sewage gets quite ripe, but it all gets flushed away in our late summer floods. Our flies and mosquitoes feast every day and our pigs and coyotes grow fat." They both chuckled.

"Guess I'll live high up then," said Gillom. Bisbee was pretty by moonlight, the houses twinkling lights two miles up the long canyon on both sides. "That the Copper Queen?"

The Copper Queen's jumbo smelter and two smaller ones hissed escaping steam and the young men heard the deep thrumming of the blowers in the smelters. The furnaces roared as white hot metal flowed under the glare of electric lights.

"Yup. The Calumet and Arizona mining company's just been formed and they've struck a rich ore body on their Irish Mag claim, so there's gonna be two big mining rivals in town. *The Electric Age has dawned and the world cries out for copper!*" Ease yelled, leaving both young men grinning. "There's even talk the town may incorporate, become official. Hell, the Improvement Company's extending electric and telephone lines all over town, and they're starting to dig wells south toward Naco to pump us up fresher water, put an end to our deadly epidemics. Our air will still be smoky, but the rest of Bisbee will be fully civilized, damn it."

"I met a man from Anaconda Copper on the train. He said Phelps Dodge is building a bigger smelter down in Douglas, gonna shut these smelters down."

"That's what I hear," agreed Ease. "But these companies will remain close to where their ore, their money, is and that's around Bisbee."

"Me, too," puffed Gillom as they tramped up a long, three-stage wooden stairway to a small wooden house on the southern hillside across the canyon from the smelters.

"You like our endless stairs?"

"You do get your exercise."

"Indeed! Sheriff's rule is, a drunken miner gets three chances to climb the stairs home before being taken to jail for the night."

Gillom laughed. "How'd you get your nickname?"

"Oh, as a kid I'd always figure the easiest way of doin' things first, before doin' my schoolwork or chores."

"Or not at all?"

Now the young barkeep laughed. "That, too. So the name stuck." Ease Bixler stopped on the stairway near a small, whitewashed house to catch his breath.

"This is Missus Blair's. Widow dressmaker, has her little millinery above the bank, downtown." The lanky bartender pointed through the darkness toward more lamplit dwellings farther along the hillside. "That's my house up there, third one over. Nothin' fancy in this neighborhood, Youngblood Hill."

He rapped loudly on the front door and it was opened by a middle-aged woman in a fancy dress of crimson silk, with streamers of pinned black lace dangling loose from its neck and sleeves.

"Who's banging on my door at night?"

"Pardon, Missus Blair. It's Ease Bixler, from three doors over." He pulled his new pal forward into the dim light. "This is Gillom Rogers. Just in from El Paso. I thought after what happened to poor Mister Peavy, your spare room might be available?"

"It is. Come in. Pardon me, boys. I am tacking trim on this dress for a customer."

"Very pretty," agreed Ease. Peering around the lamplit front room, the youths observed lace scraps on her rug, and scissors and sewing boxes lying in front of a full-length glass mirror, which tilted on wooden hinges.

"Sorry to bother you at night, ma'am," added Gillom, removing his Stetson.

"I've got a two-room cottage out back, up the hill. Use my privy, too, but you have to buy your own stovewood and water off the burro trains. Linens provided, but you gotta wash 'em and keep the place tidy. Twelve dollars a month. In advance." She didn't appear to be in the mood to negotiate, so Gillom agreed, sight unseen.

"I don't want any short-timers. Mine is not a hotel. Couple months' stay at least."

"He intends to get a job, Missus. Bank guard or somethin' respectable," interjected Ease.

"Let's go see it then." Handing her neighbor a coal oil lamp, the woman, still dangling lacework, pulled sheets and several worn towels from a chiffonier, handed a quilt to Gillom, and led them through her kitchen and out her back door.

"Ain't fancy, but it's suited several miners just fine." She unlocked the door to the two-room shack, reached inside to strike a match, and lit another lamp. The boys followed to look in the moving lamplight. The only standing furniture was a bench and rocker in the front room. Two single bunk beds, cupboard, settee, and chest of drawers were built into the wooden walls. The wood-burning stove in the smaller kitchen also had a wooden table to eat off of bolted to the wall, several pine chairs, and a big tin washbasin perched atop two sawhorses. Cups, glasses, and cooking utensils were stacked in another built-in cupboard.

"Nothing much here to destroy, all built-in. Since you know Mister Bixler, I'll let you stay tonight for free, see how it suits. I'll take my twelve dollars first thing in the morning."

Gillom nodded. "Probably be fine, ma'am. See you first thing. Oh. Where's the—"

"Privy's right up the hill. No peeing in the bushes, or late-night cards, or entertaining women all hours. I know how young men like to do, but I live right next door. Like my peace and quiet."

Neither Gillom nor his new buddy met her stern eyes. She'd embarrassed them. Mrs. Blair merely nodded, dropped her sheets on one of the bunks, took her lamp back from Ease, and swept from the room.

Gillom put down the old quilt, pulled a mattress up on its side for several hard bounces and a shake to see what might be living inside.

"Thought I'd left my mother back in El Paso."

Ease chortled. "She's just puttin' you on notice, sport. Bark's worse than her bite. Get a job, start makin' money, you can find somethin' more suitable, maybe bunkin' with one of our painted cats, up the Gulch." He winked.

The teenager didn't take his bait. "Thanks for the help, Ease. I owe you a good dinner, anytime you'd like."

The redhead grinned. "Tomorrow night then. When I get off my shift. Friday night always jumps. Show you some of our high life."

"You bet." They shook hands again at the door. "Need a light?"

"No, this is my neighborhood. Don't slip on a dog turd in the gully, I should make it home all right."

"See you tomorrow night about eight at the Bonanza then."

After his new pal disappeared into the dark, Gillom kicked his saddlebags into a corner, quickly tucked in the sheets, pulled off his boots and pants and cotton shirt. As he blew out his lamp, he pulled the quilt up over his long johns and dirty socks with a sigh. *I'll make the best of this, even if I do miss my mother and Bee and Ivory and even ol' Johnny Kneebone, just a little bit.*

Twenty-one

He paid Mrs. Blair next morning. She warmed to the feel of his two gold eagles. He left her dobie silver dollars from his change to pay the Mexican burro drivers on their daily rounds with supplies of firewood and twenty-five-gallon canvas sackfuls of fresh water, to get him started stocking supplies.

As he sat in the outhouse taking his morning ease, peeling off his merino wool underwear, separate top and bottom, he was pleased to discover no other house guests had come out of his thin mattress to bite him in the night. *Maybe I should try the stage line first?* Gillom wondered. *That could be an exciting job, stagecoach guard, fighting off armed robbers and the occasional Apache.*

So, even if he still smelled a little ripe in his roady clothing, Gillom clomped down the long, almost vertical flights of wooden stairs from his new home atop Youngblood Hill. He stared around at the warrens of wooden houses with their gingerbread trim the residents had gouged and blasted out of hillside ledges. One neighbor's roof was perched just below another's front door. He looked over the twisting dirt trails, steep stairways, and tortuous streets connecting these homes, the big mines across the canyon and the businesses downtown. In the sparse foliage woodcutters hadn't stripped clean, Gillom could hear mockingbirds, wild canaries, and linnets spraying melodies in the thickets of red oaks along Mule Pass Creek as he strode into the heart of Bisbee.

His first stop was up Mule Gulch at the Warren Laundry, where the white ladies let him change out of his dirty duds in back and leave them behind, wearing the clean set they'd just ironed. By asking, he learned these were the widows of foreign miners who'd been killed on the job, and the town traditionally supported them by letting them do their washing.

Gillom walked farther up Mule Creek deeper into the canyon, where he could hear an Arizona canary singing as he approached the O.K. Livery, Feed, and Sales Stable, right next to the O.K. Harness shop, whose sign proclaimed "We'll hitch you up *right now*!" A heehawing burro was one of several being shoveled grain in a feed trough in a corral. He approached the hefty teamster wielding the shovel.

"Howdy, mister. I'm looking for a job on the stage line comes in here."

The rough-looking man with a pockmarked face spit tobacco juice.

"Might use some help muckin' stalls."

"I'd like to be a stage guard, preventing robberies."

The big animal handler laughed. "Kid, we don't hire

guards no more. Our stages only go where the train don't, like over to Tombstone. Our wild Apaches have all been shipped to Florida and stage holdups are a problem mostly of the last century's. It's *1901,* son. Gangs are going after bank express cars these days. Them big Wells Fargo safes on the trains. That's where the smelted gold and money rides now."

Gillom frowned. "I didn't realize."

"Yeah, you look a little young. Try the train depot."

It was the same story at the Arizona and Southeastern office. The railroads had hired most of the experienced stagecoach shotguns to ride as gun guards inside their express cars at a pay bump to twelve dollars a day. They were an easier ride than a bumpy stagecoach, with better, regular meals on the trains, too. Wells Fargo's heavy traveling safes were a more secure way to move serious money and valuables faster and cheaper. Under twenty, Rogers was too wet around the ears for such dangerous work. Sorry.

Gillom was a mite discouraged as he walked back down Main Street to the two-story Angius building. The bank was right next door to the busy Copper Queen Mercantile, the "Merc," the miners' company store.

A small crowd idled on the one bricked street Bisbee had been able to pave so far. They were admiring the town's first automobile, parked not far from an iron hitching rail. It was a white 1901 Locomobile, powered by a small steam engine in a wood-framed compartment under its two-passenger leather seat, with a retractable cloth top folded down behind. Gillom had never seen anything like this vehicle and wondered how it had even gotten all the way to isolated Bisbee.

"Okay, M. J., fire it up." A hawk-faced gentleman in a brown three-piece suit issued the order. The younger driver adjusted his straw boater and swallowed hard. The small steam boiler inside had a pilot light lit by a blow torch, so it was always ready to move as long as steam was built up. There was no ignition key for the Mason two-cylinder gasoline engine. The driver released the foot brake and shoved it into forward gear, holding on to the metal steering tiller in front of him, which turned steering rods attached to the front wheels. With the *chuff-chuff* of a steam engine, the lightweight little car jerked forward as the buzzing crowd stepped back. Twenty-eight-inch spoked white rubber tires spun on the slick bricks, then grabbed traction as the seven-hundred-dollar runabout was off down Main Street at a gallop—twenty miles an hour!

"Cunningham's fleeing with our money!" yelled the bespectacled man in the suit to appreciative laughter. As the automobile disappeared, so did the crowd. Gillom caught up with the gentleman as he climbed the bank's steps.

"Sir, excuse me! Who would I talk to about a job as a bank guard?"

"Me. I'm this bank's president."

"Oh. Gillom Rogers, sir." He extended his hand but the president just looked at it. "Just got into town from El Paso. Looking for security work, which might make use of my gun skills."

The older gentleman pulled a handkerchief to polish his wire-rimmed spectacles.

"We already have a uniformed guard inside. But, well, a couple weeks ago, one of our town butchers, big guy, too, was robbed right up the gulch there, trying to walk down here with a late deposit from his till. I've been thinking, maybe if we did offer private guard service, to our better customers, for a small fee, they would feel safer."

"I can bodyguard anybody."

"You look young. What guard experience have you had?"

Gillom leaned back on his bootheels to make himself taller. "None, sir. Just out of high school. But I make up for that with my gun speed and friendly countenance." He smiled wide.

"Prove it."

They were standing on cement steps underneath the bank's granite columned portico, and Gillom stepped down to let a customer enter. Slowly withdrawing his right-hand Remington .44-.40, he opened its nickel-plated cylinder and pulled one brass cartridge. Resnapping the cylinder into place, he made sure there were two empty chambers now in his six-shooter, one under the hammer and an empty one for the next rotation. He reholstered his weapon. Placing the spare cartridge on the back of his right hand, he stuck it out in front of him. Gillom looked at the bank president, who was watching curiously.

"Don't blink." Yanking his right hand out from under the bullet, Rogers fast drew his pistol, thumb-cocked it, and pulled the hair trigger, dry-firing the big pistol before the bullet hit the ground. *Click*.

The banker licked his lips. "I think we might find use for you, young man. For twenty-five dollars a week."

Gillom bent to pick up his bullet. "Need a little more than that."

"What! You're just *starting*. If you get along well, become known around town, you can probably pick up extra work nights, escorting some of our gamblers and their winnings safely home."

"Later. *Maybe*." The young gunslinger looked the banker directly in the eye. "Some of these miners make twenty-five dollars a day now."

"But that's hard work, digging and blasting ore. You're just going to be babysitting some of our merchants, walking them to and from their stores." The banker was becoming frustrated, suddenly in a negotiation he hadn't expected this morning.

Gillom drew both pistols in an instant, threw in two forward rolls, a pinwheel transfer with each Remington revolving one full turn while crossing in midair, caught them in opposite palms and concluded with double reverse spins back into both holsters. Perfectly.

"All right, all right! *Fifty* dollars a week."

"To start," added the young shootist.

"To start. First thing Monday morning, 8:00 A.M. I'll send customers letters over the weekend. See if extra protection doesn't stir up some new business after that last robbery scare."

They were distracted by the Locomobile chuffing

back down the street and skidding to a squeaking stop on the brick pavement nearby. The banker frowned at the showoff.

"That's my cashier. Have to tell him to put you on the payroll."

The banker started to walk up the steps to enter, but Gillom stuck out his hand again.

"Thank you, Mister . . . ?"

The bank president hesitated, finally stuck out his hand to shake with the teenager.

"Sumner Pinkham. Your new boss."

"Much obliged, Mister Pinkham."

"*Cunningham!* Leave that toy automobile alone and get the hell in here!"

Gillom celebrated with a breakfast of eggs and bacon and a rasher of potatoes at a small café, then started back up to his hillside home, a bounce in his bootsteps, puffing less from this elevated hike. The birds trilling in the bushes along the creek below certainly sounded sweeter this fine afternoon, saluting him.

He discovered two stacks of firewood and a half-filled water barrel beside his kitchen door. While he unpacked his limited possessions, Gillom lit his Franklin stove and heated several buckets of water. He dumped the hot water into his big tin tub he'd placed on the wooden floor, threw in some Gold Dust washing powder he'd found on his shelves, grabbed a bar of Ivory soap and a pig bristle brush, and treated himself to a refreshing scrub.

Dressed in his black wool pinstriped pants, his

black-and-silver-threaded shirt, and brown calfskin vest with the silver conchos, Gillom was back in the Bonanza before 8:00 P.M. Ease was behind the long bar cleaning up from his day shift. The barkeep smiled and poured his new pal a free beer.

"Sleep well, pard?"

"Dandy. Landlady took a shine to my money this morning, so it looks like I'll be there awhile. No bedbugs, either."

"Good! Makes me as daffy as a duck lost in Arizona to have a new friend handy just across the hillside. Just don't pee in her bushes!"

They both laughed. Ease took off his apron and checked out with the senior bartender, before drawing himself a beer and joining his young friend on the other side of the hard wood.

"Welcome to the Golden West, where a few folks have more money than they can spend in the daytime!" They clinked pint mugs.

"Appears that way tonight." They looked around the big saloon, where the gaming tables were filling and tarted-up women were filtering in to flirt with the amateur gamblers and entice them to drink.

"Well, long as your ore holds out and the price of copper stays up, Bisbee'll keep booming," Gillom agreed.

"You betcha! And we'll make our fortunes here along with her. I intend to *own* a saloon better than this someday." The boys clinked glasses again, but were interrupted in their mutual admiration by a slap from the tables that resounded like a firecracker's report. They turned to see a big man in a black suit rising from one of the faro tables to confront the dealer behind the felt layout.

"You've got that squeeze box rigged!"

Threatened, the gray-suited dealer shoved his right hand forward like he was shooting a starched cuff, but the big customer grabbed his wrist and twisted it, pushing a hideout gun from the spring mechanism inside the dealer's suitcoat's wide sleeve. The din died down due to the confrontation and the boys could hear the gambler growl.

"William, open that faro box. Let's see how it's stacked?"

The dealer started to protest, but the beefy gambler leaned and thrust the dealer's over-and-under derringer right up his nostril.

"I want my money *back*!"

The Bonanza's floorman and its burliest bartender were already on the move, the latter holding a wooden cudgel behind his apron tied in back. The dealer's "lookout," the man who sat on his right corner of the faro table and collected and paid off the bets, was also on his feet with his hand on his side gun.

The gambler's buddy opened the faro box, a small metal rectangle inlaid with abalone shell designs, removed the cards, and examined the insides. At the bottom William found a metal plate that, when pressed with a finger, sprung up slightly to allow him to pull out a hidden card, an ace of spades, concealed in a smaller stack beneath the plate.

The gambler yelled, "Lookit *that*! He's pullin' two cards out of the slot! Whichever he needs to win! Bastard's *bracing* the deck!"

The big man with the Roman nose pulled back the derringer and with both meaty hands shoved the green felt faro table hard at the dealer, pushing him suddenly back into his chair and pinning him right up against the saloon's wall.

"I want my money *back*!"

The floorman leaned in, took the angry gambler by the shoulder of his gun hand to restrain him. Right along his other side was the bartender, thrusting his cudgel.

"Okay, Luther, calm down. We'll give you your money back if it's justified."

"*Justified!* His box is gaffed to double-deal! *Look!*"

A crowd had gathered around this faro table, wanting their look, too. Luther's partner demonstrated the spring plate card concealer to the elbowing barflies and floor boss, who stared hard at the sweating dealer pinned against the wall.

"You're through, Simmons. We don't allow gaffed faro boxes in the Bonanza. Be on the next stage out of Bisbee." There was nothing more to say, so the dealer wisely didn't. The gambling manager was making good on everybody's losses while Luther held the rigged faro box high as his trophy. The din returned as bettors loudly demanded to examine the boxes at other faro tables.

"C'mon. I'm not supposed to drink much in here after work, and the owners'll be coming in, they hear about this mess."

"Let's put on the nosebag then. I'm starving!" The boys chugged their beers and were outside the Bonanza in a burp.

"Who was that spotted the fix?" Gillom wanted to know.

"Luther Goose. One of the biggest gamblers around. They say he comes down here to recruit our girls for his parlor house up in Clifton, the other big copper town in Arizona."

"Funny name for a gambler."

"His whorehouse in Clifton's called the Blue Goose."

They chuckled as they strolled farther up the dirt lane comprising Brewery Gulch, Ease explaining it was the next street in town scheduled to be brick-paved. They stopped to watch a fierce dog fight erupt from an alley. No one claimed the territorial mutts so a few miners paused to watch, even started to make bets on the barking, biting combatants.

"How do you know so much about Bisbee, Ease? Were you born here?"

"Nope, grew up in Tucson. My dad was a bartender, part owner of a saloon. Mother was a barmaid there awhile. She's still over in Tucson, lives with her sister after my pop died a few years back. Heart went. Saloon business is a hard one, never stops, but the money's good if you can stand the late hours. I learned from the bottom up, mopping vomit and washing out spittoons. I came over here right after high school. There's more promise here in Bisbee with all its mining money, although Tucson's still the biggest trading town in Arizona Territory."

They pushed their way through the dozens of men sitting along the boardwalks outside the twenty saloons and rooming houses lining the lower end of the gulch. Miners off their day shift clotted in groups smoking, chewing, or passing round a bottle as they watched their brethren make the rounds of the bars this fine Friday night.

Ease steered him into one of the better establishments, Tony Down's Turf Saloon. Gillom was soon digging into steak and potatoes and steamed vegetables washed down with another beer.

"Hell, you got to be a little on the rustle to make your fortune in Bisbee now it's being dug out and built up. I'm just training on the day shift, where I miss the better tips at night, but eventually I'll meet some well-connected gentleman through the Bonanza who can get me a head bartender's or a manager's job somewheres else."

"Same here," agreed Gillom. "Hope to bodyguard enough wealthy businessmen during my day job at the bank, to slide into something more lucrative nights."

"Just don't end up an enforcer, a fast gun for somebody like Luther Goose. He's put the evil eye on the Bonanza now. Rigged faro, gollee."

"Does he really steal girls from your saloons for his own joint?"

"Yeah, but lots of professional gamblers take up with prostitutes and make money off them. Doc Holliday had Big-Nosed Kate following him around the West. Over in Tombstone, the famous Earp brothers were known as the fighting pimps."

"Huh." Gillom leaned back and wiped his mouth with his linen, well satisfied with his supper. The boys ordered dried plums soaked in water overnight, dessert fare in an arid country where fresh fruit was a rarity. "Well, I'm no dirt digger. I aim to keep my hands clean and make my fortune aboveground."

Ease wiped foam off his bare upper lip. "Me, too, pard. *Waitress!* Bill, please! I feel like goin' on a tear tonight!"

Twenty-two

They tumbled from the Turf Saloon into the night.
The upper end of Brewery Gulch was beyond a sharp
bend in the gorge that cut it off from the street of that
name as if it were in a different mountain range altogether. Ease explained this was Bisbee's red light area
of twenty dance halls, cribs, and whorehouses known
as "the reservation," all licensed and taxed by the city
fathers to keep a lid on their licentiousness in one boiling kettle. Consequently, it was the part of town notorious for robbery, assault, and drug use, so they had to
watch their tails. Bisbee's wickedness beckoned these
young men this fair spring night with a wide red smile.

Gillom had strolled El Paso's notorious Utah Street
at night with his pals, so he wasn't shocked when he
passed the rows of cribs on both mountainous sides
of the gulch. These were frame rowhouses about the
size of boxcars, fifty to seventy-five feet wide, parti-
tioned into ten to twelve cubicles, each with an entrance to the street and a bedroom in front and a small

washroom, closet, and stove in the back, with privies and clotheslines out behind. Women posed in the doorways and front windows displaying their charms, soliciting customers with lewd gestures, whistles, and insistent entreaties.

"Hey, I'm Cassie, an awful nice friend to you boys." Or, "Say, sweetheart, what's your hurry?"

They were different shades, brown or white, some overweight or worn, others fresher, lingering in the lamplit openings in skimpy nightgowns or colorful kimonos, rocking on their front porch pulling up silk stockings and stifling yawns.

"Come in and see me, cowboys! Two-for-one special tonight!"

Ease walked Gillom to the bitter end of the gulch to take it all in, the bright lights and the depravity, giving him a good look at bad Bisbee by night, but now he took his new friend by the elbow and turned him around on their evening constitutional.

"These tramps ain't for the likes of us. I'll show you the Red Light dance hall, back near the bend. Nicer, younger girls to talk to, dance with, and you don't have to fuck 'em to have some fun."

Gillom grinned. "Sounds about all right."

As they entered, Gillom saw the Red Light was a little bigger and better decorated than most of the Western dance halls of 1901, for this narrow frame building had a long bar on one side of the dance floor. It also featured a bandstand for music and no nude paintings on its walls of harlots posed in prostrate beauty common to frontier gambling establishments. Some of the Red Light's younger dancers were of foreign, European extraction or, this close to the border, Mexican. Gillom and Ease admired the flashier girls whirling about the wooden floor, trying not to bowl over their lead-footed partners.

"Howdy, Ease," said the plump, mustachioed barkeep. "What'll you boys have?"

"I believe I'll have a Stone Fence, Fred, thank you."

Gillom looked puzzled. "Whatever that is, make it two."

"*That* is a shot of rye in a mug of hard cider with some ice and a dash of lemon. Couple of Stone Fences and you're ready to try buildin' your own," Ease explained. The lads laughed. "Know whose favorite drink that is?"

Gillom shook his head.

"Buffalo Bill Cody's."

Their drinks appeared and Ease paid and they clinked glasses.

"To *love,* wherever her pretty ass may be," toasted Gillom.

"Maybe right in here!" chortled Ease, as up on the bandstand, Swart John bowed his plaintive fiddle, and Ramon and his kid brother their melodious guitar and guitaron, as another chili-flavored stomp commenced.

Gillom turned to admire the ladies spinning past them. "Are these girls whores?"

"Some of them are, sure, but not all," advised Ease. "You've gotta know which ones do the deed. There's small rooms with beds in back up there. Three dollars a poke, plus tip. Ten dollars for the whole night, after hours. You hafta buy 'em a drink before each dance, see, but it's only cold tea, so they don't get too drunk to maneuver." Ease pointed toward a wall sign. DANCES AVAILABLE! ONE BUCK A SPASM!

"A dollar gets her tea and a dance with her. Whiskey, beer, or mixed drinks extra."

His younger friend looked perplexed. "I thought all hurdy-gurdy girls were prostitutes?"

"In the cheaper joints, yes. There's those in Bisbee. But some of these dance hall queens are so popular they don't hafta make their money watchin' the ceiling. And they're insulted if you ask 'em to go upstairs, so be careful you don't get slapped."

There was a disruption as one of the drunken miners tripped over his heavy boots and took his partner down to the floor with him. The fast music played right on, and except for a ripped stocking, the girl appeared to be okay as she stalked off from her clumsy partner while he rolled to his feet grinning loopily.

Then Gillom saw her, a heart-quickening eyeful in a dress of white satin as she whirled by with a better-dressed, older gentleman. Her lighter brown skin was clear and her coloring shone around the lipstick she had smeared across her warm prettiness. Many of these bar belles favored too much makeup, rouge and eye shadow, but the ones with the most face powder to cover their wrinkles were more likely to be "painted" ladies of the evening as well as dancing partners. This girl looked lighter-skinned than most Mexicans, so there had to have been a white European in her family's generational woodpile somewhere. Her long, black hair spun out as she swung from her partner on small, light feet. He was a skilled dancer and got her spinning faster so the bell shape of her knee-length skirt spun out, giving the attending men a good view of her ankles and calves and, more excitingly, her ruffled white bloomers.

"What about her? The beauty in the white dress?"

"Don't know 'er. New girls are always popular. You'll have to get in line to meet her." Ease pointed to another sign on the wall—NO DRINKS, NO DANCES.

So Gillom imbibed his liquor and inhaled the powerful odor of tobacco, stale drinks, cheap perfume, sweat, and stained clothing that a Western dance hall mixed in strong doses, while the patrons thrashed about the dance floor under the allure of yellowish lamplight. And it was often more thrashing than ballroom dancing with these clumsy miners, so some of the gals wore work boots just to keep their toes from getting mashed. When the five-minute song ended, he watched the enchanting girl return to her bench along the wall and her partner to refresh himself at the bar. Whistling and applause came from some of the watchers for this dancing gal's lingerie display, which would increase her tips this busy night in the Red Light. Gillom walked over to join her.

"May I have your next dance, ma'am?"

The *señorita* smiled, but pointed a slim finger at the sign nearby.

"Oh yes. What are you drinking, ma'am?"

She smiled coquettishly. "Sweet tea."

Gillom now knew the gambit, and at least she was honest, not calling it liquor. He hurried to the end of the long counter, got a bartender's attention, and pointed back at who he was buying a phony drink for. There was a five-minute interlude between dances so business could be transacted. But now the music was starting up again and her missing partner was pulling her out onto the dance floor once more. Gillom shook his head, frustrated. *This is gonna be difficult*, he figured. *She's so damned popular*.

But he bought the glass of tea the bartender poured from a pitcher under the bar and watched as the man chalked a quick mark next to a name he couldn't read on a small blackboard he hadn't noticed behind the glassware. It was the Red Light's scoreboard for which girls had had how many drinks when it came time to split the proceeds at night's end, fifty-fifty. For an energetic evening of sweet tea and tips, a few of the prettier girls could make as much as fifty dollars, good money just for dancing their feet afire.

Gillom took his tea and mug of hard cider back to her empty seat, getting a high sign from Ease as he passed, and proffered it to the young lady as she waltzed off the dance floor again, out of breath. Her partner gave Gillom a cold stare as the beauty accepted his drink. The middle-aged gent started to protest, but the dancing queen cut him off by pointing at the no drinks sign once more. He knew the house rules. In a huff, the gentleman in the blue suit stomped off for more refreshments, as Gillom moved in.

"What's your name?"

"Anel."

"What?"

"Ana Leticia. *Mi papá* put them together. So, Anel."

"What's it mean? In Spanish?"

"Nothing. Is made up."

"Ah. Pretty name, though, like you. I'm Gillom Rogers. From El Paso."

"Ah. *Tejano*." She presented him a bent wrist. He didn't know whether to kiss it or bow? So he tried to shake it instead. Then, a pause amidst the din, both of them looking away, then back at each other, sipping their drinks. The music commenced and they could put down their glasses, step out on the dance floor. This one was slower, a waltz almost, so they could converse as they danced.

"Where are you from?"

"Zacatecas. Where I was birthed. Then Minas Prietas, La Cananea, to Bis-bee. Mining towns. *Mi papá*, hees a miner."

"Ah, *sí*. So your family is here?"

"No. *Mi familia* ees in Mexico. La Cananea. Work the mines."

Gillom swung her around under his outstretched arm, even if it wasn't the proper move for this dance. Anel giggled but seemed to enjoy him. At least he wasn't tripping over his own feet, but following her lead. The whiskey, hard cider, and beer were rising from his gut to his head when he waltzed her off the dance floor as the music ended and back to her bench.

"Thank you, Mis-ter Vaquero." She curtsied, having fun with him. They took up their glasses, thirsty from the exertion.

"No, no cowboy. I'm the new bank guard. Starting Monday."

"Guard?"

"Bodyguard. Bank of Bisbee. For the customers. So they don't get robbed."

"Ah, *sí*." And then he was back, her first dance partner, bearing a fresh tea and a shit-eating grin. That was enough for this impatient teenager, this constant changing of partners.

"Okay. See you around."

The cute Latina gave him a little wave as he walked away, then turned back to her work. He found another spot at the bar and ordered a last beer, watched Ease reel by in the arms of a muscular Amazon tossing about a mass of flaming red hair to match his own. His buddy was beaming as he thanked his Lorelei after this dance ended and panted back to his *companero*.

"Who's the big gal?" inquired Gillom.

"Red Jean. Tougher than a mesquite root, pard. Jean could grind my stem to pulp if she wanted to. I'd never cross her, but she's fun to dance with. How'd you do?"

"Anel's pretty, but she's getting play from the sports in here."

"Yeah, it's Friday, crowded." They watched Gillom's beauty dance by again with her older gentleman. "Older bucks just won't leave the new does alone."

The young bucks rued their luck. But Mr. Bixler was still full of fire.

"C'mon! Finish your drink and let's go find some more fun!"

The lads stepped outside to clear their lungs of the smoky, stale smell of the dance hall.

"This place must rake in money."

"You bet. Dancing miners just pour down the booze,

and there's not as much overhead as with a gambling saloon or a parlor house. The noise is such a nuisance the neighbors complain, so the Red Light has to pay a higher tax to the city council for more deputies to patrol this action," Ease explained. "You can't open up a dance hall just anywhere. Come back on a quieter week night, Gillom. If that's gal's workin', she'll have more time for you then. These girls make most of their money on weekends."

"Figures."

"Let's go have a toddy downtown. Joe Muheim's is where Bisbee's important men like to drink. No dancing girls there, though."

"Lead the way, pard."

And Mr. Bixler did, off the lighted porch. They were crossing a dirt alley between buildings when a voice hissed out of the darkness.

"Reach for Heaven, if you value your lives."

The threat wasn't shouted but it got their attention, halted their stroll. A pistol poked from the black night, beckoned them back into the inkwell. The boys did as instructed, slowly.

"Hurry up. Hands against the wall. Your wallets, boys." The pistol's owner wore a dark suit and a heavy black mustache. All they really noticed, though, were mean eyes glaring from beneath a slouch hat.

Ease wasn't armed, coming off his work shift, but he was in front and so was shoved against the wall first. Pulling up the tails of Ease's wool coat, the footpad spied the bulge in Bixler's back pocket and groped for it. Whether he didn't notice Gillom, still facing him, was packing iron covered by his coat, or the thrill of finding his first victim's money distracted him, but the moonlight bandit forgot to keep an eye on his second prey as he ripped Ease's wallet from his pants.

Gillom's hands brushed back his coat and dropped to his revolvers and yanked both from his holster and thumb-cocked them so fast the robber couldn't react as the Remingtons roared! One bullet to the upper chest! Another to the stomach, paralyzing the bandit as he was blasted backward from the concussions.

"*Aieee! Aieee!*" The footpad screamed in pain as he thrashed about in the alley, which quickly attracted a crowd of gawkers, heads poking around corners, men running into the alley from the street.

"*Jesus!* Gillom!"

"Let him die! He deserves to!"

The thief rolled onto his stomach so they couldn't see him bleeding, but they could smell him, the strange odors of bloody flesh, singed wool, and soiled trousers.

Ease Bixler was still worked up. "Bastard tried to rob us! He yanked my wallet!"

Someone brought a kerosene lamp to illuminate the downed man, and there was the bartender's horsehide wallet lying nearby. Ease picked up his money as a bystander rolled the moaning robber faceup. He was still breathing, but had two bloody holes in his midtorso.

"Somebody raise the sheriff!"

Another gawker trotted off to do so, and spread the hot news. Nobody called for a doctor.

"Jesus, Gillom, you're quick!" yelled the intended victim. "The guy had his gun on me, but you whipped out your pistols and were firing before this jasper even moved."

Gillom reholstered and now buttoned his coat over his matched revolvers on his hips, not wishing to draw more attention to them.

"He was grabbin' *your* money, Ease. He forgot about me."

"A fast draw artist," somebody opined. Another bystander patted Gillom on the back.

"Mebbe so. But you're greased lightnin' with those six-shooters. Thank *you*, pal!"

The sheriff wasn't so complimentary. Gillom was taken before Scott White in his downtown office next to the jail soon after the shooting. The bandit had expired before anything could be done for him and was already being undertaken. White had just returned from viewing the corpse and making burial arrangements. The sheriff, a well-dressed, slightly overweight man, seemed more businessman than a tough law enforcer to Gillom. Certainly not the toughest hombre in what seemed to be a lively nest of thieves.

Sheriff White chewed a toothpick as Gillom finished retelling his side of the deadly encounter. "Uh-huh. We've had several street robberies these past couple months. Even got a bulletin here from Tombstone for one Rollie 'Hard Luck' Harrison, a known footpad. Description matches, but we'll send a death photograph over to our sister city."

Ease grinned. "Hard luck indeed."

"If Harrison's identified in Tombstone, you've got $250 coming, kid," announced the sheriff.

Gillom lit up like Christmas.

"What'd you say your name was, El Paso?"

"Gillom Rogers."

"Uh-huh. I don't take kindly to shoot-outs in our streets. Even 'exhibiting a pistol in a threatening manner at another person' wins you a week in my jail. This is a mining community, well financed and sophisticated in its tastes. I'm a Democrat in Democratic Cochise County and usta gettin' reelected. This isn't one of those bang-bang cowtowns on the Great Plains, where the marshal occasionally gets swept out of office along with the corrupt city council. We do things *business*-like in Bisbee, savvy? So, soon as you get your reward money, *if* you do, you'll be drifting elsewhere, Rogers, correct?"

The teenager shook his head. "No, sir. Just got a job this morning. Starting Monday I'm the new guard at the Bank of Bisbee. Mister Pinkham wants me protecting their better customers."

This was displeasing news to the sheriff.

"Uh-*huh*. Just full of yourself and God's own grace, ain'tcha? And this dustup will only polish your reputation around town, won't it? All our swells will be wanting to meet you, maybe test your weapon skills. I could skin you of those fancy pistols right here."

"Then I'd lose my new job."

The pudgy lawman rose and leaned across his desk.

"Kid, Governor Murphy's forming a new detail of Arizona Rangers here right now, but you're too young to join 'em. And I've got deputies bigger and better with guns than you to handle any rough work here in Bisbee. So don't go making any armed bank withdrawals yourself. Or testing your gun skills against some of our rougher customers. It's a new century, sonny. The Wild West has been *tamed*."

Gillom didn't like being bullyragged. "What if one of your bank's depositors was being robbed?"

"Any more shootings in my town, Rogers, I'm confiscating those fancy pistols and throwing your tail in jail, regardless of your good reasons."

"On *what* charge? Doing my job? Defending myself?"

Sheriff White flashed an insincere smile. "Disturbing *my* peace."

Twenty-three

Mr. Pinkham awaited Gillom's arrival at the bank first thing Monday morning.

"Heard about your shoot-out Friday night. You may have gotten the bastard who robbed our butcher two weeks ago. Congratulations."

"Thank you, sir. Just tryin' to do my civic duty in my new town."

"Except now all our other customers want to meet you. I sent out that mailer advertising your services. They heard about your killing, and now every old lady in Bisbee wants you to walk her down here to deposit her egg money."

Gillom smiled. "Well, things will settle down, once they get used to me bein' around. That's what you wanted, Mister Pinkham, your customers to feel safer. Maybe you can start charging for my services."

"We'll see." The bank president smiled accidentally and Gillom sensed his boss was actually pleased by all the attention his new employee had brought to his banking business. "Go talk to Cunningham. He's drawn up a list of the customers you're scheduled to protect today."

And that's how it went all day, walking the butcher, the baker, and local candlestick maker from their stores to the bank to deposit their day's receipts, or accompanying them back to their small shops with fresh cash for their registers. The older ladies Gillom tried to discourage, after walking them up one damned mountainside or down another, telling them this new service was really for the merchants. Many just wanted to meet the young man who bested that bandit, and he could stall them with an autograph and a tip of his Stetson. But several middle-aged widows and spinsters were more persistent about his company, effusive in their praise, and invited him to dinner to celebrate his success. Gillom wasn't much interested in older women, so he fended them off with excuses of pressing business or in one pushy lady's case, a flat "no thank you, ma'am."

He was leg weary when he hit the long bar in the Bonanza after work on a Wednesday. Ease lit up when he saw his pal shuffle in.

"Hey, *Gillom*! You look like the walkin' deceased. You gettin' used to our sulfurous air? Folks say this furnace smoke protects 'em from diseases, like the smallpox, but I don't know. They built us a pest house on the outskirts of Bisbee, just in case. Price of prosperity."

Rogers shook his head. "Up and down these mountainsides escorting ladies to the bank is wearing me out. I'll either turn into a mountain goat or have to have my boots resoled."

Ease Bixler chortled as he opened the beer spigot on a draft for his pal. "Widows are givin' you a run for their used money, eh?"

"They want to meet the man who shot that awful bandit, and then they're surprised I'm so young. I should be meeting their daughters, not them."

"*Me,* too!" interjected his young friend.

Ease dried his hands on a bar towel, rolled down his white shirtsleeves, and stashed the black silk garters of his uniform.

"Well, the boys are still talkin' about your shoot-out. Let's pray none of his criminal pals come lookin' to avenge their dead pard."

"Don't think so," said Gillom, shaking his head again. "Sheriff White said footpads are usually lone operators, maybe just one partner. They aren't like train robbers, which takes gangs of fellers."

Ease slapped his pal on the back as he emerged from behind the bar.

"Hope not. Or I'll have to start goin' armed, too, just to go out to supper with you."

They made do with stringy beef sandwiches and the free countertop fare at Cavetto's Saloon, first door north of the city jail. With Ease as his chaperone, he was being introduced to all levels of society, high and low, in this bustling burg. Gillom noticed men were murmuring, pointing him out to their friends. He enjoyed the sudden attention, the false camaraderie of men who liked hanging around somebody a little dangerous.

They were feeling their hops when they hit the Red Light around the upper bend of Brewery Gulch. It was a midweek night, slower, so the proprietor didn't hire a band. Live music came from a hurdy-gurdy man, who played a hand organ with strings, twenty-three keys in two rows similar to a piano keyboard with wooden wheels inside the machine. Any tunes that came out of the contraption sounded like a bagpipe, only with a better melody and faster rhythm.

Wednesday night didn't provide a full complement of hurdy girls, but Gillom spotted Anel talking to another girl on the dancers' bench. The boys ordered more beers as Ease elbowed his partner.

"That's her, ain't it?"

Gillom nodded.

"Gotta be a dancin' queen to make her money. Wednesday night's about the slowest it ever gets in here, so take her a cold tea, pard, and warm her up!"

Ease laughed and Gillom did just that.

"Anel, you're looking pretty tonight."

She couldn't blush under her face powder, so she batted her eyelashes. "Thank you. Dance?"

Gillom handed her a glass of tea, the price of a spin round the floor.

"I'd rather get to know you. Where do you live in town?"

"I live with Rosa." She pointed to a plump, older Mexican gal in a red skirt and mass of petticoats, sashaying around the dance floor on a cowboy's arm to a sprightly tune from the hurdy-gurdy man. "She works in the Brewery, most nights."

"Whereabouts you two live?"

She pointed upward. "Top of the mountain."

"Uh-huh. I'm up the far side of Tombstone Canyon. Near my friend, Ease, over there. He's a bartender in the Bonanza. I'm the new bank guard, remember?"

"*Sí.* Where I esave *mi* monies."

"Yes. Come in and say hello sometime."

"Hokay. *Ahorita.*" (Soon.)

He didn't know what else to ask her. But the man in the blue beret and striped shirt onstage cranked his instrument again to drum up business. It was a popular song, "Pop Goes the Weasel," so Gillom extended his arm and off they went. He twirled her right up to the less crowded bar when it was over. Several customers saluted their dancing prowess with upraised drinks.

"Ease, this is my new friend, Anel. What's your last name, darlin'?"

"Romero."

"Romero. From Zacatecas."

"Famous silver mines down there," agreed young Bixler. They continued chatting up the lovely, buying her and themselves drinks, and didn't notice new arrivals to the Red Light. Only when these new men elbowed in beside them did the lads pay them any heed.

"Two whiskeys, bartender, and a drink for the lady here."

Gillom was still bending Anel's ear. "Maybe you an' me an' Ease here, and one of these other gals, could go out on a picnic sometime? Nice May weather, Sunday afternoon, we'd rent a surrey."

The heavyset man in a black suit and black Stetson leaned in to their conversation, passing the drink glass to the dancer. "Dance, pretty lady?"

"What do you think, Anel? About a picnic?"

"Maybe." She took her new customer's arm as he led her onto the dance floor while the hurdy-gurdy man began strumming a more sedate tune, a waltz. The big man was surprisingly light on his feet dancing in his soft leather, pointy "toothpick" boots.

Gillom leaned close to his buddy, frustrated. "Damned hard to talk to her. Somebody always cuts in."

"You've got to meet her outside, pard, on her day off."

"What about a picnic?"

"Sounds fun to me. I'll rustle up a dancing queen, you set the date."

They watched as the dance ended, but the couple remained on the floor, her partner conversing animatedly with wide hand gestures. Ease was startled.

"My God. That's Luther Goose."

"Who?"

"Remember last weekend, in the Bonanza, the guy who braced our faro dealer for cheating?"

Gillom nodded.

"Luther's a heavy gambler, so the casino owners don't bother him. But he tries to recruit our saloon girls to take up to Clifton, to work in his own brothel there. Bar owners and madams don't like him comin' down here, hustlin' our women."

"*Me*, either."

"Well, you can argue her out of dancin', but be careful of him." Ease was now aware of a shorter man right at his other elbow wearing a derby, listening to them.

Luther Goose walked Anel over to the dancer's back bench instead, where he continued his earnest appeal.

Gillom counterattacked. "Bartender! Another tea for the lady." He was irritated at his picnic offer being thwarted by an older man. When the short glass was filled, he grabbed it and walked it over to his intended, ignoring Ease's warning.

Gillom presented the beauty her fresh drink. "Miss Romero. I believe this next dance is ours."

Luther Goose peevishly pulled his large nose. "Young lady's talkin' to me."

"Doubt you'll have anything to say she wants to hear."

"You wet-earred pup! Get the hell out of here before I put my boot to you!"

Swart John on stage had started cranking his hand organ, but stopped at this altercation.

The man in the cheap suit at Ease's elbow was suddenly at Luther Goose's side. Gillom was focused on the large diamond mounted on a stickpin in the pimp's flowing tie. This was his "headlight," a top gambler's very expensive affectation, if it wasn't pinchback jewelry, made of paste. Gillom's hands came to rest on the butts of his Remingtons.

"Save the bullshit for your garden, mister."

From a corner of his mouth, the gambler talked to his side man. "Can't believe this whoreson's brass. You have any notion who I am, kid?"

Gillom smiled, a little cocky. "Yeah. I'd say some deck is shy a joker and you're it."

Suddenly florid of face, Mr. Goose took a step toward his young antagonist, his big hands coming up outstretched for a throttle.

Gillom's quick hands pulled both revolvers and stretched them forward. Two clicks in the silence announced he'd earred their hammers back.

Ease stepped in to suppress any bloodshed.

"Hey, *hey*! Gillom, he's *unarmed*. Give my friend a little room here, Mister Goose."

"He's vexing me."

"Well, all's fair in love and war, especially in disagreements over women. So I'll jus' escort this young lady back to her seat, while you gents cool off." The young barkeep took Anel by the elbow. She shook her raven hair in admonishment.

"Crazy gringos. Always hurry." But she allowed Ease to walk her away from the argument. The dance hall's bouncer showed up to intervene.

"Why don't you gentlemen both take a smile, on the house. Opposite ends of the bar, though, please."

Luther Goose's brown eyes were as hard as rocks. "See you again, buckshot. *Around*." Gillom now noticed a dark mole over Luther's right eyebrow, to go along with his big ears and long nose. Nothing was very attractive about this big hustler, besides his penchant for flashing his fancy jewelry.

"Counting on it," agreed young Rogers, reholstering.

Goose's companion, the smaller man with the longer arms, looked Gillom Rogers up and down, estimating his weight and fitness, saying nary a word.

Twenty-four

Gillom slept fitfully that night. After a first hour of turning on his feather mattress, the darkness was rent by gunfire, shots echoing up Tombstone Canyon, cowboy yips in the night and clattering hooves from up near the livery stable. A stray bullet busted one of his neighbor's glass windows and he quickly rolled out to hit the floor. Gillom groped for his holstered pistols and pants on the floorboards.

Peering warily through his one front window, Rogers could see coal oil lamps being blown out in shacks in Chihuahua Town atop the denuded hillside across the canyon, so they wouldn't become targets of these wild cowboys on a midweek toot. His landlady, Mrs. Blair, had forewarned him this was a regular midnight interruption; that the sideboards of these miners' shacks were so thin that gunwise residents hit the floor when sport-shooting forays erupted. But he couldn't spot any shooters in the dark below, so Gillom crawled back into his built-in bed with his jeans and pistols still on, ready for trouble. With a nervous shiver, nature's sweet restorer finally overtook him and he slept well past dawn.

Walking to work, Gillom watched a water train climbing uphill, the short-legged, stout little burros each rigged with an iron frame and a ridge pole from which hung a heavy canvas sack on either side, twitched along by Mexican muleteers. Each sack held seven gallons of water from the wells up Brewery Gulch and sold for twenty-five cents, to be poured into the barrel outside the back door of every dwelling.

He paused to watch the Mexican women gathered at the narrow, polluted river in the canyon to beat their clothes clean by hand on the wet rocks. The women gossiped with their friends while smoking hand-rolled cigarillos. Naked babies splashed happily in the gurgling waters at the ladies' bare feet. It was a soothing scene after a restless weekend, and the young man drank it in for a long moment before trudging on to his bank. *Today is gonna be a warm one,* he realized. *Luckily it rarely hits a hundred at this high elevation, Ease said.*

Lucky his boss, Mr. Pinkham, hadn't heard about his run-in with the big gambler in the dance hall, so it was an untroubled day. Near closing time, before 3:00 P.M., Anel Romero dropped in.

"*Anel!* Nice to see you."

She was wearing a shawl over her head, although it was too warm for that this late spring day, trying not to attract attention in her flashy dress, but she recognized him.

"Oh, *sí,* Mister bank guard."

"It's Gillom. Gillom Rogers."

"*Sí,* Gillom. Putting *mi* monies safe, from last weekend."

"Good. Are you on your way to work? Tonight?"

"*Sí.*" The Mexican miss looked about, unwilling to discuss her place of employment in public.

He smiled. "I'll walk you there."

"No *necessario.*"

"Bank's just closing. I'll get permission."

While Miss Romero made her deposit, Gillom wheedled an okay to escort one of its good customers to work.

"Which good customer?" M. J. Cunningham looked up from his ledger and scanned the bank's floor. "Oh. One of those dance hall girls."

"Hey, they make good money entertaining. Miss Romero's dollars spend just as well as anybody else's."

The young banker hesitated. "Don't make a habit of escorting young dollies all over town. You were hired to attend our *better* customers."

"Yes, sir. But certainly none prettier."

Next they were strolling Main Street where workers were bricking to pave the entrance to the dirt acreage that was to become the Copper Queen Hotel, still in blueprints. With seventy-five rooms, it was intended to become the territory's biggest and most luxurious.

A knot of miners standing about the empty lot smoking and passing a bottle watched the young couple pass. They knew she wasn't one of the town's respectable ladies, not someone dressed that sexy in daylight. Gillom ignored the wolf whistles she was causing.

"Starting to warm up. I heard Bisbee gets more rain in the summers due to its higher elevation. An oasis above these dry valleys around here."

"Summer rains heavy, yes. Floods."

"*Si. Muy malo.*" He essayed a little Spanish to impress her.

She smiled. "*Por supuesto.*" (For sure.)

They were climbing the steps to a two-story brick building with a façade of plastered arches. It was at the south end of Brewery Gulch, where its posters and hanging signs could be seen by everybody. The Orpheum was Bisbee's opera house, erected in 1897 and containing one of the biggest dance floors. Its main attractions were the traveling shows which arrived several times a month for four-day runs, sometimes held over depending upon ticket sales. Frush's Oriental Circus from San Francisco had just been there, and the couple paused to admire its colorful posters plastered on billboards outside. Shakespeare's plays, minstrel shows, wrestling, and boxing matches had all played to good crowds at the Orpheum.

"Anel, look. Another show coming. Wanna go?"

"I work."

"Aww, you can get a weeknight off. Opens Thursday. I'll buy tickets. The Raymond Teal Musical Revue from Chicago. Sounds like fun."

"Thursday. Hokay, I try."

"Bueno."

They were soon at the Red Light's front door.

"Thank you, Mister Gillom."

Gillom's excitement over their first date was contagious. "Drop by the bank tomorrow, Anel. Tell me you've got the night off, so I can buy those tickets. And tell me where you live, so I can pick you up Thursday evening. For dinner first."

"Hokay, mister. Bank, tomorrow."

"Swell!"

His reward was a kiss on his smiling cheek.

When he returned to his miner's cottage that night, Gillom got his rags and wire brush and gun oil out and cleaned his Remingtons. Reholstering but not reloading, the young gunslinger retrieved poker chips from his warbag and placed one of them upon the back of his right hand, which he held out waist-high. His holster was still on, hung low on his waist with the leather tie-downs tight around his thighs. He let the chip drop. Before it hit the floor, Gillom had his revolver in his right hand, its sightless, nickel-plated barrel thrust forward, as he cocked and dry-fired the single-action .44 twice. *Click-click.*

Hell. Harvey Logan of Butch Cassidy's Wild Bunch could supposedly cock and fire three times before his poker chip dropped. "Hafta practice," he grunted.

And so Gillom Rogers did, right hand, left hand, both together under poker chips, cross-draws, midair exchanges, forward spins, backward, over-the-shoulder tosses, thumb-cocking and dry-firing at the end of each trick. *Click-click-click.* By the glowing lamp-light, as the night slowed to a lonely crawl, he practiced his gunplay. *Click-click.* Until his arms were too tired to pull iron anymore. *Click.*

Anel dropped by the Bank of Bisbee next day to tell him she'd gotten Thursday night off. She would meet him at the theater instead, so he wouldn't have to pick her up. *Maybe she doesn't want me to see where she lives?* he thought.

Gillom also dropped by Sheriff White's office to pick up his reward. "Hard Luck" Harrison's photograph had been identified in Tombstone, so a money order worth $250 was all his now, although the sheriff wasn't in to congratulate him on his killing.

Twenty-five

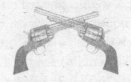

Gillom was outside the Orpheum at quarter to eight the following night. He'd stopped by Bisbee's only flower and seed shop to pick up a rose. Milling in the crowd entering the theater, he kept the flower cupped behind his back, not wanting to look like some smitten country bumpkin. Gillom hadn't attended a variety show before; his widowed mother never had the money to spend on such frivolities in El Paso.

Someone plucked the flower from his fingers. He turned to find it was her! Anel wore a more subdued dress with a higher neckline, not emphasizing her bosom. It was pale green, the color of her eyes under the boardwalk's yellowish lamplight.

"Anel."

"Thank you, Mister Gillom. Left your *pistolas* home. Good."

"Yes. I'm off-duty."

She let him pin the rose on her chest, fumbling so

as to not prick her. She pirouetted around flirtatiously. "My dress. Flower matches."

"We like our roses yellow in Texas."

Gillom took Anel by the elbow and escorted her up the stairs and inside the second story. The Orpheum was shaped like a wedge, squared off to an entrance with the ticket booth inside. Across the small lobby from the ticket booth, a young ticket taker directed customers up the stairs to the third story if they'd bought seats in the small back balcony. Atop that stairwell awaited "wine girls" to usher the biggest-spending patrons into curtained boxes along both sides of the three-story concert hall.

The young bank guard towed his date across the second story's main floor and found a couple of wooden chairs off to one side, nearer the stage. Gillom beckoned a wine girl brushing past to bring them two glasses of white wine.

In the small orchestra area to one side of the raised stage, the musicians struck up Von Suppé's *Poet and Peasant* Overture, and the hubbub began to die down as the patrons found seats. Anel's eyes widened as the heavy curtain was drawn aside to reveal all thirty performers perched around the stage on papier-mâché rocks, standing under fake trees or seated on camp stools. Even some of the Orpheum's wine girls were onstage, dressed alike in white dresses with red stockings and a red sash across a shoulder, spinning red parasols. A blond ingénue in curls under her bonnet and a yellow dress of ruffles and petticoats strolled from the wings singing "Mother Has a Sweetheart, Daddy Is His Name."

She waltzed off to loud applause and a few whistles from the mostly male crowd. The young thrush was followed by Frank Bryan from under his tree, a comedian known for his self-composed parodies.

A song that always gets my goat . . .
Though some folks think it's fine
To get stewed and bust your throat
While singing "Auld Lang Syne."
They wore tight pants and homemade shirts
And went to bed at nine.
And I'm damned glad I never was born
In the days of "Auld Lang Syne."

Gillom Rogers paused, laughing with the crowd, to explain to Anel what this ditty referred to, but his young lady was distracted by a banjo player walking onstage picking a lively tune. It was Raymond Teal, the proprietor of this musical revue. This strolling musician led the orchestra and wine room girls into a hoedown dance with younger males from the regular cast. The flying petticoats, whoops from the young men, and squeals from the girls as they crossed hand-in-hand to twirl on their partners' arms and circle and cross again in tricky combinations absolutely captivated Anel. Eyes shining, she rose from her seat to applaud the dance troop when they finally sashayed off. Gillom joined her on his feet to shout approval and get a hug from his girl.

Their rousing praise caught the attention of two men just settling into a large upper box across the hall. Luther Goose was dressed again like a prairie knight

in a black suit and a bib-front cream shirt with pearl
buttons. The big man ostentatiously shot his French
cuffs. It was the shorter man in the nondescript gray
wool suit and gray derby who pointed out the young
gunsmith below to his boss.

"That him?"

Mr. Goose peered into the yellowish gloom cast by
the coal oil footlamps on stage.

"That *is* the kid who gave me the hard time in the
Red Light."

"Out with the girl you fancied," added his companion.

The brothel owner squinted. "Is he armed?"

"Don't see any pistols. Could have a hideout."

"Perhaps you should say hello, William. For me."

"Yes, sir." William got up from his front chair just
as a wine girl arrived with their drinks. The blond
pixie handed William a beer, poured champagne from
an iced bottle for Mr. Goose. Luther had eyes on the
distant bank guard. He swallowed a gulp, but immediately spit it on the floor.

"This is swill! Awful pear cider! Tell the bartender
I want *real* French champagne up here. Immediately!"

"Yes, sir." The chastened waitress followed Luther's
bodyguard out of the balcony box.

Gillom waved to one of the wine girls coming off
the stage for another round. His ladyfriend was riv-
eted, watching a feisty brunette march about the stage
to a snare drum's beat, carrying a rifle. From backstage
a stagehand pulled a barely visible black string to rip
off her costume to reveal a washerwoman's shirt and
blouse. The music changed, her rifle was tossed, a

broom caught, and she began performing an Irish jig. Another pull on a strip string and presto!—the pretty gal was in a short skirt and skipping a rope tossed her by the stagehand. Gillom's and Anel's mouths were open, having never seen anything like this transformation dance. Yet another rip of her costume and the miss was a policeman in shorts and buttoned-up tunic, singing a patriotic song. She marched off to whistling, foot-stomping applause.

"Anel! Here's two dollars for our drinks. I'm going to the washroom."

She nodded and smiled as Gillom pushed his way through the miners, cattlemen, and gamblers milling about the center aisle to the back of the dance hall. This variety show was continuous throughout the evening, repeated once entirely, so patrons wandered in and out through these lengthy shows.

The men's room was in a back corner, off to one side of the raised main stage near the backstage dressing rooms so the performers could use the two large lavatories as well. Ease had mentioned one of the Orpheum's attractions was its tiled washrooms, for even by the turn of the century, Bisbee still didn't have much indoor plumbing in its restaurants and businesses, let alone its hillside homes. Some patrons were known to purchase an occasional ticket to a variety show just to enjoy its fancy indoor restrooms.

Gillom strolled inside to unbutton his best black wool pants to use the long urinal along one wall. Another gent was washing his hands at one of the porcelain stands across from it, but quickly left.

The restroom door opened again and William

walked in. The shorter man noted the teenager buttoning up, and that he was not wearing any revolvers as he smoothed his sparse lip hair in the framed mirror above a washstand.

"Mister Goose sends his greetings."

Gillom froze. He knew that name.

What *was* unusual about William were his extraordinarily long arms for an average-sized man, sort of like an ape's. He grabbed Gillom by the belt and yanked the kid toward him, at the same time thumping him in the upper chest with the bottom of his outstretched palm. The blow knocked a surprised Gillom back on his bootheels while raising his center of gravity. The fighter released his prey suddenly with that shove, knocking Gillom to the hard wood floor with a *woof*!

Before the seventeen-year-old could recover his breath, William reached down to grab the top of his trousers, yanking him up with a crotch grab, while with his right hand the bodyguard flipped Gillom over so that his back was to him. The teenager struggled, but this grappling was happening so fast, and with his wind gone, he wasn't resisting very well.

"Hey! Let me . . . loose! Unhand me!"

William had him upside down, arms forward, unable to reach around behind to try to grab his opponent's legs, as the grappler began to walk him forward. Gillom was game and fit, and he suddenly jerked upward while trying to bend backward from the waist to claw the attacker's face with his hands. Countering, William lifted the young man up with his arms clasped tight around his waist and rammed him toward the floor in a piledriver. Gillom's hat had fallen off in the scrabble, so the top of his head hit the tiled floor with a notable thump.

Still Gillom resisted, trying to swing round and grab one of his attacker's legs. He failed and got another head-banging. Legs wide like a sheepshearer's, William walked the upside-down teenager over to the three flush toilets in the theater's men's room. Each sat in a wooden-sided stall with common walls but no doors. Near the ceiling above each porcelain bowl was an oblong porcelain compartment which stored the water. A pipe of sizeable circumference ran down the wall from the water compartment into the rear of each toilet bowl. Under the overhead compartment hung a pull chain with a white porcelain handle. Dazed by several hard bangs to his brain, Gillom groaned as he was clutched lower around his crotch, wrenched upward again, and then rammed down, his shoulders bumping into the wooden toilet seat, his head thrust through the seat's hole into the water.

Another bathroom visitor started to walk in, took one look at the two men poised over a toilet, one with his head in the bowl and groaning, and quickly backed out.

William flushed the toilet. The cascade of water racing through the pipe and out below into a distant septic tank hissed and echoed through the tiled lavatory. Gillom reared up, both hands bracing the toilet seat, sputtering, before his captor heaved him up and dropped him down again into the toilet seat before letting him loose. Essaying a back flip, Gillom tumbled over onto his knees in front of the toilet bowl where he shook like a wet dog.

The grappler bent to be sure the bedraggled young man heard.

"Remove yerself from Mister Goose's *bisness,* kid. Or yer'll fare *worse.*"

Dizzy and confused after his attacker left, Gillom staggered to his feet to grab hold of a washbasin and check himself in the wall mirror behind it. He could feel several large bumps forming atop his head. Red skin at the base of his neck and around his collarbone meant he'd have bruises where he got banged into the toilet seat.

Gillom retrieved his felt Stetson from the stall and placed it gingerly atop his wet hair, which he slicked back with a hand.

Anel remained engrossed in the variety revue when he limped back to his chair. Onstage, a "bender" was contorting himself into amazing and amusing positions to a flautist's encouragement. Gillom kept craning around, rubbing his sore neck while trying to spot the strange man who had so rudely accosted him. The teenager sucked his white wine through clenched teeth, unable to concentrate on the show, wary of another sneak attack. His gaze finally elevated to the box seats above and across the hall from their chairs. He could see figures moving between partially opened curtains, girls on men's laps, the swells laughing and drinking. But there, in the end booth above the stage, he was. Luther Goose sat front and center as a wine girl poured him another glass of real champagne. Right behind him, drinking beer from a mug, sat the short grappler, his derby cocked over one eye. Giving his hostess a squeeze, Mr. Goose looked directly at Gillom and his girl across the hall below and smiled, raised his flute of bubbly in toast. The insult was too much to bear.

"C'mon. Let's go."

"What? Gillom. I like to see, very much." Anel looked disappointed.

"Show's almost over. We've both got to work tomorrow. C'mon."

She sighed, but got up. "Hokay."

Dancing onstage in wooden shoes, two Irish tenors, Needham and Kelly, in Prince Albert coats, pants of different colors, weather-beaten plug hats and short sidewhiskers, began one of their showstoppers.

Oh, we are two rollicking, roving Irish gentlemen,
In the Arizona mines we belong.
For a month or so we're working out in Idaho,
For a month or so we're strikin' rather strong.
Oh, we helped to build the elevated railway,
On the steamboats we ran for a many a day.
And it's devil a hair we care the kind of work we
*   do,*
If every Saturday night we get our pay. Right there!

Both lads stuck their bare hands out and clog-shoed into their chorus.

We can dig a sewer, lay a pipe or carry the hod,
In the Western states our principles are strong.
We're the advocates of all hard-workin' men,
And if that's the case you cannot say we're wrong.
Are we right?

The Irish gents waltz-clogged around the stage, repeating their rousing chorus to loud, stomping *huzzahs* from the hard-digging miners in the hall, as Gillom and his girl shouldered their way out through the raucous crowd in the Orpheum. Still smiling, Luther Goose waved them goodbye.

Anel and her beau walked across the wide brick junction of Bisbee's two main business streets at the mouth of Brewery Gulch. It was before midnight. The streets were quieter than they would be on a weekend. Gillom walked her up the boardwalk of Brewery Gulch past the Miner's Saloon, from which raucous laughter issued, the Wave Candy Company, and the Bisbee Ice Cream Parlor, which were both closed.

"Where do you live, exactly?"

She raised a slim arm, pointing through her lacy ruffle at sleeve's end. "High up."

The young man peered upward through the darkness at the bigger houses along the eastern mountainous side of Brewery Gulch, some ostentatiously ablaze with new electric lights. Other dwellings, small shacks mostly, squatted on a bench of land near the top of the ridge, maybe one room aglimmer from a coal oil lamp.

"*Chihuahua* Town?"

"*Sí.*" She lowered her eyes, embarrassed by the name always given to the jerrybuilt collection of goods boxes, tin cans, *carajo* poles, ocotillo ribs, and mud adobe bricks that housed most of the Mexicans in southwestern mining towns.

"Is it safe? I'll walk you up."

"Safe, *sí*. I live with . . . girlfriend. An *otro* dancer."

"Ah." Even on the darkened street, she could see he was crestfallen. "Like to see you again, Anel. When we have more time to get acquainted."

She batted her eyelashes, seemingly shy for once.

"What about this Sunday afternoon? We could go on a picnic. I can rent a buggy." He talked faster. "I could ask Ease, my friend. And he could ask a girl. Four of us. Find a pretty spot, have lunch."

"I like that. *Sí*."

"Okay! I'll make arrangements. We'll let you know, Saturday night, at the Red Light."

"*Sí*. Thanks to you, Mister Gil-lom." She leaned up and left him a smear of red across his cheek.

Then she was off into the moonlight, around the store's corner to climb the first of several long sets of wooden stairs up the steep hillside toward the south-of-the-border-looking shacks near the top. A flash of white leg hose made Gillom feel a little better.

Twenty-six

Friday was always busy, but at least the widows and unmarried spinsters had slowed demanding the handsome young guard escort them back and forth to the town's only bank. Gillom was able to hurry a couple blocks up the hill to see Ease in the Bonanza an hour after his bank's 3:00 P.M. closing.

Sun filtered in to the dim saloon from dirty upper glass windows as he entered one of Bisbee's biggest drinking establishments. Gillom surveyed one table of card players along the empty row of faro and roulette tables, just to make sure Luther and his minions weren't about. The day shift at the mines hadn't gotten off yet, so the vultures weren't around to loosen their pay. Gillom elbowed up to the mahogany between a couple of day drinkers for whom one drink was too many and more were never enough.

"*Compadre!* How was your date with the dancing queen?" Ease Bixler drew his pal a tall mug.

"We didn't stay the entire show. But it was a good

one, singing, dancing girls and a guy who twisted him-self like a hot pretzel."

"Sounds like a wonder." The barkeep winked. "You walk her home?"

Gillom shook his head. "No. It's a hike up to Chihua-hua Town. We're gonna go on a picnic, though, Sunday. Won't be so noisy, so's we can get better acquainted. Why don't you and that big redhead from the dance hall come with us? We can hire a carriage, split the fee, have some fun?"

"Sounds gooder than gum. Let's stop over at the Red Light tonight, see if Red Jean wants to go."

"Anel knows her, but she's got other girlfriends, too. She said she lived with one of the other dancers."

"Well, maybe. If she's not Mexican?"

"Roommate might be, Ease. What's wrong with brown-skinned gals, if you're just playin' around?"

The young bartender paused in drawing more beers from a keg.

"I got into too many fights with Mexican kids from across the tracks in Tucson, growin' up. That's a race line we were raised not to cross."

"Yeah, was the same with us kids in El Paso. We didn't mix much with the Mexes, went to different schools. Unless they worked for somebody we knew, maids, gardeners, tradesmen, we weren't around Mex-icans much. But, I'm cuttin' my own trail now. You won't turn unfriendly due to me seein' Anel?"

Ease shook his head. " 'Course not. She's a comely *chiquita*." He grinned. "Your *niños*'ll have to be raised Catholic, though."

They dined on complimentary sausages and cheese

at Lem Shattuck's St. Louis Beer Hall after Mr. Bixler got off work. Gillom stayed wary, keeping his back to walls and his eye on the front glass doors of this upper-crust saloon. Ease had many friends from his Bonanza customers who bought the boys ice-cold Anheuser-Busch beers and helped them enjoy their free meal. Gillom was reassured by his twin Remingtons, for he had resolved after last night's debasement never to appear again in public unarmed.

The Red Light had gotten a jump on the weekend. Gillom and Ease elbowed their way across the dance floor to the pumping Western music of Swart John and his four-piece band. The boys ordered more beers at the long bar. A brewery was located right in this gulch, hence its name, so the malt liquor didn't have far to travel. They sleeved foam off their lips as they watched revelers cavort around the dance hall.

"I don't see Red Jean in here. She's just a pal, but maybe someday, if I play my cards right . . ." Young Bixler flashed a hopeful grin.

"Thought Jean was one of 'em went upstairs?" Gillom nodded toward the stairway beside the band-stand which led to an upper floorway of small rooms where some of the girls entertained their lustier dancing partners.

Ease held up both hands. "Not with me! I *never* pay for it!"

"Me, neither," joshed Gillom, punching his friend in the shoulder. "You get a little liquor in Jean, maybe she'll let you squeeze it outta her later."

They laughed. The Western music strummed to a

halt and Gillom saw Anel being deposited back on a bench by her partner.

"Save my beer."

Gillom pushed through the couples changing partners.

"Gil-lom! Nice to see you, *señor*."

"You, too, Anel. You ready to venture forth with us Sunday? Ease is looking for Red Jean right now, to ask her along on our picnic. You like her?"

"Jean, *sí*. Older *amiga*."

The young buck smiled. "Good. If you ladies will pack some savories, Ease and I will rent the carriage, bring the drinks."

The band struck up a favorite, "Turkey in the Straw." Cowboys yipped and gals squealed as couples swung out onto the hardwood dance floor. Gillom and his girl gave themselves up to the music, sashaying around the loud hall. Anel's black hair flew out to match her swirling white petticoats under her yellow-checked dress as he swung her round. Gillom was transported in her arms into being a better dancer than he normally was, his boots pivoting across the dance floor, barely keeping time with his enthusiasm. His dancing partner could have been a happy farm girl at a hoedown, except for her darker coloring. Four bits a spasm *indeed*!

As they caught their breath after the song ended, he escorted his lady back to the bar. "Gosh, that was a rouser!"

Anel's sweet tea magically appeared from a waitress.

"This'll be fun, Anel. I want to see the countryside.

Don't fancy living in this smoky, smelly town forever. Rather have a ranch south of here, near the border, maybe ride into town for work."

"So you hope sell cows, thieve horses?"

"No, no horse thievin', or cattle rustlin', thank you. I'm an honest cowboy."

"*Bueno.*" She flashed him a Cheshire cat's smile.

He could tell she was foolin' with him. The band commenced again, but they sat this tune out, engaged in each other's flirtations. With his back to the bar, Gillom saw them enter through the batwing front door, swung wide to accommodate the bulk of the man in the lead, Luther Goose, with his henchman William right behind.

"Anel, that's the man gave you trouble."

She turned to look over the dancers to spot the tall, heavy man in the Prince Albert coat. The gambler smiled slightly when he saw the young couple and nudged his partner toward them.

"No. Is no *problema.*" Her smile had vanished. She stared at Gillom. "Don't make *problema, por favor.*"

Where is Ease? he wondered anxiously.

"Well, well. It's the Texas hellbender." The gambler's smile spread into a sneer as they walked up. The teenager watched Mr. Goose wrap and unwrap a gold watch chain thick as his little finger around another digit, betraying his nerves. "I want a dance with this young lady."

Gillom was quick to respond. "No."

"*Sí, señor.*" She noted her young man's scowl. "Gil-lom. I *must* dance. Make monies."

Luther Goose licked a lower lip. "See. Little lady's

smart. Keeps an eye on her bottom dollar." Then to his henchman, "buy us drinks." Luther proffered an arm and led Anel onto the dance floor. The youth was left looking at the stoic William, who hadn't said a word. Gillom backed off a couple steps, pushed his wool coat back clearing his revolvers, and nodded to the bodyguard with the apelike arms.

"Care to stand up to the iron tonight?"

William just smiled, tipped his gray bowler forward at a rakish angle, and ordered whiskies and a tea from a concerned bartender. Luckily, Ease Bixler pushed his way between them just then, with his auburn-haired vixen in tow.

"Gillom! Meet Red Jean. She's goin' picnicking with us Sunday."

"My pleasure, young man. Little country outing. You boys show me a good time, I'll pack us a nice lunch," offered Jean.

Gillom shook hands with the lady, impressed by her strong grip, never taking an eye off his smiling adversary behind her.

"Thank you, ma'am. We will have some fun." Normally he would have been bowled over by a damsel as pretty as this one, but he was distracted by the bodyguard and trying to watch Anel flashing past on the dance floor.

"Is Anel going with us?"

"Uh, yes, ma'am. Why don't you talk to her about the groceries?"

The song ended, but Luther kept the girl out on the floor in animated conversation. Gillom motioned her to come back.

230 © Miles Swarthout

"I'll bring the libations. Gillom's in charge of the carriage. Meet you at your house at noon, Jean. After church?" Ease grinned at his little joke. Red Jean cuffed him in the arm.

"Sure, Ease. You can even take me to church *first*, if the good Lord will let us *both* in."

Anel led her demanding customer back to the little group before she had to dance again.

The redhead piped up. "Anel! You an' me's gotta talk, honey, about this picnic."

Luther Goose butted in. "Ohh, a picnic?"

"You're not invited," Gillom interjected.

"I didn't ask you, kid." The brothel owner frowned. "You should be nice to me, ladies, for all the money I've passed through this joint, and gambled in the Bonanza, too, fella." He addressed Ease. "Recognize you from behind the bar."

"Yes, sir, Mister Goose. We appreciate your business."

"But *not* my company?"

"I didn't say that, sir. It's just a . . . private party."

"And these ladies are already spoken for," added the kid from El Paso.

Luther nodded. "We can take our business to friendlier saloons. Come along, William." But his tight brown eyes warned.

As they brushed past, the short Cornishman made a sudden feint at Gillom's legs, as if he were going to take him down again. Gillom jumped backward, both hands jerking to his pistol grips and pulling them. The quick move caused William to smile, since he'd deceived Gillom as to his intent. The two older men bulled their way out through the crowd forming on the dance floor for the next tune.

Gillom blew hot air. "I'm tired of running into those jaspers. Got into a wrestling match at the Orpheum last night with that damned bodyguard."

"Oh, yeah? That William Pascoe's a champion wrestler, Gillom. Hell, most of 'em are. Cornish miners are *strong,* pard, big arms and shoulders from hammering iron spikes into rock all day. Wrestling's their national sport!"

"Found that out the hard way, when he dumped me in the toilet."

"He *didn't*?" Ease chortled and even the gals were amused.

"Yeah, well, I'd never seen him before and the bastard just tackled me suddenly, no warning. Wasn't wearing my guns."

The wiser harlot weighed in. "Just stay away from them then. You, too, Anel. Luther Goose is bad trouble."

They had fun the rest of the evening in the Red Light planning their menu, where they'd go, details Gillom was unfamiliar with, having never double-dated before. When he and Ease pulled out after midnight, they hiked back downtown and then uphill to their miners' cottages, nearly talked out.

He was exhausted when he pulled up his wool blanket and quilt atop his feather pad, but his sore legs were too jumpy to go to sleep immediately. He had to get up again in his long johns to relieve a beer full bladder. With the door open to the outhouse uphill, Gillom rested in the one-holer, contemplating the few lights still on in the large mansions on Quality Hill across the canyon. In the dark, the "dirtiest air in the West" wasn't so noticeable.

Bisbee's a booming town, he thought. *Everybody here's trying to elbow their way to fortune and not being too choice about how rough they have to play to grab it. I want a little of that luck, too. I cannot allow myself to be pushed around in public by this gambling Goose joker and his thug. All's I got to build on is my reputation as a fast gun, and I've got to protect that at all costs.*

From somewhere down the canyon, an accordionist pulled his bellows and pressed the keys and a haunting Mexican air echoed up the Mule Mountains. The song provided mournful contrast to the deep thrumming of the mines' blowers and smelters, which he'd gotten used to. A shout in the night—*"shut the goddamned up!"*—made him smile.

His bladder relieved, his confidence bucked up, Gillom Rogers padded barefoot back into his cottage, retreated under his bedding, calmed by the night air. As he relaxed finally, before Morpheus took him, he remembered his one scrap with John Bernard Books in his mother's downstairs guest room. Books had learned from the old El Paso stableman, Mose Tarrant, that Gillom had sold Books's horse one spring morning without his say-so. The old shootist made him give the hundred dollars back, humiliated him right in front of his mother! Books turned the fraudulently obtained money over to Bond Rogers for the trouble he'd caused her by staying in her rooming house. After his mother had been dismissed, the gunman berated him further and Gillom sassed back, which had gotten him slapped. This precipitated a tussle, banging them both against a chiffonier. Surprisingly, the teenager's strength and suppleness had prevailed over the bigger, cancerous older man as he threw him onto the bed. Gillom hadn't forgotten what he'd yelled at J. B. Books.

"I'm as good with a gun as you! And you can't fight for sour apples, not anymore you can't! So just remember, Mister Blowhard—I've got my own laws now, just like you, and I live by 'em. I won't be laid a hand on, either, or showed up! And I won't be treated like a kid, ever again!"

He meant every word and had lived on those very terms since. After that little dispute, the great gunfighter had given him no further grief. That was the way men dealt with their difficulties and those causing them, straight on, heads-up, and devil take the hindmost. J. B. Books respected that dominant style, too. *From here on, the cautious, the weak, the inferior type of man can just swallow my dust,* he promised himself. Gillom Rogers drifted off with a contented smile.

Mrs. Blair was sweeping her porch the next morning as Gillom went out late to do some errands. The widow fixed him with a hard eye.

"At least you're quiet when you bump in so late."

"Yes, ma'am. No singing or playing the gui-tar."

Her gray hair up in a bun, she smiled, in spite of herself. "Start boiling any water you drink, anywhere. There's a touch of typhoid in town again, they're sayin'. Spring down at Castle Rock's tainted. That fever can kill you, young man, so be careful of what they pour you in restaurants."

"What about the water off the burro trains?"

"It's supposed to be drawn from the one uncontaminated well way up Brewery Gulch, but I wouldn't trust it. Unless you'd like to die with your brain on fire."

"No, ma'am. I'll stick to coffee then. And beer!" he yelled back up at her, now brushing her front stoop.

"They've gotta hurry digging those wells south near Naco, pump us clean water up here before we're all diseased." Mrs. Blair was talking mostly to herself, for Gillom was already taking the wooden stairs two at a time to get out of focus of his landlady's all-seeing eyes.

The same pockmarked man was mucking mules' stalls when Gillom strolled up to the O.K. Livery that Saturday afternoon.

"Howdy. I'm lookin' to rent a carriage tomorrow. Gonna have four of us to pull, so we'll probably need a matched team.

"A *matched* team." The liveryman leaned on his rake. "Kid, we don't rent show horses here."

"Well then, the best you've got. Taking some ladies on a picnic."

"Ah, well then. An unmatched team should work just fine for you. Picnics are pretty popular on summer Sundays. Our surrey and two spring buggies are already spoken for, tomorra."

He left his rake and escorted Gillom to the side of

their barn next to the mountain where this commercial operation stored its wheeled conveyances in space not large enough for corrals.

"This here's a Jersey wagon the railroad used to haul baggage and passengers to the Bessemer House. They've bought a couple lighter carriages now, with that spur rail in closer. This'n still's a smooth ride, though, and we can put the leather top on 'er if you want? You got plenty of room for your baskets and gear in back."

"How much for the day?"

"Oh, three dollars, since it ain't our fanciest rig."

"That'll be okay, I guess. Fix a top on it and I'll pick it up around eleven tomorrow morning."

The teamster showed stained front teeth, essaying a smile.

"Okay, son. We might even find you a matched team to pull this heavier wagon."

Gillom decided to stay home Saturday night to rest his weary legs after a long week escorting bank customers, inflating their sense of self-worth, that they actually made enough money daily to require armed protection getting it back and forth from their tills to the bank's safe. He didn't need any more late-night confrontations with the big gambler from Clifton, either. He wanted to be fresh for the morrow.

Twenty-seven

Next morning as he walked along the road to the stables in the upper portion of Tombstone Canyon, Gillom came upon his bank's cashier, M. J. Cunningham, sitting in his white Locomobile peering back at whisps of steam seeping from the brass exhaust pipes beneath its rear boiler compartment.

"Mister Cunningham."

"Gillom! I could use a little assistance, young man. This automobile stalls sometimes, trying to get up hills. If you could help me push, turn her around, I can coast back down to town."

Gillom went to the back of the boiler compartment, while the driver in his seersucker suit yanked the metal tiller hard to the right, turning the forty-spoke bicycle tires in front to the left. The wooden car body weighed about seven hundred pounds, plus the two passengers, so the teenager had to put his shoulder to the frame as the banker released the band brake under his foot. It was difficult for Gillom's boots to get traction in the dirt, so the driver hopped off and helped push against the dashboard from the right-hand side.

"Is it in gear?" asked Gillom.

"No, in neutral."

Together they got the vehicle turned sideways, but Cunningham had to jump back in to hit the brake and stop his automobile from rolling into a ditch across the road. The teenager walked around to the front of the seven-foot-long Locomobile and smiled at the young lady perched on the cushioned seat. His bank paymaster looked perturbed.

"Okay, shove!"

Gillom placed his hands on the painted wooden dashboard from the front; Cunningham let off the brake, cranked the steering tiller to the other side, and jumped down to help Gillom push the wooden frame backward.

"Salesman said this Locomobile would do forty miles an hour and climb steep grades, but I think he was exaggerating!"

Grunting, boots slipping, the men got the Locomobile backed up as M. J. leapt onto the seat again to set the foot brake. Gillom held the vehicle steady as the young lady on the front seat looked him over as she smoothed her polka-dot dress. She graced the young bank guard with a smile. Looking down the road, the driver saw an older Mexican leading a string of ten burros toward them up the dirt track.

"Damnation," muttered Cunningham. This was a wood train, empty of stovewood now, trailing up into the mountains to cut another load of juniper and oak to warm Bisbee.

The two automobilists sat there until the woodsman's son, moving the burros along from the rear with his switch, had passed. Gillom stepped aside. The Bisbee Bank's cashier let off the brake and with nary a "thank you" steered the town's only automobile back downhill. The young beauty, though, did turn slightly in her seat to give Gillom a little wave.

He thought about yelling, "Might be faster walking!" but restrained himself.

Gillom and Ease picked up their mountain wagon later that morning at the O. K. Livery and paid the stableman. As promised, he'd put on the removable top, which was a simple leather cover with foot-long flaps tacked onto wooden poles that slid into metal holders at the four corners of the rear wagonbed. The tough stableman had one last surprise for the lads when he walked out their "matched" team—a pair of gray mules.

"*Mules!*" groaned young Bixler.

"Now, boys." The stableman held up a big paw. "Mules ain't as pretty as horses, I admit, but they are lots steadier haulers. These two have pulled this wagon full of freight or folks many a time. 'Sides, we're busy on Sunday an' these mules are the best we got left."

Ease climbed up to take reluctant reins. Both lads were frowning as he gigged the mules and set them off at a smart pace down the dirt road back to town. The stableman's grin bid them farewell. More money in his pocket renting horses to wealthier adult swains.

Ease had experience driving horses hauling beer

kegs and supplies for the Bonanza, one of his tasks mornings at the bar, so he stopped the mules on a side street back of his saloon and handed the reins to his pal beside him.

"Gotta get our refreshments."

He soon returned lugging two metal pails secured by tops and wrapped in wet towels to keep the beer inside cool. Ease also toted two bottles of clear liquor, which he packed by stuffing a blanket around them in the cargo compartment.

"Beer for us, wine for the women. Boss wouldn't lend me any glassware. Said we'd just break 'em, so don't forget to ask Jean to bring glasses. Ladies don't like to drink from the bottle."

"You know where Jean lives?"

"She's got a cottage up Brewery Gulch. Lives with her pet parrot." Taking the ribbons from his pal, Mr. Bixler clucked to the mules.

The parrot greeted them from the scrub oak outside Jean's green-roofed cottage farther up Brewery Gulch from the cribs and *bagnios* that Gillom had only seen at night. It was a quiet Sunday noon in the "territory," with the whores and their customers still sleeping off Saturday night's dissipation.

"Hit the trail, hombre!"

Gillom started at the squawk, but Ease just laughed. "That's her bodyguard. Miners have taught this bird naughty stuff when they're carousing around here at night."

The yellow-head flapped its colorful green wings

with splashes of red at its shoulders and flew to a higher perch.

"Keep your pecker in your pants, pardner!"

Gillom had to smile as they walked to Jean's front porch. The dance hall queen hailed them through her screen door. "Howdy, fellas. Don't let that bird intimidate you. Fibber's just a saucy talker, not a biter."

"Colorful bird, ma'am. What kind?" asked Gillom.

"He's a yellow-headed parrot, all the way from the Amazon. Probably would like to fly back to South America without a girlfriend up here, but I keep lookin' for one for him." Jean gave Ease a welcoming buss and handed him a wicker basket. She looked almost like a man in riding pants, boots, a white blouse, and a short-brimmed, brown felt hat, which covered only part of her pile of red hair.

"Noisy, though, ain't he?" opined Ease.

"No noisier than the daily dogfight in our streets," countered Jean.

"Manny at the Bonanza wouldn't lend me any glasses, Jean, so can we use some of yours?" asked Ease.

"Sure. Let me pack 'em in something."

"Hullo, amigos." It was Anel, walking quietly up behind them.

"Anel! Just in time." Gillom got a fast kiss on the cheek before he led her back to their wagon.

"I bring fruits. Oranges, grapes. And cookies I bake." She handed up her little wooden crate.

"I'm already hungry. No breakfast today."

Ease packed away Jean's lunch basket as Gillom

helped his *chica* up the side step and over the padded backrest to sit in the cargo bed, her back against a side panel. He stood in back of the freight wagon admiring her yellow dress, the petticoats ruffled over her high-buttoned light brown shoes. Anel looked up to anoint her smitten squire with the sunniest of smiles.

Red Jean wasn't so happy. "*Shoot!* Mules! I wanted to bring along my saddle for horseback riding. I can't ride one of these ornery critters."

Neither young man had an answer. Gillom took her box of glassware wrapped in hand towels, while Ease helped his beauty onto the front seat beside him.

"*Hasta la vista,* Red!" squawked the parrot. This brought laughs, too.

"Says that every time I leave," grumped Jean.

"How come he's named Fibber?" inquired Ease.

"Because he *lies* all the time, you saucy bird," admonished his owner.

Ease snapped the mules' reins, causing them to lurch into their heavier load. The Jersey wagon pulled out from under the scrub oaks and onto the road back down Brewery Gulch, which wasn't crowded on a Sunday after church.

From his moving perch, Gillom noted the flaked paint on some of the houses and dance halls in the red light district, the rusted brass on their outdoor fixtures, a shabbiness he hadn't noticed at night. Bisbee's tenderloin was run-down, like the clothes on the customers idling on its boardwalks, or the drab chemises hanging off the whores languishing in the doorways of their workplaces, watching their little world stroll by. A few waved or yelled when they spotted Jean in the front seat. *Imagine, one of our own tribe lucky enough to have a day off just for fun,* they probably thought. A couple sports still on a weekend bender whistled at the pretty girls rattling by on the big painted wagon.

Twenty-eight

The grazing range south of Bisbee was where Ease Bixler drove them that May afternoon, to a miners' shack halfway the eight miles to Mexico atop a little hill. Ease let his passengers and supplies off at the old shack and then drove the empty wagon up the little hill to a water tank with a wooden windmill next to it, where he unhooked the mules but left them in harness so the animals could refresh themselves but not run off easily.

Gillom was pouring his pal his first beer from a lunchpail as Ease hiked down from the windmill.

"How was business last night at the Red Light, girls?" Ease asked.

"Exhausting," groaned Jean. She passed her friend a plate of fried chicken as Ease helped himself to some of her potato salad and honey biscuits.

"The miners have come down with spring fever, the way they were trying to stomp my toes last night."

"I agree so, yes," said Miss Romero.

Gillom didn't look at her directly. "Did Luther Goose and his buddy come in?"

"I not see him."

Ease uncorked the bottle with his pocket knife and poured the ladies wine. "This white sparkler may be a trifle sweet, but it's refreshing on a warm day."

The older courtesan toasted the group with her wineglass. "To fun and friends in the merry month of May."

"I'll drink to that," smirked Ease. They all drank deeply and tucked into their lunch.

Miss Jean changed the subject. "Anybody here ever ridden a bicycle?"

Gillom burped his beer and didn't excuse himself. Anel giggled. "I have not ride, how you say, these bi-cycles. But I like to."

"Don't you gals have to wear bloomers to get on a bicycle?" asked Ease through a mouthful of chicken.

"We had some gals riding bicycles Sundays in El Paso in their bloomers," offered Gillom. "A couple of our pastors said they'd disgraced themselves."

Red Jean's cheeks flared, to match her hair. "The Women's Club would say the same if we tried it in Bisbee." Freckled hands fluttered in front of her face for emphasis. "Loose women, riding around town in their underwear. *Shame and disgrace!*"

"I dunno, those society ladies try to do some good, improve our foul air, put in more water fountains and horse troughs downtown, built a playground for kids," mused Mr. Bixler.

"Their good works are fine," snapped his girlfriend, "but those bluenoses are tryin' to run us giddy girls out of the saloons, even if all we're doin' is dancin' with a bunch of lonely miners. If they get the town incorporated, Ease, and pass a bunch of blue laws, it's going to cut into your business, too, deep."

"I know, darlin'." Ease winked at Anel. "Gotta keep an owl eye on those snotty old ladies stalkin' around in the dark, *watchin'* us."

Anel frowned. "You think is possible, they shut the Red Light?"

"Sure they could." Jean nodded with a toss of her signature hair. She swallowed more wine. "They'll get their husbands to vote to outlaw us *darlings of the demimonde*, as the newspapermen mockingly call us, and run us outta the dance halls. The cribs and parlor houses would be shut next. Then Bisbee's big party is *over*, boys."

"What would we do?" The Latina was suddenly concerned.

"What us painted cats have always done, girl. Get on the train or stage to the next Western boomtown, one that has fewer matrons to get prissy with the entertainment."

"Where is that?"

"Oh, in these parts, Clifton maybe. It's another copper bonanza a ways north, more isolated than Bisbee. But I wouldn't work up there for Luther Goose and his gang. Heard bad tales."

Their distress floated right over Gillom's head. The afternoon was warm, the slight breeze soothing, and after a tasty lunch and a bellyful of beer, Gillom Rogers was drifting. His eyelids fluttered beneath the crease of his silverbelly Stetson. When the rattle on his snakeskin hatband began to vibrate with his breathing, the others noticed he was taking a little siesta.

Even Jean smiled when Anel giggled again at Gillom's light snoring. A finger to his lips, Ease got to his knees, leaned down to his pal's ear. *"Holy smokes! Look out!"*

Gillom jerked up, eyes popping open as both hands instinctively sought his guns, which weren't there. He'd taken his gunbelt off to better enjoy his repast. His friends shared a laugh at his expense.

"This is just so pleasant." He smiled, embarrassed.

"Give us a show with those *pistolas,* Gillom, boy. Wake *us* up!"

Gillom reluctantly agreed to redeem himself. He found his feet as he strapped his gun belt back on. Stepping away from them, off the blankets, he planted his boots. He shifted the double rig on his hips. He began slowly, pulling one six-gun, then both, spinning them on each index finger, forward and backward, returning them to their holsters.

"Show us how fast you surprised that *bandido* tried to rob us next to the Red Light."

The matched revolvers almost jumped into Gillom Rogers's hands, so fast was his draw. Then came the tricks, spinning the guns in the air and catching them by their handles, one of black gutta-percha, one of pearl. Pinwheeling them crossing in the air, so that the butts dropped naturally into the palms of his hands. Over-the-shoulder spins, from behind, dazzled his small audience. Maybe it was the beer, or his brief nap, but he was relaxed and didn't miss any moves or drop one of his pistols.

Ease's mouth was open, and all three applauded as he slid his Remingtons back home.

"Jesus, Gillom. Never saw those tricks before."

"Well." Young Rogers wiped sweat off his palms on his jeans. "I been practicin'."

"May I shoot one?" It was Jean again, reasserting her venturesome self. Gillom turned, looking about the empty terrain, then down at his friend.

"I guess. Nobody else around here to hit."

"Besides us chickens," said Ease, sitting up. He lit one of his cheap cigars, offered more around to the other three, who all turned them down.

"I can not esmoke," apologized Anel. "Dance too hard."

Gillom handed a .44 to the oldest among them, whose brown eyes flashed. "Hit the shack. Should slow a bullet."

Jean lifted the three-pound revolver in her strong hand. The muscles of her forearm strained as she hefted it, squinted, cocked, and blasted a jagged hole in one of the thin wallboards of the old shack.

"Easy pull on the trigger."

With another toss of her red hair, Jean followed his instructions—taking her stance, cocking the big pistol, and easing the trigger. More splinters flew.

"Now see if you can put one through that knothole." The teacher pointed. The calico queen blasted away and whooped with delight when one of her shots clipped the knothole's inside edge. She handed the empty weapon back to Gillom with a smile as big as her daring.

"I try, too?" asked Anel.

Gillom swallowed. "Sure." He showed off by pulling his left-handed pistol and quickly reversing it in a road agent's spin to hand over butt first. More grins from the girls at this little trick. Ease was on his feet now as well, shading his eyes to search the distance, seeing if anyone in the vicinity was bothered by their gunfire. But he missed the flash of light off a glass lens in the small grove of trees about a mile distant, back toward town.

Anel tried the other Remington, first gripping it in both her smaller hands to steady its wobble. The recoil and concussion jolted the smaller woman, sending her first shot up into the air. Gillom and Ease ducked.

"That's okay. Now steady your aim, catch your breath, let a little air out, cock it and *squeeze* that trigger."

At least she hit the shack's side, prompting Gillom's applause.

"Good! Now pepper that knothole." Anel did, cocking and firing the revolver and gradually hitting closer to her target, while Gillom reloaded his first pistol.

"That is fun." She handed back the empty revolver. "Heavy. Tired, *mi* arm."

"So let's see *you* hit somethin', Mister fast gun." Always the redhead.

Gillom stopped smiling. After a moment, he nodded and moved to Ease.

"Stand sideways to the shack and don't move."

Ease Bixler froze. "Oh boy . . ."

Gillom walked backward five long paces. "I'll aim for the tip of the cigar, not your nose."

Ease removed his derby hat, placed it carefully on a blanket, and inhaled the slender Mexican cigar between his lips. He exhaled nervous smoke. "Wish I'd made out a will."

"Don't stick your chin out, pardner, or I might make it cleft."

Ease struck his pose and the lit cigarillo bobbled as he talked. "No fast draw now."

"Quiet. You requested a performance." The Remington was in his outstretched right hand as Gillom closed his left eye, paused, and fired. The lit cigar half flew up in the air. The girls cheered and clapped.

His pal let out a deep breath. "Damn. Ruint a good cigar."

"Stand against that ol' shack and I'll paint your portrait."

"Not me, pard. Already run through today's luck."

Ease plunked down next to his girlfriend, who tousled his shock of red hair playfully. Gillom pointed his pistol at Red Jean, inquiring?

"No thank you, sir. I've seen your crack shooting, but I'm nobody's target practice."

"I try eet." Anel's offer surprised them.

"Okay. Just stand there, back against those boards, and be very still."

Gillom replaced another cartridge in his pearl-handled revolver. The young Latina stood up and walked resolutely to place her spine against the weathered boards, gritted her teeth, and squinted her eyes closed. Gillom gave no warning as his first shot splintered wood about six inches from her right elbow.

Anel flinched, but no splinters struck her and she

didn't jerk away. Four more shots banged out in fairly close succession, moving up her arm, over the curve of her right shoulder, alongside her rounded, light brown face.

He reholstered his empty weapon, pulled the left-hand gun with the black handle, began reloading.

Ease was consternated. "Gillom, enough. You've proved your skills today."

"This is a portrait in lead we're all gonna remember."

Anel Romero opened her eyes to stare at the artist. Beads of sweat had formed, matting black hair on her forehead. Gillom focused on the small dark beauty mark on her left cheek, just below the prim line of her lips. *I wonder if that mark is real or makeup? I'd like to lick it to find out.*

Anel squinted and gave him a slight nod. The young man fired again, using his right, dominant hand outstretched, to lessen the chance of deadly error. His next shot was a little close, sending a splinter through her long black hair into her left earlobe. She grimaced but didn't let out a peep of pain, allowing him to continue, placing bullet holes around the curve of her left shoulder and down her other arm. One last shot, in the space between her legs, thigh-high, made her jump.

"Done," he exhaled.

Anel stepped away from the sidewall, shaking her head and arms slightly to see if all her digits were still attached and not bleeding.

"Outstanding," said Jean, admiring the bullet-holed vaguely human figure. "Crazy, but outstanding."

"I wouldn't have believed that kind of marksmanship," agreed Ease. "Barroom lies."

Gillom smiled, loaded three more cartridges from his holster, and then completed the outline with his off hand, adding one hole over the crown of the head, another two a little indented, where her bare neck would have been.

"You're my silhouette girl, Anel. Brave one, too." He walked over to playfully buss her lips, lick the spot of blood off her earlobe where the splinter had pierced skin.

"This calls for a toast!" Ease rummaged in his burlap sack and pulled out shot glasses. He pulled the cork from a clear, unlabeled pint bottle with his teeth and poured light yellowish liquid into the little glasses.

"This is what the Mexicans call *tequila*. Made from the heart of the blue agave. The most refined cactus liquor from Mexico we can get our hands on. Supposed to be good for your health. Three whole dollars a small bottle and it ain't been watered. Ladies?"

The bartender poured them all shots. Gillom seemed transported, larger than life. He raised his shot glass.

"To our fearless, feisty ladies. Gunslingers and living targets. I'm mighty impressed."

Anel and Jean blushed at the compliment, raised their glasses, and grimaced as they sipped the fiery liquor.

"This'll put hair on your nipples, girls!" chortled the bartender.

"Just what I need," frowned the blousy redhead. Anel was slicing up a couple of Salt River Valley oranges on a plate, which she passed around to sweeten their mouths after the tart liquor. Then Anel, who'd tasted tequila before, pushed her shot glass forward for a refill.

"*Por favor*. Calm *mis nervios*."

"You bet, honey. You earned it."

Gillom finished reloading the last of his cartridges into his pistols, just in case.

"Do you have any lip paint I can borrow, ladies?"

Jean looked at Gillom quizzically, but dug into her leather purse to pull out a tin of carmine rouge that complemented her flaming hair.

Gillom took the tin and dabbed some on the tip of his finger as he walked to the bullet-holed silhouette on the old miner's shack, where he smeared two curves of a heart right where his girlfriend's would be. Anel came up when she saw what he was doing. Gillom took more rouge and printed his first name in red lip paint below the heart, added a plus sign, and handed the tin of lip polish to her.

With a shy smile Anel daubed a fingerful and painted her first name beneath his. Impulsively, they sealed their signatures with a lingering kiss.

"C'mon, loverboy. Help me hitch our matched mules."

Gillom let Anel's slender hand slip from his grasp before ambling after his friend.

When the boys returned in the wagon, the girls had packed up the picnic, except for the desserts. All four of them sat in the bed of the rented Jersey wagon under the shade of its leather top, enjoying Anel's grapes and oatmeal cookies while the young men polished off their pails of warm beer.

"I was reading about Colonel Hooker's hot springs on his ranch up north around Sierra Bonita, below Mt. Graham," said Gillom. "Anybody been there?" Headshakes no. "Well, newspaper said the colonel had a gospel minister come visit and this pastor said the hot mineral waters there had healed him. He believed those soothing waters would cure any ailment, even 'wash away sin.'"

The girls laughed. "*Any* sin?" inquired Jean.

"I guess so," said Gillom. "I think we should all plan a trip to Sierra Bonita."

The ladies helped themselves to the crystalized fruits, lemon slices Jean had bought from the candy store.

"Boy, I could use a healing scrub."

"Might be a little hot for you, Ease, burning out all that sin," smiled Red Jean, insincerely.

"Scorch my tailfeathers for sure." Her friend grinned back.

"Would you go to the hot baths with me, Anel?" asked Gillom.

She smiled fetchingly at her young gunslinger. "*Sí. Manana es otro dia.*" ("Tomorrow is another day.")

"*Okay then!* Spiritual refreshment for all!"

They laughed as Ease slid onto the driver's seat. He grabbed the reins and clucked to their mule team, a lemon slice stuck between his teeth.

"I was reading, too, girls, that they've made a scientific discovery of alfalfa tablets that fatten human beings just like they work on hogs. We should get some of them pills for our next picnic."

"That's just what we girls need, Ease, fattening pills. Then you can take us up to Hooker's hot springs and boil the lard off us just like they render them hogs."

The mule driver chortled. "Sounds fun to me. A pinch and a squeeze and Ease always aims to please!"

The four were laughing so hard they didn't notice the horse nearly hidden in the small grove of trees they passed on their slow roll back to Bisbee. William Pascoe pushed back his derby and peeked around a couple entwined tree trunks with his binoculars as the merry wagonful made for home. His boss would want to know exactly who had enjoyed themselves out here this Sunday. After church.

Twenty-nine

After they'd dropped Jean off at her cottage and palavered with Fibber again, they left Ease at the Bonanza where he had to pull a rare night shift. Gillom managed to drive the wagon back up Tombstone Canyon. The mules scented their bed ground and pulled the now lighter freighter with some urgency, anxious for their nightly feed.

Anel was still with him. Gillom picked up the blanket and slipped the half-empty bottle of tequila into her dessert crate while the stablehand was unhitching the animals.

"Come to my rooms up Youngblood Hill. There's a nice breeze, so the smelter smoke won't linger. The stars should be pretty."

"Need my esleep."

"Tomorrow's Monday. You don't work Monday night, right?"

"Hokay. For a leetle time. Then I walk home."

"Sure. We just got to be quiet. My landlady doesn't want me entertaining guests late."

They hiked up Youngblood Hill's wooden stairways, whispering to each other in the milky moonlight, giggling often from a long afternoon of beer, wine, and tequila tasting. They climbed off the stairway halfway up to the highest landing, to cut across the grass hillside and sneak in behind Mrs. Blair's house. Anel tried to keep her high-buttoned shoes from thumping the planks to Gillom's back door, when he burped. The rude eruption set off more giggles and whispered *sssshhh*'s while he keyed his lock to slip inside his sparsely furnished rooms.

He lit a coal oil lamp and made sure his window curtains were pulled, when he spotted Mrs. Blair next door, peeking out her lit window now she realized Gillom was home. He lit another coal oil lamp, showed his girlfriend his built-in living room and kitchen.

"Nice home for you, Gil-lom. I need use, outhouse." She squinched her eyes. "Too much wine."

"Me, too. But my landlady's up, listening. So no light, no talking." A finger to his lips, he opened his back door, but the dark-haired beauty had plopped down on one of his kitchen chairs to unlace her calf-high boots to lessen any noise. Gillom didn't wait for her but left the door open as he tramped up the hillside in the dark to the one-hole privy, doing what his landlady might expect.

He clomped back down to his doorway where his Mexican miss waited, backlit by smoky lamps.

"Wait." Following her inspiration, the kid from El Paso sat down on a chair to pull off his own boots and socks, dump his holster and hat, so that he could join his girlfriend on her barefoot trip up to the little privy. There he patiently stood guard while she relieved herself, then led her over to a grassier slope the other side of the wooden structure, far enough away from Mrs. Blair's back door so they could quietly converse without being overheard.

"Beautiful night."

"*Sí.*"

"Full moon. Make a wish."

She was silent a moment, thinking of something good. She could hear change jingling in his pocket. "You've gotta jingle silver coins, to make it come true. Whatcha wish for?"

"*Us.* . . . Just us."

Gillom smiled and nodded. "Breeze is freshening, blowing that smelter smoke away. A big, dark cloud headed this direction, though. Smells like rain."

The Latina followed his pointing finger. "Rain? You smell eet?"

"Moisture freshens the air and a charge builds in the air from the lightning. Oh yeah, I can smell rain. It's comin'."

She shook her head. "We weel see."

Gillom sat down and pulled the cork from Ease's bottle of Mexican cactus liquor. He took a swallow to wake himself up.

"*Hooo.* Care for a little more tarantula juice?" He passed the bottle over. Anel took a tentative sip of the yellowish liquor and gasped. She handed the bottle back, wiping her nose.

"Why did you come to Bisbee, Anel?"

"In Estados Unidos, I can make monies. I wish more to see. If Jean say right, Bisbee shut Red Light, I move. In Mexico, Zacatecas, the *señors* dig silver, drink, the women take care *niños*. I wish more."

Gillom took a pull on the bottle. "Feel the same. I was bored with high school, wanted to see more of the world. Then I had some shooting trouble in El Paso. Got out of Texas quicker than I planned, but here I am." He bowed facetiously, but could hear her frown in the dark.

"Guns bring *mucho problema*."

"They got me my bank job. I don't want to shoot anyone, Anel. Really, I *don't*. I was just showing off this afternoon, tricks."

"You play with guns, be fast, shoot good, you weel use them."

"Only to protect you, missy. Or the bank's customers."

"You weel bore soon, estanding that bank house all day."

"Not with you as our prettiest customer." He reached an arm tired from all the gunplay and pulled her into him. This time their kiss was more urgent, forceful. Whether it was the foreign liquor, the sudden chill in the night air, or the heat of their skin rubbing, they got into each other's essence, entwining in the dry grass like snakes in heat, running their hands all over, inside each other's clothes, nuzzling necks, arms, any bare skin. Gillom was sweating, moisture on his forehead, running down his underarms, staining his cotton shirt.

Or maybe it was the electric charge in the night air?

He came out of his sex haze to catch a breath and realized it had started to rain. Gillom stuck out his tongue to catch big fat drops on a stiffening breeze.

"Rain."

She opened her eyes, trying to get her bearings, breathless. Anel rubbed her moist face.

"Eet *is*!"

"Sssshhh. It's gonna get wet. Storm blew in fast. Come."

They were up and moving when the first lightning struck the hillside above them, flaring the darkness. They were inside Gillom's cottage when the thunder banged, smothering Anel's frightened squeal. He pulled her to him, covering her mouth with his. He hoped his landlady hadn't heard her shriek? Gillom picked her up in his arms, swung her slowly around several times before depositing her gently atop the feather mattress and blanket on one of the single beds built into the wooden cottage's wall. He rolled over on top of her, scrunching himself next to the wall. Just in time, too, as another lightning strike and clap of thunder hit the hillside nearby, making them both jump with the sudden *bang*.

"Can't go home now, honey. Not until this rain stops. This one's gonna be a gullywasher."

Anel nodded in the flickering lamplight. "Scare me."

Gillom smiled. "We'll just ride it out here."

Another thunderclap made her cringe, cling to him. They could hear the rain hitting the roof hard, his glass windows pinging as wind drove the water on a slant. He hoped to God there were no big leaks, wash them down this hillside. *Be tough climbing back up here,* he thought, *through steep mud.*

Their wet bodies warmed the blanket and they were quickly kissing, groping one another again through their damp clothing, between moist sheets, helping each other undress. Gillom had to rise to get his jeans off, and he crabbed over her to blow out one of the lamps. Then he got up to take the other lamp around in his kitchen, see if there were any wet spots on the floor. Finding none of consequence, he turned down the coal oil lampwick, returned to their little bed to sink again into her arms. There, on that thin mattress, as the thunder rolled and the rain poured, they salved their lust, consummated their passion under a summer monsoon. He was awkward, not knowing quite how to proceed, not wanting to hurt her, but she helped fit him inside her. It was a little painful for her, but it was beautiful, and it was over fairly quick. No matter, it felt like love.

He awakened in tangled sheets, just before dawn. He could see well enough to see her face, rouge running from her night sweat, her lip paint smeared beyond the corners of her mouth. Gillom did what he'd dreamed of and licked the beauty spot on her right near cheek. It *was* real, didn't smudge.

Anel opened a weary eye. "What?"

"Lick you like a cat."

"Nooo. More esleep."

"Gotta use the privy. I'll fill a bucket in the kitchen, you wanna wash."

"Come back . . . to me. . . ."

"*Momentito.*"

Gillom put on his shirt to barely cover himself, padded out the back door into a wet dawn. He walked up to the outhouse, glad his landlady wasn't up yet.

Back in his kitchen, he filled a small basin and soaped up for a cold water whore's bath. Anel was up wanting water so he poured them a couple glassfuls from a ceramic pitcher on a shelf. This was water from his outside barrel he'd taken time to boil, to kill any taint of typhoid from the local well. It tasted cool and sweet in his sex glow. Gillom stroked her bare shoulder like you'd pet a cat, admired her pouty breasts. *Goddamn she's pretty naked,* he marveled. Anel padded out into the morning mist wearing nothing at all to hike up the hill herself.

She came back to the bed, which he'd straightened, shaking out the sheets. It was even better this second time. They could see each other for one thing, and their loving wasn't so rushed, fumbling in the dark. Most of yesterday's liquor was out of their systems, so they could better feel each other's hot, sensitive skin. Their coupling was easier and he quickly fell into a natural rhythm with her body. Soft moans inspired him and he built up to his coming by degrees—long, slow, long, fast—and finally, as she urged him on with her feet raking his bare buttocks, spurring and pulling him into her deeper with each thrust, an ecstatic release!

After a moment catching his breath, nuzzling her smooth neck, Gillom rolled off her, fell back on his mattress and laughed. His new girlfriend was confused. "You laugh at me?"

"No, honey. It just feels so great. What love is."

"Sex. You mis-take, for love."

"No. Sex. Love. Together. Now I know how love feels."

"Maybe you change your mind."

"Maybe. But it sure will be fun to find out." He tickled her bellybutton, sending her into spasms. "They say making love during a rainstorm will produce a girl, but sex during sunny weather results in a boy."

"No, no *niños*. Not now. No need."

Gillom suddenly turned serious. "How come you stood up there yesterday, let me shoot at you?"

"Because you need help, to show what you do. How good *pistoletazo* you are."

"But you could have been killed."

Anel smiled. "No. I believe you . . . are the best."

He could only nod. And give her another kiss.

Ravenous, they dressed to go downtown for breakfast. It was Monday, so Anel didn't have to work after her weekend shift at the Red Light. But Gillom was due at the bank. They slipped out his back door quietly, then got stuck in the mud trying to cut across the wet grass to get to the long stairway down Youngblood Hill. Anel swore in Spanish about getting her high-button shoes dirty. Gillom looked back over his shoulder to see Mrs. Blair peering out one of her windows into the gray morning mist, watching them leave. *Maybe I can excuse my way out of this,* he thought. *Just providing a wayward miss shelter from a bad storm, ma'am.*

The creek running from the spring at Castle Rock down Tombstone Canyon rushed by wider and faster, muddy red water racing toward the mouth of Mule Gulch. The two got off the bottom of the stairway and made their way slowly toward downtown, slogging along the muddy hillside, trying to keep from slipping and falling over. Anel's yellow dress was muddy at the hems and Gillom's jeans were spattered with dirt. They saw tree limbs and wooden siding floating by, even a soaked dog paddling hard for the far bank in the rushing water. Bisbee's hillsides had been denuded by woodcutters and every heavy rain now caused a mudslide. Sulfurous smelter smoke had killed the canyon's root plants as well. This flash flood was dangerously dirty, too. Cesspools overflowed and up Brewery Gulch on the right side of the dirt street, businesses had built their rear bathrooms on stilts over the creek with enclosed structures below. When a flash flood like this occurred, the owners went below and opened the up- and downstream side doors on their hinges to let the storm water give their outhouses a good flushing.

"I cannot go home!" Anel shouted as they neared the downtown junction of the canyon and the gulch, where two flood streams joined to run south onto the floodplain below Bisbee.

"Bank's not gonna open today, either." Nearing Main Street they could see the bank's big wooden doors shut. The sheriff already had his chain gang out, trying to clean up the business streets, supervised by deputies. They noticed carcasses of dead animals washed up in doorways, a cat, a young steer, plus items of discarded apparel, from hats to stray shoes, being sniffed by a foraging mongrel dog that had ridden out the storm.

"There won't be many restaurants open today, till they get this mess cleaned up."

He pointed to several hand-painted signs some wag

had planted outside the Bonanza, Ease's saloon near the now sandy, watery bottom of the Gulch. NO FISHING ALLOWED HERE, stated one. FERRY LEAVES EVERY HOUR, another. Gillom grinned in spite of this municipal disaster.

"Let's go back to my place, till this mess dries out. Maybe I can get my landlady to cook us breakfast. She enjoys my money, if not my female guests."

"Boil water," his girlfriend reminded.

"Already am. Now all the town's wells will be tainted."

Mrs. Blair *did not* cook them breakfast. She was so perturbed by the first big rainstorm of the summer and the leaks it had divulged in their roofs, she said nothing about Gillom's entertaining. But her renter promised to get out the tar brush and help her caulk the new holes, so his premarital sinning was ignored. For the time being.

Next day, when the water downtown had subsided, one of his new duties was shoveling mud off the bank's cement steps so customers could come in. But Gillom had more important things on his mind. So smitten was he, he arranged to get off early later in the week to meet his lady love at the Atlantic and Pacific Portrait Studio, a small shop just north of Castle Rock up Tombstone Canyon. Gillom told Anel to look her best, but she later had to go on to work at the Red Light, so the red satin dress with black lace trim she showed up in was pretty sexy.

Their photographer, C. E. Doll, was a short man

with an overbearing attitude. *Prissy*, Gillom thought. He posed them just so in front of his compact Pony Premo camera as he adjusted its rectilinear lens. Their backdrop was ornate flocked wallpaper on one wall. Then Gillom changed his mind and asked Mr. Doll to put up a drop sheet of black velvet instead. This set the little photographer clucking his tongue, since he no longer had decisive control of his composition. His paying customer ignored the artistic tension.

Electric lights were rigged in the studio so the portraits didn't require smoky flash powder often used for formal photographs at the time. Gillom went whole hog, ordering full-length portraits of them together and alone off the five-by-seven-inch glass plates. Plus face shots, from the shoulders up, one of them even kissing! For his solo portrait, Gillom made sure to hike Books's matched pistols higher on his waist, reversing the gun butts forward, and pulling back his black morning coat he'd brought along so Books's famous pistols were on display.

The bill came to twelve dollars, in advance. The teenager paid and they floated out the photographer's after an hour's hot work.

The couple celebrated, memorializing their carnal togetherness in the fancy Senate Saloon in the Gulch. Gillom ordered a Rocky Mountain Cooler.

"We can have more photographs printed, Anel, if you want to send them to your family and friends in Mexico. I want to send one of us together to my mother. Show her my new girlfriend."

266 of Miles Swarthout

"Kissing?"

He grinned. "No, not kissing. That's just for us."

The young lady smiled and quaffed her Egg Flip.

"That one of me, sporting my guns, I may send to our sheriff in El Paso. Bastard tried to steal these pistols off me."

"Why?"

"Because these are J. B. Books's matched Remingtons. He was a famous shootist and I helped him die, so he willed 'em to me."

She wrinkled her cute nose. "Help heem to die?"

The young gunfighter nodded. "Long story. But his guns are famous now, too, and valuable. No one else gets 'em unless they pry 'em from my cold, dead hands."

"Why you push thees big men?" Anel punched him in the arm, irritated. "Thees sheriff, thees gambler, from Clif-ton? You wish to fight, get killed?"

"No, no, I don't want to shoot anybody, or get killed. Sometimes you just have to show your skills, so bad people won't bother us."

She looked worried. "No more fights."

Her boyfriend tried to reassure. "Not if I can help it."

Thirty

Work that May week was slow, since the entire town was preoccupied cleaning up and repairing homes and businesses from the early summer's deluge. Anel took Wednesday night off due to slow trade at the Red Light and their difficulty bringing up Mexican musicians from Naco after the big storm. So they caught a quick meal at a hole-in-the-wall taqueria and then went to the Bank Exchange for drinks. This saloon was famed in Brewery Gulch for the owner's wild animal menagerie, which he penned elsewhere and then brought to a cage outside his establishment on a rotating basis—a young lynx, a mountain lion, a rattlesnake, a peccary—any desert animal he could display for a few hours to entice interested tipplers to enter for further excitement and one more libation.

The Bank Exchange had also circulated flyers around town advertising an "intimate" performance tonight, to pump up business during a slow summer midweek. The show was under way when Gillom and

Anel arrived, so they stood at the long bar to watch. On a small, elevated stage in back normally used by a piano player or musical trio, an elderly gray-haired man was standing behind a diminutive woman seated in a chair, running his fingers through her long brown hair.

Gillom ordered mint juleps while they listened to the old gent describe this young lady as "emotional and flighty" due to the shape of her small head. Her organ of philoprogenitiveness, which was located in the middle posterior of her skull, just above the occipital spine, he pointed out, was small, and its diminutive size showed that she was not overly fond of children or animals and could be severe when they misbehaved. The woman's concentrativeness, though, was larger, manifesting a power of concentrated application to just one thing. The phrenologist had the young lady turn to the audience as he demonstrated, parting her hair on the crown of her head. She was thusly suited for precise work like bookkeeping in a store. The old boy coaxed the name "Sarah" out of her, and Sarah offered that she was indeed a clerk at the "Merc" and enjoyed working the cash register best. This fact met with mumurings of approbation. But her skull didn't evince the emotional stamina necessary for schoolteaching or raising a large family, he added.

"You are not yet married, correct?" This troubling question caused the unfortunate's face to redden as she teared up, which caused spectators to nod knowingly at the sage's wisdom as the young lady fled the stage crying.

The old blind phrenologist babbled about his expertise in "the living science of studying the shape of the skull to learn what is on one's mind. Phrenology teaches that the mind acts through organization of bodily instrumentalities. And there are, so far as is known, nearly forty mental faculties, each of which has a special and separate function." He paused to study the crowd with his gaping eye sockets. An older lady was helping him with his act and she had spotted Gillom arriving late to the performance.

"*You*, sir! You in the back, yes, standing at the bar with your girl. We need another young head up here."

Gillom pointed to himself, surprised. *Me?*

"Yessir! We need your help with a reading, please. A free drink for you two, if you will."

Smiling amiably, Gillom walked past occupied tables to join the elderly couple onstage.

"What's your name, lad?" the old gent asked as he seated Gillom right in front, facing the bar patrons.

"Gillom Rogers."

"And how do you earn your daily bread?"

"I'm a guard, Bank of Bisbee."

"You stand watch over all our money."

Chuckles from the boozy crowd.

"No, I don't touch the money. I make sure our customers get *their money* back and forth safely to our bank."

After removing Gillom's Stetson, the old man's long, wizened fingers were in his victim's thick blond hair. He rubbed and traced the teenager's scalp like a mind reader.

"You have the head of a mule, young man. Long ears and a long jawline, mulish. I feel a large organ of combativeness, at the posterior of the parietal bone, about an inch and a half upward and back from the external opening of your ear. A continuation of the length of the head from above the ear backward indicates a strong faculty to defend, oppose, and resist. That will make you a good sheriff or newspaper journalist someday when you're finished with this first job. I don't forsee you guarding a bank forever, young man. You have a fairly thick neck, corresponding with a broad base for your brain. We also often find in the fighter a wide, rather straight, and very firm mouth, like yours."

The old man's thin fingers played over Gillom's face like spider's legs. "The moustache on some of our important military men partially conceals their straight mouth, but it is evident enough in the portraits of Caesar, Wellington, Napoleon, and Ulysses S. Grant, among others. A firm mouth indicates good development of the nasal cavities and especially of the jaws, and the great masticating power which allies such great men to the carnivore, and makes them not averse to blood."

Anel stopped sipping her julep.

"To sum up, you're not a fast, sleek horse who will readily gallop through life and friends, Gillom, but a steady, mulish plodder whom one can count on being steady in a tight spot. Law enforcement may be your game. That about right, son?"

"No. I'm more racehorse than mule. But I *am* steady in a fight."

Laughter and a smattering of applause as Gillom sauntered off the stage.

"Get a bull up there to go with that mule!" yelled a drunk from the rear bar. The lady assistant quickly began coaxing a stolid cattleman onstage to cover Gillom's dissatisfaction. Anel and he quickly finished their free drinks, wished good night to the Bank Exchange's gila monster, and breezed outdoors for a long stroll hand-in-hand down Brewery Gulch and up the squeaky wooden stairways to his miner's cottage.

They snuck in quietly and didn't go back outside to enjoy the summer's starry night, for Gillom still wasn't certain Mrs. Blair would permit his entertaining a girlfriend often. They gulped glasses of boiled water from his ceramic jug and undressed quickly without even lighting a lamp, so hungry were they for lovemaking. This time he stayed with her better, climaxing as he matched her rising excitement, so they both collapsed with a final shudder in a tangle of sweaty sheets. Anel panted in the sticky air and Gillom inhaled lying on his back.

"That was better than wrestling," he grinned.

"Who wres-tle?"

"Oh, that henchman of Luther Goose. He surprised me in the men's room of the Orpheum, night we saw that variety show."

She squinted in the darkness. "I no remember?"

"He banged me around some before I could even fight back. I didn't have my guns on that night."

"A good thing, no? No lose you to a *bandido*."

She could see Gillom's frown in the moonlight. "He in last night, Luther Goose. Say come with heem to thees mining town, north. Have saloon there."

"He bother you?"

"No, just dance, buy drinks. I need earn money, too, you know."

"He may promise you more money, Anel, but Luther is a bad man. Red Jean said so. Doesn't treat his saloon girls well."

"I no go with heem."

"Clifton's a smaller copper mining town. Rougher, isolated, up in the mountains, north and east of here. Never been there, but that's what I hear." She saw his eyes slit in the darkness, gleaming like an aroused cat's.

"I something have for you." She rose from his single bed, fumbled in her handbag. He admired her soft curves in the moonlight filtering in from his front windows. Then she was back straddling him naked as she dangled a chain in his face.

"What's this?"

"A loc-ket."

"For a girl?"

"No. You wear eet, round neck. Or keep eet, under thees pillow." She took the filigreed silver oval and snapped open its hinged case. She leaned forward, her bare breasts distracting him as she put a small photograph in front of his eyes. "Pictures we made. I pay for small one, to fit. See?"

Gillom squinted. He could just make out her long hair and features.

"Very pretty. Looks like you. I *will* wear it. Always."

Anel then lifted her left hand to show him thin strands of silky, curly hair she'd tied with a pink ribbon. "Is from here." She patted the triangle between her legs.

Gillom was flabbergasted. "Your muff hair?"

He could almost see her blush in the dark. "*Sí*. I know dancer did this. Mean I be faithful. Only to *you*."

"Ohhh, Anel. That's beautiful."

"*Sí*. No matters who I dance with, only *you* I let in me, in my heart."

He pulled her down for a long, tongue-sucking kiss. She eased his manhood back in and then, braced up on her knees, took her sweet time, rocking back and forth atop him, moaning like a contented puppy, until their passion passed.

Thirty-one

After work at the bank the next day, Gillom hit the Bonanza just as his pal was finishing up his day shift. Ease pulled them two drafts and they sat at its long oak bar.

"Goose is bothering her, Ease, least once or twice a week, trying to get her to go up to Clifton, work in his brothel," Gillom peeved. "She thinks it's just a saloon."

"Well, she has to drink tea with all kinds of customers, bad men even, to make a living in that dance hall."

"I know, but Anel says he's become more bothersome, trying to get her to go upstairs at the Red Light."

"Can't she tell the manager there?"

"She did, but the owner doesn't want to bother Luther. He spends too much money."

"Huh." The young barkeep turned to another customer. "Hey, Mickey! You ever work the mines up in Clifton?"

A wiry Welshman down the bar nodded. "Certainly did. Phelps Dodge pays better down here, though, and Bisbee's mines are better run, safer."

"Uh-huh. You ever frequent a joint up there called the Blue Goose?"

"Yep. Snootiest saloon in eastern Arizona."

"Was it a whorehouse, too?"

The roughneck rubbed his chin stubble, remembering. "Yes, it was. Upstairs. Never ascended to those heavenly chambers, though. Too expensive."

"See?" Gillom nudged his pal. "He wants to turn Anel into a painted cat, pimp her."

"What are you going to do about it?"

"Warn him off. Like he did me, when his sidekick caught me in the men's room at the Orpheum. This time I'll have my guns on and it'll be public. No sneak attacks."

Young Bixler looked worried. "Ummm. Trouble. Bad for our business."

"Not in here, Ease. Luther won't be back in the Bonanza after he braced your faro dealer for cheating, remember?" Gillom was aggravated. "I just need your support. Like I backed you when that footpad attacked us."

"Yeah, yeah, all right. I don't want any shooting, but I better borrow a *pistola,* just in case. I don't wrestle any better than you can."

They clapped each other on the shoulders and Ease went off to borrow a sidearm for the evening.

Soon Bixler carried a '78 Colt Frontier .45 double-action revolver in the side pocket of his black cotton coat as the boys stepped onto the boardwalk heading up into the netherworld of upper Brewery Gulch. A warm dusk was gathering along with a crowd of miners just coming off the day shift in the Copper Queen or Irish Mag shafts. The boys scouted the St. Louis Beer Hall with no luck. Ease had heard Luther Goose was still in town and he was a known high roller, so they decided to stalk him in Bisbee's best saloons, where there was slightly less chance of gunplay.

Their second stop, the Senate, they hit pay dirt. The Senate was Bisbee's fanciest restaurant, which offered wild game along with regular beef and chicken dishes, served on silver platters by white-jacketed waiters. The brothel owner from Clifton idled at the back bar, hoisting whiskeys with William and a couple other hard cases in coarse wool suits. Mr. Goose, anticipating further trouble, had beefed up his protection.

William spied Gillom and Ease stalking through the front barroom, peering about at the customers dining.

"It's that pissant kid and his pal, boss."

Gillom halted fifteen yards away from the smaller bar in the Senate's back room, where few were dining midweek that warm early summer evening. In the bar's mirror, Luther Goose watched Gillom drop into his gunfighter's stance, feet apart, long fingers dangling at his sides. His work coat was pushed back behind two gleaming gun handles, butts forward, leaving them ready for fast work. Luther's henchmen put down their whiskeys, leaving their own hands free.

"If it isn't the kid gunslinger."

"Mister Goose, you've been bothering my friend at work. I want you to leave her alone."

"Who might that be?"

"Anel Romero. Works the Red Light."

The hefty gambler finally put down his tumbler, turned slowly round to face his accuser. He saw Ease's right hand fingering his coat pocket.

"She's a saloon girl. Belongs to anybody with a dollar for a dance."

"No, she's *my* girlfriend! She dances with anybody she chooses to. And that's no longer gonna be you, since you're constantly bothering her. Anel doesn't wish to see you again, here, or in Clifton, or anywheres else."

Luther's mouth twitched upward into a false smile. "She needs to tell me that herself."

"*I'm* telling you. Right here, right now." Gillom saw that Luther's three henchmen had slumped into partial crouches, ready to spring. His were the only guns on display, though.

"Kid, you ever grow up, you'll see she's just two tits, a hole, and a heartbeat, like all the rest of those dance hall whores."

"Not *my* sweetheart."

The big gambler started rubbing his mole over his right eyebrow with an index finger, a nervous tick. At frantic waves from the bartender behind the short counter, the saloon's owner came striding up.

"Gentlemen. No trouble here?"

Luther was gruff. "No. He's spoken his stupid piece."

The restaurateur was curt, sensing the threat. "Good. Because if there is a disagreement, please take it outside or the sheriff will be called. The Senate's a fine dining establishment, as I'm sure you're aware, Mister Goose, owning a saloon yourself."

Luther nodded, his eyes not straying from Gillom's gun hands. "It used to be."

Ease tapped his buddy in the arm, breaking Gillom's glare, and the boys backed off. As they were walking slowly back through the now quiet front room, the big man from Clifton got in a final jab. "Walk careful, sonny. I *will* see you around!"

The young men passed out the Senate's front door, trailed by the owner to see that they did, and watched by the now silent diners in that restaurant.

In the back bar, Luther Goose gathered his men close.

"Take 'em down tonight. Break something this time. Don't kill 'em unless you have to, since you boys are no use to me in jail. I don't wish to be called out in public by either of 'em again. You know where they live?"

"Near each other up Youngblood Hill. We can ambush 'em up there," offered William.

"That two-gun kid is dangerous; he's ready to scrap. I think his bartender buddy is packing, too. Saw him fingering his right coat pocket."

William the wrestler nodded, speaking to the other two rough miners. "If they split up, Frankie and I will trail the gun boy. Duggan can follow the nervous one."

Luther interjected. "Anybody armed?"

Duggan edged a revolver from his coat pocket. Frankie flashed a small pistol, too.

"Good." Mr. Goose passed his .41 Remington derringer to William Pascoe with a couple extra rounds. "Hurry. Before they reach home."

Grunting, his henchmen left their boss to finish his excellent whiskey.

Thirty-two

Their encounter wasn't a complete surprise, for the lads could hear heavy breathing from the darkness as they climbed the long second tier of wooden stairways up Youngblood Hill. They'd ambled home, dissecting their encounter with Goose and his thugs, wondering what might happen next. Bisbee sat at fifty-three hundred feet and the tops of these Mule Mountains were two thousand feet higher, so climbing partway to their cottages always left even these fit young men a little winded.

Gillom hesitated before stepping out onto the wider platform where one stairway ended and another began again up to the hill's top. He could hear noises, but there were no lights on this steep staircase and he couldn't see much in the darkness besides coal oil lamps glowing in the nearby miners' cottages. No moon out tonight. Ease bumbled up behind him on the stairs, pushing Gillom out onto the platform, which is where they got ambushed. Three men heaved up and came vaulting over the wooden railings around the platform from all sides, trapping the two young men in the middle of the square. Ease got in one good punch to a stranger's jaw before he was driven to his knees by a grab at his legs. Frankie had a mugger's choke on Gillom—a left arm around his throat with his right arm reaching over Gillom's shoulder and locking up the hold, using the radius bone of his right arm as a lever against the kid's windpipe. Before he began to black out, Gillom drew, cocked, turned the barrel around, and fired, right into the big man's gut.

"Ahhhh!" The shot shocked Frankie into releasing him, but Gillom had to thrust off the heavy man who was pinning him against a railing. The escape gave him a view of Duggan astraddle Ease, slamming the young bartender in the face with punches as he tried to cover up. Firing again, Gillom executed Ease's attacker with one bullet to the back of his head. The two shot men went down heavily, bodies collapsing, the reports echoing up Tombstone Canyon.

The bank guard was then slammed against the wooden railing so hard he could hear a couple ribs crunch. He reached toward his new attacker with his right arm and revolver, but William Pascoe stepped outside his stretched arm to snatch his right wrist with his right hand, thumb down and palm facing Gillom. William jumped forward and chopped hard with his left hand to make Gillom bend his elbow. The wrestler snaked his left arm on top of Gillom's forearm, between his forearm and biceps. Reaching under his own right hand William grabbed his own right wrist with his left hand, forming his arms into a shape like the number four. Snapping the right arm down quickly, he drove Gillom to the platform with this move, yelling in pain, *"Owwwww!"*

A figure four armlock is a restraint and control hold and could have broken Gillom's arm, except William forgot the kid's two guns. Gillom dropped his Remington as his right arm was about to break, but got his left hand working and pulled his other six-gun, cocking and snap-shooting a .44 slug into William's right thigh from up close. Now it was the wrestler yowling as he crumbled, releasing Gillom's bent arm.

It was hard to see in the darkness in this ringed open space with bodies banging about, anguished cries, flashes of gunpowder, and the scent of blood. Ease Bixler rolled out from under the dead man who had collapsed atop him. Bleeding from his nose, Ease managed to get his borrowed Colt from his coat pocket. Frankie, meanwhile, holding his stomach wound with his left hand, got his pistol out from under his waistband with his right. Braced against a corner post, the mugger aimed at Ease sitting across the platform with his pistol pointed, too. Both gunmen pulled their triggers simultaneously, muzzle flashes brightening the night for a long second. Younger Bixler was the better shot, finishing Frankie off with a bullet to the throat, severing his jugular in a burst of blood. Ease took a bullet in his upraised calf.

"Yowww!" The bartender grabbed his wounded leg as Gillom staggered, watching wounded William fling himself over the railing and then slide down the weed-thick hill, limping off into the darkness, no match for Gillom's two guns.

"*Ease!* You gonna make it?"

"Shot my leg." Ease wiped his bloody nose on a sleeve, so the red smear on his face matched his sideburns. Dogs were barking furiously, doors were opening, and lamps held high to see what in God's name was going on outside? The gunfire came from nearby, so the hillside's residents knew this shoot-out wasn't some drunken cowboys downtown on a toot.

"My ribs are stove in," groaned Gillom as he gingerly felt round his aching chest. He moved near Frankie and noticed the assassin's trigger finger still twitching convulsively.

"I gotta get that bastard, Ease. He's wounded and he won't give us any chance next time." Gillom looked at the two miners seeping dark blood, dead from shots to their heads. "Somebody will help you down to a doc. I'll be there later myself."

"God's grace on you, Gillom. Don't let that Cornishman gitcha, or I'm all alone with that sonofabitch Goose."

Then Gillom Rogers was gone, stepping gingerly down the long stairway, pearl-handled .44 in his left hand for balance as he rotated his right arm back and forth, trying to work out the ache. For the first time in his young life, he was on a vengeance trail.

Gillom could hear his prey sliding clumsily down the mountainside when he stopped clomping down the stairway to catch his breath and reload. *Must be close to midnight,* he thought, *and it's Thursday, so fewer miners will be out carousing.*

When he reached the bottom of Youngblood Hill Gillom listened again and could make out a limping gait heading toward town, where the dirt road turned into the bricks of Main Street.

Passing store windows lit by electric lights, Gillom could see who he thought was William Pascoe, limping due to his leg wound. The man crossed the tracks of the railroad spur running south from Bisbee proper and limped along beside another short track laid uphill into the Copper Queen's smelter works, not far from their original glory hole shaft. *He can't go to the hospital,* Gillom surmised. *He'd be recognized and reported with a bullet wound, then connected to tonight's shooting. Maybe he's looking for his miner buddies to treat and hide him? Gotta be careful up there. I don't have any friends yet who dig copper.*

Gillom followed as fast as his aching body would allow, stalking in the storefronts' shadows until he had to move out in the open on the train track up Sacramento Hill to the vast Copper Queen diggings.

The Cornishman hadn't stopped to scout his trail, unconcerned that anyone was able to follow him after this evening's bad confrontation, which had left all five combatants wounded, dead, or banged up. William limped inside the nearest of the big tin-sided buildings as his pursuer walked through the mine's entrance and then slipped back into the same building's night shadows. Gillom entered the southwest's biggest mining operation, which was easy to do, since hundreds of miners came and went on three different shifts without being checked, twenty-four hours a day, only Sundays off.

The steely teenager was determined. *This thug has to be stopped. This miner has beaten me up twice now*

*and a third fight will surely end kill or be killed. Maybe
I can get the drop on this wrestler, turn William in for
attempted murder, but I doubt it. This Cornishman is
too slick. He'd escape the law's grasp just as easily as
he can break an arm hold in an unfair fight.*

Gillom was blinded by bright electric lighting and a
deep thrumming of heavy machinery inside the building. Farther in he saw William bent over a long wooden
bench in front of a wallside of multiple hooks on which
hung cleaner clothing the miners changed back into
after their end-of-shift showers. The thug's back was
to him and he was rummaging in a white wooden box
with a red cross. His wool pants were loosened about
his knees and his hands held a bandage and a bottle of
antiseptic.

"Cousin Jack!" William froze, turned to see Gillom.
He put the medicine bottle down. "You need to see
Sheriff White. Or hear the music of my .44's."

"The hell with you," growled the wiry man, not
quite so fearsome with his pants down. From his suit
coat pocket appeared a derringer, just as Gillom aimed
his revolver. William's specialty wasn't guns and his
short-barreled shot missed. But he immediately dove
to the floor, overturning the oak bench. The kid's bullets splintered thick wood. Behind the bench, the miner
hastily splashed astringent over his wound and grunted
loudly as he wrapped his bloody thigh tight with a
bandage.

Gillom retreated around a wall corner, knelt, and
peeked around it to pepper the overturned bench with
a couple closer shots. Behind it, William had his pants
back up. Digging into his other coat pocket, he pulled

out a round tin container and from it a blasting cap crimped around a fuse. This thin metal spike of primer explosive was supposed to be inserted into a stick of dynamite to ignite it after a time delay and blow rock apart in the mines.

Gillom could hear a hissing, and after a long moment something burning came sailing over the bench in his direction. *What in hell?*

The detonator's explosion reverberated in the high-roofed tin shed, generating more dust than damage in the changing room, but the surprise and shock to Gillom's ear drums allowed the tricky Cornishman to scoot. Some of Gillom's top hair was burned, he could smell it, and one eyebrow was scorched. He peeked around the corner again to see William limp out a side exit.

The teenaged gunman hurried after him and outside saw William limping into the Copper Queen's biggest building, their third smelter. This building was open on one side and men were working inside. The thrumming of air blowers inside this big smelter made hot work only slightly cooler. Smelter workers kept the molten copper flowing, so they paid little attention to William limping past them and stopping behind one of the huge Bessemer converters. But when Gillom followed the bodyguard, Remington in one hand and holding his aching ribcage with his other, they looked up from their dangerous work.

He couldn't hear a fuse hissing again, what with all the noise of the copper processing, when another lit blasting cap came flying at him. Gillom hit the dirt, but the surprised smeltermen did not and the nearest was knocked down by the detonator's blast. Before the assassin could light another, Gillom was back on his feet, running and firing both revolvers as he rounded the big iron converter with its red-hot copper cooking inside.

The frontal assault surprised the Cornishman, six-guns blazing at him, one shot hitting him in the chest, another in the groin. As he went down, the escape artist fired a last shot from his hideout gun, clipping Gillom's coat shoulder high. The impact didn't slow the kid's steps as he skidded to a stop next to this thug who'd twice tried to kill him this grim night. No hesitation, either, as he repaid the favor. Gillom Rogers bent over his fallen foe, put his .44 right into William Pascoe's hairline, the same way he'd done John Bernard Books.

"Say your prayers."

"See you in Hades, you sonofabitch, or some other seaport," groaned the bodyguard as he spit up blood.

"Fair journey then. And better luck." *Click.*

Somebody from the smelter crew snuck up behind Gillom as his final gunshot echoed and put his lights out with a two-by-four to the back of his brain pan.

Through a dark mist, Gillom was vaguely aware of a bell ringing as he was carted down Sacramento Hill, going somewhere? Two slow bells, which in miner's terms, rang when someone died on the job.

Thirty-three

When he awoke again, Gillom had a bandaged goose egg on the back of his skull. The chunk of wood somebody had brained him with had broken his scalp, so the cut had been sewn up while he was knocked out. The teenager squirmed as he rose in bed.

"*Awww.* . . . Head aches."

"Easy, son. You took a good blow to the bean. Rest and water and your headache will gradually go away. No alcohol, though, until we see how you do." This opinion came from a slim, bearded man sitting on the next bed over, sewing up Ease's wounded leg. Dr. Frederick Sweet was the mining company's doctor.

"Least you don't have a hole in you," his buddy offered.

"You gonna walk, Ease? Still chase girls?"

"Just can't catch 'em for a while. Doc here says the bullet went right through my calf, didn't break any bones. *Ouch!*" The bartender twitched as the nurse assisting dabbed astringent on his bare calf the doctor was stitching, to staunch the bleeding.

Gillom was concerned. "You see the sheriff?"

"No, but a deputy came about the gunfire and helped me in here. Told him we were ambushed."

Gillom looked around. This hospital was Bisbee's first, located near the old Rucker Mine, about a half mile from Main Street. The facility had opened the year before and was a four-winged structure with a well-lit operating room. It was paid for by the Copper Queen Mining Company and its small staff hired by the same. Dr. Sweet no longer had to go to the patient's home and operate on their kitchen table.

"Ahhh. . . ." Gillom felt round his sides and ribcage through his unbuttoned shirt. "Couple ribs might be busted, Doc. Pains in my chest where I got slammed into a stair railing."

"I'll take a look." With scissors he clipped his last black stitch in Bixler's holed calf.

"There. Just walk easy, with a crutch or a cane for a while, so you don't tear these stitches open and start bleeding again."

The middle-aged surgeon polished the glass lenses of his metal-framed glasses on a shirtsleeve.

"Your employers probably aren't going to compensate you boys for late-night gunplay. Either of you have any money for your treatment today?"

Ease gave him a rueful smile. "Always heard 'M.D.' meant 'money down.'"

"I do, Doc. Work at the bank and have a savings account," replied Gillom.

"Fine. Pay my secretary on your way out. Now let's see these sore ribs."

Sheriff White arrived in a three-legged tear as Dr. Sweet was finishing applying liniment and wrapping long strips of bandages around Gillom's bruised ribs. The lawman was, as usual, in a bad mood.

"*Heeere's* these young gunslingers like to shoot up my town nights."

Ease spoke up. "It was an ambush, Sheriff. We got attacked just hikin' up Youngblood Hill to our homes."

"For what reason? Another stick-up?"

"No sir," answered Gillom. "I told their boss, Luther Goose, last night in the Senate, to leave my girlfriend alone. Those three thugs who surprised us work for Luther, as muscle."

"They also work as miners. William and Frankie, whatever their last names are. We don't know the third jasper yet. But you crack shots didn't have to shoot 'em dead."

"They knocked us down, Sheriff. Were beatin' on us in the dark. Hard to see what's suddenly going on up there," explained Ease.

"We were just defending ourselves, best we could," added Gillom.

The sheriff grew angrier. "Maybe at first, but then *you* stalked William all the way up to the mine. Copper Queen Consolidated doesn't appreciate having its miners gunned down on its own property. Upsets the workers and makes 'em concerned for their own safety."

"Hey, their worker was throwing blasting caps at me, could have blown away anybody up there!" Gillom slid off the bed and stood like a mummy in his underwear and wrapper. Sheriff White poked a stubby finger into his bandaged midsection.

"You're not understanding me, boy. Phelps Dodge is the most powerful company in this territory. And you're *fucking* with their mother lode! Arizona's trying to become a state. There's a United States Senator from Indiana, Senator Beveridge, who's filibustering Congress we're unfit for statehood, too primitive to join civilized society. So we *cannot* have shoot-outs in our best mines, in the middle of our nice town. Scares the workers. Scares *me*. And it's bad for business, which pays *all* our salaries." He gestured at the two *medicos,* listening intently to the sheriff's oration. "So I advise you to buy a trunk, kid, soon as my investigation's concluded."

His dander up, Gillom Rogers stood his shaky ground. "What about my girlfriend, Anel Romero? Luther Goose has been bothering her at the Red Light. She didn't want to go away with him. He's a damned *pimp*!"

"I'll check that. Dance halls pay a liquor license fee and the city council doesn't want their good business disrupted, either. But if this whole dispute is over just one painted cat, it has gotten way out of hand." The lawman put his hand down, stepped back from his threatening closeness. "Your family's known in these parts, Bixler, so you can still work at the Bonanza, if you stay out of more shootings. But *you*, El Paso, tie up your affairs and get the hell gone."

Sheriff White turned on a bootheel and stalked from the new hospital. The nurse assisted a glum Gillom into his pants and boots and guns so he could help Ease home. The bill for patching them both up came to twelve dollars, which Gillom paid since he'd gotten his pal into this trouble. Ease groused they were being overcharged for misbehaving.

As they wobbled out, the doctor stopped the young mankiller.

"You may have trouble breathing with those two bruised, maybe fractured ribs. Take a deep breath occasionally to get air way down in your lungs, even if it hurts. Use pain liniment on the site, or ice if you can get it, and keep your ribs bandaged. May take a couple of months to heal, but broken ribs come around. Lay off the whiskey and stay out of fights." The surgeon stared hard at both young men. "You'll live longer."

The lads lay low in their cottages over that weekend while the sheriff's investigation of their shootings continued. They snuck out after dark for their one meal a day, and went together for protection. They ate in out-of-the-way restaurants so as not to attract undue attention. Gillom and Ease were healing and went armed, but because of their stiff gaits and pained movements, neither would have been much of a match for anybody else in another fight.

Monday morning, Ease was moving well enough to attempt his day shift behind the bar in the Bonanza, since it would be a slower weekday. Gillom lathered on more Tiger Balm, a Chinese painkiller he'd picked up in the Bisbee Drug Store, mummified himself in fresh bandages, and headed off for work. He was there at 9:00 A.M., before the bank's doors opened at 10:00, but was immediately confronted by Mr. Cunningham.

"Pinkham wants to see you." Gillom didn't care for the gleam in the treasurer's eye.

Sumner Pinkham's office wasn't regal, but it was distinguished by several large wooden lamps with fancy laminated shades atop his big oak desk for night work. The young man noticed cut glassware and several bottles of vintage whiskey on a side table in a corner, evidently for night work, too. The boss wasted no time on formalities.

"Heard about your *contretemps* last Friday evening. How you feeling?"

"Better, sir. Lathered on Tiger Balm for a couple bruised ribs, but the doc says I'm serviceable."

"I can smell it. Self-defense again, was it?"

"Yes, sir." The president hadn't indicated a seat in one of the heavy oak chairs for customers, so Gillom stood. "Thugs ambushed me and my buddy in the dark near home, so we had to shoot it out. I'd warned their boss to stay away from my girlfriend, who's a customer of ours, by the way. This Luther Goose is a gambler, and I guess he didn't like me objectin' to him pressin' his affections where they weren't wanted. Those bodyguards worked for him."

"Those thugs were miners, Gillom. Heard about this mess over the weekend, when I was paid a visit by Ben Williams, Copper Queen's superintendent. They don't take kindly to their miners being shot on their property. Killings get the company unfortunate publicity. Your shoot-out is in the papers, and the Copper Queen at this moment has the reputation as an unsafe place to work."

"But I had to get that wrestler, or he'd have kept coming after me on Goose's orders. Bastard already banged me around once before, besides this ambush. Hell, he was throwing dynamite caps at me up there, trying to blow me up, hurt other miners on their night shift, too. I couldn't have turned him in to the sheriff in that predicament. That jasper wasn't going to be taken."

The bank's president nodded. "Well, I'm glad you came out of your scrap relatively unscathed. And that your girlfriend won't be bothered anymore. But you've become more trouble to me now than you're worth, Gillom. So I'm letting you go, with two weeks' severance, to help you move on. I'm sure your gun skills will be useful elsewhere. I'll even write a letter of recommendation. Shootist *extraordinare*!"

"Did the sheriff put you up to this?"

"I haven't spoken to Sheriff White."

"Well . . . it's not fair."

The bank officer was perturbed. "Fair? *Fair?* Phelps Dodge is our *biggest* customer! Their interests are *my* major concern."

"And my interests aren't."

"Wish you a safe journey, son. And better luck." This time Sumner Pinkham offered his hand to shake, but Gillom Rogers didn't take it. The insult raised a scowl on the banker's face. "Cunningham has your pay."

· · ·

Gillom didn't bother Ease at his workplace with this latest bad news as he climbed slowly up Brewery Gulch in the bright morning's light. His ribs ached as his sore chest rose and fell from the climb. His pockets and the hidden moneybelt on his holster were full of greenbacks and gold coins from closing out his bank account. But he wasn't worried about being accosted even in the dangerous red light district. Nobody was going to fool with young Gillom Rogers in Bisbee, not with his sudden reputation as a three-time killer in just two months! Not unless they worked for Mr. Goose.

The parrot didn't bother him approaching Jean's green-roofed cottage. The bird must have been sleeping off a raucous weekend itself. Red Jean greeted him in a housecoat, with curlers holding up her mass of auburn hair.

"*Gillom!* Your shoot-out's the talk of the tenderloin! You all right?"

"Coupla sore ribs, but I'm still walkin' and talkin'. Ease got shot in the leg, but it went clean through. He's already back behind the bar. But I lost my guard job at the bank."

"*No!* Why?"

"Two of Goose's thugs we shot were miners. Copper Queen's manager complained to my boss, and that mine does the biggest business at the bank, sooo . . ."

"So what will you do now?"

"Probably be movin' on. But I gotta talk to Anel first. Do you know where she lives? I don't know if I can make it up Chihuahua Hill with this chest pain. Hampers my breathin'."

"No, but I'll find out. We were busy at the Red Light this weekend, but I don't remember seeing her, now I think of it. Why don't you stop by there tonight?"

"Can't risk running into Goose again, Jean. Bastard's probably already hired more bodyguards."

"Don't recall seeing him after Friday night, either."

"Was he in then?"

"Yes. By himself. Drinking, dancing with Anel."

"They leave together?"

"I have no idea, young sir. Had my own business to attend to." The bar belle lowered her eyes.

Gillom chewed a lip. "Suppose he fled up to Clifton with her?"

Now Jean looked concerned. "Let me get dressed, pay a visit when I locate her lodgings, see if she's okay? I don't work tonight."

"If you can track her down, bring her along tonight to the Turf Saloon at eight. I'll get Ease, too. I'm hosting a farewell dinner."

"So quick?"

"Well, Anel's missing, and as of this morning I have no job here. When the sheriff starts making threats, I pay attention. Time to vamoose."

The dance hall queen managed a half smile. "Then I'll see you young foxes at dinner."

It was the bird who wished him a fond farewell from his perch up the scrub oak.

"*Adios, pendejo.*"

If he'd felt better about everything, Gillom might have grinned.

Thirty-four

He dropped by the Bonanza and tipped Ease off to the evening's dinner, asked him to pass the question about his missing girlfriend. He left out his imminent departure.

Gillom stopped by the post office to close his account, get any mail forwarded. There was a letter from his mother. He went back outside to sit on a bench with some aging loafers who liked to roost there daily, crankily commenting on the world passing by.

Gillom—How are you, dear? I am feeling better and busier. El Paso is booming and since the bad news about Mr. Books's tragic shoot-out has died down finally, new residents and job seekers are needing a nice place to stay. So our boarding house has filled up again and I'm able to pay off bills and even hire a Mexican girl to assist with housekeeping and in my kitchen.

You can have Mr. Books's room again downstairs,

if you'd like to come home. I think it's safe now. Marshal Thibido dropped by once, but I said you'd headed west for parts unknown. He seemed to accept that, good riddance. He didn't inquire about those pistols.

I miss you! If you returned you could sell those guns and have money to live on while you finished your last year of high school, look for a decent job. Something quiet behind a desk, please, instead of one involving dangerous weapons.

Your future awaits in El Paso, Gillom. Come home!

Your loving mother,

Bond

There was a little breeze blowing up the gulch that June day, moving the miasma of red-brown smelter smoke out of town, but Gillom's eyes watered anyway.

He puffed up the stairway on Youngblood Hill, noting the bloodstains on the wood landing where they'd killed men a few nights before. The two bodies had been undertaken.

Gillom huffed slowly across a weedy patch to his cottage to rest a few hours, but as he unlocked his door, an armed man suddenly stepped out from behind their outhouse uphill, a Winchester repeater held to his chest, port arms.

"Gillom Rogers?"

Gillom's hands immediately went to his pistols. "Who wants to know?"

"Got a message for you, kid."

"You from the sheriff? Come to arrest me?"

"No. Just a note." Guy was maybe 5'6", small-boned, but had an intense demeanor. He held out a square envelope. Gillom didn't pull his revolvers, but his left hand remained on his pistol butt as he took the note and removed the folded stationary with one hand. He read the warning, glancing up at the gun-man's rifle.

> Gillom Rogers! Be on the stage or train
> out of Bisbee by noon tomorrow, Tuesday.
> —The .45-.60

"Who wrote this?"

"The Committee of Safety. Named for our rifle cartridge loads."

"*Vigilantes.*"

"Call us what you like. But me or somebody else will be watching you, round the clock, till you're gone from Bisbee. By our deadline."

Gillom scratched a pimple he'd just found behind his ear. "This is *legal*? You're a deputy?"

"No, I'm not a deputy sheriff. But I *am* applying for the Arizona Rangers. Governor's organizing a detail of Rangers here right now."

"Hell, *I'd* like to join that bunch. I need a job."

The committeeman almost smiled. "Not on the best day of your life. You're already cutting your notches pretty deep, kid. At too young an age. Just leave Bisbee pronto and we'll let these bad killings pass."

Pursing his lips, the young gunman nodded. "All right. Tell Sheriff White to come see the Tombstone stage off tomorrow, wave me goodbye."

. . .

"I found her Mexican shack, Gillom, several rooms in a hovel up in Chihuahua Town. No running water or electric, just a bathtub and a woodstove, pretty primitive. Talked to Rosa, her roommate, waits tables at the Brewery. Anel hasn't been home for three days. All her stuff's still there, clothes, family photos, and Rosa doesn't know what happened to her. So she's going to report Anel missing to the sheriff tonight, like I advised." Red Jean finished her report.

"Could she have gone down to Mexico, family emergency?" asked Ease.

"Not without some clothes, traveling money, do you think?" They were sipping Veuve Clicquot, real French bubbly, at a table in Tony Downs's Turf Saloon, their favorite Bisbee haunt.

Ease Bixler shook his head. "You've got the sweetass on that girl bad, pard."

"Cupid *has* given me a couple jabs under the ribs with his dart." Gillom nodded. "But I'm afraid Luther Goose has kidnapped her, taken Anel up to his brothel in Clifton, against her will."

Red Jean played devil's advocate. "You don't think she might have gone up there on a whim, to check his saloon out?"

"Not without telling me or her roommate first. We're in love, Jean! Or we said we were. If she got offered better money, that's not a good enough excuse to fly the coop that quick." Gillom looked worried.

"So what do you aim to do?" asked his buddy.

"Take the stage up to Clifton, see if she's there."

"But, that's Goose's roost. He'll kill you if you try to take her back, if he so much as sights you again. You've burned his play in Bisbee now, and he'll want to get even. He can hire more shooters or wrestlers from the copper mines up there to put your lights out, pardner."

"I'm just gonna sneak into town, move around at night, see if I can spot her. Then spirit her out of Clifton, if she'll have me."

The darling of the demimonde frowned. "How romantic. And dangerous. Just like in a dime novel. Where would you flee to in the moonlight?"

Gillom sipped his champagne thoughtfully. "Oh, I guess back to El Paso. My mother wants me to come home, finish high school, get a good job, guarding if I have to, maybe join the Texas Rangers. Anel can find a better job, store clerking, but not dancing, I won't have that. My mother runs a boarding house. There's room for us there, till we both get working again."

"Boy, this is all very fast," worried Ease.

"*If* you find her in Clifton, bring her back down here. Give your love time to blossom," advised Jean.

Grimly, Gillom explained his new predicament. "I can't come back to Bisbee. Got a visit this afternoon from a member of the .45-.60. Said I had to be out of town by noon tomorrow. They've got an armed vigilante watching me outside here right now."

His two friends were stunned.

"The Safety Committee warned you out of town?" Ease sounded plaintive.

"I'm a marked man in Bisbee."

Ease shook his head again, dazed. "Can't let a couple killings disrupt their mining."

His friend reassured him. "I think you're okay, Ease. Your family's respected in southern Arizona, like the sheriff said. I'm the two-gun stranger they're worried about, who has to ride on."

"This ain't right," disagreed Jean.

"Or legal, either. It's just the mob's rules."

"They enforce them, too," agreed Ease. "Back in '83 during the Bisbee Massacre, the robbery of the Goldwater and Castaneda general store here, five innocent citizens were killed in that shoot-out. Our posse captured five robbers, several in Mexico, and the law tried and executed them all. The .45-.60 was formed after the head desperado, John Heath, was given a life sentence to Yuma Prison for planning the robbery. The Safety Committee didn't want to let him get away alive, so they pulled him out of jail one night over in Tombstone after sentencing, and strung him up there from a telephone pole. The .45-.60 are *very* serious citizens of ours."

They were silent after Ease's troubling local history. The waiter arrived with their meals to break the glum spell—pork chops, ribs, and a steak to help Ease replenish his blood.

"A toast," said Gillom. Three good friends raised their glasses. "To better times in different places." They drank champagne to that. "*And,* it's my birthday."

"Ohhh, happy birthday!" chortled the redheaded dancer.

"Congratulations! Which one?"

"I'm eighteen." The birthday boy smiled.

"Nearly legal, kid," beamed Jean. "You deserve cake."

"I'm amazed you made it this far," agreed Ease.

"I've grown up since hitting Bisbee. Feel like I'm making adult decisions now."

"This rescue ride doesn't sound like one of 'em. Awfully dangerous," disagreed Red Jean.

"I'll be in and out of Clifton before they know I've arrived. *If* she's up there."

Ease polished off his bubbly. "Well, good luck, pardner. Hope you make it to twenty."

Gillom said goodbye next morning to the landlady, Mrs. Blair. The graying seamstress stood on her porch watching, not waving, as an armed watchman appeared from up the hill to follow the young gunslinger down the long stairway from Youngblood Hill.

Gillom trudged down the Gulch's busy boardwalk a last time and back up Tombstone Canyon. He was winded from carrying his saddlebags and warbag full of accumulated gear. He hoped the man with the rifle following a discreet distance behind wouldn't be the only person to see him off.

At the O. K. Livery and Stable, the stage from Tombstone had arrived and teamsters were exchanging baggage, dumping mail in the boot, switching horse teams. Gillom bought his ticket, five dollars to ride a thirty-eight-mile loop south and then north round the Mule Mountains to the town "too tough to die."

Tombstone *was* slowly dying, though, with its nearby silver mines flooded and petering out, while copper mining was still booming in Bisbee's mountains.

Gillom slung his leather bags into the leather-sided rear boot of the Concord coach, but he was too restless to take a seat inside with the other passengers yet. So he climbed on a corral fence to wait, eyeing the watcher who was now resting against a fence pole, far end of the corral.

He saw her at a distance, trudging up the canyon road to the stable, long red hair tied up in a scarf, carrying something under a cloth. She wore men's blue jeans, brogans, and a very short-sleeved tunic which showed off the muscles in her arms and shoulders. *Good ol' Jean.* Gillom grinned. *At least someone's come to see me off.*

He eased gingerly down from the fence to greet his ladyfriend, his right arm and ribs still sore from last week's fight. "Jean, you look fetching this morning. Ready to work the mines."

She frowned at his joke. "Ease is working, but I'm on night shift so I don't have to dress up today. I thought someone should say fare thee well on your fool's errand." With a flourish she whipped off the linen covering two chocolate cupcakes on a small china plate. "I didn't have time to bake, so I picked these up at City Bakery. Happy day-late birthday."

"*Swell!* Send me off in style." They were all chocolate smiles as they gobbled the cupcakes in a few bites. Jean cleaned her fingers on the napkin while Gillom licked his.

"Make it to your next birthday, Gillom, okay?"

He nodded, not smiling now.

"Let me know if you find Anel. Post me a letter, care of the Red Light. I know you can't come back to Bisbee, at least for a while, but if you make it down to Tombstone, or Tucson, let us know. Ease and I will ride over to celebrate your survival."

"You bet I'll do that, young lady. You let me know, too, if Anel suddenly shows up here again. Mail my mother, Bond Rogers, in El Paso." He squeezed her hands, gave her cheek a kiss. A new driver climbed up on the coach's front seat while the liveryman checked harness on the anxious six-horse team.

"All aboard for Tombstone!"

Gillom opened the stage door to help another lady up in the coach. He swung up inside, latching the small door shut. "I'll absolutely be seein' you an' Ease again."

The driver whistled sharply, got six horses moving in a slow left turn inside the corral as the shifty stableman threw open the wooden gate and they were off, down the dirt road through town.

"Clear the road!" The coachman cracked his whip over the fresh horses' heads to pick up speed and put on a show for any watching townsfolk.

Sticking his head from the rear coach window, young Rogers saw only Jean waving goodbye. *To hell with Bisbee,* he groused. *There's friendlier towns to nest in.* Just for the hell of it, Gillom pointed at the vigilante from the Safety Committee and shot off his finger pistol.

Thirty-five

The stagecoach from Bisbee was nicknamed the "Sandy Bob," and its jolting six-hour journey involved two relay stops fifteen miles apart, where horses were changed and the passengers could use the outhouse or purchase a quick snack and a drink at a ranch. In between, Gillom tried to ignore the chatting ladies inside the coach and straighten out his own jumbled thoughts.

What will I do if Anel's not in Clifton? Sure can't go back to Bisbee. Guess I'll sell these collector guns first, return to El Paso, try to work things out with the sheriff, so I don't have to do more jail time. Maybe take a slower stagecoach back to west Texas, stay off the trains. Like to see Silver City in New Mexico. Hear that's a bustling burg.

Gillom pulled down the brim of his Stetson and closed his eyes, but the hoofbeats of the galloping horses and shocks to the leather thoroughbraces snapping support beneath the heavy Concord coach only allowed him to doze fitfully.

They reached Tombstone about suppertime, but Gillom didn't go sightseeing. Scott White was sheriff of all Cochise County and had too many confidantes in town. The youth didn't wish his presence noted. So he grabbed a meal of beans and biscuits and coffee during their hour layover. The twenty-mile run up to Benson on the "Modoc" was mostly men on business, so they could catch next morning's train out of Tucson headed east to El Paso. Since this night run was nonstop, the new driver handling the ribbons up top put the six horses into their collars, never allowing them to slow to less than a hard trot unless going uphill. Their fast pace through the night finally lulled Gillom and he dozed—remembering what J. B. Books had told him about the only time he'd ever been shot.

Full of laudanum a spring afternoon behind his mother's boardinghouse, Books had rested on the back stoop atop his red satin pillow like a potentate.

"I was wounded just once, Gillom, in a restaurant in Bisbee. Two butt-ins braced me at a monte table in the Free Coinage, fancy saloon up Brewery Gulch. I won't stand for an insult, but bartenders intervened and we three took our drinking elsewhere. I ran into those two loudmouths later, don't even know their names to this day. I was having a quiet supper around midnight at the English Kitchen when those two jaspers came in, still drunk, and their insults commenced again. Only this time they drew pistols to really bullyrag me, so I had to respond, chair against the wall, right over the bone china. I killed 'em both, several bullets in each—they dropped right inside the Kitchen's front entrance. It was a helluva noisy mess inside that little restaurant, diners diving for cover under the tables, linen pulled down, dishes flying, but they gave me no choice. Never know what a drunk will do."

Gillom Rogers was entranced. "And one of 'em plugged you?"

J. B. Books shook his head violently. "*No!* That was the crazy thing. It was some *other* thumbhead, a complete stranger who probably also had too much to drink. This joker lurched up from his meal, pulled his pistol while I was shooting the other two, drilled me right in the belly. I fell down. Stomach's a bad area to get shot in, because the shock to your nerves is immediate, paralyzes you from fighting back. Doc Hostetler was called and removed the bullet, which is why I rode in pain all the way down here to El Paso from Colorado to see him again, a doctor I trusted. I was lucky then to have a good doc patching me up. Lots of gunmen have bit the bullet from a stomach wound."

"What happened to the guy who shot you for no reason?"

"Never saw him again. After the mayhem that shooter just wandered off, picking his teeth after a full meal and not paying for it probably." The notorious gunman paused, troubled by the bad memory. "That's what makes gunplay so dangerous, Gillom. It's unpredictable. Too often, when weapons are pulled and working, it's some nobody, some butt-in with a secret compulsion to use a gun once in his piss-poor life on another human being or to die spectacularly, some six-fingered bastard who couldn't hit a cow in the teats with a tin cup when sober, who has the final say in the drama. I have no idea who that other sonofabitch was, but he was close and accurate enough to nearly kill me."

J. B. Books fixed his young worshipper with a solemn eye. "Yes, speed, aim, and deliberation are all critical in a gunfight, but you've also gotta have an awful lot of luck to live long as a shootist. It's not an occupation to aspire to, son."

Gillom Rogers woke in a cold sweat from his dream. Tipping back his silverbelly Stetson, he saw the other passengers across from him were dozing, too. The eighteen-year-old roused to pull aside the leather curtain next to his back seat. Outside, sagebrush and sand flashed by under a new moon and he shivered.

They arrived in Benson around midnight, so Gillom recovered his saddlebags and unlimbered stiff legs down to the train depot. He decided to save money instead of looking for a flophouse. He found an empty wooden bench outside near the end of the train platform, put his warbag up for a pillow, pulled his wool coat over on top of him, and gradually fell asleep.

So here I am exactly where I was four months ago, sleeping outdoors with no job and no good prospects. And even more bastards looking to snuff out my candle. What a life!

A wagon pulled up after dawn to drop off luggage and freight. Gillom opened an eye on dusty sunshine. He hit the washroom to splash water on his face and arm-pits. He was starving, so stashed his coat and bags in the freight office and hurried into Benson for a forti-fying breakfast of steak and eggs. Wasn't much to see, since Benson was a trans-shipment point for people and equipment and supplies moving south to the mines. Cattle, sheep, and horses were penned here, too, by Arizona ranchers, for shipping east in freight trains re-turning from the West Coast. The big dollar item was the tons of smelted copper coming up from Bisbee and soon Douglas, Arizona.

Gillom bought a two-dollar ticket to Bowie, the next depot east. The Tucson train wouldn't arrive un-til 10:00 A.M., so the young man spent time writing his mother. He wrote he was pleased her boarding-house was back in business. He missed Bond and his school pals and guessed he would return to El Paso in a few weeks when his affairs in Arizona were con-cluded, before school began again in the fall. Gillom kept his words to Bond Rogers enthusiastic and brief, neglecting to mention being out of a job, killing three more men and being run out of Bisbee. His mother was turning gray and had enough to worry about him already. Instead, he included a photograph of himself and Anel, saying he had a new girlfriend. But it wasn't the photo of them kissing. He wasn't quite sure how his mother would take to his dating a Mexican girl.

Gillom mailed his letter and caught the eastbound train. He was only hitching a ride on the Southern Pa-cific for a couple hours, sixty-odd miles, so he kept his bags with him in the second-class car and spent the time oiling his old brown leather holster and cleaning his .44 Remingtons, admiring again their balance, custom grips, and nickel-plated beauty. He deserved these precision weapons. He'd killed six men with these revolvers! Now J. B. Books's six-guns truly belonged to him.

His gun work caught the disapproving eye of a middle-aged woman seated across from him, as well as the fascinated attention of her young son. Gillom Rogers paid neither any mind. This might be the last chance to do his gun care on a stable surface before he reached Clifton. If there was to be a showdown with Luther Goose, he'd better be prepared.

As Gillom stood atop the train's steps at Bowie depot, he could see old Ft. Bowie up on a hill to the south, twelve miles away. He stepped down and walked toward a waiting Wells Fargo stagecoach. The teenager paid the driver, climbed aboard, and the six-horse team was soon rolling north up the trickling washes off San Simon Creek through the valley of the same name.

Gillom figured it would take them until evening, with two stops at relay stations to reach another town, Solomonville. He realized he'd be exhausted by the time he got to Clifton, so he pulled his Stetson down again. The two other men inside the stagecoach were excited, though, about riding into Apache country, as Gillom dozed.

Solomonville was another small dusty town with one Valley National Bank, the gateway to trading at the

San Carlos Apache reservation way to the northwest, or the booming copper mining country around Clifton and Morenci to the northeast. Gillom didn't need to see its limited sights, so he gobbled a restaurant dinner and retreated to bed in a tight room in Solomonville's only hotel. His ribs ached, his right arm still twinged, his butt was sprung, and his head was confused, full of worries. Somehow he fell asleep, but it wasn't restful.

Young Rogers rode another Wells Fargo stagecoach early next morning, heading up a valley along the Gila River, which ran down from Clifton's higher elevation forty-five miles northeast of Solomonville in the Gila Mountains. This toll road had no bridges or culverts, so was prone to washing out during storms as it ran alongside the Gila River. Gillom looked out his window at the Peloncillo Mountains to the south, but no rain clouds were to be seen.

Two relay station stops lay along this route, so the eighteen-year-old had more time to reflect on his two magic nights with Anel in his moonlit cottage, having sex during that deluge, the smell of her wet, naked body when she came back to bed from outside in the rain. Such thoughts aroused him. He prayed she wasn't a prostitute now, ensnared in Luther Goose's promiscuous web. He couldn't conceive she'd done that willingly, sold herself in a strange town, leaving all her clothes behind in Bisbee on a risky lark. But who could tell with young women, although Anel Romero hadn't struck him as flighty. *Not after she'd had the guts to pose as my silhouette girl!*

Hours later they hit another stage road as they made the left turn up to isolated Clifton, nestled between mountains twelve miles north. Gillom emerged from his dark thoughts to engage a rough-looking passenger seated across the coach wearing a tired flannel shirt and old denim jeans, who he thought might be a miner.

"Sir, what's the railroad out there?"

"That is the Arizona and New Mexico line. They're expanding it this summer to standard-gauge, three-foot rail. Arizona Copper, which owns the railroad line up in Clifton, will make two daily freight runs down to Lordsburg faster and cheaper with bigger trains soon. They make connections in Lordsburg with the Southern Pacific, to ship our smelted ore through El Paso to the east coast for more refining. Copper business is booming, boy. We'll set another production record this year, easy."

Gillom pointed out the coach door's little window. "What's that river there?"

"That's the San Francisco River, whose water we gotta have to keep our smelter furnace jackets cool, from all that heat refining our copper. Water's more drinkable north of town, for we've got salty hot springs around town and we dump our mine tailings in that river, too, so it doesn't taste so good down lower."

Out their stage window Gillom could see the approaching town nestled in a deep canyon walled in by rock and chalk bluffs, two to three hundred feet high.

The hillsides were gray and brown, treeless, austere, but the air was cooler, due to their increasing altitude.

"What are those two mountains?" he asked the gabby local.

The man craned around in his front seat, stuck his head out the side window for a good gander. "That's Clifton Peak to the north, and Mulligan Peak, another thousand feet higher, to its right. You obviously haven't been here before, kid, so I'll tell you Clifton's only got three streets, one each side of the river and another along Chase Creek, which has cable bridges across it." The miner pointed and Gillom stuck his head outside, too. "You can see one bridge up there. They wash out every spring melt. The Mexicans have burrowed into the hillsides along that lower creek, cheaper land, but they're the first to be washed out when our summer rains come."

Both men pulled their heads back inside for easier discussion. "Are there a lot of Mexicans in Clifton? There weren't that many in Bisbee."

"Yes, many of our miners are Mexican, but not the shift bosses, like me." The muscular roughneck snapped his suspenders with pride. "You from Bisbee?"

Gillom nodded. "Worked as a bank guard down there."

"Well, Bisbee's a white man's camp, more organized. Clifton's so remote, we have to go down to the Mexican mines in Sonora to recruit many of our copper diggers. The Mexes are hard workers, I'll give 'em that, and they get paid fairly equal. But they stick to themselves, got their own cantinas and cribs."

"What about Chinamen? Do they work the mines, too?"

"No sir. We won't let 'em undercut our wages. But celestials do own the laundries in Clifton and some restaurants, have their own tong societies and secret hop joints. They stick to themselves, too." The mine boss pointed out the window again at the acreage planted in vegetables the stagecoach was passing along either side of the dirt road.

"That is Metz's Flat. Chinamen rent this old stable-land to grow their vegetables they sell in town. Shannon Copper's just raising its new smelter down here, too, so we'll have three copper companies competing round these parts. Should keep wages decent. You lookin' for work, son?"

"No sir. Just up here visiting, looking for a friend."

"Don't like to get your hands dirty, uh?" The work-man grinned as he spit out the window.

Thirty-six

The Wells Fargo stage rolled into Clifton early afternoon. Gillom put his lightning-striped boot down from the coach and walked into yet another dusty Western town. He pulled his cowboy hat down low, hoping he wouldn't be recognized. He checked into the Clifton Hotel under another name, for all the good that would probably do him. Built in the 1880s and still the only hotel in town, the two-story frame building was notorious for its resident scorpions who had moved in during construction and still held regular dances there, nights. After washing off road dust, Gillom took a nap in his two-dollar-a-night room to catch up from his restless sleep in the stagecoach.

Gillom tried the chow mein at Jim Mammon's Chinese Café in South Clifton. The noodles and chopped vegetables had some stringy chicken in it, which he found quite tasty in its sour brown sauce. This establishment, run by a wealthy young Chinese who owned several restaurants in town, was recommended by the hotel clerk. Inside, booths ran along a long hallway. Each booth had heavy curtains that were never open while eating, after an old Chinese custom offering complete privacy to a man who might be entertaining a paramour. The restaurant was perfect for Gillom, who didn't wish his presence known in this rough town. His waiter, an Oriental of indeterminate age in wide-legged blue pants and tunic, didn't have many customers to serve early, but he didn't seem overly friendly to this young white man, either. *Just like they say, inscrutable,* Gillom thought. But as he paid his cheap bill, he tried conversation.

"Mister, I'm sore from my last few days riding stage-coaches. Can you recommend a bathhouse where I can soak my weary bones?" The teenager wasn't certain he'd been understood, as the Chinaman stood next to the table stroking his long braided hair.

"No bath, no. Laundry?"

"No. I need a hot bath." Gillom held his back. "Sore bones."

"Ah. River. Hot." The waiter pointed vaguely north, uptown.

"Hot springs? In the river?"

The Chinaman nodded, took his money and dirty dishes away. Gillom left him a good tip, hoping to strike up a friendship later.

The scrawny desk clerk in the hotel confirmed. "Yeah, there's hot springs along the river on Potter's Ranch, little over a mile north of town. Take a towel and bathing attire, or go bare as you dare. Mineral water's free, but don't drink it, not pure. Never know who you'll run into at those springs after dark. Parties been known to get a little wild, late nights." The clerk grinned. "Just what I've heard."

"Thanks for the advice."

Gotta get these bent ribs healing faster, Gillom decided, *after banging around in stagecoaches these past three days.* So he took a towel and soap from his room, exited the hotel, and stopped in a saloon to order a bottle. The bar's business was just starting to pick up as the day shift from the mines got off work, so the youth got his whiskey without being bothered about his age. With his hat pulled down and towel tucked under his arm, he set off north up the main street of Clifton along the west side of the river, trying to disappear into the crowd. He noticed the street was dirty, empty cans, and rubbish around, for this town evidently had no sewers or trash collection. He wanted to get to the springs about dusk so he wouldn't have to bumble around in the dark without a light, trying to find a bathing spot.

As he hiked the dirt road north toward the mines higher up in Morenci, Gillom wondered how this river got its name, San Francisco? It couldn't run across this wild territory all the way from that major city in northern California?

Two boys were using slingshots made of y-shaped pieces of wood with rubber innertube attached to rocket small stones across the river from its east side, trying to hit the tin roofs of houses in North Clifton, the best residential area. The boys didn't shoot at him when Gillom approached what looked like an old wooden ranch house back among the trees, away from the riverbank. Several rock pools were spaced alongside the river thirty yards or so apart and he could see wisps of steam rising from the biggest of them. Gillom sat and began pulling off his boots and dirty socks. He was careful to keep his holstered guns within reach as he removed shirt and pants, but kept his long johns on for decency's sake.

"You youngsters git on home, or your mothers will paddle you for being late for supper!" Two heads jerked up like otters' in his direction, and then realizing he was right, the youths scampered off toward town. As darkness fell, Gillom had the springs to himself, some peace and quiet at last, after several long, confusing weeks. He stuck his foot in the water, agitating more steam and bubbles from the bottom.

"*Ahhhh. . . .*" A sigh bubbled up from deep within as he levered his body into the mineralized waters. It was warm, not too hot, just the right temperature to take some of the ache out of his sore muscles, if not his heart. He tasted a drop and found it salty. *Gosh this feels good, just what the doctor ordered.* He smiled. This water north of town looked fresher, cleaner, for slag from the Arizona Copper Company was granulated and dumped next to their smelter. Gillom had seen it massed along the riverbank in Clifton, leaving the river water there dirty. He gave the underwear on him a good soaping, trying to cleanse his body and socks along with his mind.

Lights were coming on in town, the amber glow of coal oil lamps and some that looked to be brighter electric. The electric age had reached even remote Clifton. Then, a whistling in the night. *Someone's coming!* It was an old cow tune about Texas he vaguely recognized. A tall man in a cowboy hat he could barely make out against the darker backdrop of the town's mountains wandered up.

"Mind if I join you in the spring, pardner?"

"Nope." Gillom put the soap down and rested his free left hand next to a holstered Remington. He still wore his big hat, so he might go unidentified.

"Long ride up from Silver City, where they celebrated these hot springs."

"Good for saddle sores," Gillom agreed.

"Yep. I became fond of hot springs breaking horses over in New Mexico, up in the mountains."

Gillom squinted in the gathering darkness, trying to make out the stranger's face.

"Which mountains?"

"San Andres. Little horse ranch up top run by a compadre. Pretty country up there."

"*Sam Graham!* Thought I recognized your voice!"

Graham was partially undressed but he hesitated, naturally cautious due to his popularity with law enforcement. "Who?"

"Gillom Rogers, you *bandido*!"

"Gillom! You young sonofagun, still kickin'!" Sam Graham splashed into the hot pool in his long johns, gave the teenager a wet *abrazo*.

"What the hell you doin' up here, Sam? Thought you were headed back to Texas?"

Blackjack's older brother settled down into the hot spring up to his neck.

"Kid, I told everybody where I was *really* goin', I'd a-been bushwhacked long ago for the reward money on me. So I usually tell 'em someplace, then head the opposite direction. Thought you went to Bisbee?"

Gillom uncorked his whiskey bottle and took a sharp swallow. "Knew I brought this bottle along to celebrate somethin'." He passed it over to his outlaw friend. "I *was* in Bisbee. But a pal and I got into a gunfight and killed some jaspers who ambushed us one night. Couple of 'em were miners, and that caused me to get run out of town by the .45-.60, their Safety Committee. Had a nice job, too, guardin' their bank, and was makin' a name for myself around town." The teenager removed his hat and even in the dark Sam could see he looked peaked.

"*Vigilantes! Sonsabitches!* Those .45-60's just do the copper companies' bidding, beating and killing and running any folks they don't like right out of their tight-assed town, to hell with any laws to the contrary. They're notorious across the West."

"But *you* recommended Bisbee to me, Sam."

"Well, you wanted an honest job and Bisbee *is* boomin'. Gene Rhodes didn't want you ridin' the outlaw trail with me. You heard him chew me out, Gillom, and I don't cross my friend, Gene. But I didn't tell you to go shoot anybody there." The tall Texan took another big swallow and passed the bottle back.

"How is Gene?"

"Feistier'n a snared bobcat. We busted a last cavvy of green broncs and drove 'em down to the Bar Cross for summer roundup after you left, and I branded their cows a couple weeks, which I don't like doin' much, jus' for travelin' money. Then I drifted west, Lordsburg, up to Silver City, lookin' for employment." Even in the moonlight, Gillom could see the outlaw wink. "Gene's back down in Tularosa, cuddling wife and new baby."

"Boy or girl?"

Graham shook his head, spread his hands wide, full of no answer. "Jus' know they welcomed one."

"What brings you to Clifton, Sam?"

"Oh, this is reputed to be some wild place, so I had to see it. Lotta money runs through these eastside saloons from these miners. Kid Louis and his strong-armed band of rustlers used to rule this remote mining district. They got a few Laws in Clifton and Morenci, but they ain't as effective as Bisbee's. No vigilantes up here."

"Glad to hear that. I noticed nearly everyone's packin' a pistol. I came up lookin' for my girlfriend. She's a cute Mex, Anel Romero. Met her dancin' in the Red Light Saloon. She doesn't even know I got fired from the bank; she just disappeared on a Friday night one week ago. Left all her clothes behind in Bisbee, no word for me or her roommate. I'm afraid she might have been kidnapped by a pimp up here, Luther Goose. He runs a whorehouse, the Blue Goose. Bastard was leaning on Anel to come work for him, probably not dancin'."

"So why don't you go there tonight, see if she's in?"

"Those three guys we shot in Bisbee were his body-guards, following his orders to kill us. Luther Goose had me roughed up twice and I ain't laid a finger on him. Those jaspers were wrestlers, bruised a few ribs, wrenched my arm. That's what I'm doin' in these hot springs, tryin' to heal up."

Sam Graham seemed to soften, his blue eyes almost melancholy in the moonlight.

"Wasn't that just the best place, those hot springs on Gene's ranch? Only thing we had to worry about up in those mountains was getting' bucked off."

"Sure was. Gunfighter trainin' with you, Sam, an' listening to Mister Rhodes's wisdom. Like going to school."

The older outlaw nodded. "What do you aim to do about this gal then, whether or not she's now in the soiled sisterhood?"

"Well, just got into town today on the stage. Stayin' at the hotel. Thought I'd ask some questions, quietly, keep my head down. Don't dare go into the Blue Goose. Minute Luther spots me, he'll try to gun me again. I saw him brace a crooked faro dealer in the Bonanza in Bisbee, where my buddy bartended. Goose is one mean, loudmouthed pimp."

Sam Graham stared at his young friend a long moment, took another philosophical sip of cheap whiskey. "How many men you killed now, Gillom?"

"Uh, let's see. . . . Six."

"Whaddya think about that?"

"Well, J. B. Books said he never killed anyone who didn't deserve it, and that's my feelin', too. Just defendin' myself from some bad sonsaguns who were tryin' to make me bleed. Gunfightin' sure is excitin', Sam, but not very pleasant business. Killin' isn't somethin' I want to make a livin' off doin'. Mister Books warned me not to expect a long life if I did much of it."

"He was right. Most of us robbers and *pistoleros* harbor some kind of death wish. Got to or we wouldn't keep at it, for it ain't easy work. How old are you?"

"Just turned eighteen."

"Umm . . . well, you're no longer some green gun kid, that's for sure. What'd you finally name your two Remingtons?"

"I didn't. Just a foolish whim."

The outlaw nodded, took another sip. Gillom realized he wasn't getting his money's worth out of his whiskey, for Sam was drinking most of it.

"This girl, she really worth causin' more bloodlettin' death for, *if* you can find her?"

There was no hesitation. "You bet. We decided pretty quick we were in love."

Sam Graham raised his borrowed bottle to his young pal. "Then to *love*, wherever her pretty ass may be."

Gillom walked Sam back to the Clifton Hotel, up the back stairs to his room so they could look at photographs of Anel he'd paid for in Bisbee. He even showed him the picture of them kissing, which the outlaw appreciated. Sam was saving money by brush camping until he got better acquainted with this tough town, nearly hidden between these wild, mineral-laden mountains. Gillom's sore ribs felt better after their soak, but he still needed a good night's rest after his long travels. He offered to buy his outlaw friend breakfast tomorrow and they parted on their first night together again with a strong handshake.

· · ·

Gillom met Sam Graham over a late breakfast in Jim Mammon's Chinese Café. He liked its curtained booths, so nosy people couldn't watch you eat or overhear what you were talking about. Breakfast was standard American, eggs or pancakes, nothing Chinese-flavored.

"Didn't spot her in the Blue Goose last night, Gillom, or a couple other saloons thought I should check. 'Course I wasn't flashin' her picture around you gave me, or mentioning Anel's name. No sense warning this bad hombre you're searchin'."

"I'll put word out, quietly, if I'm gonna get anywhere tracking her. I shouldn't be seen around town with you, Sam. You're my undercover man."

"Where will we meet up, to exchange news?"

"Hot springs again, dusk. My ribs are still achin', so I can use a hot soak every day."

"Me, too," agreed the outlaw. "Whaddya gonna do today, kid?"

"I need a haircut, and more pain liniment. I'll show her photograph to the druggist and the barber. They have lots of customers. I'll stay out of the saloons, better lie low. Don't want to get shot in the back in broad daylight, just walkin' around."

Sam grinned. "Me, either. I gotta buy some clothes, get these dirty ones cleaned. Then I'll be out in the brush, nappin'. Had a late night." He winked and Gillom smiled for the second time since he'd run into his outlaw pal again. He couldn't quite believe it, having breakfast in public with a very wanted man.

"Breakfast's on me. Thanks for your help, Sam. I probably couldn't find her without you. You leave first, so I can talk to this waiter."

The handsome outlaw nodded and got up to part the velvet curtains for a peek. "Dusk. Hot springs."

Gillom took the time to get his Chinese waiter's name, Young Ah Gin. He showed him Anel's photograph.

"Sorry. No see."

It was the same at the avenue barbershop where he got his long blond hair cut shorter, even indulged in his first professional shave, had his sparse mustache trimmed. His skin felt good, clean, and the tonic Mr. Springer slapped on his face woke him fully up. No, the barber hadn't seen anyone who looked like Anel. But he only served men. Mexican women, he didn't pay much attention to.

Gillom bought more Tiger Balm at the apothecary's for his sore ribs, then slipped into the back hall to rub it on under his shirt. Its sharp odor clashed with his bracing face tonic, so anyone could really smell him coming. A bottle on a back shelf caught his eye, Casonet's Candy Cathartic. TRAIN YOUR BOWELS TO DO RIGHT! the label shouted. "Constipation leads to lethargic liver and eventually, Bright's Disease," it warned. *Whatever that was?*

Maybe that's my problem, Gillom thought. *My bowels are tied up from riding these stagecoaches. Everything's bottled up inside me, and it's going to make me crazy if I don't calm down.* The druggist agreed a good laxative never hurt, so the teenager bought a small bottle and chewed a candy. The young, bespectacled druggist shook his head looking at Anel's picture. She wasn't a customer.

Gillom was smart: he decided to rest in his hotel room that afternoon, where he wasn't far from the lavatory, right down the hall.

Thirty-seven

"Reverend New!" **Bond Rogers** greeted her pastor as he came out of the Fair dry goods store in downtown El Paso with a wrapped bundle under his arm. The widow crossed the dirt street, pausing until one of the city's street trolleys passed, pulled by Mandy the mule.

"Missus Rogers. Nice to see you, dear. Another hot day, is it not?" He mopped his brow with a handerchief. "Feels like I'm being punished for my sins."

"Yes," she agreed. "We are summering in Hell."

The Reverend smiled in spite of his rectitude. "Let's hope not."

"I just heard from Gillom. He wrote to say he was heading home soon, when his affairs in Arizona are tied up. He missed his young friends and hoped to be back here before school starts in the fall."

"Capital! *If* they let him back in Central School. Has he shot anybody yet?"

Bond Rogers was taken aback. "I don't think so. Gillom's working in Bisbee as a bank guard."

The parson placed a finger to his pursed lips. "Ahhh. Bank guard. So he found those missing guns, Books's revolvers?"

The mention of those unlucky guns again flustered Bond. "I don't know. Gillom must have gotten a gun to guard a bank, but certainly nothing to go to jail in Bisbee for."

Reverend New favored her with a righteous smile. "For God shall bring every work into judgment with every secret thing, whether it be good or whether it be evil."

Gillom's mother frowned and turned away, not even wishing her pastor a good day.

"When he returns, Missus Rogers, remember, spare not the rod from the wayward evildoer! See Marshal Thibido if you need help!"

Another quirk about this mining town crammed into a canyon was its lack of sunlight. Gillom noticed the surrounding mountains of the Gila Range cut off its sun for many hours, so Clifton got fewer hours of daylight even during longer summer days. Almost half a normal day this tough town rested in shade, which was perhaps symbolic of its violent reputation, which he'd heard about. For throughout the 1890s, a corpse a day was often pulled out of this bullet-riddled canyon.

Unlike in Bisbee, the sixty-five Chinese in Clifton were allowed to reside in town and they stuck together for safety, most residing in shanty houses pitched together on the riverbank. Their real socializing, tong meetings, and pleasurable interludes took place in a network of caves and tunnels the celestials had dug underneath their houses, where they were wont to retire evenings for a peaceful pipeful. Fat Choy, who'd gotten his name from a Chinese New Year's greeting—"*Gung hoy fat choy*," or "Good fortune"—was indeed fat and jolly to the white citizens who knew him, but his real good fortune came from running the biggest opium den in town.

His stonewalled basement was reached via a trap door and stairwell under Fat Choy's otherwise unimpressive house by the river. It was there Young Ah Gin hurried after his breakfast shift at the Chinese Café. The waiter was an irregular opium smoker. He couldn't afford to indulge much on his tips from Mammon's restaurant. But he knew the elderly Chinese lookout on the back porch of Choy's house and thus had no difficulty entering and pulling aside the oriental rug in the kitchen, knocking three times, and then raising the trap door in the wooden floor and descending into heaven, or perhaps hell if you smoked too much.

Little kerosene lamps lit the smoky gloom of the den he climbed into down the stairs. It wasn't fancy, some cheap rugs on the dirt floor, greetings inked in Chinese characters on rice paper banners stuck to several walls. The proprietor greeted him at the bottom. Mr. Fat Choy wore a mauve satin tunic accented with gold braid, too flashy for street wear and unusual for him in the daytime. Most of his regulars smoked nights, after a hard day's work. Ah Gin could see only one Chinese smoker reclining on a bamboo mat on one of the board beds propped two feet off the floor, against the stone wall. The dope fiend was lighting a stained bamboo pipe by moving a small lamp wick under the small porcelain bowl near the end of the pipe to heat a bead of refined opium held in the bowl by a needle. The little gumlike ball of opium bubbled from the heat. The Chinaman took a deep draw on the pipe's metal tip and motioned Ah Gin to join him. The waiter shook his head, but he could smell the pungent black smoke in the damp room. Smoke issued from the fiend's nose and seemingly, even his ears. Relaxed, the *yen shee* man lay the pipe down and put his head back on a wooden block that served as a headrest, as he drifted off again to an exotic dreamland.

Always ready for business, Fat Choy asked his customer if he wished a pipe?

"Not now," was the waiter's answer. "Is woman here?"

"Which one?"

"Mexican girl."

The proprietor gestured toward a beaded curtain covering a doorway to a smaller room.

"She not ready yet for customer."

"Somebody looking. Young man show me picture today, in restaurant. Eat Chinee dinner last night, too. Never see before."

"He say why so?"

"No. Only want find her. Girl-friend may-be? Not family. He white. Carry two gun."

Fat Choy patted his customer on the shoulder. "Thankee. Next time, smoke free."

Young Ah Gin grinned.

Gillom walked downstairs refreshed from his long nap, his bowels certainly cleansed. He nodded to the desk clerk and strode through the short lobby to the front door, when who should appear from the street but his best friend from Bisbee.

"*Ease!* What in hell you doin' up here?"

The road-weary barman grinned as they shook hands. "Came up to check on my buddy's health. Manny at the Bonanza gave me more time off to heal this calf. Wound was paining me standing behind the bar all day. Now I'm a known gunslinger, boss wants me to help keep order in his saloon. See, even bought my own pistol."

He showed Gillom a Colt .41 Thunderer contained in an open-front Lightning Spring shoulder holster under his coat. "Just have to practice my fast-draw and learn a few spins and I'll be as fancy as you, amigo."

"Good. I've got just the spot to heal you up, pal. Local hot springs. Let's put up your luggage and grab another towel. I was just on my way out there to soak my bent ribs."

In short order they were walking along the board-walk up Conglomerate Avenue, the town's only street on the east side, soap in their pockets and both carrying towels. Gillom moved a hand around under his longsleeved cotton shirt. It was too warm for his wool coat, and he noticed moisture as he checked his sore chest. *Sweatin'. Must be nerves,* he figured.

"Feels dangerous in this town, Ease. Clifton's got a long reputation for violence and its few Laws evidently look the other way. Everybody here knows everybody else, and the few I've asked haven't seen Anel. Haven't run into Luther Goose yet. Not sure he even knows I've arrived."

"If he doesn't, he soon will. Might as well finish it here, Gillom, cook this Goose. So he doesn't have someone come stalking me again after work, when I'm alone in Bisbee."

The young men paused to check the display windows in the Arizona Copper Company's store, dry goods and sundries for miners on credit. Gillom looked down the street and across it to the two-story Blue Goose Saloon, where he saw a large Chinaman in a navy blue tunic waddling into the entrance. No batwing doors outside that fancy-looking establishment. Conglomerate Avenue was the business center of Clifton and also its saloon row.

"Gotta get us somethin' to drink." Gillom popped into Hovey's Saloon next door, which from the crowd inside he took to be the town's social center, full of workers eager to cut the smelter smoke from their throats at the end of another hard day in the mines. He came back out wrapping three pints of whiskey up in his bath towel.

"I could use somethin' to drink with hair on it, but *three* bottles?" Ease inquired.

"Want you to meet somebody." They limped on, or Ease did with his leg wound, heading north toward the residential end of town. "Can't tell you how much I appreciate you showin' up to help me, Ease. This rani-caboo is gonna be over pretty quick. Anel's either here or she ain't. I don't need to get into a gunfight just to learn that."

"Me, neither. But I've been lookin' for a reason to see this lonely part of Arizona." He slapped Gillom on the back. "I guess what Doc Holliday said to Wyatt Earp before that little fuss over in Tombstone applies."

"What was that?"

"Pardner, I will back your play." Laughing, the two injured youths ankled off into a dying day.

Thirty-eight

Fat Choy tasted trepidation entering Luther Goose's back office. Luther had his pointy kid leather boots up on his desk as he chewed a silver toothpick. Mr. Goose was the owner of the fanciest cathouse in the eastern side of Arizona Territory and ran a temper to match that entitled roost. So the Chinese boss made sure to bow low as he was ushered into the sparsely furnished office by one of Goose's honchos. Luther did not get up to greet his guest.

"Mister Choy. What can I do for you?"

"This girl, Mexican. Somebody look for her."

"Oh? Someone bothering you?" The brothel owner put down his boots, sat up.

"Young man ask waiter at Mammon's, show picture."

Mr. Goose stopped picking his teeth. "When was this?"

"Breakfast. This morning."

"And he came to your house?"

"No. Waiter tell me. Young Ah Gin, customer of me."

"I see." Luther Goose stood up. "How's the girl?"

"Sleepy. Want me give more?" He pantomimed giving a shot.

"*No.* No more injections. We'll move her here, after dark. Don't know if she's ready to take on customers, but she can smoke that dope here. Send a pipe and kit along."

The saloon owner reached into his pocket and pulled out a double eagle, a twenty-dollar gold piece, slapped it in Fat Choy's hand.

"Thank you, Mister Choy. Come Chinese New Year, let me know if you'd like anyone special."

Realizing the meeting was already over, the Chinaman bowed again and left. Goose's main man, Sunny Jim, a hard-eyed hombre with a thin mustache framing a steady smile, awaited orders.

"Get Hite, Cripes, Dan the Duck, and that old man runs errands, what's his name?"

"Sofus somethin'. He's a Swede. Got dusted lungs."

"Get 'em all in here, pronto. We gotta button Clifton up."

The outlaw awaited them, six feet of him immersed up to his coffee-soaker of a mustache in the water, as the boys arrived at the hot springs in twilight. The two-hundred-foot-high bluff close to the San Francisco River threw long shadows across the open canyon.

"Just us chickens, Sam! Don't get jumpy . . . Ease Bixler, this is my friend, Sam Jones, who I broke horses with this past spring up in the San Andres."

They didn't shake hands, merely nodded, as Gillom handed the outlaw his gift bottle of whiskey.

"Ahh, tongue oil. Thanks." Graham uncorked it with his teeth.

Gillom sat down and quickly began yanking off his clothes. "Ease was with me in that shoot-out in Bisbee, Sam, with Luther Goose's wrestlers. He came up to these medicinal baths to help heal his leg wound from that affray." Both men could see the bandage wrapped around Bixler's calf as he undressed.

"Another triggerman. Foundation of your own gang, kid."

"No, no." Gillom held up a hand. "We ain't outlaws. Promised my ma and Gene Rhodes I'd ride a straight trail. Ease is gonna own his own saloon someday. We're both just up here to rescue Anel."

Sam took another slug of whiskey as the other two men eased their naked, bandaged selves into the bubbling water. "How you intend to do that?"

"Well, thought we'd check all the saloons tonight, just lookin'. Don't know if Luther knows I'm in town yet? But you'll have to check the Blue Goose again, Sam. We'd be recognized."

"Okay, but if your girl doesn't turn up tonight, I wouldn't hang around Clifton looking to tangle with this bad honcho. Never met Mister Goose, but he's got the fanciest muff mansion in these parts and is sure to have some tough jaspers to help him run it. You're both young fellas, got a lot of life to live yet. Gunfights over gals who may be long gone just ain't worth it, boys."

"Anel may even be back in Bisbee, Gillom, by the time I return. I'd sure let you know quick," added Ease.

Gillom Rogers nodded. "Can't argue with either of you. If she doesn't turn up tonight, or tomorrow, the day after Ease and I will be on the stage to Silver City. We want to see a little more country before headin' home."

"Silver City's cattle country now. Government repealed that Silver Purchase Act back in '93 and overnight thousands of silver miners went broke. So that area's silver boom petered out. Butch Cassidy and his Wild Bunch used to work on a ranch down there between robberies, and the Laws tamed the Hall Gang from around there six years ago. Good outlaw territory."

"I'll drink to that plan." Ease clinked glass pints with Gillom, then Sam joined, all tapping bottles like good old boys.

"You sure know all the hottest spots for outlaws, Sam," said Gillom.

"Well, I like to keep track of my friends."

"*Ahhh,* this hot water feels good! My wound's healing already." And then young Mr. Bixler slid almost fully under, one hand holding aloft a half empty pint.

The boys didn't dine with Mr. Graham that night. Gillom and Ease ate in a little steak joint the south end of Clifton. The outlaw had advised them not to return to the same restaurants, the same businesses, so their movements wouldn't be easy to track around town. Picking their teeth afterward, the young gunmen hit the rest of the saloons on the eastside, having a friendly drink in each. They didn't ask any questions, or catch many hard looks, and kept their coats buttoned óver their weapons. They checked the Midway, the Office, and the Richelieu for Anel Romero, but didn't spot her.

After cooking a steak and beans at his campsite, the wily Mr. Graham rode back toward Conglomerate Avenue, hitching his horse at the edge of town and walking behind the lit buildings of business row, staying just inside the edge of darkness. Sam made a beeline for the Blue Goose, where he was pretty certain any action would be with the girl, if she were even around. It was a warm summer's night. A light breeze finally stirred the smelter smoke in the air, and he sunk into shadow under the eaves of the building next door. He wished he had a whiskey to occupy his time. He turned his head slowly from the saloon's back entrance to its front door, watching who came in and out.

He'd been there maybe a half hour and needed to take a piss. Across the street from another alley a small cluster of people hurried toward him. Somebody was in the middle with a cloak and hood over their head, being hustled along by two rough-looking cowboys. They didn't go to the Blue Goose's front entrance, but jounced into its side alley. Sam pulled back against the wall, not breathing as they whipped past. As the trio reached the back stairway to the second-floor landing, what seemed to be their captive suddenly spun from the men's grasp.

"I want to *dance*!" Her hood fell off as she twirled in the moonlight. Peering intently, Sam could make out a younger woman's darker skin, her long tresses. One man grabbed her across the mouth and literally dragged her up the second flight.

"*No!*" she squealed. The captive appeared to swoon, slumping down like she was passing out, but the guard shoving her from below pushed her up onto the top step. Graham heard another smothered squall, then the second story door was yanked open and she was pulled inside the building. The rear door banged shut. The outlaw took a deep breath, pondering this new problem, then stepped out into the alley. Nothing moved nearby, so he lit out.

Sam caught up with his young pals having another get-acquainted beer in the Gem, a miner's saloon farther south along Conglomerate Avenue. No upholstered furniture or dancing girls in this smoky, low-ceilinged joint, just working men off the day shift at the mines or smelter, drinking beer in loud groups. The place reminded Graham of the old Brewery, Bisbee's original beer hall.

Gillom had had a few and greeted the outlaw like his long lost friend.

"*Sam!* She ain't in here!"

The Texan grabbed both young men by their biceps and hustled them to a darker corner table. "Think I just saw her."

"*Where?*" Ease shouted.

"Quiet down, boys. . . . In the alley beside the Blue Goose. Coupla toughs were dragging her up the back stairs, but her cloak fell away and I saw her face.

Looked Mexican, but it was dark out. Couldn't be sure enough to start shootin'. Gal struggled, yelled 'I want to dance!' Then they grabbed her again, dragged her inside."

"*Bastards! Let's go!*" Gillom Rogers rose from the bench, beer mug in hand, ready.

"Settle down, kid." The older gunman pulled him back down. "Nothing hasty, we've gotta plan this. And not tonight, you've both had too much to drink. You'll never win a gunfight on a bellyful of beer."

Gillom was belligerent. "We *can't* let her stay there, captive!"

"Yes we can. Let things quiet down with her there, put them off their guard, then tomorrow night we'll strike."

"How?" asked Ease.

"I'll have to go up those back stairs, try to find her in one of the bedrooms of that cathouse, pretend I'm a lost customer if I'm stopped. Nobody knows me in this town. You two will have to keep his *pistoleros* occupied downstairs."

Ease nodded. "Simple enough."

"Yeah, *if* that back door's not locked. And *if* I can find her without gettin' noticed. And *if* you two don't get into a shoot-out while I'm trying to spirit her off. Yours will be a diversion, a trick to give me time while I'm rooting around upstairs."

"Lot of problems," mused Gillom, more reserved now.

"Yes there are. And then how do we all get away? *If* we get lucky and don't get shot up."

"Train," thought Ease aloud.

"Not a chance," argued Sam. "His bad boys ain't going to let you get a good night's hotel sleep after her disappearance, catch a train the next sunny mornin'. Or wave you all goodbye on the stagecoach to Solomonville the day after tomorra."

"Horses," guessed Gillom.

"Yes. I've got mine, but we'll have to find three more. And saddles, tack, grub, more ammunition. *Mucho dinero*, amigos. Unless you're into horse stealin'."

"I've got money," said Gillom.

"How much?"

"About five hundred dollars."

"Give it to me."

Gillom hesitated. "Uh, it's all I've got."

The outlaw frowned. "Don't trust me, huh?"

"Look," the youth answered. "First thing tomorrow, we'll meet at that stable south of town I noticed on the stage coming in here. See what horseflesh they've got, if it's any good? Ease and I will pick up food, cartridges, enough for four. Then we'll go camp with you, cook dinner, rest up till dark."

Young Bixler nodded enthusiastically. "Anybody watching will think we left town."

Sam Graham slammed a palm down on the table, sloshing their beers.

"All right! Meet me at that stable early, bring your money. Go back to that hotel and sleep with your guns ready tonight, boys. I'm bettin' they know we're here."

They left the Gem separately, didn't shake hands, hoping nobody had noticed them together. If Sam hit another saloon for that whiskey he savored, no one knew. He made sure, though, watching from a distance atop his horse, that these liquored-up youths made it safely back to their hotel first.

Gillom had changed rooms to a bigger upstairs suite with two single beds after Ease arrived, so they could protect each other. They rolled through the Clifton's dusty parlor around midnight with an arm around each other for support as they slipped unsteadily on a big Navajo rug. The night desk clerk stirred off his stool, pitched Gillom his room key since he was the guest paying. Over his shoulder Gillom noticed an old man, seemingly asleep in a stuffed leather chair when they entered, now sitting up and eyeing them from under a brown slouch hat as the youths climbed the hotel's stairs.

The boys slept off their inebriation and luckily their locked door wasn't rattled during the night. Gillom awoke to a rooster in a nearby henhouse saying hello to the rising sun. He felt pain behind his eyeballs as he rubbed water over his face from the pitcher on a dresser. He wore his guns belted over his long johns as he walked down the slumbering hotel's hallway to the lavatory. As he returned he crept halfway down the stairway until he could scan the hotel's lobby from above. The old watchman from last night was gone.

Gillom washed up in their room as Ease roused and stretched.

"I could use a little hair of that dog that bit me last night. Any whiskey left?"

Gillom shook his head. He tried to shave stubble off his unlined cheeks, but the barber had removed any stray hairs professionally the day before. He still managed to cut himself near one ear and had to clot the wound with a bit of paper. The sight of his own blood woke Gillom Rogers fully up. This could be the most dangerous day of his young life. He'd better be alert for it.

Gillom paid for his room, five dollars for two nights, dollar extra for the bigger room he'd moved into with Ease. He mentioned to the sleepy night clerk they'd done their business, enjoyed their stay, and were headed back to Bisbee. That was the false trail they'd decided on and it wouldn't hurt to start laying it.

Thirty-nine

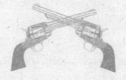

Out on the street the boys hiked along with their warbags and saddlebags. *Leñeros*, or woodmen, were selling bundles of mesquite off their burros, and housewives were buying produce from Chinese vegetable men who had wrapped their lettuces, tomatoes, chiles, and squashes in wet burlap and loaded them into bamboo baskets dangling from either end of a thick wooden pole. The 130-pound loads these slender Chinamen carried reminded Gillom of the extra weight on his own shoulders, and his sore ribs. A loafer enjoying a morning cigarette on a bench against the front wall of Mammon's Chinese Café watched them stroll down the boardwalk, not stopping in for breakfast. The watcher spit, got up to hurry across the street toward the Blue Goose to report their passing.

Hop Yick's grocery at the south end of Clifton's commercial strip provided foodstuffs for their long ride home. Burlap sacks full of slab bacon, hardtack, beans, bread loaves, and steaks for today, salt crackers, coffee, even a wheel of hard cheese. *At least we'll eat well,* Gillom thought, *if there's enough left of us to enjoy it.* Ease remembered to buy several boxes of .44-.40 rounds and .41-caliber cartridges for his lighter Colt. Gillom even gifted his friend with a gun-cleaning kit.

In the Blue Goose's back room, too, preparations were under way. Luther had an oiling kit out on his desk and had his Remington derringer and a .38 Lightning, a smaller, lightweight, double-action Colt, apart for cleaning when Cripes hurried in. This middle-aged man in soiled, raggedy clothing couldn't stand still as he made his report.

"They was walkin' south, Mister Goose, carryin' saddlebags and toting goods. Didn't stop for breakfast."

"Maybe they've checked out?" Luther chewed this thought while Cripes scratched his scraggly red beard. "See what the hotel clerk says, if they've gone? Then check the train station and stage office, see if they're buying tickets? *You*"—he pointed a cleaning rod at Sunny Jim—"check the stables. They might take a long ride home, but I doubt it. I wanna make sure those bastards are outta our hair, so we don't have to sit here jumpy, waitin' for 'em to pop in to give us a six-chamber hello."

"Should I plug 'em I get the chance?" It was Sunny Jim, his chief bodyguard.

"No. Let's not get Sheriff English aroused if we don't have to. If those young jaspers haven't heard anything about her, they might just leave town, spare me more grief."

"Boss, we'll let you know."

Luther Goose stood up behind his scarred wooden desk, indeed a little jumpy as he poked a stiff thin brush down the barrel of his small revolver and squinted through its empty hole, pondering eternity.

So the boys were well laden when they walked up to the stable corrals south of town. Sam Graham awaited them, looking over the horseflesh. The horsebreaker had already picked out a couple five-year-old geldings from the limited string there, a bay and a buckskin, and Gillom quickly liked a paint pony for his missing girlfriend. Since they were buying several mounts, they were able to wheedle a deal for saddles and bridles and several well-used saddlebags to carry their food from Henry Hill, the stable owner. The bill rounded off to four hundred dollars, greenbacks, with a sack of oats and a morning's feed for Sam's nervous stallion, which he also talked the stableman into. This big, skinny racer was the best of the bunch he'd broken for Gene Rhodes over in New Mexico, and Sam had trained the new horse well on his long ride west. Gillom felt lighter in the moneybelt sewn inside his holster as he buckled it back on. His worldly wealth was now down to seventy-five dollars, and his posse expected him to keep paying for this rescue ride as long as it was under way.

After adjusting saddles and bridles and tying saddlebags to the new mounts, the boys practiced on these three horses, reining and starting and stopping them around a side corral to ascertain how well these animals handled before the men were finally ready to ride.

"Looking forward to greeting old Bisbee again," Gillom said loudly, making sure Henry Hill heard him as they loped away. The saddled paint pony ran on a long lead rope trailing Ease's horse, carrying no rider. The three amigos rode south, on the stage road that would soon angle off to the right, southwest, toward Solomonville. As soon as they were out of the stableman's view, though, the young men looped around north, riding back toward Clifton through the brush.

The trio dry-camped north of town, where they could see Clifton in the distance from atop the low hill they squatted behind, hoping no one would come out to investigate a midday campfire. While Sam cooked fresh-cut steaks and beans, Ease tried his new gun-cleaning kit while Gillom oiled his leather holster. Over a sizzling pan, the outlaw eyed Ease working on his new pistol.

"You like that Thunderer?"

"Just bought it used, but it hefts lighter than a bigger Colt and has an easy double-action pull. Rubber grip, six-inch barrel, shoots straight, I like it. Now I have this sudden reputation in Bisbee as a shooter, my boss at the Bonanza wants me to display a sidearm, to help prevent shootings inside. I tried a hip holster, but it got in my way mixing drinks. This shoulder holster fits better, but I don't fancy toting this lump of metal under my arm for eight hours drawing beers. You ever drink in the Bonanza?"

Sam Graham shook his head.

"It gets rowdy weekends sometimes. Last Fourth of July, they picked one guy out of a corner next morning, thought he was just sleeping off a drunk. Little bullet hole under his left ear and no one heard a thing."

"I thought the Bonanza was a *gentlemen's* club, Ease?" Gillom added.

"Not *every* night." He and his pal chuckled.

Gillom looked over at their cook. "How you wanna do this, Sam? Take 'em about midnight, after they've been drinkin'?"

"No. Early, just after dark, when they're still thinkin' about what they'd like for supper. We get away clean, then we'll have all night to ride southeast, hide out at daybreak."

Ease's curiosity got the best of him. "You goin' to Silver City with us, Mister Jones?"

"Might. This Goose may send men on the stage to check Solomonville, or wire ahead to have the trains watched for you all in Lordsburg. Silver City's the most unlikely spot to be caught right off."

"Or head the *other* way, up into Apache country north a' San Carlos," said Gillom. Graham just smiled. "Gonna ride that outlaw trail till you die, Sam?"

"I dunno. Gettin' worn down. Robbin's hard work and now they've gone and put numbers on the banknotes. Makes stolen money easier to trace by the damned bankers. I may retire to a life of leisure, runnin' cows back in Central Texas, where my brother's got a ranch."

"I'd *pay* to see you proddin' cattle for an honest living. We're not breaking any laws, you know, rescuing a girl held against her will," argued Gillom.

"Brothel owner won't see it that way," answered Sam. "Think of whores as *their* property."

"She's *not* a whore!"

"Just explaining that a fickle woman is like a careless man with a gun. They're both apt to hurt somebody."

"She's not *fickle*, either! Whatever the hell that means?"

After a good meal the three drowsed in the summer sunshine, resting on blankets or propped against a rock. A temperature inversion was holding the warm air still and close to the ground so the smelter smoke lingered, irritating their noses and throats with sulfurous acid in the air. Nobody moved around much, hoping for a cleansing breeze. Gillom nudged Ease and they both watched dumbstruck as Sam stirred his hot coffee with the barrel of his .45, absent-mindedly flicking off the wet drips before reholstering.

"Still not too late to pull out of this, Gillom. No shame in that. You ain't married to Anel," said Ease.

"I might like to be." The young gunslinger got on his knees, reached into his Levis. He pulled out the silver locket and showed it to them. "We had our photographs taken in Bisbee and Anel had this keepsake made for me, a surprise."

His pal looked it over. "Very nice."

"Gave you a lock of her hair, too," admired Mr. Graham, lifting it up.

"That hair ain't off the top of her head. Trimmed it special to prove she'd always be faithful."

The outlaw dropped the hair clump tied with a tiny pink ribbon back into the silver oval and snapped it shut. Even the tough Texan looked a little shocked as he handed the locket back.

Ease Bixler was open-mouthed. "Jesus, Gillom. You *are* serious about this girl."

The young gunslinger looked grim. "That's why I'm here. I know Anel's faithful, not whorin' for this bastard. She's my silhouette girl, Ease, trusts me to aim true for her."

His buddy nodded, remembering. "That was quite a picnic, you two challenging each other, your tremendous target shooting."

"Tonight ain't gonna be easy or fun, my friend."

"I'm aware of that, amigo."

In the Blue Goose, glasses were being polished behind the front bar, food prepared in the kitchen for Friday night's business. Upstairs the ladies began to get dressed, putting on their war paint for the night's festivities. Luther Goose was busy, too, checking rooms in his two stories for shuttered windows and locked doors, securing his castle, when his chief henchman reported.

"Cripes didn't see 'em catch a stage or a train," announced the boss.

"I know. They bought horses this morning. Three mounts, saddles, tack for 'em, had supplies in their saddlebags. Henry at his stable said there was another man with 'em, older, knew horses, riding his own black stallion. They rode off south together, one of the youngsters saying they were going to Bisbee."

"*Three* men? *Four* saddled horses?" Luther Goose was figuring hard as he began working his eyebrow mole again with a long finger.

Forty

Darkness swept over the Gila Mountains from the east and three men spun cylinders and holstered their revolvers. They ambled to their horses, re-adjusted the used saddles and bridles they'd just purchased that morning, giving each mount a last hatful of oats to chew after grazing in hobbles most of the day. A fresh boost of good feed would have to last them all night, for there would be no rest for these horses till the morrow.

Gillom deferred to the train robber about tactics, although it was *his* mission. Sam Graham pulled his weathered brown Stetson down to seat it firmly on his forehead, then looked his two compadres in the eyes.

"You rakehells ready?"

They rode. Coming in on the north side of town at dusk, they hoped they wouldn't be watched for from that direction. The men dismounted and walked their horses to make themselves less noticeable as they neared the first commercial buildings at the north end of Conglomerate Avenue. They approached the rear of these buildings and the first saloon they came to, the Office, had a hitching post and watering trough out back, so they were able to refresh their four horses before tying them up. The Blue Goose was in the middle of this long block next to an alley, and Sam gave them final instructions as they walked toward it the back way.

"Ease, you stay in the alley, back end of the Goose. While I'm up trying to get in that second story, whistle if you see anyone coming along the rear of these buildings, any danger. Gillom, you stay in the shadows up front, watch who comes in their front door. If I can get inside upstairs, don't do nothin' unless you hear a commotion, like they're trying to corral me. They haven't seen me before, so I stand a chance, unlike you two. But if there's a ruckus, any shooting, then you're both going to have to come in that front door with your guns pulled, but not firing unless you need to. Maybe you'll buy me an escape."

Gillom blinked at Ease. "We can do that."

"I hope I can locate the girl, sneak her out that upstairs back door, while you two cover us coming down those outside stairs. Maybe we'll get lucky and get away with no shooting at all."

"That would be nice," agreed Ease. "Just don't be ridin' some downy couch while we stand out here all night, eyeballin' the dark."

Sam ignored the riposte. They reached the alley between the Blue Goose and a one-story, wood-framed office building. Peering down the alley to the west, they could see lights coming on and hear music from a saloon as the weekend's entertainment began revving up in Clifton. Except for people passing along the main street, no one else was out back of these businesses yet to bother them.

Graham asked them again. "Ready?"

Gillom gripped each man by the hand. "I sure appreciate it, fellas, you takin' this risk for me and Anel. Nobody else would have, 'cept maybe Gene Rhodes."

Ease Bixler grinned loopily. "This *is* the gunfighters' way, pard."

The remark caused even Mr. Graham to smile. "We'll see if either of you *is* a gunfighter, has that kind of sand. Just name your first two kids after us, Gillom. That's enough for me."

Then Sam was striding to the back stairs of the Blue Goose. Gillom drifted off into the shadows to watch the saloon's front door. Ease watched them both go, swallowed hard, and sprung his Colt from its shoulder holster beneath his work coat.

Sam crept up the back stair landing on his boot tips like a cat. Windows were lit in the rooms upstairs as the girls got ready for their night's labors. Graham reached the second-floor back door, but found it bolted from inside. He pulled a hunting knife from a sheath attached to his holster, but its long, pointed blade couldn't jimmy the metal bolt open. Sam held his knife in front of him as he looked round the narrow, two-foot-wide balcony rimming the saloon's whole second floor. He looked over the railing at Ease guarding the back alley, opened his hands wide to indicate he was flummoxed. Peering round the back corner, Sam spotted it. One of the prostitutes had vented her room to catch some cooler evening air. Lace curtains fluttered out an upraised window.

Graham scuttled along the balcony to that opened window, put his knife through the window first, then his head, holding his black hat aside in his free hand. His eyes adjusted to the dim light inside the whore's bedroom, but nobody was home. Sam withdrew his head, bent back over the railing to catch Ease's attention across the alley below to indicate by hand gestures that he was going inside.

Ease saluted he understood before Sam disappeared again. Whistling up the alley to Gillom, who was hugging a dark wall just off Conglomerate Avenue, Ease got his pal to turn as he pointed and indicated their outlaw friend was going inside. Gillom waved he understood, turned his gaze back to the saloon's front door. Nobody was going in or leaving the Blue Goose. It was still early to be visiting a whorehouse, especially on a Friday night when some men didn't have to work the next day and were probably having a cold one with their pals somewhere else. The wait gave Gillom the fidgets. He restlessly drew each of his Remingtons in their oiled holster pockets and reversed the gunbutts to face forward for a cross-handed draw. He remembered Sam's lesson—real gunfighters carried their pistols butt forward.

Sam Graham got his long legs in through the window frame one at a time without tripping on anything with his roweled spurs. He paused a moment to let his eyes accustom to the gloom thrown by a tall candle melting in a glass-chimnied holder. The small bedroom was standard for a high-end brothel, one level below the more luxurious accommodations in parlor houses in bigger towns he'd visited, like Denver's. Sam sat down on the white linen summer bedspread and tested the brass bed's bounce. He lifted the glass candleholder so he could look around the vacant bedroom. An oak lamp table beside the bed contained female accents— stoppered perfume he could smell, a bottle of Godfrey's Cordial, an opium-laced elixir he was familiar with, Pine Knot Bitters to treat venereal disease, a bottle of rosewater douche, another bottle of Yellow Dock Sarsaparilla claiming to cause miscarriage. Atop an oak bureau with three big drawers certain to be filled with extra towels and sheets and the resident's fancy undergarments rested a "peter pan," a china bowl containing a bar of soap, plus a pitcher of water next to it for washing the customer before consummating business and herself afterward.

Sam was more interested in two smaller china bowls, one containing several long, thin condoms made from sheep's intestines, and the other cradling a yellowish curved plug of beeswax hopefully to prevent pregnancy.

The outlaw got off the bed, moving his candle lamp toward the cane-bottomed chair against the wall at the end of the bed for a customer to drop his clothes on, and a full-length wall mirror in which to admire his manly glory. There was also a small woodstove in the corner, vented through the ceiling, to keep undressed customers cozy in the winter. Sam was interested in the prostitute's large trunk, which he knew contained most of her valuables. Kneeling next to it, he lifted the buckled lid and quickly rifled the contents with one hand, finding a wad of greenbacks in a small wallet inside a leather purse, and then a small jewelry chest. His instinct for thievery overcame him. He slid open the little drawers and helped himself to the best items he examined in the glowing light. A small diamond stickpin in the shape of an owl and an opal ring circled by diamond chips went into his jeans pocket, plus some gold earrings and a thin golden neck chain supporting a gold, heart-shaped photo locket. Sam left her cheaper silver jewelry behind.

Footsteps along the hallway outside caused the bandit to rise to a crouch, but he heard a woman's thin heels clatter down the wooden stairway heading below. He'd been wasting time so he shut the trunk again, put the candle lamp back on the side table, and picked up his pigsticker. As he moved to this whore's closed door, his boot banged a chamber pot partially underneath the bed. Sam froze while his gaze wandered to framed photographs on the wall of nude women in risqué poses, prostitutes demonstrating various sexual positions at which this inmate was evidently talented, for the right price. Sam Graham frowned, for such pornographic advertising was more common in cheap, back-alley cribs than in nicer brothels. An ear to the doorjamb to listen, but he could hear only faint music and singing coming from downstairs. Taking a deep breath, the train robber opened the bedroom door and stuck his head into the upstairs hall.

Gillom was really restless, too impatient for his own good. No one was entering the Blue Goose across the way, which surprised him. He wondered what Sam was doing? Gillom began pacing, in and out of the wall's shadow. Down the alley he could see Ease slouched against the same building, only his head moving as he peered into the darkness behind these row establishments, scouting for intruders to their reconnaissance. As he chewed his lip, his worry got the best of him. *They've had a whole day to torture Anel up there. I can't let that happen to my girl tonight!* Gillom stomped into the alley, hissed at his best friend.

"*Ease!*" He motioned him to come and Bixler hurriedly did. "Nothing's happening."

"It's not supposed to," muttered his friend. "Sam told us not to move, till we heard some commotion."

"I can't take it anymore! They could be rapin' Anel up there, breakin' her in." The teenager was so agitated he couldn't stand still. "Let's go in and distract 'em. What'd Sam call it? A diversion."

"Then we'll have to shoot our way out, Gillom, while Sam gets away with your girl."

"We always knew it was going to come to a fight, didn't we? You figured on burnin' some powder, right?"

Ease pulled a poor face. "Yeah, guess I did."

Gillom grabbed his pal's arm. "Then let's show these hired hands what *real* fast guns look like." With that pronouncement he was off, marching toward the brothel's front door.

"You're just achin' to shoot somebody again," muttered his glum partner.

Forty-one

No one was in the hallway upstairs, so Sam slipped out of room number two, shutting its door carefully. Coal oil lamps were affixed to the corridor's walls, illuminating the carpet runner down the wooden hallway. Behind door number one across the hall Sam could hear mattress springs squeaking and a brass bed clinking. *Some cowboy riding a downy couch,* grinned the outlaw.

He took a chance at the next door, another of what looked like three bedrooms along each side of the hallway in this upstairs brothel, six rooms total. Sam didn't knock, his only chance being surprise in any affray. To sharpen that edge, Graham kept his long knife hidden up the shirtsleeve of his left arm, point forward. As he opened the door, a young woman lying fully clothed atop her brass bed rose slightly off her pillows and lifted several green leaves with purplish edges from her eyes to see who was at her door? Experienced prostitutes used belladonna leaves to

make their irises big and glassy, dilating their pupils
and giving their eyes a "bedroom look" Western men
liked. Sam realized this big blonde wasn't the Mexican gal he'd seen in Gillom's photographs.

"Oh, sorry, ma'am. Wrong room." He pulled his
head back.

"Okay, cowboy. Change your mind later, come back
and see me, won't you?" She winked a glassy blue eye.

"You bet." Sam smiled as he shut her door.

Ease Bixler followed his disgruntled companion
through the heavy front door. No glass front windows
or swinging doors into this brothel, only a solid oak
door which could be barred from the inside to stall unwanted armed entrance by irate customers or the au-
thorities. The Blue Goose was more like a fortress than
an open saloon. Gillom was surprised to find no gambling going on, although there were chairs around
tables where poker could be played. Instead, the Blue
Goose operated as a brothel where the profit was made
trading in flesh rather than pasteboards. Two tough-
looking men wearing pistols sat drinking at one of the
tables, not talking. Across from them was a long, black
oak bar with the requisite brass cuspidors and foot
railing. Behind it presided a burly colored bartender.

The young men stood near the front door, returning
the stares of the few other patrons this early evening.
Gillom noticed the action seemed to be in the back
half of this main floor in a parlor sectioned off from
the main barroom by neck-high wooden partitions.
A *portiere,* a fancy gold braided rope hanging from a

brass bar across the ceiling, provided a decorative barrier in the threshold between these two barrier walls.

They couldn't just stand there, so Ease nudged Gillom and they walked to the bar and ordered short beers. These they merely sipped, focusing on the music and singing coming from the back parlor. The boys couldn't see over the partial walls, but through the roped entry they could see a white man in a dark suit and derby hat tinkling an upright piano. It had to be the whores singing "Oh Heavens!," a popular ditty.

> Don't you think she's awful,
> Slightly on the mash?
> See how close her lips are
> To that young man's mustache.
> Oh Heavens! He has kissed her!
> Her parents are away
> But if they saw her actions
> What do you think they'd say?

Titters of laughter from the parlor caused the anxious Mr. Bixler to grin. His partner nudged his arm and picking up their beers, the young men walked back to the parlor. Gillom noticed one of the toughs had left his drink and walked through a doorway at the bar's end to their left, leading to rooms on the alley side of the building.

Sam Graham was in a quandary. The girl had to be in one of these upstairs rooms, for if she was still in this brothel, where else would they hide her? Trying to keep his spurs from jingling, he tiptoed across the hallway to listen at the fourth doorjamb. Silence, except for musical accompaniment drifting up from downstairs. The gunman moved in what felt like slow motion to the last door on this far side of the hall, next to the upstairs back door. Ear again to the door, but still no sounds.

Breathing frustration, Sam moved across the hallway again, pausing to unbolt the back door in case he had to flee—fast. This final door, number six, he now noticed was farther apart from the door next to it than the ones across the hall, indicating perhaps a larger room. Behind this last door Sam heard low voices, murmuring. He realized he was nervous, not concentrating well enough. He sucked in a lungful, held his breath and then released it, trying to calm his beating heart. Luckily these bedrooms didn't have bolts inside their doors, so the women couldn't hide from the brothelkeepers if they didn't feel like fornicating.

Sam opened the door. Two women sat on a king-sized bed, the nearest, with her back to him, in crimson silk bloomers and a partially untied corset. This big-boned gal was also a blond. She appeared to be heating the bowl of a long-stemmed opium pipe with a small oil lamp.

The other woman looked Mexican. She had on a white blouse with puffed sleeves too big for her and men's woolen pants held up by leather galluses. This younger girl with long black hair did resemble the gal in Gillom's photographs, and her borrowed clothing indicated she'd come from somewhere in a hurry. She looked asleep until her eyelids fluttered atop her pillow when the blonde leaned in to place the pipe's metal tip between her lips.

"Suck, honey. That's a girl. Suck up all this good *yen shee* smoke."

The Mexican was a looker all right, and Sam stood transfixed in the doorway, neither of the women aware of his presence. The American gal began to cook another bowlful of opium for herself when Graham interrupted.

"Hey, girls. Havin' fun?"

The blonde looked over her shoulder. "We're havin' us a little smoke here, cowboy. Come back later."

The gunman smiled as he moved inside and closed the door.

"I'm to look up Anel Romero, and I'm pretty damned sure that's you, miss."

Hearing her name, the Latina sat up to give him a sleepy hello. This irritated her keeper.

"Mister, you're not supposed to be *in* here. This girl's not in the lineup yet."

"You're right about that. She ain't ready yet for whorin'."

Sensing trouble, the busty blonde put her opium kit down and turned round, but Sam was already pulling his pistol.

"Hey, fella, this is a *private* session. Go downstairs and pick one of the other girls, you're feelin' frisky."

"*Shut up!*" The outlaw backhanded the broad across the mouth with the butt of the gun in his fist, rattling her front teeth and bloodying her lips. The big whore was so shocked she forgot to scream.

"Get off that bed and unhook your corset."

The blonde felt her lips with her fingertips, tasted her own warm blood, and looked like she was going to cry. "*What?*"

"You heard me. *Do* it."

The American girl was too drugged to move fast and Miss Romero had roused herself, but the younger girl was so doped up from the opium, her movements were in slow motion.

"Easy, missy. Boyfriend's looking for you."

The young *pistoleros* pushed through the hanging gold ropes to the back parlor. The gals had stopped singing, but the "Professor" was still tickling the ivories.

"Company in the parlor, girls!" yelled a middle-aged brunette bulging from her corseted yellow dress. This older gal was evidently the madam, supervising her flock. Her loud call was the signal to assemble, for all four younger girls stood up and arranged themselves in a loose line. Gillom saw Anel wasn't among them. Ease, more interested in the saloon's business, noted that none of the brocade chairs and red velvet sofas the girls had been sitting on matched. He did like the smaller crystal chandelier hanging from the ceiling, though, and the hand-cranked victrola on a side table.

A clatter on the stairs leading down from the second floor landing heralded the arrival of the big blonde from room number one, her bedroom eyes glistening.

The madam came toward them, took the friendlier

looking Ease by the elbow, leading the young men into her lair.

"You young gentlemen haven't visited us before. Don't recognize either of you?"

"No, ma'am. Never been to Clifton before. I'm Ease Bixler and this is my pard, Gillom."

"Welcome, boys, to the Blue Goose. Finest girls in all the Arizona Territory. Where you handsome fellas from?"

"Uh, Bisbee," answered Ease, not thinking too quickly.

"Texas," nodded a tense Mr. Rogers, chewing his lip again.

The hefty brunette brushed back some wanton hair. "*Uh-huh. Wandering* cowboys. You didn't look like miners to me."

"No, ma'am. What about these girls?" asked Ease.

"Ah. To business. Five dollars an hour, twenty for the entire night. Tip what she deserves for your pleasure. Can you handle that?"

"Little higher than I pay in Bisbee," offered Mr. Bixler.

"Well, this is a high-end house, boys, not some cheap crib. You get what you pay for in the Blue Goose. Why don't you have a drink with us, meet these nice girls. I'm Ethyl, the madam, and this blond just joined us is Kitty. Our redhead here in the flame dress is Irish Mary, this elegant brunette is Lady Jane Grey, she's English, and this busty little spitfire answers to Sweet Annie."

"Howdy, cowboys!" enthused the latter, who was chewing gum.

The stout madam was still shilling. "Sit down, boys, enjoy your beers, have another and we'll get acquainted, then you can make your selections."

Ease did as commanded, sitting down in an over-stuffed armchair and resting his beer on a side table, so his hands remained free. Gillom remained standing beside him.

"I'm partial to Mexican girls," said Gillom. "Got any?"

"Why no, young man, we don't."

Gillom frowned. "Thought you'd have a brown-skinned gal or two, all these Mexican miners in Clifton."

"Oh, they've got their own cribs in Clifton. We don't cater to colored customers. Our painted cats are too expensive." Trying to be genial, the plump brunette winked at Ease and Gillom relaxed a little. He wasn't going to get any information out of this wily flesh peddler.

Upstairs, the blond whore had removed her straight-front corset so she was naked above her silk bloomers. Sam had unstrung her boned corset and was using the strong cord from its back to wrap her ankles and tie them to a brass bedpost. He cut the cord with his knife and her wrists were next. This tight binding between bedposts stretched her out full-length on the covered horsehair mattress.

"Now don't get feisty, try to move around or you could roll off this mattress and really hurt yourself," he warned.

Miss Sherrie wasn't happy. "Why you tying me up half-naked? I'm not gonna screw you now. You ain't getting a free ride offa me, cowboy."

Something had to be done about her big mouth, so

Sam pulled up the corner of the cotton sheet and started slicing it into wide strips with his knife.

"Or you gonna rob us sweet girls? Take advantage of poor, helpless women."

"Not a bad idea," he muttered.

The big blonde was trussed like a steer for branding, but Graham had to shut her up or they'd never get away clean. The Mexican girl managed to rouse from her drugged languor and was moving on the bed, trying to rub pipe dreams from her eyes.

"What happens? Why you doing thees?"

The outlaw balled up sheet strips to cram between Sherrie's bloody lips, while questioning the other. "What's your name, honey? 'Anel'? Your sweetheart, Gillom, wants to see you."

Sam wrapped cut sheet in layers around the prostitute's head like a mummy, to keep her from spitting out her gag and yelling for help.

The Latina struggled to shake off her languor.

"Gil-lom? *Gil-lom* ees here?"

"You betcha. I'll take you to him. Give me a *momentito*."

Forty-two

Luther Goose was preceded from his back rooms by his two gunmen, the always smiling Sunny Jim and Dan the Duck. The proprietor was dressed to kill in a low-cut silk vest decorated with painted flowers over a white shirt bedecked with diamond studs behind a flowing black silk tie. Perhaps he hoped to intimidate the two youths by flashing his wealth in his fancy brothel, running them out of town without a fight. But if it came to trouble, well, at least he might go down in high style.

Tall "Wood" Hite took up a position peering over a wooden partition to the parlor as his boss entered it. Cripes, the red-haired spy, headed for the front door at the far end of the Blue Goose to bolt it from inside and keep anyone from leaving. Seeing Luther Goose appear in the doorway to the parlor with his two henchmen moving either side of him, blocking easy exit, Ease Bixler gulped a frog of fright and stood up.

"So. You whoresons are back to devil me some

more." The proprietor wasn't serving southwestern hospitality this evening, and the high-spirited prostitutes quieted quickly at his harsh tone.

"No sir. We just rode up from Bisbee to sample your wares," offered Ease.

"I doubt that."

"Lookin' for one special girl, Anel Romero," countered Gillom. "Believe you know her."

"I do. But I believe she's back in Bisbee."

"Why don't you shame the Devil and tell the truth," said the young man from El Paso.

The whores were nervous and Gillom could see Lady Jane Grey rubbing her fingers below her waist near her crotch, which she didn't realize she was doing. Ease lifted a hand to wipe sweat from his upper lip, causing Goose's two gunmen to flinch. The moment was feeling mighty tight. Dan the Duck's prominent lips opened and closed rapidly, making nervous popping sounds, which is how he'd gotten his nickname. The owner needed to make a statement in front of his employees.

"I *am* telling the truth. She's *not* here."

"Anel was seen last night being dragged upstairs by a couple of your gunmen."

"*Liar!* Seen by whom?" Luther's icy composure was melting. He had rubbed his eyebrow mole so hard that the skin on his forehead around it had reddened, a telltale sign of his jangled nerves.

"Let's go have a look."

The madam attempted to calm the boiling situation. "All our girls are right here. Only *customers* get invited upstairs. You cowboys got some gold for me?"

• • •

Unaware of what was transpiring downstairs, Sam Graham was again unable to resist the lure of whore's loot. With the prostitute hogtied atop her bed and Miss Anel getting up to steady herself against the flocked red wallpaper, the outlaw was on his knees rifling Sherrie's trunk, yanking clothing out with both hands. He found what he was seeking near the bottom in a velvet jewelry bag. Sam dumped what looked like paste jewelry and crammed the gold chains, diamond brooch, and pearl earrings into his jeans pockets. Seeing her entire jewelry hoard being stolen, Miss Sherrie squirmed against her corset tie bindings. The bandit turned at her muffled oaths and got back on his feet, throwing a turquoise bracelet and several silver necklaces back in her trunk.

"Okay, okay, I won't take it all." Pulling up his bulging pants, Sam moved to the bed to tickle the blonde's bare tit, causing her to lurch again. "Or take a free ride on you, either, honey. You worked hard for that jewelry."

"No, ma'am," answered Ease in the parlor. "We'll just take Gillom's girlfriend and head on back to Bisbee, no fuss."

Luther Goose had had enough sass for one day in his own establishment. Some unhappy miners were banging on his front door to be let in and serviced, and these young toughs were costing him money. It was past time to get 'em gone or get to it.

"Like Hell." The proprietor ran an index finger across his hand-painted silk vest. "Which flowers are your favorites, fellas?"

The inside of Gillom's lower lip was beginning to bleed, he had chewed it so hard. He could taste his own mortality. "Those two there . . . over your heart."

Sunny Jim couldn't take the tension. Luther's lieutenant drew his double-action Colt and fired awkwardly from his hip, but he was close enough to Ease to hit him in the left arm, tipping him down to one knee.

Gillom Rogers reacted instinctively to the other gunman's motion, pulling both his .44's in a second and getting them cocked and working. Dan the Duck fumbled his long-barreled .45 Colt up to aim when a lead bullet exploded in his stomach, paralyzing him in shock as he fell back onto his rear. His teenaged antagonist was into the moment, calling upon his hand speed, coordination, and sharp vision to work his thumbs and trigger fingers without flinching or considering. Crouched, Gillom took out Sunny Jim with two shots from his extended left hand, rolling the gun over after each, the first bullet hitting the henchman's groin and another piercing his breastbone, cracking it. Sunny Jim was smiling no longer as he let out a squawk like a kicked chicken!

Whores began bailing out in all directions amidst this mayhem, squalling in fright. Irish Mary's temper matched her flame-colored dress. Yanking one side of her skirt up, the spitfire pulled a small dagger from a garter tied round her thigh and with a sharp cry leapt toward Gillom, burying its sharp point in the first part she contacted, his raised knee and thigh. Gillom yelped at this wound and at this woman yelling bloody murder and clawing at him. Luckily she knocked the kid backward as Luther thrust the .41 derringer he'd stolen from the crooked faro dealer from inside his coatsleeve, firing at Gillom just as he was being knocked to the floor. The brothel owner's errant shot hit Ethyl, his madam, in the breast instead, spraying blood across her ample bosom and staining her yellow dress.

Irish Mary was on her knees trying to straddle Gillom in her petticoats, raising her dagger to plunge into the gunslinger again, but Ease turned to blast the shrill prostitute right in the gut from the gun in his good hand, knocking her off his friend with a .41 caliber bullet.

"Wood" Hite was working himself into a frenzy, shooting into the death pit from behind the wood partition, barely able to see over it to aim. The gunman's shots from his horse pistol drilled the combative prostitute, nailing Irish Mary right above her ear, killing her instantly. The cacophony of yells and screams and gunfire at close range was earsplitting and unwounded whores trying to run or crawl out the one entrance left behind false teeth, false curls, and false palpitators in their panicked rush from this parlor of death.

Luther dived behind the overstuffed couch and extricated his smaller .38 Colt from his rear waistband, but he was still aiming his over-and-under hideout gun at his skilled foe when Gillom lurched to his feet and took two big strides on his bloody leg to leap atop the sofa's red cushions with his good front leg hitting the top of the backrest, toppling the sofa over with his momentum. The toppling couch jolted Luther out of its way and as he flung his arm up, his second bullet from his little Remington derringer banged upward, missing Gillom but blasting crystal fobs on the small ceiling chandelier into smithereens.

Glass showered down as Gillom ducked, but so intent was he on his prey his aim didn't stray. His first shot took Mr. Goose in his closest upper leg, but then the Remington in Gillom's right hand jammed and a .44 cartridge misfired in the cylinder. His move was instinctive, dropping the useless, pearl-handled revolver and tossing the other with its black gutta-percha grip from his left hand to his right. Instantly Gillom was cocking and triggering the second of J. B. Books's custom pistols as Luther Goose heaved up, throwing his empty derringer at Gillom as he tried to get away. Another bullet into his belly had the brothel owner squealing in pain.

"You want that, don't you!" yelled Gillom.

A third bullet into his chest was all the truth Luther Goose ever deserved. It jerked him backward onto his bootheels, crashing him into one of the coal oil lamps hung from the partition to cast the parlor girls in seductive lighting. Luther smashed the oil lamp to bits, spraying ignited fuel from the glass container all over his bare neck, the wallpaper, and the Spanish carpet.

"Nooooo!" Their boss's scream stopped the bloodbath cold for a long moment as everybody still moving paused to comprehend the carnage that had just occured. Taking advantage of the terrible stillness, the Professor jerked up from beside the small piano and

picked his way quickly over the sprawled bodies, the slippery pools of blood, walking through the entryway straight for the front door. Like a black-suited phantom drifting through a deadly fray, the pianist didn't seem bothered at all.

Driven out by all the gunfire, Sam Graham suddenly appeared at the top of the stairs. He recognized the blonde, Kitty, whimpering in fright, crawling out the parlor entrance on hands and knees to seek safety between wooden chairs under one of the main saloon's tables. After reloading, Hite was again trying to aim over the parlor's wall, so Sam bent to cock and sight his Bisley target pistol atop the balcony railing, listened to his heartbeat, and touched off a bullet, straight into the gunman's kidney. "Wood" went down like a poled ox, flopping on his belly in agony until Graham paused and finished him off with two more long-range shots, lead slugs thudding into Hite's long body stretched out on the barroom floor.

Atop the stairs the outlaw grabbed the girl's hand, but Anel pulled back, disoriented and reluctant to enter the fray. Sam yanked her arm hard, dragging her down the stairs.

"C'mon, girl, you're hopped up! This bloody mess is all about *you*!"

Gillom surveyed the death and destruction in the parlor—two whores killed and Sunny Jim shot dead. Dan the Duck had managed to prop himself against an armchair where he rested with his index finger stuck into a bullet hole not far from his belly button. Dan's fat lips opened and closed with labored breathing as he fought to keep himself from bleeding to death. Luther Goose was dead, blood trickling from his Roman nose and the hair on the back of his head smoking from lamp oil. The brothel owner's eyes were popped wide open as if he had just sighted Hell itself. Smoke rose from the burning rug and flame crawling from the broken oil lamp was beginning to eat into the stuffed furniture.

Gillom bent to pick up his jammed pistol and re-holster, but his stabbed leg was bleeding and he felt the gash now as his excited energy dissipated.

"C'mon, Ease." He pulled his best friend to his feet. Bixler's wounded left arm hung limply at his side, but he carried his newly purchased Colt in his right hand.

Ease was in shock. "Godalmighty. Look what we did."

Both young men were too exhausted and wounded to do anything about the fire licking fitfully around the parlor. As they limped out the parlor entrance past the dead and dying, there was a scuffle at the front door as the piano-playing Professor and Lady Jane Grey and Sweet Annie all yelled and pushed at Cripes to unbolt the door to get out of the damned whorehouse. After they'd fled, the street vagrant took one scared look back at the two young toughs limping toward him and took his hurried leave, too.

Satisfied with his gun work, Sam Graham jumped quickly to Gillom and Ease in the saloon, his eyes shining with success.

"Nice shootin', boys! We *did* it!" His glee was

snuffed immediately by a shotgun blast from a slide-action Winchester, blowing Graham forward as 12-gauge lead pellets ripped into his back, shredding his shirt. Gillom caught Sam falling into his arms as Sofus, the old Swede retained by Mr. Goose to spy on them, stepped from the doorway to the back storerooms and pumped his shotgun once more.

Gillom cradled his dying friend, so Ease was forced to do their fighting, raising his Thunderer in his good hand and shooting the angry old Swede once in the shoulder, spinning him as he exploded a second round of buckshot into the floor. These lead pellets ricocheted upward, catching Graham in the legs as he slumped in Gillom's arms.

"*You sonofabitch!*" Ease blasted one more .41 slug into this Charon's back and then another into his chest as Sofus rolled over on the hard wood, crying in pain. Anel yelled now, too, finally awake to all this mayhem she had caused.

"Stop eet! Stop eet! *No mas!*"

Sofus was dead and Sam was quickly heading across the river Styx to join him, as Gillom laid the gunman down and turned him over onto his bloody back, his shredded skin hanging in strips. Ease noticed the black bartender standing behind the counter with his only weapon raised, a flat-headed bung mallet, but too frightened by this shoot-out to move.

"You want some unshirted Hell, too?" screeched Mr. Bixler, aiming his nearly empty Colt at the bartender. The black man shook his head, lowered his cudgel.

"Sam, *Sam*! You gonna pull through for me?" There

were tears in the teenager's green eyes as he knelt on his good leg beside his dying friend.

"No . . . I'm not," groaned the robber chief. "Get gone, Gillom, before the Laws come."

"We'll get you doctored."

"Too late," the older Texan burbled. "You ain't cut out . . . for the outlaw trail, kid. Get back to Texas, where you belong."

"We had a fine time with Mister Rhodes up in those pretty San Andres Mountains, didn't we, Sam?"

Sam Graham nodded as he choked on his own blood, his pale blue eyes starting to fade. But he reached into his jeans pocket and pulled out two small diamond earrings entangled in a golden neck chain.

"Wedding . . . gift." The gunman did his best to grin through teeth-grinding pain. A charming thief to his bitter end.

Ease menaced the bartender with his pistol. "*Gillom!* Got to git!"

"Okay." The kid put his arm around his anguished girlfriend's shoulder, gathering her in.. No time for affection; the parlor behind them was starting to burn fiercely. His leg still bleeding, Gillom Rogers pulled his sweetheart toward the front door, with Ease covering their rear in case any more backshooters appeared.

A few gawkers attracted by the gunfire were on the boardwalk as they stumbled out into the night. Smoke curled from the opened door to the Blue Goose, for the wallpaper inside the brothel's back parlor had caught fire.

Someone yelled, *"Fire!"* This warning caused other

patrons to step outside a nearby saloon to see what was going on.

"Somebody needs to help the wounded inside, before they burn up!" shouted Ease, the last one out.

"How about you?" replied some wiseacre.

"We've been shot ourselves," said Ease, following his friends around the corner and up the dark alley. "On our way to the doctor's!"

Three young escapees limped and coughed along the dirt track behind the buildings of Conglomerate Avenue toward its northernmost saloon.

"Don't have time to find a doctor, Ease, unless you want to see one in jail," panted Gillom.

"I know that. Just tryin' to throw them off the chase. Can you make it to Silver City?"

"There's no bullet inside to poison me. I can ride." Gillom noticed Ease was holding his bloody coatsleeve with his gun hand over his limp left arm. "Your arm?"

"Think the bullet went through again. Feels like it anyway. Hope she still works. Ain't acquainted with any one-armed bartenders."

They reached their horses, still hitched.

"I take whis-key, clean your blood," offered Anel.

"How are *you*, honey?" her boyfriend finally asked. "Can you ride tonight?"

"*Sí*. That smoke, stoo-pid make *mi*. Like drink too much, not know where I am? That Goose, that *culero*, tie me up in wagon, meeny days. Where am I?"

"That's why we came up to Clifton. Did he . . . did he rape you?"

"No sex. I say vir-gin, he like. Give me needle, make me sleepy."

Gillom liked it. "You're a peach." Then Gillom remembered his manners.

"Thanks for savin' my life, Ease, shootin' that crazy whore offa me."

"Shootin' women. My folks didn't raise me for that."

"Well, she wanted my heart's blood."

Gillom helped his girlfriend into the smaller paint's saddle. He decided to use Sam's stallion as their spare. He wasn't ready to handle that much horse in the dark.

"We lost Sam Graham back there. Tom Graham's older brother."

"The notorious *Blackjack*? Sam was his *older brother*?" Ease was amazed to learn who their companion really was.

"Train robbers from Texas. Some vulture will surely turn his body in for the reward."

Gillom got his edgy buckskin to let him mount from the right, so he could hoist his good right leg in the stirrup and drag his bloody left leg over the saddle without too much pain. He reached down to unhitch Sam's anxious black racer.

They were quiet as they fast-walked four horses behind the Blue Goose, heading south, out of town. Flickers of flame could be seen inside a lower window to Luther's back office as smoke enveloped the back alley next to the saloon. Up the alley on the main street they could see the volunteer fire department running up pulling a pumper carriage. Spectators were yelling, several men struggled outside coughing with bodies draped over their backs, male and female.

Hope they're too late, Gillom thought. *Luther*

Goose's legacy, burned to the damned ground. So if he's remembered here at all, it'll be badly.

Anel crossed herself as they passed. *"Gracias a Dios."* (Thanks be to God.)

Forty-three

The three youths rode at a slow trot, drinking deeply of the cooler night air, trying to take their minds off the bloodbath they'd just suffered, the loss of their outlaw friend. Gillom was reloading his Remingtons, extricating the misfired cartridge from one cylinder. Anel Romero cleared her opium fog by pouring half a canteen of water over her head, rubbing the refreshing water around her face, and shaking her wet, black hair to dry off. The darkness was illuminated by a growing fire flaming up against north Clifton's night sky, but they didn't care what happened to that *pozo* and the pimp's employees.

"Can't believe I shot those jaspers without usin' many gun tricks. Moving so damned fast, I forgot to show off," muttered Gillom.

"'Fast is fine, accuracy is everything,' said Wyatt Earp."

"Wyatt said that?" wondered Gillom.

"Yup, after that little fracus at the O.K. Corral. But

you're the best shootist I've ever seen, Gillom, your speed, accuracy, and nerve, just sensational. Least as good as ol' Wyatt ever was," admired Ease.

"Thank you." Gillom Rogers sat straighter in his saddle, basking in the first compliment anyone had paid him in a very long while. "Like J. B. Books warned, gunfighting's a sorry way to make a living."

The riders were now in Metz's Flat, a mile south on acreage which had been leased by the livery stable owner for the local Chinese's vegetable gardens. Additional acres Henry Hill had sold to the Shannon Copper Company, the third new mining conglomerate in the Clifton-Morenci area, which had just blown in its first smelter down here near the banks of the San Francisco River for the needed water to cool the furnaces refining their new copper ore.

Gillom slowed their fast walk to lead the horses off the stage road to Guthrie, then over railroad tracks from the mines in the north down to this new copper-processing facility.

"Where are we going?" inquired Ease.

"Need to bandage in some light. I'm still bleeding."

They could see a fiery glow ahead from two blast furnaces. Noisy rock crushers weren't operating within the wood-framed, tin-roofed buildings, too dangerous work at night, but the young riders could see a few carbide safety lamps moving about as night workers smelted valuable ore around the clock.

The three reined their mounts outside a corner of the nearest open-sided building. The cooling water jackets to these two furnaces were thirteen feet high, and the glow reflected out of four charge spaces on the feed floor gave them enough light to doctor by, after the two wounded youths gingerly dismounted.

"Get whiskey from my saddlebag," motioned Gillom to his girlfriend. He snapped open the Barlow knife he'd won from Johnny Kneebone, oh so long ago, to cut wider the stab hole above the left knee in his heavy denim jeans. Anel had the whiskey pint open and an unused bandanna to soak the alcohol in.

"Hold up. Will hurt," she ordered.

He lifted his knee and braced himself against the horse's flank. She splashed liquor directly on his leg wound, then swiped the soaked cloth around its edges to clean it.

"Aaahhhh!" It hurt like blue blazes. His girlfriend reached inside his ripped pants to wrap the bandanna tightly around his thigh several times and tied the stab wound off with Gillom's belt for a pressure bandage to staunch further bleeding.

"Help Ease, wouldcha?" Anel began rifling saddlebags to find something else to use for a bandage.

Gillom tested his bandaged knee to see if he could walk. Ease slipped the torn wool coat off his holed upper left arm as gently as possible.

Gillom was drawn toward the heat from the furnace being stoked by several workers on the feed floor. He saw metal cooking through the *tuyère*, the indentation in the furnace's metal jacket through which a metal nozzle was inserted to blast air like a bellows to superheat the ore that then flowed into a metal crucible below it. The glowing red mix of lime and flux waste and molten copper was alluring, and the gunfighter was drawn closer. He halted, staring into the hellishly hot maw wrenched from the bowels of the earth. His heart was high in his gullet, and he chewed his lip as he squinted into the fiery glare.

Suddenly, in a split second, Gillom Rogers drew his Remington, spun it twice to flip forward in the air and catch by the butt on its rotation, then wound up and heaved the custom revolver straight in through the *tuyère*, the side opening in the blast furnace. Gillom could see the famous gun sink in the molten metal, heard three loud pops as cartridges in the cylinder ignited, quickly swallowed by the burning flux.

This rash act got several smelter workers' attention. "Hey, kid, what in hell do you think you're—"

But the man was too late. From his left-hand holster Gillom Rogers pulled the second Remington, the pearl-handled one, and flipped this nickel-plated .44 in the air with a backspin transfer, caught it by its barrel, and then threw this beautiful pistol, too, right into the furnace after the other weapon.

"Hey! Fella! *Stop* that!"

The trick shootist didn't linger to hear those bullets popping. He limped back to his friends, who were watching him, amazed.

"*Gillom!* Those were valuable guns!" Ease's upper left arm was bandaged in another bandanna, and Anel was tying his bloody coat to the back of his saddle.

"They were *cursed*. Those revolvers brought nothing but blood, death, and bad luck to me and Mister Books. Don't need 'em in my life anymore." The young man seemed calm as he checked his horse's cinch, then remounted carefully from the right side again, forgiving his bandaged leg.

Ease was confused. "Can you risk going unarmed?"

"*Si!* No need *pistolas,*" Miss Romero agreed, remounting as several smelter workers carrying safety lamps high approached for a better look at these gunslinging intruders.

"J. B. Books said I was a sorrow to my mother. Well, I don't intend to be anymore. And I sure as hell don't wanna be ridin' the night train to the big *Adios.*" Gillom turned his buckskin gelding, pulling Sam's black race horse along behind by its reins.

Ease Bixler was having a little difficulty mounting with only one usable arm to clutch his saddlehorn. Gillom's girlfriend gigged her paint pony over to pull him up onto his saddle.

Gillom Rogers straightened in his saddle, feeling calmer, refreshed. It almost felt like being reborn.

"C'mon, Ease! El Paso *awaits!*"

With a clatter of hooves and whoops in the night, the three friends rode away fast, whipping their reins, galloping now, out from under a black cloud toward clearing southwestern skies and a pearly white gibbous moon.

Afterword

I knew the toughest thing to convince Western fans of would be the alligator pond shoot-out, so here's a 1954 photograph of the famous alligator pond in El Paso's downtown San Jacinto Plaza. Note the little boy on the left attempting to climb over the concrete railing to get in and "play" with the alligators. Wonder if he's still got all his fingers and toes? That concrete railing was an improved barrier from the original low chain-link fence I've described, which was erected in 1883 when the plaza was relandscaped to contain this tourist attraction. The original gators had grown large and were still in the plaza in 1901. There was a wooden plank from the pond's concrete rim over the water so keepers could walk out to the fountain to do repairs or reach the animals for feeding. Yes, a group of dentists really *was* turned away by the police late one inebriated night way back when they tried to decide a bet about how many teeth an alligator actually had. El Paso history records that the alligators were eventually moved to quarters at their city zoo in 1965 after two were stoned to death and another had a spike driven through its left eye. Students also kept "borrowing" them to put in lucky professors' offices or the pool at Texas Western College (now the University of Texas at El Paso) before swimming meets.

My late father's, Glendon's, famous novel has had an impact on the Western genre since it was first published by Doubleday, winning a Spur Award as the Best Western Novel of 1975. The Western Writers of America ranked *The Shootist* no. 4 in their sixtieth anniversary member survey in 2013 of the ten greatest Western novels written in the twentieth century. This Western classic is now available in its fourth paperback edition (different covers, different publishers) from Bison Books, the University of Nebraska Press. It's available online from Bison's website (www.nebraskapress.unl.edu) and is an e-book on Amazon's Kindle.

Where this Western title has really become well known, though, is as John Wayne's final film. May 22, 2007, was John Wayne's centennial, one hundred years of the Duke! The bulk of Wayne's 176-odd films were Westerns, and all the studios and video distributors rushed out DVDs of most of his movies in a one-hundredth-birthday celebration, some in newly remastered special editions. *The Shootist* received a DVD edition from Paramount Home Video, in which I appear in their "Making Of" segment talking about this film. The film featured a sterling cast of famous actors who came together to support Wayne when word went round that his health wasn't good and this might be his last movie. Many of those stars worked for less than their normal salaries in this eight-million-dollar picture, which wasn't that large a budget even back in 1976.

By all accounts it was a tough shoot, with Wayne having difficulty breathing at Carson City's five-thousand-foot altitude. He had to be oxygen-assisted regularly and had a nurse with him round the clock. The Duke was cranky with his costars and demanding about script changes and the hiring of bit players. He'd never worked with action veteran Don Siegel before, and those two hard-headed guys soon had a showdown over who was actually going to direct the picture.

John Wayne calmed down and filming went a little easier when the company moved down to sea level on the back lot of the Burbank Studios for some of the interiors and the Carson City street scenes. The novel is set in El Paso in 1901, when it was the last of the roaring border towns, but the script changed the locale to Carson City to match the mountainous exteriors they had filmed in Washoe Lake State Park north of the Nevada state capital. Big John caught the flu during filming, and he was already down to one lung from an earlier operation for cancer due to his lifelong smoking. The producers had accident insurance to cover his two-week absence and filmed around Wayne using body doubles and every trick in the cinematographers' handbook. Finally Wayne returned to film the final saloon shoot-out on a very tense back-lot set.

Robert Boyle received a well-deserved Oscar nomination for his $400,000 set design for this film, and Wayne was reportedly in close competition for another Best Actor nomination; however, he'd already won for *True Grit* seven years earlier, and the Duke's conservative politics didn't mesh well with more liberal, younger Academy voters, so it wasn't to be. Released in September 1976, usually the slowest movie month of the year with students back in school and the beginning of football season, *The Shootist* didn't do that well at the box office, grossing thirteen million dollars in the United States. Producer Dino De Laurentiis kept the international box office for himself, and cofinancier Paramount Pictures only had North American distribution, so the studio didn't spend that much on advertising. Wayne found the energy to do twelve days of TV talk shows and press interviews around the country to promote the film as the mostly rave reviews came in. *Variety* called *The Shootist* "one of the great films of our time." Another film critic called it "the finest valedictory performance by any major American actor in a role hand-tailored for him."

And indeed, *The Shootist* became John Wayne's final film, outside of a few last TV commercials and antismoking ads. His last appearance was presenting the Best Picture Oscar in April 1979 at the Academy Awards. Duke looked like a walking cadaver then, after having most of his stomach removed earlier in the year because of his spreading cancer. John Wayne died on June 11, just a few months later, and the world mourned a film legend's passing.

Where *The Shootist* has really aged well has been in the aftermarket, on TV networks worldwide and in DVD and video sales. Film historians have widely praised this Western, deeming it a classic, and today it's considered one of John Wayne's ten best Western films.

Several times since my father died of smoking complications, too, in Scottsdale, Arizona, in September 1992, the Swarthout estate has been contacted by book packagers wanting to put out quickly written paperback series of Shootist novels or a compilation of short stories by well-known Western authors about the adventures of John Bernard Books as a younger gunfighter. We turned them down, not wishing to tarnish this famous title via hacked-out tomes. I wasn't ready to attempt a sequel until I won a Spur Award myself from the Western Writers of America for *The Sergeant's Lady* as the Best First Novel of 2004 (Forge Books). That frontier romance, set against the backdrop of the final months of Apache raids into Arizona Territory in 1886, was also based on one of Glendon's forgotten short stories, which ran in the old *Saturday Evening Post* in July 1959.

Glendon Swarthout never wrote any sequels to his

sixteen novels, although the 1960s *Where the Boys Are* had editors beseeching him to write *Where the Girls Were. The Shootist* is one of his few novels that really sets up for a sequel. The endings, however, differed between the movie and the original novel. In the movie, the teenaged youth played by Ron Howard follows John Bernard Books (John Wayne) into the fancy saloon where Books has assassinated all the gunmen he's invited to try to kill him but enters just in time to see a sneaky bartender blast the already wounded Books in the back with both barrels of a shotgun. Ron Howard picks up J. B. Books's Remington .44 and kills that back-shooting bartender, giving him what he deserves. After a moment of indecision, the teenager throws the gun away, to John Wayne's approval, before Wayne, too, dies on-screen. Gillom Rogers (Howard) then walks out of that saloon, having renounced gunfighting and further violence, and goes home with his mother, played by Lauren Bacall. No sequel possible to *that* filmed story.

The novel, however, was *not* tailored for John Wayne. Glendon's J. B. Books character was loosely based on the last few years of the notorious Texas gunfighter John Wesley Hardin, the only gunslinger to ever write his own autobiography. Hardin was known for his custom-made leather skeleton vest, onto which he had sewn leather holster sleeves to hold his custom .41 Colts, among a number of types of pistols Hardin used throughout his man-killing career (high estimate on John Wesley was forty-four kills, but no one knows for sure). Glendon changed the guns to matched .44 Remingtons, and the dust jacket illustration on the hardcover *Shootist* novel from 1975 shows these re-volvers and their special holster vest.

They tried to rig up such a vest for Wayne during costume fittings before filming *The Shootist*, but Duke was overweight and too awkward trying to pull big revolvers out from under his coat easily, so they dumped the special vest and he went back to a single six-shooter on the hip. In the novel, the teenaged boy has already worked out a trade with J. B. Books for his prized weapons in return for running the invitations to all those gunmen for this final shoot-out. Gillom Rogers (in the novel) enters the saloon, and at J. B. Books's last request, he issues the coup de grâce to the famous shootist, who is already dying of prostate cancer and his bullet wounds anyway. The teenager then walks outside the saloon (*doesn't* shoot the bar-tender first) and shows off these matched Remingtons to an awed crowd, thus becoming the last shootist. The novel's *different* ending absolutely lends itself to a coming-of-age sequel about what then happens to this teenaged gunslinger carrying these famous six-shooters during the next six months of his exciting young life. I included the last scene of Glendon's orig-inal novel as my prologue, so readers would know they're reading a sequel to the novel, *not* to the famous movie ending they might be more familiar with.

John Wayne wouldn't have anything to do with the book's original ending. My father and I didn't know this when we had several debates with the film's pro-ducers, Mike Frankovich and Bill Self. I was the origi-nal screenwriter on the film, and when we declined to change the story's ending (no possible *sequel*!), director

Siegel brought in his favorite on-set rewriter (credited as a "dialogue coach" on a few of Don's earlier films) to make changes. Scott Hale made just enough changes (one-third) under the Writers' Guild adaptation rules back in 1976 to qualify for a screen credit, and I was too green a screenwriter to protest much. So it too often goes in Hollywood.

What was never explained to us was that John Wayne had made another Western in 1972 called *The Cowboys* in which he trains eleven schoolboys, aged nine to fifteen, and in the process of toughening them up into men while driving his Texas steers to market also teaches them how to fight and kill. *The Cowboys* was the first picture since the 1960s *The Alamo* in which Wayne's character dies on screen, and these no-longer-young innocents go after Bruce Dern and his gang of cutthroats, slaughtering them graphically to avenge the murder of their father-figure trail boss. Well, Big John evidently got so many letters from outraged PTA mothers about his setting such a bad moral example and poor movie role model for their youngsters in *The Cowboys* that he wasn't about to make that mistake again. So, as dictated by Wayne, Ron Howard throws John Wayne's six-gun away, does not execute the famous shootist, renounces violence, and goes home with mom, to live happily ever after. And thus we have a sanitized but perhaps less realistic movie ending to a great Western tale.

Weapons owned by notorious outlaws and expert shootists were valuable to gun collectors even back in the nineteenth century, as long as their provenance could be proved, so fictional El Paso marshal Walter Thibido's burning ambition to get his hands on Books's matched Remingtons for resale is set up in the original novel. The guns mentioned in this sequel were authenticated by an excellent book, *Flayderman's Guide to Antique American Firearms* (8th edition, 2001).

The best histories of old El Paso recommended to me by Leon Metz, who wrote the finest biography of Hardin—*John Wesley Hardin: Dark Angel of Texas* (1998)—were C. L. "Doc" Sonnichsen's *Pass of the North: Four Centuries on the Rio Grande* (1968) and *El Paso: A Centennial Portrait* (1972), containing essays by members of the El Paso Historical Society.

El Paso Daily Herald journalist Dan Dobkins's pointing Gillom Rogers toward the outlaw town of Tularosa to seek out another aspiring writer is also quite plausible. Eugene Manlove Rhodes was *the real Western deal*. Rhodes's appearance, college schooling, and interests (horse breaking, poker, and great literature) are taken from several biographies of the man I tapped (*Eugene Manlove Rhodes—Cowboy Chronicler* by Edwin W. Gaston, Jr.). Gene *did* train one of his wild horses to be mounted only from the right side instead of the left to foil a saddle thief in Old Mesilla, as recounted in W. H. Hutchinson's *A Bar Cross Man*. Rhodes made his living breaking horses as a young man in his camp up in the San Andres Mountains twenty-five miles above Tularosa. This actual horse ranch Gene described in one of his novels, *Stepsons of Light,* which I've reused. Periodic trips down to Tularosa for supplies Gene took to visit the widow he'd courted by letter, May Davison Purple, caused Gene to leave his daily horse chores on the mountain to whichever outlaw happened by that remote rest stop on the Owl Hoot Trail. Word spread and soon Gene was trading food and a safe hideout for horse wrangling duties to such big-leaguers as the Ketchum Brothers, two of the Dalton Gang (Dick Broadwell and Bill Power), and Bill Doolin, King of the Oklahoma Outlaws. Gene befriended these bad men and heard their wild stories, which was grist for his writer's mill when he began publishing short stories in 1902 in famed historian Charles Fletcher Lummis's *Out West* magazine from Los Angeles. In 1906, along with a new baby by May, the family returned to her parents' farm in Apalachin in Upstate New York, where the bulk of Rhodes's Western novels were written and first serialized in the old *Saturday Evening Post* and then compiled into books.

Eugene Manlove Rhodes was the Louis L'Amour of his day, but his flowery prose and anecdotal digressions read somewhat dated now. Several of Gene's novels were filmed after purchase by the Western actor Harry Carey, and the best of his novellas, *Paso Por Aqui,* was released after Gene's death in 1948 as *Four Faces West,* starring Joel McCrea. I like to scout the actual settings of my stories, but Rhodes's real San Andres horse ranch is difficult to get to anymore, located inside the government-restricted White Sands Missile Range in south central New Mexico. The Alamogordo Chamber of Commerce runs bus tours twice a year out to Trinity Site, where the first atomic bomb was detonated, and evidently they pass by a large boulder (*without* stopping) upon which Gene's family and fans have placed a bronze plaque to memorialize his burial spot in what's still known as Rhodes Pass through those same mountains, but I didn't make that special trip.

Western historian and novelist Bernard DeVoto later wrote in a sympathetic *Harper's* magazine essay that Rhodes's Westerns were "the only body of work devoted to the cattle kingdom which is both true to it and written by an artist in prose." Gene Rhodes's fourteen novels and shorter novellas about the Southwest he knew so well stand as reflections of a cowboy author who lived during the last days of a freer ranching era and could easily evoke the Western spirit and rugged physicality of that region in his stories. The Bard of Tularosa's inclusion is my tribute to one of the Western's great *originals*. Old Tularosa has been remodeled now, too, but the best history of that bandit town (*Tularosa: Last of the Frontier West,* 1968) is again by historian C. L. "Doc" Sonnichsen, whom I had the honor of meeting at a Western Writers' convention as a friend of my father's.

The notorious Ketchum Brothers are called the Grahams in this novel, and Blackjack *did* have his head yanked off in Clayton, New Mexico, on April 26, 1901, so Gene Rhodes would have just heard about that botched hanging. The best new history about this deadly outlaw family from West Texas is Jeffrey Burton's *The Deadliest Outlaws* (University of North Texas Press, 2nd edition, 2012). Tom "Blackjack" Ketchum was so mean that when he was about to be hung, he asked Union County, New Mexico, sheriff Salome Garcia to dig his grave very deep and bury him facedown so that Frank Harrington, the train guard who shotgunned Blackjack during a solitary, fouled-up robbery (leading to Tom's capture the next day and the eventual amputation of his right arm) could "kiss my ass."

Both Ketchum brothers spent time hiding out at Gene Rhodes's mountain horse ranch in New Mexico various times and even asked the would-be writer to join them in a train robbery in the summer of 1897, but Eugene turned them down, saying he was "flush just then." I had to change their last names since Tom's older brother, Sam, whom we *do* meet in this story, actually died of blood poisoning in 1899, after being wounded in another train robbery with his brother Tom and Elzy Lay, a member of Butch Cassidy's Wild Bunch gang. This novel is set in the spring and summer of 1901, two years *after* both outlaw brothers were dead, so the Ketchum boys had to become the fictional Grahams. Sam Ketchum probably wasn't quite as friendly an hombre as I depict him, but he was certainly good with guns.

Gillom's first ride on the Southern Pacific out of Deming to Benson was typical of long-distance trains at the turn of the century, which were infested with cardsharps and their cheating cronies. Doc Davis was a notorious crooked gambler of the late 1800s known to ride those same rails fleecing suckers. The mighty S & P Railroad had to sell tickets to these card cheats, but the conductors were by then warning inexperienced travelers against playing cards with these devious gambling professionals.

When the Citizens Reform League got rolling in El

Paso in 1904, by year's end they had leaned on the city council to outlaw houses of prostitution and saloon gambling. Many of the resourceful pimps and whores and gamblers got on trains and headed west—to Bisbee, Arizona.

Bisbee was still a wide-open mining town with legal gambling in fifty saloons operating round the clock and prostitutes available in "the reservation," the parlor houses and cribs and dance halls at the upper end of Brewery Gulch. Bisbee's elected law enforcers were controlled by the three big mining companies, and nothing was allowed to interfere with their immensely profitable dirt digging. After the infamous Bisbee Massacre of December 1883, when the Goldwater & Castaneda General Store was robbed and five innocent people killed, the citizens formed their own Safety Committee of local vigilantes and caught and hanged all six murdering store robbers. The .45-.60 were thereafter in business and began to run troublemakers out of town after a formal warning, with the nonlegal approval of the county sheriff and the mining concerns. Gillom Rogers runs into these urban vigilantes, and they are the reason well-organized Bisbee suffered nowhere near the robberies, shootings, and murders of nearby wooly Arizona towns like Tombstone, Nogales, or Tucson. Sheriff Scott White (who ruled Cochise County at that time) explaining the local political situation to young Gillom and Ease after their two shoot-outs and how Arizona was trying so hard to become a civilized state in the Union separate from New Mexico is accurate regarding congressional frontier politics of those years.

The names of Bisbee's saloons (except the Bonanza),
restaurants, stores, and the construction of their show-
place, the luxurious Copper Queen Hotel, are also
factual to the town at that time. Traveling variety
shows did pass through their big new Orpheum
Theatre, which featured the fanciest restrooms in
the whole Territory, a sight to see and enjoy. M. J.
Cunningham *was* the cashier of the new Bank of Bisbee and owned the first automobile in town, although
it was a big Stanley Steamer instead of a smaller Locomobile, because the bigger car would have been
much more difficult for two men to push up a slippery
dirt track.

The Arizona gunman known for making a "silhouette girl" out of his new wife after killing her husband
over their affair was Buckskin Frank Leslie, thought
by some to have also been the unknown murderer of
his gunslinging pal, Johnny Ringo. Drinking and then
tracing his wife's profile in wooden siding with bullets was Buckskin Frank's fun thing to do, but luckily
their marriage didn't last that long.

Dr. Frederick Sweet *was* Bisbee's surgeon when
Phelps Dodge built their first hospital in 1900 so that
their company physician no longer had to operate on
kitchen or barroom tables. C. E. Doll *did* operate his
Atlantic and Pacific Portrait Studio north of Bisbee's
Castle Rock in 1901.

Ease Bixler and Anel Romero are fictional characters, representative of the young people who flocked
to the booming towns along the Mexican border to
make their fortune catering to the miners and ranchers creating this new wealth. Red Jean, though, *is*

based on a famous prostitute, Irish Mag, whom one of the best copper claims in Bisbee was even named after. Irish Mag kept her small cottage up Mule Pass and her parrot in a scrub oak outside. The bird was known for its salty remarks the rowdy miners had taught it.

The better histories of the great copper boom in Bisbee are *History of Bisbee, 1877 to 1937* (University of Arizona master's thesis by Annie M. Cox) and *Bisbee, Not So Long Ago* by Opie Rundle Burgess. Carlos A. Schwantes's *Bisbee: Urban Outpost on the Frontier* (1992) and *Bisbee: Queen of the Copper Camps* by Lynn R. Bailey (2002) are filled with old photographs of the mines and businesses and unique mountainside houses, plus stories about the colorful residents' lives in that famous copper camp. The only period novel set in these southern Arizona mining towns I found was *Tacey Cromwell* (1942) by two-time Pulitzer Prize winner Conrad Richter. Richter's descriptions of the turn-of-the-century social life in the old mining town are by a famous writer who obviously spent time there. I did, too, with a Scottsdale High School pal, Rob Uhl, and later my mother, Kathryn, on several trips to scout Bisbee's old library and mining museum. Microfilm of their old newspapers, *The Arizona Daily Orb,* succeeded by *The Bisbee Daily Review,* as well as the weekly "Bisbee Jottings" in *The Tombstone Epitaph,* I read in the University of Arizona's excellent library in Tucson.

The incorporation of the city Ease Bixler mentions

took place in Bisbee in 1902, and their new council's first act was to ban women from saloons. Gambling was outlawed in Bisbee in 1907, prostitution was banned there in 1910, Arizona became a state in early 1912, and Prohibition hit the newest state in America right between the eyes in 1915. Free-wheelin' days in that famous old mining mecca were *officially* over.

Much less has been written about mining in remote eastern Arizona, although *The History of Arizona's Clifton-Morenci Mining District, Volume 1: The Underground Days* by Ted Cogut and Bill Conger (1999) covers early copper mining there thoroughly. *History of Clifton* by James Monroe Patton (University of Arizona master's thesis, 1945) was also enlightening. The descriptions of the saloons and businesses on Conglomerate Avenue and the incredible violence in the brothels and saloons along Chase Creek, from which "a body a day" was pulled in one three-month period in 1883, came from Patton's later published graduate thesis. Clifton's amazing level of murder and violence slackened but continued blazing through the 1890s. Henry Hill *was* the stable owner in South Clifton, and a new Shannon Copper smelter *had* been blown in along the San Francisco River just after the turn into the twentieth century.

Up-canyon, Morenci was just as rough and lacked water and sewage facilities during its formative years. Even into the 1950s, Phelps Dodge operated a private brothel for its miners in that isolated, totally company-run town. The Chinese *were* allowed to live in Clifton (unlike in Bisbee), and the only hostelry Gillom rooms in, the Clifton Hotel, did host an alarming number of scorpions. Fires and floods periodically wiped out parts of both towns, but the rival copper companies and their supporting businesses quickly rebuilt along the polluted San Francisco River to continue their lucrative operations. The mining must never stop was the copper companies' motto and continues in Morenci to this day.

Luther Goose is fictional, but there were rough pimps like him investing secretly in parlor houses or operating them openly with equally tough madams. And a Blue Goose Saloon *did* exist in Clifton at the nineteenth century's finish.